ALEX FERGUSON

FOUND
NOT
GUILTY

A Crime Fiction

To my wife, Irene,

To my friend, Alanna Keegan Cooper,

And to all of you.

Thank you for supporting my work.

"But nothing makes a room feel emptier than wanting someone in it."

- Calla Quinn (All The Time)

"It is estimated that some 8 million children go missing around the world each year."

- Melanie Grayce West.

1

The door behind him jolted upon those rough knocks, with his broken voice affording a whimper. "Out of service!" He had to lie. He was not giving this small space – not at least until he was done. A public restroom would keep a man with a shitty reason, no pun intended. Jacob Brownfield did not have a shitty reason. He was gagging not because of the clogged bowl. He closed his eyes, with a heavy swallow down his burning throat. And he repeated, once and twice before settling into a practiced trance while his fingers crinkled that thermoformed blister pack. The restroom spun the moment he looked at that wretched print on the foil.

"*Peter Piper picked a peck of pickled peppers,*" he said, a hoarse prayer as the buzzing lamp flickered during a thunderclap. Hot air escaped his nose, casting vapor over an accompanying reflection. The prayer wheezed in this musty air on a loop, again and again, and his hands steadied. Regaining, Jacob looked at himself in the mirror for the final time and forced a swing toward the trash can. The blister pack landed on top of the pile, its drug label in full view.

"She'll always be with me – now, then and forever. Nothing happened. Her fucking mother called. That's all."

With that, he left bracing through the weather for a black Honda in the parking lot. "Everything's fine. *Peter Piper picked a peck of pickled peppers.* Everything is fine."

He made out the glowing outline of a girl's face, illuminated from a phone. She made a hurried move to unlock the car. "Took you a while!" said Miriam, almost gasping. "You didn't hear some guy knocking on you?"

"I didn't," he said.

"He went back to his truck I thought for a gun or something."

"Yeah? Hope he put it in his mouth."

"Are you okay, Dad? Your eyes are red."

"Could use some coffee."

"Oh. There's a gas station coupla miles from here," she said, thumbing along a road on Google Map. "I gotta buy something. I'm starving. I think Spud's starving too." The King Shepherd in the back gave out a low whine.

Jacob eased on the gas for 40 mph. The trees since Lewiston were swaying in the winds. Water drowned those wild grass by the embankments, where road debris boated in a violent flow. Miriam had a wool blanket over her arms. She pulled back a boogie blob, breathing but not smelling caffeine, carcinogen and peppermint in this warmed car cabin.

"Is it always like this?" she said, gazing through the pattering ponds on both sides of the road.

"The rain?"

"No. The ponds. Of course, the rain!"

"Get used to it, hon. They can flood too."

"The ponds?"

"No. The rain," quipped Jacob, sticking his tongue out. "I remember going fishing around here."

2

"I thought you hate fishing."

"How ya' figure that?" Miriam paused for a brief look.
"Lemme guess," said Jake. "Your mom told you?"

"Yeah," she breathed.

"I love fishing. Learned everything from Uncle Obie.
Remember your Uncle Obie?"

"I just got here, Dad. C'mon."

"He ain't your real uncle," he said. "Gee, he ain't mine
either. Let's just say he's a better dad than your Grandpa Abe.
Obie took me fishing, hunting, hiking – Jesus, he nearly got me
killed one time."

"Can we go fishing some day?"

"Sure. We get settled first and I'll show you everything you
gotta know."

The gas station was not far from the crashing Androscoggin
River, right after a faulty traffic light. Miriam held her Ybenlow
crewneck sweatshirt together for a headlong run to the
RestoMilk. With three clicks on the screen, the smart machine
started dripping oat milk mocha and hazelnut latte into fancy
recyclable cups. Meanwhile she zigzagged by the shelves for
club and tuna sandwiches.

"Sorry, Dad. It's all they have."

The triple-shot coffee glued their eyelids to the underside
of both brows. They spotted everything along this dull
monotony of trees, wind, churches, trees and wind again. The
Honda struggled for traction, once dodging a Styrofoam box.

"Don't go too fast, Dad. I feel like you're gonna get me
killed!" After a crisscrossing traffic, they came upon a grim
building with little light. "What's that over there?"

"I was hoping you wouldn't ask," said Jake. "It's where
Grandma Rhoda, you know, went."

"That's the hospital?"

Jake exhaled. "Yep. That's the one."

"She ever asked about me?"

"A buncha times. Tell you the truth, I really wanna bring you to see her."

"Why didn't you?"

"Why else? Your Grandpa Abe. He didn't like your mom. Two of us had a big fallout."

"You didn't call him back?"

"Hey, this is me you're talking to," said Jake. "I called, Miri. I called and called and called. He was always that dead-end cliff. By the time he died, your grandma's cancer relapsed. She can't remember a damn thing. She even thought me and your mom are still together."

Miriam turned away. "Bless her."

"Amen."

"Would've crushed her if she knew mom is a ho."

"C'mon, hon. That's harsh."

"Oh, puh-lease! Don't go moral on me. The bitch told me you cheated on her." Her breath started racing. "I'm really, really glad you won custody! I'd probably kill myself if I ever had to hear them banging their brains out. Jeez, I can't brain why you fell for her!"

"I been askin' myself the same question." For a time, his marriage with Rachel blossomed into something promising. "Married people have this spark, you know? I guess she just lost it because I was working," he said, twitching in a blast of frost Miri did not feel.

"You always came home late, slept on the couch, got back to work before seven! Ain't no way you're two-timing her, no way!"

4

The Honda stopped that pulsating Eco hum when Jake took a foot off the gas. "Screw her, Miri," he said. "We're here. Let's have a fresh start. Anything you want – just tell me, okay?"

Their fresh start in this part of town was a house in the middle of Court Street. It stood like a haunted vigil in a jungly darkness, coming to sparse life upon those thunderbolts. The Honda skidded in a momentary panic toward the rattling garage.

"Here we are. Just get your bag and go on ahead. I need a smoke."

"I'm not going inside by myself!"

His jittering hand shoved the pack of Marlboros into a pocket. A leaking hallway linked the mildewed garage to an interior space. He felt the wall for a switch. "Probably the circuit," said Jake, after flicking. With the flash from Miri's phone, they got to a panel board near the front door. "And then there was light."

Miriam's mouth dropped with a fleeting glance over the entryway. She stood unmoved, a gaze on those framed pictures in a crockery cupboard. There was a photo of an old couple, with the same house in the background. "Are they–?"

"Yup. Abraham and Rhoda Brownfield. When they bought the place." The rest of the gallery revealed decades of an untold prologue. Pointing at a baby in monochrome, he said, "this was Uncle Ike. Never got to know him. He died as a baby. German measles, from what I heard."

"Rubella," whispered Miriam.

"I'm gonna get some sleep. Don't go wander around. The last room upstairs – that's where your great uncle Reggie died."

"What?" exclaimed Miri.

"He's still there."

5

"Dad! You serious?"

"That's your room." Jake left Miri rooted in dread. For a brief moment, Miri was sure the house moved. She chased after him, with Spud loping from behind for a room next to her father's master. "Anything you want – just give me a knock."

"There is no Uncle Reggie, right?"

A thunderclap stirred. "Not anymore," Jake growled, closing the door.

Miri did the same, locking herself and backing away straight to a bed where she sat on something fluffy. A scream was held behind her tightened lips, subsiding when she heard Spud's whine through the rain. "Sorry, doggo. This place gives me creeps!" Spud barked. "You too?" A whine escaped him. "You're not the only one."

After hitting the showers in the adjoining bathroom, she spent an hour unloading her luggage into the dusty dresser. Spud helped around the best he could, gripping her favorite baseball in his salivating mouth. And Miri found it the next morning floating in the Kohler bowl.

"Morning, Dad. Spud been an idiot like your ex-wife."

"I take it you met Uncle Reggie?"

"Enough, Dad. Nobody died here."

Spud started whining when Miri had a bite of tortilla. "Stay back, doggo. You're cleaning my baseball!"

Rain sprayed all over the casement window next to the dining table. Miri sat right there, tempted with the sound – before she saw the neighbors running around in their backyards.

"Jesus Christ!" Miri turned away, her cheeks burning with flush.

"That's the Robins," said Jake. "That woman over there – she's Tara."

Her eyes widened. "Ten Tummy Tara? She doesn't look fat!"

"She been yapping about Atkins on Facebook."

"But Dad! They're naked!"

"I've seen her mom. They had this jungle fever thing going."

"Mom would have a meltdown–"

"She doesn't find out about this, okay?" snapped Jake. "I mean it, honey."

She nodded, then sneaking a peek. "Is it legal, Dad?"

"Grey area. There's a lot to be said about this place."

Tara Robins rolled on the grass, confident without shame even for a mother of four. Her trimmed body coiled and curled like an hourglass goddess of perfection in ivory and peachy pink. The fun ended after she saw Miriam who flinched with a gasp. That stab of discomfort was obvious within those awkward moments.

And the following doorbell shut Miriam's blood flow for a blanching suspense. Her teeth racketed as Jake approached to greet a baldheaded man who whooped for a big hug. "Uncle Obie!" screamed Jake. "Come on in! You must be freezing!"

Obadiah Parker walked with a small hunch to the dining room. "Hello there!" he said, pocketing a kippah into his cloistered clothes. "I heard so much about you. What's your name, angel?"

"You heard a lot about me, but you dunno my name?"

"Miri–"

"Whoa, hold it, hold it there," said Obie. "I like a witty niece. Reminds me of your momma." A horrible laugh coughed

7

out of his dry throat. "Of course I know my Miriam. How was the drive last night?"

"It was scary. I thought we'd never make it."

"Just one of those storms you can fly in it, Unc."

"O-yeh. Bad weather at Pottapaug. Can't get a catch!"

"Catch?" asked Miri.

"Me and my buddies go to this pond at Quabbin Reservoir. Some bass fishing. You know stuff old people do to feel younger. But this time was bad. Raining, raining, raining we started singing rain rain go away. Seeing as y'all are here, I ducked out early."

"You coulda told me you're coming," said Jake.

"Why? You woulda gotten me the same cheap tortilla anyway."

"Or I can do what Dad did."

Uncle Obie sprayed a laugh. "That asshole woulda give you some water in plastic cup thinking it'll do!"

"Yeah. Until he found that dude in the basement."

Obie exploded. "You heard about this, Miri? Some card game with your Gramps before Rosh Hashanah. Pat Berger – god rest his soul – got drunk and gone we all thought he went home or something."

"What, he went to the basement?"

Miri cringed as another laughter rang out. "Yeah! Rhoda found him there the next night – still sleeping! She even called the cops!" More stories came out as he finished the tortilla. "So many memories, Jake. So many memories. I'm glad you ain't selling this place."

"You were gonna sell?"

"I thought we won't be here anymore."

Obie whistled. "Well, Miri. I think you gotta excuse us before I start spilling more tea!" Obie declined a cigarette in the alfresco next to the kitchen. "Just wanna talk to you, kid. How you two been? The truth now!"

"I just gotta ride it out, Unc. I'll be fine."

"You really should've stayed with me in Waltham. I mean I'm all alone there! Ezra's moving out next week!"

"It's okay, Unc. I know you'll be happy to have us."

"Very happy!"

"But it's just – really wanna be with Miri for now."

Obie tsked with a small smile. "Always a hardheaded kid, are you?"

"Enough about that, Unc. I didn't get a chance to talk to you about Mom."

The smile disappeared. "Urgh. Your momma told me uhh some things. You know, some nightmares." Obie shook his head. "Wasn't easy for her, you know? Those migraines were hell. And there was this doctor she called Ruth."

"God," breathed Jake. "She really missed Ruth."

"She kept talking about Ruth in those last weeks. Ruth this, Ruth that. Had to pretend it's our first time hearing."

"You tried calling Ruth?"

"Heh. We all did," replied Obie. "That girl hates the family so much she'd probably shoot me.

"Don't blame her. You know what happened."

"Of course, Jake. She wanted nothing to do with Farmington. Still your mom wanted a piece of this house for her. You read Rhoda's letter, didn't you? The one I told you about?"

"Yup. Twenty percent. I was ready to fly out to Utah but we didn't close the sale and my marriage fell apart."

"A mother's love, boy, is a touch from the God."

"I'm considering a lot of options, Uncle. You know all those things in Alabama," said Jake. "Been thinking about applying in Boston. Won't be far from you. But without a job, the rent's gonna dry me up real good."

"I've known you since a boy. You'll pull through. You're good with money. I never worried about you. Heck, even your dad never worried about you."

"What the hell did he ever worry about?"

Obie tapped on his shoulder. "Remember what I said, kid. A mother's love is straight from God. Not your mom. She's gone. I'm talking about Miri."

Jake turned to look as she browsed through her phone. "Got it, Unc. Got it."

2

Shopping with Uncle Obie was a seven-hour nightmare because he never stopped being a tour guide for Farmington. He knew everything here, perhaps from his stay during Grandma Rhoda's final weeks. For clothes, he brought them westward on a 45-minute drive to Oxford County where there was a town named after Mexico.

There was an untold greenery in between Farmington and Mexico. Mist hung over the treetops with a natural hymn from those combed pines. The US-2 maintained a consistency of houses on one side and humble establishments on the other. It was the kind of "small businesses" mentioned so adamantly during election seasons.

The Opera House between Taylor and High Streets had a spooky vibe, much like their home during the storm. Miri took a walk around the littered lawn that midmorning, stopping to smell those daffodils, hyacinths and hydrangeas in the backyard. "Uncle Obie, can I ask you something?" she said at a burger joint.

"Eh?"

"You said grandma got very sick since March. But her flowers looks pruned. She took care of them?"

"Oh, yeah, yeah. There's this girl. Pretty lil thing," said Obie. "I uhh – I dunno her name. Just calling her Lottie like you'd call a puppy. She always came around taking care of everything."

"I gotta thank her."

"Damn right. She can tend the flowers if you ain't staying. She loves them."

Jake smiled at Obie's attempt to lure them out of there. He insisted that Miriam would be schooled in Farmington. "Can't do much, Unc," he said. "I already declared it in the divorce papers. If I stay with you, Rachel's gonna say I'm homeless." They returned home after Obie fetched six pairs of winter gloves for Miri. "Don't you think this is too much, Unc?"

"Gotta prepare for anything – winter storm, tornado, nuclear war," said Obie. "After they got Crimea, it's only a matter of time." He kissed Miri on both cheeks and bid farewell before sunset. His 1998 Ford pitched and lurched from a cranky transmission. Jake remained at the porch, blinking, contemplating and ruminating at the clutter all over his yard.

The evening draft sounded like an omen of another storm. His arms ached as a trembling fit started from the pinky finger. He reached into his pocket out of habit and sighed. "Shouldn't have thrown it away," he breathed.

"Threw what away?"

"God. You still here?"

Miri sat up from the rocking chair. "I never got up, Dad. Wait, what did you throw away?"

"My diazepam."

"Those are for anxiety, right?"

"Yeah. Don't need them anymore."

Jake lied. He needed the whole pack if he was to make through the juridical language in his suitcase. A headache was beginning within minutes; his brows locked, trying to understand. Then he stared at the ceiling with both hands by the clammy nape of his neck. The answer was not up there; it was not even in his bank account. The sticky note upon every page was a simple instruction from his divorce attorney. Even with those, he had questions.

"Mr. Pyke? You free?" he said over the phone.

"Yeah, Mr. Brownfield. What's up?"

"I'm taking care of the thing you asked me to. The get-her-to-school part," said Jake. "Just asking, I listed a school in the custody document. I don't really have to put here there, right?"

"Not that particular school? No. You can put her wherever you want. Done moving in?"

Jake took a slow breath. "Not yet. There's tons to do. School. Internet. Some other stuff about my mom. Some leakings."

"Ah, I understand. It's been sitting there for months."

"I'm still worn out from the trip to be honest."

Pyke laughed. "It's all right, Jake. We can talk about your arrears some other time. I'm about to head out anyway. Good luck there."

"Yeah. Bye." He dropped his phone onto those papers and cupped his face. "Gotta pay him," he breathed. "Gotta pay him." The wind from the balcony door put him on a spell that ended with a flinching gasp. Those small arms were strong around his shoulder, clasping and clutching. "God, don't scare me like that! How'd you get in here?"

"Is this why Uncle Obie bought everything we need?"

"What?"

"I heard you talking to that Pyke. I'm so sorry, Dad. How much you owe him?"

"Not too much – you ain't got to–"

"I did my googling. Divorce lawyers cost thousands!"

"It's okay. You ain't got to worry about anything." Her breath convulsed against his chest, now soaking in tears, mucus and saliva. "Shh. Don't worry about it, okay?"

"I have an idea, Dad," she said, her nose swollen. "You don't have any mortgage. The car's already paid. I'll try cooking. That way we don't have to eat outside. We'll save a lotta money! Whatever I can do, I'll help you pay him!"

"Miriam it's just a speed bump! We'll be okay."

"Fuck, Mom!" said Miri. "You spent so much to get me! Shh-she didn't just cheat on *you*! She cheated on us both!" Her eyes enclosed into wrinkled slits, oozing with tears. "She's a bitch! Don't stop me from saying that! What d'you think I felt when I saw him at *our* home? The home *you* paid for! Fuck, he's even showering there!"

"I know, I know. It's all her fault. But we'll survive this, hon. Just gimme some time – I'm good at this."

Miri sat sprawling upon the carpet, a hand over her face. "How much we have left, Dad? Please tell me. I can't stop thinking about it."

"Sixty grand," he said, with a grin. "We had some cracks. But we can patch 'em. We're safe."

Her ruby red face crooked into a menacing stare. "Just you know – mom never got the mail," she said. "I put those bills, tax, bank mails on your desk. I felt so dirty thinking about it but I did go through the numbers back then. That's how I know mom's a fucking liar when she said you spent on women! Now again, Dad – how much we have left?"

"Okay." Jake started. "Things are pretty bad. That's as far as I'm gonna tell you. But Mr. Pyke ain't demanding everything at one go." The pressures at her nasal cavity covered the whole face. For a moment Jake saw her expression pausing before that panic. "Hey! Hey!" Miriam was flailing. "Miri! Oh, God! Breathe! Breathe!" He tossed her aground and rubbed upon the small of her back. "Miriam! Breathe! That's it, girl! Take a deep one, slowly – from the nose – that's it."

The thrashing abated; her legs went limp. She was fighting for air in a fetal position with a hand upon her stomach. "Hurts!" she said.

"Damn it, girl. I told you not to worry about it!" snapped Jake. "Come on. C'mere. Up the bed." He held a glass of water over her mouth as her arms quivered. "Lie back, Miriam."

She obeyed, pulling a blanket to feel his warm touch sweet upon her constricted face. "I'll do anything to help you, Daddy," she breathed.

Jake shook his head after she slid into sleep. He dragged himself back to the desk. Online via mobile hotspot, he googled all schools in Farmington to map out a small list on a receipt paper. The first to answer his call was Jen Calvert from the riverside Mount View Community School. He spoke to her for about half an hour, starting about the divorce and relocation from Alabama.

The school was gloating about its cavalier district ranking. "We balance our curriculum with the little things that matter," said Jen. "Creativity, imagination, literature, integration. Our music class is publicly funded as well."

"That's amazing. What about sports?"

"Oh, your child is interested in games, I take it. We have the best facility for some sports. To cover what we lack, say baseball, we have partnerships for a field access. But, Mr.

Brownfield – we have strict prerequisite," said Jen. "Strict but simple. Is your child properly immunized?"

"Yes, yes. Ain't got no time for essential oil here. Is there a tour we can go?"

"Yes. We're open now," said Jen. "You can come, if you're free. I'll be there shortly." Whittier Road was repurposed with fresh asphalt and yellow lines on both lanes, leading toward what seemed to be a high-tech research facility. Jake might have turned back if not for the school sign. The glass-walled buildings revealed decorated corridors from a good distance. "On behalf of Principal Katherine DeWinter, welcome home, Mr. Brownfield. I take it this gorgeous girl is Miriam?"

Miriam offered a hand. "It's a pleasure to meet you!"

"Pleasure to meet you too. I'm sure you'll fit well here."

"I really like Farmington!" Those poking perennials spoke a lot about after-school activities, a topic Jen elaborated in great depth. Aside from academics and protocols, this principal favored soft-skills. Portraits and landscapes filled the reception hall, but priority was given to an amazing 3' x 2' panorama painting of Farmington. "A student made this?" asked Miri.

"Yes, Miriam. This belongs to Amelia Morgan. It was originally an image her father took with a drone. We're waiting for our client to take it away."

"Take it away – why?"

"We sold it. More than a grand."

"You sell paintings?"

"Oh, yes, Mr. Brownfield! Money keeps this school going. We sell a lot through our networks. Imagine your daughter earning by royalties – isn't it wonderful?"

"Wish I could paint!" said Miri.

"Well, it's not just painting. Chad McCrain was heard singing one day. We gave him a push, and he's now performing in our record studio for YouTube." Jen showed the picture of a girl in her phone. "And Lorena Martins – she's pretty good with strings. We had her playing something from the Hobbit, and the video went viral with millions and millions of views. She just got her Silver Play Button three weeks ago."

"Y'all are a whole another level!"

"It's impractical to perform on the basis of a model from the Nixon time," said Jen. "This Amelia Morgan is an eighth grader. You might even be in the same class, Miriam. We have five classes. Twenty students each. Ten empty chairs left."

Leaving through the decorated hallways and contrasting student lockers, Jake asked, "you like it, hon?"

"Sounds like a competition, Dad."

"Life is a competition."

"Yeap. And couple people cheating their way."

After emailing the proof of residence on Court Street, Jake received an assuring automated response from the school management. Term would start on August 12, according to the enclosed details. "Unless stated otherwise?" said Jake.

"In case I need a reform class, Dad. Ms. Calvert was very particular about that. Weren't you listening?"

"She ain't too particular about buttoning her blouse though."

"Seriously, Dad?"

"Just because I didn't remember doesn't mean I wasn't listening."

"You're gross, Dad. See a therapist, okay? You need your mind fixed."

"Yeah. Remember this mind will put you in college."

17

"Or in a body bag," replied Miri, walking out of the kitchen.

Jake looked at the direction of the stairs, counting those footfalls as Miri headed to her room. When her door banged shut, he produced some frightening bills from a drawer. "Mom," he rasped, running the numbers with the calculator in his Samsung Galaxy. The months of non-payment resulted an outstanding. If paid in full, he would be at a disadvantage over groceries, Netflix and 400-mbps Xfinity. "I can't trim these!" he told Spud. "Maybe we can cut down on your food, eh?"

Spud titled his ears with a whine.

"Fat boy," said Jake. He wrote '-$79.99 a month' in blood ink, highlighting over the 12-month Internet plan contract. "Or else we will have no choice but to repossess your items as per the pending overdue – idiot, I just got here!"

He said the same thing to the Collections. "But we have information you visited Farmington two months ago, Mr. Brownfield."

"For my mother's funeral! You wanna know about my custody battle too?"

"I'm sorry for your predicament, sir. But unfortunately, there's nothing I can do here."

"Let me talk to your supervisor. Anyone!"

"I'm sorry, sir. I can't forward your request. You have to talk to the repossession agent."

The doorbell triggered Spud. "What, they here? Sit, boy! Stay! I'm not in the mood, dammit."

The smiling woman could never pass for a repo agent, at least not with that striking halter top. "Hello!" she said, holding a Saran-wrapped plate. "I'm Charlotte. I live across the street."

"Hi. I'm Jacob. Wow, sure smells good."

"Thank you!" she said, giggling.

"I mean, the cobbler."

"I know!"

"C'mon in." He ushered her into the dining room and set out some plates. The peach cobbler indulged him for a greedy tablespoonful. "That's one hell of a filling!"

"Little accident with the brown sugar. I hope you don't mind."

"No, no, it's perfect! How do you know I love cobblers? You musta been stalking me."

"I was. I saw you backing your car this morning."

"Yeah. You know how things are with school." He called Miri. "She's probably asleep. Miriam!"

"That's okay." Charlotte made herself welcome on the couch. "The old owner was a sweet lady. I been doin' everything for her. You know, gardens, plumbing–"

"Doing everything? You're Lottie!"

"Yeah. Everyone calls me that."

"That old lady was my mom," said Jake.

Lottie gulped. "Jesus! She never told me about you!"

"She wasn't all right up there," said Jake. "She been feeling guilty about Ike and Ruth. And Sam was the golden boy, if you wanna know. He was really good Uncle Obie petitioned him for the IDF."

"That's how he died?"

"Not IDF, no. It was the IED for a terrorist trail that went cold," said Jake. "Obie said she started seeing things. It was *that* bad."

"I was in Houlton when she died. Your uncle informed our community group. You wanna join on WhatsApp? I can hook you up."

"No thanks, Lottie. Never a fan of groups. Men talk about women; women talk about men. Until they started debating politics."

"You summed it up in one breath," said Lottie.

They talked for about an hour before she left. At the porch, she turned to ask. "When can I meet Mrs. Brownfield?"

"Nice shot there."

Lottie scratched her head. "I didn't mean it like that. This is not how I welcome neighbors!"

"Nah, I don't mind."

"I understand, Jake. I'm divorced too."

Her peach cobbler sure forgave that. Miri joined him after a round with her mobile game. "I thought you're sleeping."

"Sorry, Dad. Headphone." She turned to the news channel. "Oh, no rain tomorrow."

The broadcaster presented a meteorology forecast over a digital map of Franklin County, pointing sunshine here and there. Miriam took a picture of the cobbler on a white plate, not forgetting a warm white effect for an Instagram upload. "Been meaning to ask. How many followers you got?"

"Only three in Maine," said Miri. "Insta's easier. FB is too noisy with F-words."

"You do know Zuck owns them both?"

Miri's mouth formed a gaping circle. "That's something."

"Post whatever you like, but nothing sexy, okay?"

"You gotta promise me the same, Dad."

"Touché. But I guess you're right. My generation screwed Facebook from the bottom. It's a different dynamic. You go to Facebook for social. We go for business. You know how much hype I got from online? I didn't have to be on TV to get my voice out."

"How do you hold it together, Dad?"

"Simple. If someone barks the wrong tree, I just ban 'em. But most of the time, it's just about the news."

"You read too much news, Dad. You're still reading about El Paso and Dayton, and you're not even a reporter anymore."

"You ever heard about the Third Enforcement Act?" Miri stared at him. "I take that as a no. It's the first law in history against hate crime, curated to fight the KKK," said Jake. "That was ages ago! But what changed? Nothing. Take a look at the El Paso shooter. Find out why he did what he did. Details like this never leave you especially with my experience. God, I missed my job!"

"How did you lose your job, Dad?"

Jake took a brief look at her. "How else?" he said. "Your damn mom."

3

The weather forecast permitted a sightseeing plan. "Some weeks back you were on about a waterfall somewhere, right?" The rapids behind poking trees and whispering woods at Route Four never left her mind. But come dawn, the plan went straight to hell. If that rainy morning was hell, the next one was damnation. They set out of bed for the sprightly sun glistening through their blinders. But there was a woman with a police officer outside their door.

"What's a cop doing out there?"

"You gotta be kidding me!" snapped Jake. "Living room, Miri. Now! Say what they wanna hear and nothing else."

Something in Jake's tone put Miri in motion. The visitor unzipped her rain coat when Jake opened the door. "Good morning, Mr. Brownfield."

The officer at her side brandished a badge. "Don't give a flying fuck," said Jake. "You gotta do this today? We're going out."

"I'm afraid I do, Mr. Brownfield. I'm gonna need you to stay away until we're done."

"How long would that take?"

"As long as I need," said the woman.

Jake turned to Miri whose inquiring look brooked her fear. "Just so we clear," he told them. "If you two hurt my daughter, I'll take your head off."

The officer kept an eye on Jake the whole time. He was told – or threatened – to stay far away from the living room, where the woman spoke with a low voice. In the following hour, her tone grew harsher. And they left much later without a word. "Who the hell was that, Dad?" asked Miri, her teeth clattering.

"Child Protection," he said. "What did they ask?"

"Made no sense! They asked if you abused me!"

Jake's hand balled into a fist. "And?"

"Just that. She kept on about it," said Miriam. "They think you did something like someone – had them told, or maybe – made a false report about the whole thing!"

"Okay, hon. Breathe," he said. "Take in a deep air. That's it. Deep air. Deep air." She inhaled through her swollen nose. "Forget about them. You're still up for an adventure?"

Her face said it all. And he spent the morning in the kitchen, trembling as heat exhumed from his boiling insides. The air was toxic with his muttering curses, bad breath and intermittent bangs on the table. Facebook did nothing to cool his temper, until a funny idea got him to Instagram.

The cobbler's image on Miri's album had over a thousand likes, with a list of comments from her acquaintances.

Miriam responded to every comment. Every comment, except one from a badgering @rachraig69. Jake scrolled for more from this particular user, each one taping him with a satisfied smile. Miriam was ghosting @rachraig69.

A friend request notification dragged him out of there. "Charlotte Reade." After approving, a balloon floated in his inbox. "You're welcome," said Jake.

"What are you doing right now?"

"Nothing. Just had some run-in with the authorities."

"What's up?" she asked with a shocked emoticon.

His hands hung over the MacBook. "Ex-wife called the cops accusing I abused my kid." Three pouting faces appeared. "We been planning to go out. She's not up for it anymore."

"Shit. That's bad."

"Let's talk about something else."

"Okay. You really went to Berlin, Jake?"

The response was instantaneous. "Stalker!" Jake could not blame her. That album was the first in his photos, publicizing about a work visit in Germany. "I had some thing back then. Nothing exciting."

Three dots floated before her reply entered. "You kidding me? It's Germany! The National Gallery. The museums. The Brandenburg Gate."

"Yep. Been there."

"I'm so jealous!"

"Company sent me for Motor Show and Oktoberfest. Back and forth from Munich to Frankfurt. But that Berlin thing was on my own dime. They're pretty much overstretched at that point."

"How was the flight?"

"To Germany? American Airlines. The reviews ain't lying."

"Hahaha. I mean, in Germany."

"We go around by trains. It's Europe, Lottie."

"Like Amtrak trains?"

"No. Maglev."

The next 15 minutes saw Jake swallowing a bit of regret because Lottie took him seriously. It was wow, wow and wow from her, punching him with bragging rights about delicious

Bavarian cuisine. While chatting, a knife went through his gut because everyone was congratulating Bernard Gilpin.

He was now in Santorini.

Santorini.

The wine island, where he would have been if Rachel did not play dirty. "Fuck," he whispered, as a splitting headache caved in from his cranium.

An ice-cold glass relieved that trunk of a vein, until Facebook algorithm selected an asshole to be on his timeline. John Smith was checking into a Las Vegas casino with two busty hookers. That big smile was the same he gave when Jake received his termination letter.

"Sorry for the late reply." Lottie messaged. "Had to change diaper."

"Yours?"

She gave a laugh. "You're funny. It's my Mason."

The question slid out too fast. "You have a baby?"

"Disappointed?"

"No, no. I mean, who the fuck divorces a woman with a baby?"

"Lil bit of a long story."

"Hey, I ain't going anywhere."

"Okay. I had a knack marrying snakes. My first always beat me and got killed in a shootout, god bless the killer. I married again. Someone sweet in the beginning but abusive as fuck. I found out he was fucking a checkout girl. So I came back here."

"He's Mason's dad?"

"Yeah. Lucky me I have my mom and dad. You should stop by at our bookstore in Chevalley Road. It's not that far from the police station."

"There's bookstore down that road?"

"You been gone too long. It's a real deal now."

"Will check it out, Lottie." The conversation inclined him to know about this interesting woman, who lived a special restart at Highland Avenue. "Be sure to bring your parents next time you bring me that cobbler."

"They won't even drive down your street anymore."

"Why?"

"C'mon, Jake. I'm Charlotte READE!"

"OMG! Like the Reade Reade?"

"Duh! The Reade who read! They send their loves btw. They're still not over about your mom thing."

"I know their feeling. Tell 'em I say hi."

Charles and Donna shared true love more immortal than their ages. Their romantic moments in Lottie's Facebook album showed vibrant examples where and how Jake failed with Rachel Tempner. He expressed that thought and did not Lottie's reply. "Imagine me with two divorces!"

She kept them busy, sometimes taking Miri out for a walk with Spud that Jake could finally concentrate on those journalist-related vacancies about 50 miles from his home. Bangor, Portland and West Brook were built for someone like him. There was an opening in Norridgewock 30 minutes away. It turned out to be a bitter biter, because he missed an important detail in the bottom.

"An internship?"

Jake punched more numbers, ended those calls and shut the vacancy tabs. Google Jobs, Indeed and SimplyHired swung him to Amazon and YouTube to buy and watch nothing. Judging from his search history, @rachraig69 was lurking like an annoying scavenger. And she was forever the living proof he could misjudge those crocodile eyes for stars and heavens.

His emotion took a plunge when Rachel admitted her infidelity. "It's true, your Honor." The words echoed across the courtroom and his kitchen from the PDF report.

He kept viewing the Reades over and over again that Miri caught him one time. "You stalking them, Dad?"

"You know who this is?"

"Yeah. It's Crazy Charlotte's mom and dad."

"You think she's crazy?"

"In a good way. Come join us," said Miriam. "It'll at least take your mind off Ms. Calvert's blouse."

Jake swung for a deep stare. "I'll allow that. Wait, she tell you to ask me out?"

"Seeing as you're turning into Rachel, I asked if you can join us."

"What d'you mean, turning into your mom?"

Miriam pulled a chair for herself. "She be sittin' around mopin' all day, pretending the world being damn unfair to her wonderin' what the hell happened, like *oh where I sucked and how did I go wrong kinda way*," said Miri, in a single breath. "And she can't get the job she wanted. So yeah, hi mom. Nice gender change there."

Jake shook his head. "I get your point. I tried everywhere. Even gig jobs!"

"At least you're trying, Dad. No mortgages – no car loans - how long can we survive with your savings?"

Those wretched bills came to his mind. "Months? I dunno. I'm thinkin' about your college too."

"Jesus Christ, Dad. I'd get married and have eight kids before I hit twenty. Have mercy on yourself."

"The first guy asking you for prom–"

"You'll figure something out next month. I'm sure of that. Just don't spend your first pay on a shotgun, yeah?" Miri gave a light smack on his arm. "Okay. No more eating out. We'll buy everything on sale. Spud gets the leftovers." The whiny protest was amusing. "And I'll sleep in your room. Save our power bills. How about that?"

"I guess you're right. I was being too hard on myself. I hauled ass to pay off my student debt. Don't want you to get into the same mess I did. Sure wasn't easy, Miri."

She grabbed his hand. "We'll get through this, Dad. Come enjoy yourself tomorrow!"

"Why? What's tomorrow?"

A smile highlighted those lines beneath her naughty eyes. "I conned Lottie into buying a fishing rod."

"Hey!"

"It was only fifty bucks!"

"Hey. She ain't that loaded, you know?"

"Her parents are! But her car smelled like chicken bones. I dunno what that was all about."

Jake gave a soft scoff. "Okay. I'll go fishing with you," he said, raising a finger to cut her off. "But you gotta promise not to do that again on Lottie."

"Okay. I promise."

Refrigerator and microwave did not change the cobbler's quality. Jake spooned from the tray while surfing through job adverts and news balloons. The updates on El Paso shooting held him for minutes of unbroken focus that the next scoop heaved only air. He scraped the crumbs into a final spoon and flipped the MacBook before retiring.

On the way to pick Lottie the next day, the clouds started teasing them. Once again, the meteorologists were dead wrong. They had to pull over as road visibility worsened. "I don't believe this," said Miri. "It was hot yesterday!"

"Just a drizzle. We'll improvise."

"You can't fish in rain, Dad!"

"Sure we can. You watched Forrest Gump."

The road was a pure countryside through a virgin heartland. Looking at the rear-view mirror, Jake saw Miriam abandoning that pout when a barn appeared through the mist. "Hey, wait a sec." Miri leaned forward to swipe for Google Map. "Where we going?"

"Titcomb Hill."

Lottie managed to shut up throughout the next five-mile stretch, which ended with a breathtaking vista at Allens Mills. The rain stopped before Clearwater Pond opened up to them. Nine years ago, Jake's career took flight toward unimagined heights after his penetrating interview with a former president. And it began right here, where he met a presidential aide who made the whole thing possible.

Miriam fixed the red ribbon on her head and ran toward those food trucks for a snack.

And in the middle of Clearwater Pond, she made her first throw. She handled the rod better than any beginner, grumbling over near misses and false alarms. Lottie was the real winner that day, rocking the boat like a femme fatale in those magazines for women of power.

Her nine-month-old son tossed and turned without a fuss in an Infantino 4-in-1, which Jake had a good-angled picture. Those minutes seemed to drag as Jake fixated his gaze upon the crimped body in that slim-fit hydrophobic shirt. And he saved every picture in an iPhoto album, his first go-to in the following weeks before starting anything.

"Don't look too long," said Miri. "You'll fall in love."

Jake laughed. "I think I have."

"You kidding me, right?"

"No. I really love–" Jake pointed at Miri in one of the pictures. "–this girl." She blushed. "You look amazing, hon." He walked her out of the house for the school bus ahead the first day at Mt View Community School. Then he went to his desk, sipping hot tea from his favorite mug over vacancy columns in Bangor Daily News, Kennebec Journal and Portland Press Herald. "Same old shit."

The thing with journalism was travel, travel and travel. All applications demanded that but responded his emails with coldness. His efforts were failing. He started assuming maybe his old company issued a warning alert within 100 miles around Court Street. These days nobody needed a private investigator to have his address.

Miri's Instagram gave it away. She posted a selfie next to the numbered mailbox, unwittingly telling the whole world where they lived. But it was not her fault, to be honest. Jake was fired over an unprofessional conduct that was nothing less than free speech. Liberty and freedom were just façade in some parts of the real world.

People demanded those virtues and cited the constitution without being able to handle its holy verses. And it so happened that Farmington had fallen into this sanctimonious trap.

The Penobscot County pledged a historic Republican support to deliver a split vote in Maine for the first time since 1828. For the last in the job list, Jake typed a gentleman post to apologize and say that he was looking for work in the writing industry.

A change of heart prompted him to shut the MacBook. Pulling over at Dunkin' by the corner between U.S. Cellular and Franklin Savings Bank, his eyes went wide. "Are you outta your mind?" he told the rearview mirror.

Still out of breath, he went in for a medium cup of Dunkaccino. The woman in white behind the counter had a leering poise. Her tag caught the glint of fluorescence. And two of them gasped. "You're Jacob!"

"Cassie? What a surprise!"

"I heard you're back in town! You look great."

"Oho, I look great? Girl, you musta lost twenty–" Blood filled his face, straining, "twenty thousand pounds!"

"A diet group with Tara. She burned thousands ton!"

"Whoo-whee! The hills are alive!" said Jake in a singsong voice.

A throaty voice beckoned from the kitchens. "Cass! No talking!"

"Hey, Pete! Come out here! It's Moose."

The barrel-chested man behind those cooking appliances and pantry racks still had the same warmth. "Sonofabitch, Moose!" quipped Peter Hollington. "Never thought I'd see you again! You really made some big antlers out there, huh?"

"I didn't know you guys work here!"

"Yeah, we in the little leagues, man."

"Don't be like that, Peter," said Jake. "Why not we get some breakfast together? Hell, we have a lot to catch up."

The electronic yearbook in his Google Drive retold the longtime secrets from bygone ages. Cassie Blount and Tara Robin were pictured together, both inflated and obese with a weight-related quote: you live in your body for free.

"Oh, those were the days!" said Cass.

"I remember you took a dive at Sandy River."

"Yeah. She ended up in the E.R.," said Peter.

Cass shushed them. "Stupid thing was, I actually thought my body will be like a buoy or something!" The next laugh was the biggest. "Shut up! I'm serious!"

"How long are you gonna be here, Jake?"

"Not forever, I hope. I'm looking for a job."

"Job? Aren't you like Richard Quest in Alabama?"

"Quest? He's the king. I'm just a baron."

"What happened?" asked Cassie.

"Everyone on Facebook knows."

"Last I had a Facebook, I got fat-shamed. Nearly killed myself."

"Shit. I'm sorry." Jake munched over his egg and cheese. "It's not a good story. Pete knows. Ask him."

"No idea what you talkin' about."

Jake feigned a laugh. "What's your story, Cass?"

"I got a daughter, Addison. She's fourteen now."

"Same as mine. Mount View?"

"Yeah! Small world. Pete's daughter going there too."

"You're with Patrick, right?"

Cass soured. "Not anymore. It didn't work out. I kinda had someone else. Pat wanted a DNA test. He didn't believe Addy is his."

"Did you really cheat on him?"

"It was just a kiss. I finally found someone who didn't go the whole day fat shaming me."

"Fuck Pat then!"

"I'd rather fuck you."

"Anytime any place," said Jake.

"Urgh. Can the fantasy, Moosie," she said. "I had some complications after Pat left me. Gained ten pounds from depression. I was walking like a moving washing machine. I hated myself. Nearly lost Addy." Jake whistled. "After she was born, I put up my game face for this other guy I kissed."

"You married him?"

"He started seeing someone else. That's when I went along with Tara and shredded two hunnerd pounds. Took years, you. Years!"

"I'll be damned. What's with this town?" said Jake. "You're divorced. Someone I know here's divorced. I'm divorced too!"

"Oookay. Come to Momma!"

"Two horny bastards in Dunkin," said Pete. "What else can go wrong today?"

"Oh, fuck you, Pete. You have your coochie. Let him have his. We don't mean what we say."

"Ah, shit happens back in my life," said Jake. "Bitch hid the pickle."

"You're a cuck!"

"Fuck you. I bucked out. Got full custody. Then I got drunk. Said some things at a bar. They fired me. I'm now dead on everything else."

"Single parent shit, Jake. It stains and smells and you love it. My hands are full with Addy."

"Same here. Just wanna be the best dad in the world," said Jake. "Sometimes I feel like my daughter's gonna die or something."

4

Jake realized he was among the richest in Farmington. His savings outnumbered the Hollingtons at least ten-to-one. His friends were honest about commitments; for that, he was thankful. The conversation steered him to inquire about an alarming pattern behind this slower pace of life.

The 2008-2009 statewide retrenchments blasted a crater deep into the Farmingtonian socioeconomics. The city was now the Maine version of Benton Harbor, Detroit and Tuskegee, where singlehood prevalence pushed families to the brink of poverty. Cassie (and Lottie) represented a small piece of the pie within Jake's old acquaintances. Ally, Janice and Michelle were supermoms juggling between minimum wages and gig jobs.

"But nobody gave a fly fuck about them 'cause they're still poor," said Cass. "We ain't the story for those anti-patriarchy people. Take a look at Ally. Without Lyft, she'll be on the streets. But who cares, right?"

"We're all about paying debts here," said Pete.

"Lucky I don't have one."

"Heh. Lucky you ain't working at a doughnut depot."

"At least you guys are working."

Pete told him of a four-day broadcast for a technical writer. The company demanded a Bachelor's degree with a minor in computer science. Jake was aghast when the HR officer requested a medical checkup. "Shouldn't we do interviews first?" he asked.

"Company policy, sir."

The changing safety and health regulations rear-ended him to the nearest clinic. He stopped for a short breath after registering. His turn was up a breakfast and two short naps later. And he strode into a bright room for a red-haired man in white. "Hello, Mr. Brownfield. So sorry for the wait."

"Who doesn't love a free clinic, doc?"

"It's not free by the way. Not yet."

"Not yet?"

"I only make a small profit to keep it running," said David Morgan. "Healthcare is a fundamental human right. But we're Americans, a step ahead the evolutionary chain. You believe in free healthcare?"

"I feel the Bern, doc."

"Yeah, me too. We can't go around overcharging people for their wellbeing. To tell you the truth I'd be happy to get a flat rate from the government if that's what it takes to give free healthcare. But they told me to go back to Canada."

"Maybe you should."

"I will if Bernie doesn't get a shot," said David. "How can I help you, Mr. Brownfield?"

"Medical checkup. This company here referred me to you."

"Of course. Everyone does. Roll up your sleeve." His constant headache was drawing from his fluctuating blood pressure. "Gotta watch the cholesterol too," said David. "Any medical condition in your family? Heart disease, diabetes, perhaps? Anything inheritable?"

"My mom had a tumor."

"Shouldn't be an employer's concern. But I must say – an established reporter like you shouldn't be diving in sweatshops."

"It's not a sweatshop. Technical writer, doc."

"What does that entail? Perfecting broken English? C'mon. It's like a dance maestro learning musical chair."

"Whatever it takes to make money."

"I won't go to Iowa if I wanna do bug-trawling. Why don't you get outta here? Coming back here is a mistake if you wanna be what you always have been." David signed something in the document and called for the assistant. "Tell you what – gimme a day or two, I'll ring you a call. I have someone in Manhattan who might be able to patch you to someone."

"After what I did, I'm not too sure."

"You insulted a mayor when you're drunk. Big deal. Bill de Blasio said a lot of things about Trump and that Rudy Giuliani. And what about that Bridgegate scandal? Oh, wait, that's in Jersey – sorry. But you get my point. Many people said things, some things a lot worse than what you did."

"Maybe I should run for politics. Seems they can say anything and get away with it."

David laughed. "I'll vote for you, Mr. Brownfield."

The doctor had a good disposition around town. During Lottie's free time, they went on in length about his crusade for Farmington. "He likes helping people around," she said. "He's really good at it."

"You think I should take a job if he has one?"

"C'mon. It's New York!" replied Lottie. "Who don't wanna go there?"

"I'm saying, Miri seems to like you."

"Yeah. I guess I'm gonna miss her."

The words spilled. "Maybe you can come with us?"

He saw his eyes mooning like white melons in the adjacent mirror. "You really mean that, Jake?"

"Yeah. Why not?" he said. "You can do accounting online even. There's POS system and all."

"Gotta go now."

His hand met his forehead. "What the hell did I just do?" he said.

Miri got home in time as he was garnishing the roasted lemon garlic chicken. The side dish today was braised broccoli, a green perfection to go along with his mother's premixed mashed potato. At the table, she told him everything about her first day. "Everyone welcomed me! I already made a few friends."

"That's fast. How many?"

"A lot, Dad. The school's awesome, I'm telling you!"

"Any of them did anything to you?"

She pressed her face, as if she bit a lemon. "What does that even mean, Dad?"

"The company I'm applying told me to go medical with this doctor. He knows what I did at Alabama."

"Oh, that video thingy you got fired for?"

"So, you know." He bumped his fist upon the table. "Perfect. Mom told you?"

"Adult problems, I guess. Don't get drunk again, Dad," said Miri. "Oh, so you know – some teachers asked me your phone number. Said it's for school thing. The weird part is, they aren't even teaching me."

"Lemme guess. They're single?"

Miri tilted her head. "I don't see a ring. And I'm not a pimp. Those horny bitches can ask you themselves."

"The student management musta said I'm divorced."

"Ah! Student management! Remember Amelia Morgan?"

"The painting girl. Someone wrecked it?"

"No. Someone stole her phone!" said Miri. "She got so angry. Who wouldn't be? It's an iPhone Ten! The XS!"

"Gee. When I was in school, I only had my books and pencils."

"Yeah but look at you now, Dad."

"Very funny!" said Jake. "Be careful with your phone. I can't afford another one. Not yet."

"I know. It's okay. No one wants a Redmi, especially with this thing going on about Huawei. Just hope mine doesn't get jammed anytime soon."

"Or stolen," said Jake, with a dry voice.

Mt View Community School was on a high alert for that iPhone. The student management rented a column in major news to demand and denounce. It was a crazy story, even for Jake whose spotless medical report turned out to be needless. Out of nowhere the HR office reached him, now spouting witchcraft about applicants only had to submit such report after being accepted. He complied with honeyed words over forgivable sarcasm.

Miri listened to his phone call, half smiling half alarmed. After hanging up, Jake gave a reassuring thumb up and walked away. That was a mistake from his part; he missed that sudden change of expression upon his daughter's face. Miri sat at the coffee table over homework, pouting.

Monday blues did not spare the perpetual hate from her peers. The first to deny her a seat was a boy who looked like a pudgy bull. It was just like one of those cliched moments in coming-of-age movies. Lee Lee Hudson threw a bag on a vacant seat, shaking her head while blowing a bubblegum. A girl made some space but changed her mind upon those scowls.

The bus bumped over a speed breaker, bouncing with gales of laughter as she fell. "Quiet back there!" Miri wiped those tears with the back of her hand. She was the last to get off, as the bullies demanded. Mrs. Owens held her hand. "It'll go away if you just fight back, you know?"

"Did that where I came from. I got punched in the face. But thank you, Mrs. Owens."

The bus driver sighed. "Next time I'll save you a seat."

Miri gave a little wave before the bus reversed. At the steps leading to the locker hallway, she met a friendly face. Penny Hollington grabbed her arm to the next hallway. "You know Amelia got in a fistfight just now?" she whispered.

"About her phone thing?"

"Yeah. She been blaming everyone! Dora's nose was so bloody like it's gone!"

"Did she do it?"

"No! That's the thing. It's like a crazy murder mystery now. She's going batshit and punching people."

A large speaker up at a corner crackled before projecting the principal's voice. "Your attention. Please assemble at the gym. If anyone has information about the stolen iPhone, please report it to your teachers."

"If it happened to me, teachers will ask why I brought it to school in the first place."

"Why everyone likes her anyway?" asked Miri.

"Trust me. Even Einstein doesn't know!"

The continuing conversations struck an impression that nobody gave a damn about Amelia Morgan. Some flipped the bird to the speaker. Miri was at her locker when a group of girls jumped from behind with a loud bang. "Look who's here," said

Naomi, locking her in a big arm. "I told you roaches ain't welcomed here!"

Penny made a futile attempt to break her free. "You leave us alone!"

"Shut the hell up, four eyes!"

"Did you get my breakfast?" asked Naomi, poking her tongue into Miri's earlobe.

"N-no."

Miri clawed for breath as the grip constricted. "Speak up. I can't hear you."

"I said, no!" Miri yanked herself out, coughing. "You get the fuck outta here!"

Her scream got the attention of a teacher. "You're dead, roach," said Naomi. "You hear me?"

"You gotta hide!" said Penny, when they were gone.

"What's the point? We're in the same building."

Naomi was seated not too far away from them in the school gym. Miriam turned away from her when a curtain-haired woman entered before a brood of teachers. "Good morning, boys and girls," said Katherine DeWinter.

The students responded in the usual, singsong tone. "Good morning, Principal DeWinter."

"Now, I am sure all of you are wondering why you are here," said DeWinter. "In case some of you don't know – Amelia Morgan's iPhone was stolen last week. We've looked into this carefully. And what we can tell right now is that we know who took it." Trembling hands and fluttering eyelids welcomed DeWinter's brief scowl. "Now it is inadvisable to bring anything expensive to a public institution. But it is criminal to steal, even if you're juveniles. Our school has a strong goal. Honing, honor and honesty.

"I don't have to tell you what is right and what is wrong. But here's what we're gonna do: this thief is to come forward to my office and return what is rightfully Miss Morgan's. That'll be the end of it. No police. No disciplinary actions. Mount View should be clean from police cases, as I like to think of it.

"But don't mistake my leniency for tolerance. You have until the end of today. After that, go to any one of the thirteen churches in Farmington. Confess and make your peace with God. Because we will find you. We will pursue you. And we will get you."

There was a susurrus among the students. DeWinter's reputation shielded her from open ridicule over the palpable impersonation of Liam Neeson. Behind her back, it was the talk of the school. Every conversation in every class had the hushed touches of that subject. And it was not just that. DeWinter had an outlandish slur at times, which explained why her forced speech sounded too automated.

"She talks like Arnold!"

"Arnold?"

"The Terminator guy, you idiot!"

"What's Terminator?"

"The movie that'll be back once in five years."

They kept talking about DeWinter, except when the prima donna was around.

Amelia Morgan sat at the other end, drumming her fingers throughout the class. Teachers came and went scooping students with homework issues. Mrs. Sophia Ratzinsky pounced at the whole class. Even she left Amelia alone in a disgusting bias.

Muscle sores and chronic boredom soon turned into excitement. Mrs. Irene Dedder was the only one not to talk about the damn iPhone, preferring real issues such as climate change. Her explanations chipped a complicated subject into simpler pieces, flowing their young minds with inspiriting information.

"Y'all use Facebook a lot, I know," she said. "You ever come across a woman who did a lot of things for the environment?"

Penny raised her hand. "Greta Thunberg?"

"Very good, Penny. Greta is a wonder girl. The Thunberg effect is something to be proud of. But I wasn't actually talking about her," said Mrs. Dedder. "If you live in a country with a good education policy, you will know more and more about modern-day issues. But imagine if you live among the rural communities in Kenya, how do you channel your higher knowledge to make people, say in villages, understand something important the way you do?"

Penny answered again. "You make it easy for them to understand."

"Correct, Penny! That's what Wangari Maathai did. She founded the Green Belt Movement teaching sustainable lifestyle to many people. And I mean, many. How many, you think?"

"Hundred people?"

"Her movement trained thirty thousand women and planted over fifty million trees!"

The class sang. "Wow."

All but Amelia. When the bell finally rang, she was the first to fly out for the exit.

"Man, if I ever hear another word about that bitch's iPhone–" Penny bit her tongue upon seeing Amelia's hens. "Trust me, if I know you before you got here, I woulda told you to go somewhere else because it's all bullshit – all about the painting, YouTube thingy. The school just took credit from what the kids did themselves." A car honk turned Penny. "Later, Miri."

She ran toward a Miata and hugged her little brother in a Graco convertible car seat. Miri watched as life seeped out of the school, with foul languages from class to gate. "Don't wanna get on that bus," she breathed.

The parking spaces were bustling with freedom. But she was trapped alone in perhaps the busiest place in the city. Nobody smiled at her. No one was there to accompany, unlike many around her. She existed in flesh without a dime in her pocket to get an ice cream from the crowded vendor truck.

Then those four in baggy sweaters emerged from the steps, their eyes latching upon Miri who turned with a hiss. Naomi's grin was not human. Her drones seemed connected to her, all swerving and swearing like automated killing machines. They threw themselves in a swaying, predatory motion for a wild spoor which dissipated upon that familiar honk.

Miri's prayers were heard. Next to that driverless bus was Jake, in benevolent long sleeves and flowing slacks. She pretended she did not see those bullies, jumping out of there like a lightning bolt. "What are you doing here, Dad?"

As usual Jake carried her bag. "Something to do at the police station," he said. "Thought about picking you up."

"You're not in trouble, are you?"

"I am, actually."

Miri's face paled. "What happened?"

"Get in the car." Jake heaved a long sigh. "You know your friend, Amelia? Well, I took her phone."

"What are you talking about?"

"I thought about our money and all."

"You're not being serious, are you?"

"I am, hon. I am." Jake cannot hold it any longer. "You should have seen your face," he said, laughing. "I shoulda brought a camera!"

"Jesus, Dad! My heart – don't do that again. I thought you meant it!"

"Nah, nah. I heard the cops been asking for a clerk or something. Thought about doing it while we're here. Can't find the application online." Miri hid her face in her hands. "How was school anyway?"

"Amazing. We learned about iPhones, iPhones and iPhones. Don't even wanna talk about–" On the dashboard, she found a newspaper promising rewards for Amelia's iPhone. "You gotta be kidding me! Front page?" she said. "Five hunnerd dollars? Just buy another one!"

"You can't buy what's inside, Miriam."

"What could be so important anyway?"

Jake breathed. "I dunno. I ain't the one stealing it. Maybe she's writing a novel or something and there's a multi-million deal in the making."

"Yeah, right."

"Anyway. Wanna grab some pizza?"

"Can we afford it, Dad?"

"C'mon. Enough with the money thing," said Jake. "Lottie paid me to start fixing her car. Can't refuse at times like this."

"Hmm. It's okay if you're the one conning her."

"I'm not conning her, honey."

"Dad, when's the last time you fixed cars?"

"Shit. Did many times. But I remember fixing the limo on my wedding day."

"That's a sign!" said Miri, then laughing. "Get out, Jake! Get out while you still can!"

The pizzeria was not far from Wilton Road through a gridlock by Bridge Street and Intervale Road. Cars and buses wrestled for road space in this intersection. "From now on," said Jake, clearing his throat. "I'll be sending you, okay?"

"Why?"

"You been keepin' secrets from me, hon," he said. "Is this some kind of a tough enough thing?"

"No, Dad. You don't understand."

"That's right. I don't understand. Lemme guess, someone been takin' your money too?" She acknowledged with a nod. "C'mon, Miriam! You said you made friends!"

"I did, Dad."

"Name 'em!"

"Penny Hollington."

"And?" shouted Jake. "That it? Real smooth, Miriam! What am I supposed to do? Go to DeWinter?"

"No, Dad. Please. Don't do that," said Miri, huffing. "She's always moody as hell. She keeps taking work breaks. Just please, gimme some time and I'll deal with them."

"Them? How many bullies we talkin' about here?"

"Look!" she snapped, matching the tone of his voice. "I don't have to deal with this, you know? You don't have to pick me up even! I know how to take care of myself, dammit!"

The red light brought them to a halt; she cannot hide a shaking spell. "I'm sorry," said Jake, grabbing her hand. "You're my responsibility. And I love you. I been through some bullies back in my days. I don't want this happening to you!"

"It does. It happens a lot, Dad."

"We gotta do something about this, okay? I mean that, together as a team."

"Whatever you say."

A right turn through the clearing traffic ended them at a convenience store cornering Franklin Avenue. The wet surface sleeked into a plunge for the underground sewer. The police station weathered through time with no major touchup or renovation. In the parking space, Jake rounded a check in his suitcase for the brown file.

The officers on break greeted them with a donut for Miri. "Something I can help you two with?"

"I'm here for the clerk opening."

"Clerk opening?"

"Yeah. Says right here," said Jake. In his hand was a newspaper with a Sharpie circle. "Who do I ask for this?"

"I dunno. I think it's Rog."

"Rog. Got it. Thanks."

"You can leave your kid here, sir. It's pretty hot inside."

Jake's steps faltered as soon as he got into the station. Farmington is the place where everybody liked everybody. But here at this particular point of time, it turned into Compton, Detroit and St. Louis in one. Tables and files were scattered, with one of the janitors on all fours brushing that smear on the floor. "Can I help you?" asked an officer, looking unkempt.

"What on earth happened here?"

"A psycho got loose. Can I help you?"

"Oh, yeah. I need to see Rog." The receptionist gestured him straight to the Roger with a weird surname. Jake did not need a glimpse of that man. The personalized desk plate in front of those papers brought back old memories. "Oh, hell no! Gothy?" he said.

Roger Gauthier popped out of his work. "Who the f–" he said with a resting frown. "Holy shit – Moose! Motherf-! What you doin' here? Not in trouble, are you?"

Jake raised his eyebrows. "No bigger than yours, man."

His friend shook his head with a shrug. "Yeah. Figures. Wassup, man?"

"Yeah, goin' all right. Just wondering if you need a writing partner."

"Just like old time, huh? Me copyin' your homework," said Roger, chuckling. "Nah, man. I'm good here."

"I'm here for the clerk thing."

"Damn, man. You gone that naïve?" he said. "We already have the guy before we advertise."

"Huh?"

"That shit in paper is just a formal thing. You know how it works?"

Jake shut his eyes and nodded. "So, whose brother got the job?"

"Some jerk-off I don't even wanna shake his hand," said Roger. "Sorry, bro. Not my call. All from the Deputy Chief more or less."

Back in the car, Jake rubbed the bridge of his nose against the onset of a headache. "It's all right, Dad," said Miri. "You're too good for Farmington."

"Miri, I want you to be honest with me."

"Oh, no. What now?"

"This friend of yours - a Hollington. Is she White?"

"N-no."

"She's my friend Pete's daughter," said Jake. "You good with her?"

"Kinda, yeah. Why?"

"You'd be okay if we leave?"

"You think it's a mistake coming here?"

"The thought came to me. So, yeah."

Miri's eyes found the overcast horizon. "I'm okay if you wanna move out, honestly. But I dunno. Can we afford somewhere else?"

"What if I get a job in New York?"

"I don't know, Dad."

"Yeah. I don't know too."

5

Lottie was proud to tell Jake about her divorce settlement. The marriage was nothing short of a disaster. But she got out of it with a bag of money, which she cashed at a garage for a used car. Two days after finalizing the paperwork, she got the Santa Fe. It was, in her words, a silver angel with clipped wings.

"You got that right." Jake spoke to her. "Clipped. Cut. Sliced. The hood is like you got a surgery in a YouTube hospital."

He had been standing, hunched over the popped hood with a big question mark about everything. Even then, Lottie sang a good opera about her grease monkey.

"Grease monkey? That monkey sure is greasy."

A mechanic – her friend of seven years – taped some wires a little too close to the manufacturer-variant 2.4L engine. "And what's wrong with that?" asked Lottie.

"What's wrong with it is that you drive like a maniac," said Jake. "When you drive like a maniac, engine gets hot. When engine gets hot, the insulation coat melts off. And the cores are electric. So, that's what's wrong with it."

"Oh."

Jake stared into his phone. "Yeah. A big oh," he said. "Wait 'till you hear about the warranty."

"What warranty? I didn't buy from Honda."

"The authorized reseller should have some warranty," said Jake. "And it's a Hyundai, Charlotte."

"Right! Sorry. How bad is it, Jake?"

"I dunno. If it's a heart, it had way too many bypasses. Way too many, and I bet your friend was drunk 'cause he didn't change your engine oil. It's black as my butt crack."

"Oh."

Jake cannot put a finger for the winner. In one corner, there was an innocent woman. And in the other was "an opportunistic parasite possibly with herpes" who knew single moms were too busy for second opinions.

That was not all. The Santa Fe should have an iridium spark plug. But in its place was a weary nickel/alloy-coated copper. "Jesus," said Lottie. "How do you know about cars?"

Jake had a long conversation about his time in UMA. Sometimes having a cheapskate father was a blessing in disguise. Jake grew tired of asking for money, which he was sure Abraham had pre-downloaded those immortal excuses into that tonsured head. His part-time gigs survived him a godly Malibu. He loved that car he even gave a name.

"Really? What was it?"

"You're gonna laugh," said Jake, and she was already laughing. "Boobee."

The first time that yellow-black car stalled was at a curb where Old Man Marvey was resting. He saw a chewed wire under Boobee's overheated engine – just as Jake saw one in the Santa Fe. His hand slid by the space near the oil stick. With the key in his fanny pack, the machine should not have any electrical charge in any way. But this here was no normal machine.

And the surge zapped every hair on Jake from neck to nuts. He dropped the wrench in the other hand, screaming as smoke puffed out of his orifice.

"Fuck! Fuck!"

He was flat upon the driveway in full sunlight.

"Jake? Jake!"

He slammed the hood and lumbered back into his home. His jaw jittered as his tongue poked against the oval bulge upon his palate, something that did not belong there. He kept wiggling his toes against the tightness of his boots to stay conscious. There was blackness for at least a second, or two, or three – or maybe more than three.

Because he was on a couch staring at the fluorescent lamps. He looked around for his phone before realizing with a hiss. He found his phone next to the Santa Fe. It had been fielding calls like a network magnet. A barrage of missed calls was from Miriam, who was lined for voicemails.

The next one was David Morgan. "Hello? Jake?"

"Yeah. My phone was on silent. What's up, doc?"

"I have this offer for you. It's from Manhattan."

The spasm beneath his muscles stopped. "Whoa! For real, doc? That's awesome!"

"Told ya' I'd work it out."

"Thanks. Thanks a lot. I'll text you right away."

"Super."

His fingers labored over the virtual keyboard for a reply which returned with an immediate bluetick. He pulled the notification bar to find a warning sign of seven text messages from a blocked number. But his Gmail application chimed, receiving a forwarded email from Evanna Rhodes.

Within the minute, Jake went to his MacBook and learned that Evanna lived in the gentrified UWS with a garden-themed balcony overlooking the Central Park. "Hmm. No ring in her finger." Jake pasted a prepared reply on the body of his email and sent straight to Evanna's way.

Shortly after texting David, there was a reply. "Anytime, Mr. Brownfield. Good luck."

Jake made his way back to the couch with a hoarse laughter. Magazines, webzines and weeklies were his trade. He swiped for WhatsApp Status to update about it. That was when David's status came to his screen, a plain text over black background: *cash for my daughter's iPhone, $650. DM if you have info.*

"Whoa!"

The next contacts left their thoughts in status as if in response to David. "No one is that crazy. A little wait can get us a grand."

"650 for an X? Dang."

"Woot woot. 650. Can I hear 750?"

They were right. The reward did not make sense with a newer model around the corner. On Facebook, Jake encountered adverts promising money for crucial information regarding Amelia's iPhone XS. They even set up a page under the Community section in frenzied hope for the bloody gadget. The supportive people in Farmington asked the same questions:

"Why not get a new phone?"

"Gee. What's in that phone?"

There was also a user leaving out an abrasive comment. "I have the phone. Wire me the money." It took a surf into his profile. Ashok Ramachandran was a frog-faced introvert suffering the agrarian life for groundnuts and pigeonpeas in a South Asian out-of-nowhere valley. He was being massacred with pro-Pakistani vilifications. To express support for Amelia's plight, Jake typed a condemnation which he deleted before submitting.

"Don't do it. New York ain't Farmington," he breathed.

Google must have read his mind; its algorithm shoved a DailyMail article about a $250,000 fine against racial discriminations. Jake was about to reply to Lottie's concerned messages when he noticed a bracketed number in the Message Requests. He clicked it, half-curious half-expecting for a Bitcoin spam. But it was Emily Tempner, an ally with a good career and functioning family.

That message was a bomb of capitalized words in no way from a speech therapist. "PLS...CLMENOW! URGNT!" Jake replied with a middle finger emoji. And he did not have to wait too long. "JAKE! ITS RACHEL! CALL!"

"Leave me alone."

Jake scrunched his blood-stroked eyes after a reply. "It's about MIRIAM! Call!" And he reached for the blocklist keeping Rachel since that very afternoon. Having her message was enough to put him on edge. He knew what to expect: incomprehensible thunders.

The main question was why.

"*Peter Piper picked a peck of pickled peppers. A peck of pickled peppers Peter Piper picked.*" Rachel answered his call. "Make it quick. I don't have all—"

"Miri called you?"

"She did. I was away."

"Why? What were you doing?"

"What the hell do you want, Rachel?"

That cracked voice highlighted her agitation. "She called me! She did! I can't make a word of it. She was like running! I can't understand. She was saying, mom—"

"Rachel, slow down. What?"

"Listen to me! She called me! She's in trouble! Go to her school now!"

"I can't get a damn word, woman!"

A man took her phone. "Jake? Hey, sorry. Miriam called us."

"What's it about?" asked Jake, a bit reluctant.

Craig explained what happened. They were at the dining when Miri called. And Rachel put it on loudspeaker. "What I heard, man, Jesus Christ. I dunno how to describe it."

"What did she say?"

"Dunno. She was running."

"Running? I dropped her at school! I saw her got in."

Miri got on his nerves this morning. She crawled out of the couch where she slept last night and on the way to school insisted for a Pepsi. Jake had to stop at a Citgo after she threw a bizarre tantrum. Before leaving, she said something that stayed in his mind until he was with the Santa Fe. "I love you, Daddy. Take care of yourself. Don't think too hard, okay?"

That was all.

"You recorded it?"

"Yeah, yeah, I'll send it to you. But please, go to her school now!"

The living room spun with Jake's legs shaking in his weight. He put a hand over his nose through a hyperventilating onset. His phone spent three agonizing seconds to play Craig's audio message. The crepitation forced a churning plunge around his insides. And the Honda was revving down the road like a rogue fugitive.

The recording was a distortion of high wind and surrounding blur. Heavy voices rapped as Miri called for help. And yes, she had to be running. On a thin line of patience, all cars were poking fun at him. Everyone was driving wickedly slow at 60 mph. Red light did not stop him from honking. He nearly hit someone after a dangerous maneuver to get ahead for Mt View, where an office lady told him to wait.

"Hey, Clara. I have a parent on emergency here asking for Miriam Brownfield. That's B-R-O-." A moment passed. "What's that?" Her face tightened. "Huh. She's absent?" Jake gripped on the furniture as his heart skipped a beat. "Okay, okay, thank you." And she was stumped when he crumbled into a seat. "Whoa! Sir, are you okay?"

"Can't be absent! I dropped her off!"

"You saw her entering, sir?"

"Yeah!"

She scratched her head. "How can that be? Her teacher said she's not here!"

"You have a security camera here, right?"

"We do but I'm afraid I don't—" They were out of there after Jake played the audio. Her internship badge swung around in their haste for the principal's office. "Madam Principal, we got a problem!"

DeWinter shot to her feet. "What's going on here?"

Jake did not know where to begin. But by the time he was done, DeWinter was on her feet shining in this air-conditioned room. They sped to the security room where the guard Pat Wilson had to put away his breakfast burger for the dozens of surveillance screens. A window was brought upon the main monitor, showing the locker hall where Jake claimed to have last seen Miri.

"You remember what time, sir?"

Jake's hands trembled. "Oh, damn. Uhh."

Pat started the footage from 0730, when students started coming through the opened doors. "What were you doing before or after you came?" asked Karen. "Ordered a pizza? Any calls? Television programs?"

"I – I can't remember – but Good Morning America was on!" He said right afterward. "Oh, that was yesterday!"

"Calm down, Mr. Brownfield. The only way we can–"

"That's her!" Jake shouted, as sharp at 07:41 the camera caught a clear glimpse of Miriam Brownfield. "That's her! I told you! She came to school!"

DeWinter's hand found her mouth. "Jesus Christ! Pat, keep looking at every exit!"

"My daughter didn't run away!"

"But she was running, Mr. Brownfield," said DeWinter, more like a bark. "The last thing we want is a kidnap right at the school compound! Pat, keep looking!" She turned to the intern. "What's your name?"

"Karen Phoht. Accounting."

"Leave your desk. Help Mr. Wilson! Find that girl!"

She was seen squatting against a wall outside the footage room. "You called the cops?" asked Jake.

"Wait. I need a moment."

His mouth fell. "What the fuck? Call the cops already! She's missing, you moron!"

"I can't involve the authorities yet. We don't know what happened!"

"This is my daughter we're talking about!"

"And she's my responsibility! So lemme find her first!"

Two staff members heard the altercation. "Is everything okay, Madam Principal?" asked Mrs. Dedder.

"Please, please, carry on with what you're doing! Everything's under control."

"My daughter is missing. Eighth grade. Miriam Brownfield."

"The new girl?" Mrs. Dedder must have bitten her tongue. "I'm her soc teacher! When did this happen?"

"Irene, go teach something somewhere!" said DeWinter, pale as milk. "I'll handle this." She was pulsing from then. "Now, you look here, Mr. Brownfield. I'm doing all I can to hold this together. Trust me, please."

Jake did not trust her. Neither did Rachel. For the first time, they agreed to something. "Just tell me what's happening, okay?" she said. "Please. Don't lock me out. She's my daughter too, Jake."

"I know. I know. They're still looking at the footages."

"God, I hope she's okay."

"Me too, Rach," said Jake, hearing his ex-wife sobbing. "We know she got in. We got her on camera. It's something. At least, we know she was here."

"That's the only camera there?"

"No. They got another one about a hundred feet or so straight from there. But it was just crowded as hell and they didn't see her at all."

"Oh, fuck."

"I'll keep you updated, Rachel."

"Are you okay?"

He blinked. "What?"

"Are you okay? How are you doing there?"

"I'm okay. Just hurt. But I'm doing best I can."

"Look, I'm sorry for calling the social services."

"Now's really not the time for that."

"I know. I just want you to know that. I really am sorry."

"It's okay."

"We're on our way there."

"Wait, what?"

"We're at the airport," said Rachel. "I wanna be there."

He rubbed his face as a paralysis grew from the sides. "Okay. I'll tell you if I have something."

"Thanks, Jake. Thanks a lot."

Pat and Karen were still barreling through the footages for the plaid-clothed girl with a hair ribbon. The wait ate and spat him to meander aimlessly with a heavy throat. Nothing came from the footages. Miriam Brownfield was missing. There was just one thing to do.

And Katherine DeWinter screamed back when Pat spoke on the phone through this synchronized school network.

6

Katherine DeWinter's final hope rested in pieces when her disciplinarians gave up. They decided for a hushed approach through a cabal-like structure, clinging in a foolish gambit for maybes. Pat Wilson and Karen Phoht found themselves to be her last line – and that was five minutes ago.

In the head office, seven of the most powerful staff were present with Irene Dedder. "Call the damn cops!" she was arguing. "She ain't here!"

"I'm afraid she's right. There's nothing we can do, Madam Principal. I don't think Ms. Brownfield is here."

"We can't waste more time. Get the authorities here."

School Superintendent John Langford's hairline seemed to recede an inch further within that hour. He reached for a telephone upon DeWinter's nod for the one-number line to the authorities.

"Do we declare a lockdown?"

DeWinter took some time to answer. "Not yet," she said. "We wait for the cops."

The phone rang. "We have a suspected kidnapping," said Langford. "No, there's no school shooting. Just possible kidnapping. Send someone."

"School shooting?" asked Jake.

The going rate for that was 1.49 case per million, the second national lowest since those days when Nixon was busy censuring the press. And this Democratic state government was not taking chances – not after the Ellsworth teenager pledged to become the most notorious shooter in history.

It might have been a year since Michael Allen made his first court appearance. The police arrived as if he was still at large, with big guns holstered at ready. DeWinter was in tears when the officers Paxton McCrain and Sherman Brune knocked on her door. "We're looking for Mr. Langford for a possible kidnapping incident."

"Yessir. That'll be me."

"Have you notified the parents?"

Jake stepped forward. "I'm the parent. My ex-wife is on her way."

"Jesus. Anything from security?"

DeWinter brought Officer Brune to the dark room, while Jake remained with the rest in the office. McCrain approached them with admirable professionalism, choosing his words with great care. "Her full name is Miriam Brownfield. That's M-I-R-I-A-M," said Jake. "Lil over five feet. Maybe hundred pound."

"Eighth grade, right? That's what fourteen?"

"Yes, sir. She was born in 2005. January Twenty."

"Anything we can describe her with?"

"You mean clothes?" said Irene Dedder.

"Everything. We might find her stuff somewhere. Like cardigans and sweatshirts. Anything you can remember."

Jake clawed Miri from the back of his mind for a description. "Her hair was a high ponytail from up top," he said, not missing the color of her clothes. "I didn't see her shoes."

"Any scars or birthmarks?"

"No. Wait. Yes. A boil scar at the back. Under the shoulder."

McCrain scribbled everything into his notepad. "You're her teacher, Mrs. Dedder. Does she have a friend?"

"Penny Hollington."

"Yes. Her father Pete. He's my friend."

"Is it possible that Penny mighta hurt her?"

"God, no. She's sweet as an angel."

"Okay. Another important one," said McCrain. "Does she have inhalers, heart pills, glasses?"

"She's not asthmatic but there's this panic attack thing she goes through. Something extreme like fear or anxiety will trigger it."

"That ain't good," said McCrain. "I've saved her picture. You have that number. Keep sending me all the pictures you have. The more I have, the better. Videos. Voice messages. Anything."

"What do you plan on doing, officer?" asked Langford.

"We'll start with a search. Until we determine she's not here anymore—"

"The recording doesn't sound like she's here."

"Doesn't tell us where she is either, Mr. Brownfield," replied McCrain. "We need that recording too. Gotta magnify everything in the background. Noises like a church bell, ice cream truck - anything small is big enough. That's what we're looking for. I also need keys to her locker and I'm gonna take a look at her desk too. Now, Mr. Langford."

Irene told Langford. "I'll come with you."

"One more question. But I dunno who I should be asking," said McCrain. "The time you called us – and that audio piece, it's three hours. Give or take fifteen minutes for Mr. Brownfield to be here. Why wait that long?"

"We thought—"

"You thought?" McCrain was taken aback. "What the fuck? You already have an audio piece sounding like a kidnap!"

"I told her the same," replied Jake.

"That still doesn't excuse *you* for waiting that long. You were a reporter for Chrissake. You don't need a moron's permission to call us."

"Who are you calling a moron?"

McCrain turned to DeWinter. "If she's kidnapped, it'll be on you," he said. "If they moved sixty miles an hour, this girl will be beyond the power of every police department in the whole New England! Do you know how big that is?"

"I'm not a moron, you hear?"

"You really wanna go through this, Madam Principal?" asked McCrain.

"I have a doctorate in Educational Administration. Do you have a doctorate?"

"Guess nowhere in your course say you're supposed to call the authorities when there's even a small suspicion your student is missing?" The silence defeated DeWinter's burning rage. "What the hell is wrong with you two?"

"I'm sorry, officer," said Jake. "I wanted to call you."

"Then why didn't you? It's damn clear. Your girl is not here!" McCrain glared at DeWinter. "Y'all pray we don't find this girl dead and naked somewhere in a ditch!"

Dedder moaned with a gasp. "Officer, please. Find the girl. Please."

Those words hung over Jake and DeWinter, both looking fazed. Miriam's locker had no possible lead. "Does she have social media? Facebook? Twitter?"

"Instagram. She logs in with my Mac sometimes."

"Help us on this, Mr. Brownfield," said McCrain. "Ask anyone and everyone you think she might know. Anyone. Friends. Maybe you have a girlfriend here. The last few diners you went with her. Maybe if you promised to take her somewhere."

"Is she in any sort of a relationship?" asked Brune.

"We just got here."

"That's not an answer."

"I dunno. No, I think," said Jake. "I only see her studying, Instagramming and playing some games."

"What game?"

"An online shooting game. Something RPG."

"Find out."

Jake was out of there bursting straight to the parking space. He managed a poor landing after the steps, regaining balance for his car. A few steps away, he keeled over to retch. His hands never stopped shaking through this low traffic. He was praying; to what god he did not know, hoping it was all a sick prank from political fanatics over his disparaging rant.

Inside his house the biting cold pecked pointily at his skin. "Miriam!" There was no answer. "Miriam!" He kept calling vainly, mustering himself for upstairs. The school should be over anytime soon. In some time, Miriam would return for a hot shower. Her school clothes would be on the floor for Jake to pick up.

The empty laundry bin next to her bed shoved a sour brick down his throat. Her study desk had no clues, neither her cupboard nor drawers. He stood unmoved before the window, thinking as a breeze stung him with a flowery whiff.

"Honey, where are you?"

The doorbell poked a sharp twinge into him.

Spud barked at his thundering speed for the door. It was not Miriam, or McCrain. "Jesus, you okay?" Lottie said as he fell into her. "What happened? Jake? What happened?"

"Miri's missing!"

Lottie froze, her mouth agape. That somewhat ten-second audio crackled and crepitated. But Miriam's scream stayed for a lot longer. The air was hot in this suspense, with both of them shivering as the plastered ceiling rotated. Cold water could not ameliorate his massive head. And Lottie would not stop replaying the horrors.

"Why are you—"

"Shh. I wanna," said Lottie, clicking on the play button again.

And that very same scream amid high wind and noises reached out for Jake, who squealed. "Mommy! Mom! Help!" Those three comprehensible words protruded like a knife. For Lottie, they had a slightly ominous meaning. "Mommy! Mom! Help!" She hit it again. "Mommy! Mom! Help!"

"What is it?"

"You hear that?"

When she repeated, Jake heard the deliberate steps over grass. "The field!" he said.

"Call the cops!"

"Cops? Oh, cops!" Jake lumbered onto his feet. "You go check her room. See if you can find anything like – I dunno, anything!"

Lottie hit the same impasse. It was not a runaway situation; this room was never critical for her rescue. She searched through her folded clothes. In between her books Jake found some cash, doodled envelopes and sanitary pads. "Oh, my God!" he exclaimed. "She's having period?"

"She's fourteen, Jake! Wake up!"

They unearthed a pink book under the mattress. Her daily entries in this diary were a jump of weeks and months with nothing indicative. "I gotta tell McCrain about this bully." Jake gave his face a forceful slather. "Dunno the name! Bet that Pete's daughter—"

"What?"

"Pete. Of course. Come with me!"

He opened up about Pete and Penny on the way to Dunkin'. By the time they arrived, Lottie realized she was holding her breath. The exhalation was the longest she did, catching up as Jake got into the diner for the counter. Cass was buttoning her apron back in place. "Jake?"

"Where's Pete?"

"He's gone back. What's going on?"

"Where's his house?"

"Perham. One Fifty-Eight," replied Cass, shaken.

Jake stormed back to his Honda for ME-43. At Perham Street, Lottie called for 158 which was at the opposite of a dumpster. "Mr. Brownfield?" said Penny. "Is Miri with you?"

"Hey. Can you get your dad?"

"He's asleep," replied Penny. "Just got home."

"Penny, please. Miri is missing. Someone took her!"

The girl was next banging upstairs, which a while later Pete came down looking listlessly. "Muh-missing?" He was out of breath. "Like kidnapped?"

"Yeah, Pete!" Jake cannot put his emotion in one place. "Someone got her."

"Jesus!"

"Mr. Brownfield, what's going on?"

"I need to ask Penny something, Pete. Please?"

"S-sure. Have a seat first. Want something, man?"

"Just water, Pete," said Lottie. "For both of us."

"Okay, Penny. Miri said she's being bullied. You know who bullied her?"

"Naomi Moulin. She's involved?"

"M-m-maybe. Did Naomi threaten her?"

Penny had a troubling look. "She did."

"What did she say? Like wanna kill Miri?"

"Jake!" said Lottie, smacking his back. "For God sake!"

"She's missing, Lottie! She called me but I was fixin' your car. I got electrocuted and was knocked out! She needed my help and I wasn't there! I'm sorry if I'm blunt." He turned back to Penny. "Did Naomi wanna do something bad? Hurt Miri?"

"Naomi always hurt us, Mr. Brownfield. In the gym. Recess. At the lockers." Penny nodded. "That time Miri shouted back. People were there. They saw the whole thing. And Naomi threatened her. She said, you're dead."

"You didn't tell me this!"

"No, no, Pete. It's not her fault," said Jake. "Don't take it on her. This Naomi must have something to do with it." Jake retched after a sip, bringing himself to the floor. "But – why Miri? She just got here."

"They called her a roach."

Lottie's mouth dropped.

"Son of a–" Jake answered his vibrating phone. "You got something?"

Rachel's fractured voice returned. "Hey."

"Oh. Sorry, Rach. Where are you?"

"North Carolina. You found her?"

"Not yet, Rach. I'm asking around."

"Nothing at all? Jake, please find her."

"Trust me, Rachel. I haven't been doin' anything else."

"Get something to eat first. You gotta take care of yourself too."

"Take care of myself," breathed Jake. Another trembling fit besieged his nerves, causing the phone to slip from his grasp. "Take care of myself. Take care of myself."

"Jake?" said Lottie.

"Take care of myself."

"Pete, get an ambulance!"

"No," snapped Jake, reaching to quench an inexistent thirst. "Miri told me that. She told me not to think too hard. To take care of myself. God, she knows she's gonna die. She knows, Pete!"

"Jake. We'll find her alive, dammit. Get yourself together. Fuck, I'm shaking! What'm I supposed to do?"

His head kept still for at least a minute before he went back to his phone. "I'm calling McCrain," he said. "We need that footage Naomi bullied her. It's something!"

The line refused to connect, no matter how many times he tried. "He's probably busy," said Lottie. "Here. Lemme try."

"Penny – something you remember, like anything, tell your dad, okay?"

"Tell me? Heck I'll drive to your place," said Pete.

They shared a hug before leaving. And Jake had to be on his couch, still with his phone. He did everything, from restarting to refitting the SIM card. It was still the damn voicemail. After another failed attempt, he threw the phone away. Peculiarly the blue screen of his display hung emptily upon the air, coalescing with the three LED bulbs by the ceiling.

The light twisted and twirled for two, three elongations before taking the four sides of a perfect square. Within that very instance, the shape turned into a circle and then circles. A second later, those circles popped and merged into an oval ring of light. Meanwhile, his arms and legs floated beyond natural reams with sharp sensations upon his skin.

"There's bourbon in the fridge. Can you–"

"No alcohol. You're having a migraine."

"How'd you know?"

Lottie gave a sigh. "Your mom came to us for a chat and then snap, she started vomiting and can't see anything so she slept in our spare room." The thing on the coffee table made sense. It was not a sock, rather a silicon compress on a bowl of ice. Lottie stroked his head in a smooth motion. "Same like your mom," she said, when he moaned. "God rest her soul."

"You don't – think I have – a tumor, d'you?"

"Shut up." She knew her way for a sweet spot. "Your scalp's really hot," she said. "You need a haircut."

"Mmm."

He was not aware of the passing hours. A distinct sound caught his attention. He opened his eyes, looking out toward the window for a cab leaving the vicinity.

Rachel was here.

7

24 hours after Miri's disappearance, Farmington made headlines. Radio broadcasts picked information from the police, asking everyone from New Vineyard to Church of Nazarene and Franklin Memorial Hospital for vigilance. Those heavy clouds rolled into a manifestation of Katherine DeWinter's feelings. It was all like a bad dream to her. First a rich family breathed down her neck over a stolen iPhone. She placated them for a small compromise. "Fucking bitch," she muttered, recalling Amelia's catty eyes.

Now a child went missing within her draconian watch. And the public vented in a hot-tempered wave. "Don't go to Twitter," Irene told her.

Those usual and useless "thoughts and prayers" flew across the cyberspace, trending those hashtags for Miriam. Questions were raised. Like hungry pit bulls, they came against the school. Before long, there was that call everyone feared. "Someone should be fired!"

The first to say that was someone in Belfast – not the Linenopolis where the Titanic was built, but that soft-pedaled tourist attraction in Waldo County. DeWinter reclined against her high chair in the locked office. Her desk was now a medical dispensary, with prescription drugs from the safe she kept under her desk. She looked as the plain-clothed doctor diluted the orange CYRAMZA for an intravenous infusion. "One problem at a time, Madam Principal."

"Yeah." She took her phone out for a forcible scoff. "That bastard!" Her calls to Jake went unanswered. She resorted to messaging via WhatsApp, which was now a long line of blueticks. "Howahwish thabrat didnah school thadday."

The doctor pulled a tissue paper for her nosebleed. "Easy now, Madam," said the doctor. "The effects are starting."

"I'm heffing a faint."

"Been telling you many times," he said. "You have to resign. You're too ill."

DeWinter shook her head. "Muhbe 'fter I sort this. Tell mehif Brownfield calls."

"Sure, Madam Principal."

Jake had given him a cold shoulder since that earful from McCrain. But he was not himself, panicking like a mad moose in his Honda which barreled way above the cautionary top speed toward the station. Midway, Jake made the 59th failed attempt for Paxton McCrain. He pulled over behind a backing police cruiser, ignoring the driving officer. "Is McCrain inside?"

"You gotta move your car!"

"Is McCrain inside?" he yelled back.

"I have no idea, you idiot! Move your car or I'm towing it!"

Jake restrained his fist, turning as Craig moved the car. He was on fire the moment he got to the front desk. "Sir, don't you take that tone with me!" said an officer. "We're doing what we can for you!"

"I'm not taking any tone with anyone! I've been waiting for the whole day. This policeman. This officer McCrain told me to call him back when I have something," said Jake. "Well, I have something. I need him. I need him now!"

"Maybe you didn't pay your bills? That's why you can't reach him!

Jake's mouth quivered. "I ain't a fucking cheapskate like you!"

"Look, Mr. Blackfield!"

"Brownfield!" he corrected. "You can't even spell my name! And this fucking town gave you a job? God. I'm so screwed. I'm fucking screwed!"

The officer pointed an indignant finger. "Your bitty bitch probably ran away because this attitude of yours! Or maybe she's taken. Deputy McCrain is busy figuring out which is which. He'll call you back. If she's not back yet the next day, come here. For now, go fuck yourself at home and wait!"

Temper misfired Jake's voice and turned his face red. Craig was there to drag him out. "Come on! Come on now! Ain't worth it!" He drove Jake back. "I'm sorry, Jake. I'm sorry for–"

"He didn't even listen! That's my girl out there!"

"I know. I know. You're not wrong."

"Why can't he just patch me to McCrain?"

"I'm with ya'."

"Are you?" asked Jake. "You don't know me. You dunno Miriam. Why are you even here?"

Craig sighed. "We both got off to a wrong start."

"Wrong start? You fucked my wife!"

"I'm an environmental engineer with Masters in Urban Agriculture, man."

"Fucking impressed! I interviewed a former president!"

"Jake, I'm saying I ain't a gas attendant fucking any girl I like," said Craig. "She told me she's single, looking for a good time. That's how I got caught into this!"

"And you're still with her!"

"What do you want me to do? Dump her?"

Jake tried to reply but had to swallow hard against the acidic buildup in his chest. That bile in the midsection triggered a wavering movement around them. Twice he held a deep breath. The last thing he needed now was an acerbic throat. It did not go away even in his bedroom. He looked into a mirror, where a dead man stared back at him. The socket bags weighed a ton, giving him a droopy encumbrance.

"Hey, I got you something," said Lottie.

Ginger tea and bread toasts smoothed him into a short, dreamless sleep. When he woke up, the pummeling headache was no more. In the showers he planned what to say. "Excuse me, officer," he breathed. "My daughter is still missing. I need to see Officer McCrain. Been trying to contact him."

Luck stood with him as the officer on duty was a woman. She took him from the moment he spoke about Miriam. "Any responsible parent in your position will do things you did, sir," said Officer Olivia Tatham.

"It's a full day missing. You got any lead right now?"

"Mr. Brownfield, my next words will be very fruitless. But we're really doing all we can. And I don't know where Deputy McCrain is," said Tatham. "Yes, it is unacceptable. It's the same thing back in Phoenix where I was. Officers go missing for days and days to investigate. It's nothing like what you're watching on TV."

"The deputy asked me to call him if I have something. Well, I have something."

"Yes? What's that?"

"My daughter was threatened by the bully Naomi Moulin. I tried calling McCrain to talk about this. I have witness. Penny Hollington."

A bypassing officer must have overheard. "Did you tell us about this before?"

"I tried. No, I didn't. I tried. I asked for McCrain."

"You don't need the deputy for this, Mr. Brownfield," said Tatham, not losing that persuasive calmness in her voice. "What else have you found out?"

The law was all of a sudden new to him. Those glowing years hoisted him to the mountaintop which overlooked the pimples and scars within the system on the ground. Those defects now caught him off guard, delaying his complete statement about Naomi Moulin's threat against Miriam. And he did not return home until that night; for seven hours, McCrain dodged his calls.

"Hey, honey."

Surprise caught him on a twist after seeing Rachel. 15 years with that greeting bricked an unbreakable habit, leaving him red-faced with anger. But there was a response from a neighbor who was dressed to stay.

She joined him on the balcony upstairs. "Where are you, Miri? Where are you?" The overlapping shadow indicated her presence. "You don't have to go," he said as Lottie was leaving.

Rachel folded her hands around the Ybenlow crewneck Miri wore during the stormy night. "The police had anything, Jake?" she voiced.

"Nothing yet."

"What are they doing?"

"They said the Deputy is investigating. I'd join him if I know where he is!" said Jake, shaking his head. "My money is on that Naomi. She must have something to do with this. God,

I'm gonna burn their house to the ground! Fucking burn it to the ground!"

Lottie fought a bout of hesitation and wrapped him in her arms. Her head leaned against the hardness of his shoulder. They remained unmoved for ten slow minutes, even after that soft shut of the door. "Thought she'd never leave," said Lottie.

"You ordered burgers, right?'

"Yeah. They're on the counter.

"Can you bring 'em here – please?"

"Why here?"

"You'll understand soon."

The beef patty juiced that medium-rare ambrosia, going along with melted cheese, spiced mayo and tomato slices. It was all in silence until that perforating rumble of an argument, which had Lottie flinching with alarm.

"Jesus. You go through this every day?"

"Every now'n then for fifteen years."

The next morning Jake landed within the crossfire. He was pacing up and down the living room. "Will you stop that? You're driving me nuts!" He shot Rachel a quick look with eyes like fiery fissures. "Just stop! It's not gonna help finding her."

"You're in *my* house. Remember that."

"Well, she's *my* daughter!"

Jake placed a foot toward her but then decided against it. His bruised eyes were slits, though with a sinful wink of joy. Because he continued meandering to that point Rachel stood thumping the floor for the guest room. "You wanna say something too?"

Craig raised his hands with a look of surrender. "I dunno how the hell I got caught in this mess."

"Sure you do," said Jake. "You're not her first." Craig's flair went purpling within seconds. "You thought you were?"

The whole living room had a better semblance without them. Jake took the couch before realizing another trouble was forthcoming in a blue Porsche. The curtain-haired woman traipsed across his lawn like an intoxicated penguin. "You got my messages, Mr. Brownfield," said Katherine DeWinter.

"I did."

"Were you busy?"

"There's no point replying to a management maniac."

DeWinter's lips were thin. "Mr. Brownfield—"

"Look, I don't wanna talk to you. Whatever you wanna say won't make a fucking difference."

"I just wanna say, I'm sorry."

"No. You're not," said Jake, immediately. "You're just covering up for your image." The ten-foot distance did not drown DeWinter's exhalation. "You said what you wanted me to hear. Now leave because you ain't welcomed here until you find my girl."

"I'll do my best, Mr. Brownfield. I called everyone for a direct interview. Already did with BDN. Soon CNN, Fox – everyone."

"Great. You can let the whole damn world know that you're lawyering up."

Electrocution surged through her nerves. "I beg your pardon?" she breathed.

"Sixty miles an hour and Miri's out of New England. Thanks to the both of us. She could even be in Mexico now. Go British if you want, I don't care. It won't stop what's coming to your school."

DeWinter's visit gave him time to prepare for the press. His trained experience curated the reporters' questions, bringing them into the path he wanted to get details out without irrelevant scrutiny. He stood beside Rachel, who held the Galaxy tablet with Miri's latest picture on display. "Folks, thank you for coming," he began with a hoarse voice. "Thanks a lot for helping us get Miriam Brownfield on air. She's still missing. I repeat, still missing. I would like to humbly ask you to please zoom into my baby's picture – if you guys have seen her, please, we beg you call 911."

"We want her back," said Rachel, with a whimper. "We love her so much!"

The staged warmth between them was over after the conference. Jake retreated into his room, where he scrolled his work pictures in an album. The sickly faces afforded a blank expression with baggy, lifeless eyes. "Who are they?" asked Lottie.

"They lost their kids same way as me now," said Jake. "They were nothing but stories to me back then. Now I know what it really felt to be on their side for a change."

"We'll find her, Jake. I uploaded her pictures on all Facebook groups I'm in. The Community WhatsApp too. We'll find her."

Nobody went against his private life. Tabloids left columns for Miriam in a show of statewide solidarity. Neighbors came with food, love and thoughts-and-prayers. At high noon, Jake received Lottie's parents at long last. Donna Reade made sure Jake had enough to eat for a week. They brought a bag of airtight homecooked meals to fill up his freezer.

And Charles with those big, blue eyes kept Jake in his warm watch. Nobody stayed with Craig and Rachel, two aliens legal but unwelcomed. Before leaving, Charles told Jake. "Hang in there, kid. We hope for the best."

"Thank you, sir. Thanks for coming."

Charles tapped on his elbow. "Went through the same with Charlotte," he said, smiling that empty smile. "Keep us posted. Whatever you need."

Miriam was the top trending issue that night. Well-meaning people flocked together to prop up an online awareness campaign with Miriam's Instagram photos. While Jake read these posts, the house rumbled. Craig and Rachel got into another heated altercation over something. "Holy shit. They're at it again?"

"Not surprised," said Jake, flicking a cigarette butt from his balcony.

His inbox was full of requests asking for his viewpoint about the Amazon wildfires. It had been a thing since January, something relatable to a dangerous practice in Southeast Asia. Dry seasons greenlit industry players to slash and burn jungles for plantations. He skimmed through the messages, typing and deleting. These requests soon turned into comforting words.

"Jesus, man. Sorry. I didn't know!"

"Holy shit, Jake. Is everything okay?"

"Jake! What happened?"

A very close friend also messaged him. "Babe! Okay if I call? How did this happen?"

"Jake, I'm really sorry for what happened. If there's anything I can help you with, anything at all!"

His replies soon fumbled into a short post attaching his last photo with Miri. "I apologize I can't respond to everyone. Y'all are so amazing. Thanks for your concern. My baby is still missing. Please share this post! Please!" he added as a caption.

He slammed his middle finger upon the trackpad for a left-click function upon the post button. The loading wheel spun, and right after that, McCrain resurged.

"Hello! Deputy McCrain? That you?"

"Mr. Brownfield. Sorry for–"

Jake did not care how he sounded. "Where – on earth – have you – been?"

"Sorry. Sorry," replied McCrain. "I've been outta town looking out over something."

"And? Keep talking!"

"Some bastard called the station telling us they had Miriam," said McCrain, ten fingers poking out of the phone to clinch Jake's heart. "Turns out to be nothing. Thinks it a good joke."

"Motherfucker! He should be arrested!"

"Renbarger will prosecute him on whatever grounds he can. But this Moulin thing you told us – it's something we gotta talk about!"

It slipped his mind. He groped for a response, staring at himself in the mirror. "I found out from my friend," said Jake, wrecking his face hard to spill the things at the tip of his tongue. "Puh-puh-puh Peter Hollington. His daughter Penny is Miri's best friend. She said that a girl named Naomi threatened to kill Miri."

"Naomi wanted her dead and then this happened. You're sure this Penny said Naomi Moulin, right?"

"Yes. Why? What's up?"

Jake could hear McCrain ruffling pages and slamming keyboards. "Mr. Brownfield. I need you at the station now," he said. "Our chief been asking for you. Your ex-wife as well. We think we know where Miriam is."

He kicked the floor to break Craig and Rachel from the stupid fight. And they sped to meet the Chief of Farmington Police. Robert Tashtego was a familiar face from Jake's past, greeting them together as a friend. "Jake, I was hoping we'd meet again but god, not for this."

"It's okay, Bob."

"I'll cut straight to the chase," said Tashtego. "Naomi's dad is Willis Moulin. Deputy McCrain filled you in about the prank thing. Well, it's this Willis. He's the son of a bitch pranking us saying they have Miriam."

Both of them processed with difficulty over a cup of coffee. "We questioned him," said McCrain. "He claimed he's only messing around over a stupid bet. He never knew his daughter threatened Miriam."

"This is fishy as hell!" said Rachel.

"I agree. When I read your report, Mr. Brownfield, I start thinking maybe Miriam is with the Moulins."

"But this prank thing changed the game. We still think Naomi got something to do with Miriam's disappearance but just not in the Moulin residence," said Tashtego. "And we can't find Naomi anywhere. She's not even in school. That's why we haven't kicked down any doors yet. We have the house surrounded with surveillance. They ain't going anywhere."

"On a scale one to ten, how sure are you she's there?"

"I'd say three. That's still something!" said Tashtego. "We've taken Willis into custody. He hasn't contacted anyone. Naomi is all alone. She'll make mistake and slip up."

"Bob, don't do what DeWinter did," said Jake. "Bring the big guns and blow the house to hell. If my daughter is in there, three out of ten is good – just get her outta there. For my sake, please, help my daughter. Get her out of there!"

8

Time was never kind to Chief Tashtego. Robert was among the best students in D.T. Cornville, back in the dark ages when he had demeaning nicknames. At college, he shook off this shameful past and debuted in that one sport people least expected. The opposing side laughed when he entered the field. Even his team held in angst. But history was made; he was known as the Pocket Fireball, a redemption blasting his scholarship on a crosscut to the oath as the Chief of Police.

And he did that losing only an inch of his criminally short height. He however proved to be stainless, never a sycophant to the unholy powers in politics. He had the gift of cajolery and diplomacy, choosing words to strike the best vibes. He knew when to shout and most important thing of all, he knew when not to.

Hours seemed to make a quick pass with Craig ambulating outside, as if his daughter was the one who was declared missing. No sound permeated from that frosted glass door. Tashtego never slouched; the only motion was an arm movement as he jotted essential parts of the crime in a cream-paper notepad. "We need some bones if Miriam wasn't with the Moulins," he said, polishing for accuracy: Jake passed out while Miriam was at school, and Rachel was… "what were you doing, Ms. Tempner?"

"Eating."

"Tell 'em the truth."

"I am!"

Jake swung a glance to knife that expression on her face he knew too well. "She was banging her boyfriend," he said, an emotional hiss from the woman.

"We'll run with sleeping," said McCrain.

Tashtego shifted his position, looking confused. "You were having an intercourse on a Wednesday morning with your boyfriend who's an engineer?"

"He called in sick that day."

"What's his company again?" asked McCrain.

"Huntsville Environment."

"He was sick for work but not sick for sex?"

Rachel hit a wall. "What does this have to do with anything?"

"Better us than the media, Ms. Tempner. Well?"

"I kinda talked him into it," said Rachel, blushing.

"Okay. I know what that means. But was it tantamount to sexual abuse?"

"Well, he's still with me."

"Yes or no," said Tashtego.

"Just h-h-handcuffs and-."

"Oh, fuck. Bob, can we move on?" said Jake.

"This doesn't leak to the press, you two hear me?"

Their night was far from over. Stepping out of the chief's office, they found themselves paralyzed like a deer in a headlight. Those white flares settled in to be camera flashes from a pack of reporters waiting for them. They jumped straight for Jake and Rachel, shoving those microphones to their sallow faces. Their vision fixed against the sudden overexposure, as those barks frothed for collective noises the press were known to make.

Craig was nowhere to be found, perhaps escorted away. Jake with a deep breath met those silhouetted faces. The town immortalized Dr. David Morgan for bringing the state media. Tonight, Jacob Brownfield brought the Big Three. Every major news picked the story – but again their answers must shape the narrative of that story.

"Mr. Brownfield, you received a phone call from Miriam before she went missing?"

"Yes. But I was asleep. She called her mother who recorded the conversation."

"What did she say, Ms. Tempner?"

Rachel stuttered. "H-help. Asking f-for help," she said. "She was running."

"Our sources indicate that she has an asthma. Did she have an inhaler?"

"Not asthma. It's just a panic attack."

"Her medical record said asthma when she was six."

"Six?"

"That time she got to the attic," said Jake. "Bird infestation. It was bad I can't breathe."

"Some claim this is a runaway from an unhappy home."

"Every family has issues. Mine included," said Jake. "But the cops are investigating this an abduction. Not a runaway."

"Her Instagram posts–"

"It's easy to cook up a story from a few posts. Lemme remind we're dealing with a fourteen-year-old girl. Every dad everywhere knows how challenging it is to raise a teenager especially without a job." Jake continued. "I couldn't get a job no matter how hard I tried. And Miriam was always there telling me to keep going on and on."

The reporter showed a picture of Lottie with the fishing reel. "Might wanna tell us who she is?"

"My neighbor. She looked after my mom. She likes my daughter."

"She seemed very attached. You're even holding her baby."

"Ain't nothing wrong about that. Anything else?"

"Just this one – what was the last thing Miriam told you?"

That very thing cut deeply. His glance met Tashtego, who nodded. And he was back in the Honda, his skin tight after a slow drive through a foggy spray. The red light was longer than usual, refracting his vision to surface a memory of his travels. He learned about behavioral changes when near death. This superstition was not strange in the United States. In 2017, he was interviewing for the Nurses Day.

His editors gauged around staffing and long hours, with sexual harassments to piggyback the #MeToo movement. Jake threw a step ahead with a question. "How do people act like right before death?"

To his surprise, those nurses at the hospital near Milton Frank Stadium cited observable changes. Miriam went through the same phase. "I love you, Daddy. Take care of yourself. Don't work too hard."

When Jake spoke about that, Rachel and Craig stayed still for an absolute period.

"No shit. The cops know?"

Jake shook his head. "I'm going to bed. When Miri comes out of the Moulin's, someone's gonna pay." He stomped on his way to the showers, where he echoed. "Someone's gonna pay."

Hunger took a different turn now that Miriam occupied most of his mind. His innards were much like a pretzel. Oat biscuits filled him the whole day. Warm milk drifted him into a rampage of images, slowing for a hotdog in the middle of Central Park. Miriam sat on a park bench, smiling. A howl turned him across the grass straight at those tubular elongations balancing a space shuttle.

Jake blinked, when an unseen cinder block went through him – realizing with an opened mouth he was back in his room staring at a scale model of Apollo 11. Loud voices broke from the next room. He stole a quiet space with a pillow upon his head, tossing and turning to no avail.

His Facebook wall was blowing up with an endless update about Miriam. The press prepared, quoted and released a chronology of the event. "Until we know otherwise, I believe she's out there somewhere," said Tashtego. "She must be found, whatever the cost."

The sudden silence filled him with a hunch. He knew the television was on before getting up for the door. Craig was watching a news network in which an anchorperson was asserting about Miri. "Police officers are now on an expansive search for a fourteen-year-old girl who went missing after going to school," he said. The visual team cropped an Instagram picture as a small display. "Miriam Brownfield from Farmington, Maine, disappeared right after calling her mother.

"We're about to show you the recording of that call. Viewer discretion is advised, for what you hear is disturbing."

"How the hell they got your recording?" said Jake.

His calm tone caused a jolt. "Jesus! How long you been standing there?"

The anchorperson continued, reacting to the audio piece. "Chief Robert Tashtego does not rule out an anti-Semitic possibility after surveillance footage revealed Naomi Moulin–"

the girl's headshot appeared. "–in a tangle with Miriam. Naomi is at the moment the main suspect following a freak prank from a man who the police later determined to be her father." A live footage of a terrace was shown with the blue-red police light and yellow tapes. "Here's a little backstory about the Brownfield. Miriam's grandfather was a famous pulpiter, Abraham Brownfield."

Jake smiled when his father's pixelated picture appeared. "I didn't know your dad is a big shot," said Craig.

"What else don't you know?"

An expert was introduced to discuss about anti-Semitism. She began with a well-rehearsed statement, praying for Miri's safety. In the same minute, she made a long leap to argue about a particular kidnapping which took place in a Parisian banlieue. "Ilan Halimi was lured to an apartment block, where he was held captive by a group who demanded a ransom of nearly half a million Euros. Halimi's unclothed body was found at a roadside. He was tortured for three weeks straight, because this group believed all Jews are rich."

She bridged that argument to blood libel, before talking about human trafficking, slavery and murder.

"Of course, we don't want any of these," she said. "And we're hoping this is not anti-Semitism. Losing a child without closure is a nightmare. Every kidnapping brings us to think about Madeleine McCann. A British girl from Leicester, disappeared from her bed in Portugal. To this day, no one knows what happened to her.

"And Shannon Matthews a year after McCann, though this one in Dewsbury happened to be a sick plan to generate money from publicity and claim rewards.

"Miriam Brownfield's case is very serious. It's no easy task for the police. It can drag into twelve years like McCann. Or just ten days as Nora Anne, the Irish who went missing in Malaysia before they found her body."

These tragic ends tipped Jake to a boiling point. But a woman's voice called an end to it. "What are you guys doing?" said Rachel, standing in a bathrobe behind them.

"What does it look like we're doing?" asked Craig.

"Turn it off!"

Jake snatched the remote for the button. "It's already late, y'all. Goodnight."

"Late? Late!" yelled Rachel. "Of course, it's late! It's too late to do anything, because of you!"

"You promised!" said Craig, his teeth clenched.

"I told you, Jake! I told you! Give her to me! Give me the fucking custody! I deserve her more than you do! I'm the mother. I gave birth to her! Not you! You're nothing!"

Hot blood throbbed his pulsing temples. He fixed her a glare – the same glare from those many confrontations in their expired marriage. Rachel stood poised with both arms crossed, then her legs betraying into a falter.

"I have a question," said Jake. "How does it feel to leave tons and tons of comments and Miri won't reply to even one?" That had her. "She replies to Charlotte. She even calls her mom. How does that feel, Rachel?"

"She called that bitch mom?"

"Charlotte became a better mom than you in just weeks. You still haven't answered me. What does it feel?"

"If you love her so much, why don't you just go fuck her and leave Miriam with me?"

"Assuming Miriam even wanna look at you."

"Alright! That's enough!" shouted Craig. "Rachel, go back to your room!"

Rachel screamed back. "I'm not a fucking kid, Craig!"

That started another argument. Jake found his way out of that mess. "You cheated on him! You lied to me!" Craig yelled. "But I'm still here, so sick to death with your attitude!"

"Why are you here? If you wanna go, just go! This is none of your business anyway!"

"None of my business? You're the one begging me to come in the first place!"

"If I know you'll act like this, I woulda hitchhiked here!"

"Oh, yeah? And get pregnant with every guy giving you a fucking lift?"

Jake had to restrain a laugh. "Oh, you didn't! You fucking didn't!" He heard footsteps, picturing her pitiful stride from the living room. "You asshole! You fucking asshole!"

"Don't you walk away with me, woman!"

"Let go of me, you bastard!"

Rachel howled upon a smack. "You wanna act tough? Why, 'cause Jake left you that house? Pretty decent security, huh? Well, guess what, bitch!" Craig's shout thundered with a shudder. "It's a thirty-year loan! He left you with what's half of it! You want me to walk out? Fine! You probably look good as a whore anyway! Oh, wait! You already are!"

"Craig, baby! Please! Please!" Those heavy movements prompted Jake to get out, not stepping in as Craig dragged his ex-wife toward the front door. "Please! I love you!"

"You love me? You fucking love me?" said Craig, with another slap to her face. "You will start talking to your man like a bitch that you are! You're mine, bitch! I own you!"

"Yes! Yes! I'm yours!"

The fiasco crumbled on its own when they saw Jake. A minute was like a year, three of them in their places. "Time to get a motel," said Jake, which Craig nodded. "Tonight." Rachel shook into a racketing sob. "You two look good together. I mean that."

"I'm so sorry, Jake."

"You were right." Jake breathed. "About the Huntsville house. You didn't win it, Rachel. It's the oldest trick in the book. I figured you won't be able to pay a dime from the day you got kicked out of modeling over that caesarean thing."

Craig stood. "I need some air."

"Damn right you do," replied Jake. "Take the highway, while you still can. No turning back once you said the vow. She'll clean you out with alimony."

"Jake!"

"I wanted Miriam to have a happy home, Rachel! And we both know you can't give that. Not with him."

Craig turned toward Jake. "I don't care about Miriam not replying to any of her comments." He swung a look upon Rachel. "She got it coming, yeah. But I came here for you. I wanna help you outta this."

"Sweet, but you can't even help your damn selves. Probably you realize that now. The whole town can hear you arguing." He added. "Let me be straight with you. She's not worth a penny. She'll do anybody she wants. I'm done with you two anyway," he said. "I'm going out. When I get back, I want you gone. The both of you."

Jake gathered his wallet and keys for a night drive. Charlotte lied about living across the street. Highland Avenue was an isolated road, half a mile away in between Anson and Titcomb. The Reades owned an enviable corner to themselves, surrounded with waving pines.

"That bad, huh?"

"Yep. Your parents asleep?"

"My dad's upstairs – last door to the right."

A small Rowenta fan was blowing hot air to the art easel in the middle of the room. Charles was found adjusting the temperature and humidity on the digital panel of a space heater. "Jake, what a surprise!" he said. "Come on in!"

"Quite a setup, Mr. Reade."

"You like it? Took me a month to get it right."

"What you working on?"

The lighting balance from a combination of natural and LED was inciting the painting to life. Charles opted for varying colors to conjure a dark tone of a wrinkled man buried in wavy strands of a graying beard. "Just added some finishing," he said, while positioning an octagonal softbox 10 feet to the left. On the right was a tripod holding a Canon EOS. "Now lemme change this focal length to there – 70 mill."

"You sure know your ways with cameras," said Jake.

"Don't go ageist on me." His soft laugh rolled into a throaty rumble. "No, bad lighting. Jake, see if you can move that thing closer." A ring light was casting a soft shadow upon the canvas, well away from the camera focus. "Closer, closer," he said, waving as Jake helped for a good distribution. "Just need that triangle on the cheek."

"Oh, you mean the Rembrandt?"

"Yeah. It used to be easier when I was starting. Wait, you know about Rembrandt?"

"It's standard, Mr. Reade. Here, I'll give a try."

The final settings had that cinematographic quality. Lottie placed three shots of brandy on the study table as they were getting it done. "Have a drink, kid, "said Charles. "I'll run this on Photoshop tomorrow."

"You're doing this for social media or something?"

"Too old for that," said Charles. "I'm in some magazines. Every now and then, these magazines showcase your stuff to the billionaires in New York, Florida, California, Moscow, Beijing, Singapore – you name it."

"How much can you close for that?"

"Maybe ten grand," said Lottie. "That's some expensive acrylic I gotta tell you."

"Acrylic? I thought it was oil."

"Nah, oil gives you some of that glossy finish. I tried before but it doesn't have that feeling." Jake sensed the foreboding topic when Charles cleared his throat. "So, kid, police gave you anything?"

Jake elaborated all events from the police station to his home. "Of all the people to go missing, why not Rachel. God, I'd gladly pay someone to make it happen."

"She's a mom. I'd flip too if it's Mason out there with some bad guys."

"Trust me. She'd want that!"

"Whoa. She's jealous of *me*? She doesn't understand the whole point of being divorced! You two ain't got nothing going on," she said, chuckling. "What's her problem anyway? I mean, she moved on pretty quick."

"It's just the way things are with some women, I'm afraid," said Charles, both eyes on the engraved ceiling. "You're not alone, Jake. Too many fathers have this kind of baby mamas. Lucky you have full custody. They get partials or just visitations. And if they have a girlfriend around the kid, their baby mama will throw a big drama you can sell a movie deal! But it's okay if they get under every man in town. They're the victim on the inside, according to themselves as some fuckface judges in family courts."

The words stuck for a while. "Damn if I do this; damn if I do that," he said

"Exactly. That's the hell a lot of dads are going through, wishing they get a fair judgment."

An incoming call interrupted the conversation. The blue screen showed an unknown number over a location, which seized his nerves. It cannot be. He read again and was sure his phone stated the call came from Utah.

When he answered, his voice failed.

"Ruth?"

9

April 4, 1992.

It felt like a thousand years ago. Jake remembered that Saturday. Everyone remembered when Abe found out about Ruth. And the family lost her since then. How Rhoda insisted, pleaded and then begged – everything was still in Jake's ears. Now everyone who wronged Ruth was dead. And that mousy voice smashed Jake back to his childhood.

Ruth was crying. "I saw the news, Jake," she said. "Got your number from the posters!"

"I – it's good to – damn, girl, where the hell you been? How the hell you been?"

"I'm doing good, Jakey."

"Jakey," he breathed. "Been too long, Rooster!"

"Yeah," she said, laughing. "I can't believe this is happening."

"Me neither, Ruth. You doin' okay?"

"We're good. How's Mom taking this?"

Jake's tongue was tied. "Mom, Ruth?"

"She must be very upset."

"No one told you?" he said, shaking. "Mom's gone."

Air must have punched out of her lungs, crackling. "When?"

With a brick in chest, Jake opened up about their mother. He lost the comfortable spot after getting up for the call. That romantic inclination was in pieces. But Lottie with understanding maturity chipped in to throw bits and pieces during Rhoda's final years. Ruth fell quiet for about half a thumping minute, perhaps closing her blackened eyes in the midst of raspy breaths and heavy background movements.

Then that familiar noise permeated into this gloom. An announcing voice followed that chime-like output from an overhead speaker. Jake cannot make out a context other than something about Gate Five. "Ruth? What's that?" he asked.

"That's my flight."

"Where are you?"

"Some airport in Texas."

"Oh. You goin' somewhere?"

"We're coming home."

His face vibrated in this state of utter shock. He looked at the wallpaper upon his phone and turned to Lottie, a gesture that seemed to take forever. If Donna was not sleeping, he might have screamed. "For real?" said Lottie, gasping. "Ruth's coming?"

"Jesus! That's something!"

"Why are they in Texas? I thought they're in Utah?"

"Transit, maybe. Who cares?" said Charles. "But you can't go to the airport tomorrow. The police could call you anytime. Especially with that crazy bitch at your home."

"Dad, don't say that."

"Sorry," said Charles, his hand flying in an apologetic motion. "Just came out. The cops can call him for anything. So, I guess I'll go fetch 'em."

"N-no, Dad. I don't trust you with the wheel. I'll go."

"I dunno what I'd do without y'all!" said Jake.

The endless blackness in the spare room began nibbling at him. The whole talk, he realized, was a placebo. Now his mind faced a test with an overtaking headache. He put a pillow under both legs, which he found on the floor after finishing in the bathroom. The morning sun hovered above those pines, kissing the adjoining balcony where there was a recliner for him. He only sat for a few seconds before setting out for the kitchen.

"Morning."

"Good morning, Jake. Charles told me you're here. Want some pancakes?"

"Sure. Do you have a charger? My phone went out."

"It's in the living room," said Donna, directing him to a socket.

The phone took some time to regain power for a light use. "You at the airport?" He texted Lottie.

A moment after reading, she replied with a voice message, "nearly there. They ain't here yet. There's a delay in Boston for about four hours."

"Ruth didn't say. How you know?"

Three dots flickered. "Her son's FB."

"Okay. Don't drive too fast." A quick movement turned him to the stairs, where Charles stood before the mirror at the landing. "Going somewhere, Mr. Reade?"

"The bookstore," he said. "Gotta cover Froggie."

"Froggie?"

"I mean, Charlotte. Can't really let the staff decide everything. Sorry I can't stay, kid."

"No. I'm the one who should apologize."

"She could use some time off the 'store. Now coffee is in the coffeemaker. Look for the dishwasher for pancakes."

Jake scratched his head in bewilderment. Those clinks took him back to the kitchen, where Donna was setting his breakfast on the countertop. The Reades had an acquired taste on kitchen configurations, leaning closer toward a minimalist style with little tolerance for clutters. The interior designer embedded an induction hob in parallel to the sink atop a small Toshiba dishwasher. Everything was built-in, except for the convection oven and of course that supersized refrigerator.

"Admiring the kitchen?" quipped Donna.

"I was looking for a coffeemaker."

Donna used a kitchen roll for those black particles near the sink. "We don't have one. Too techy, if you ask me."

"Mr. Reade told me there's coffee in the coffeemaker."

At that point her face went red. "That asshole," she said. "He's talking about me!"

Jake smacked his forehead. "Oh, my God!"

"Don't mind him. He does that to everybody. You shoulda seen when he was younger," said Donna. "He rubbed a lot of people the wrong way telling them to get something to eat from the dishwasher." The pancake went down Jake's throat, hard. "I'm glad nobody shot him with that mouth he got."

Jake smiled, not looking at Donna in the eyes. The pancake filled his cramping cavity with a blueberry tinge. A while later, he asked, "where's Mason?"

"Still asleep in our room. Up all night watching James Corden."

"That's a mini-me there. I'm a Stephen Colbert guy."

Donna placed her mug of coffee. "I don't mean to pry, Jake. How's your ex holding up?"

"Not well, with this whole thing goin' and her new relationship. They been fighting and fighting. I had to run here or else, I will get arrested."

"Assaulting people don't solve anything, Jake."

"Murdering people will. They deserve it, Mrs. Reade."

Donna scoffed. "If you ask me, they should be in a motel. Not nice to have her under the same roof. But of course, I respect your decision."

"It wasn't mine to make. I never wanted them. Just can't kick a mother out on the first day."

"Yeah. I guess you're right. If only she's half how your mother was," said Donna. "The day we went to yours, I swear I felt her, Jake. I know it's superstitious. But I am spiritual. A good person like Rhoda will be there in that house so long as we remember her. To think she's watching that woman—" she sighed. "I'm sorry to say this. That Rachel is a disease."

"You chose your words too carefully, Mrs. Reade. Miriam calls her a bitch."

"Still nothing from the cops?"

"Now that you asked, I'm gonna call that chief."

A zesty tang aired the living room after he burped a miasma of butter and cinnamon. The small embarrassment slipped his mind upon checking his phone. There was a message seconds ago. "Jake. Station. Now."

His fingers were insanely quick upon the smart keyboard. "You found her?"

Agonizing moments later, the same text came back. "Station!!!"

"Jake? You okay?"

"It's Tashtego. They – I gotta go! I gotta go."

"Okay, okay."

He barreled straight for his Honda, pulling the charging cable to a full stretch that he nearly dropped his phone in this haste. Something important must have happened for Tashtego to force him like this. The Honda tore through the morning for Anson and Main. "*Peter Piper – peckled pickle* – fuck!" His sweaty hands kept slipping. "*Peter Piper picked a peck of pickled pepper.*" He swallowed, thinking, pondering, trembling and hyperventilating.

Too many questions raced in his convoluted head. Twice the small traffic screamed and honked at him. The passersby all had an abnormal character: pale and white in searing temperature.

Restaurants and diners along the way were not full. Roads were empty. And some traffic lights malfunctioned. Something was dreadful and wrong. He slapped himself for not driving first by the Moulins, forgetting about it in less than a second. Perhaps Miri was finally found. Maybe she was tied up. But he was not going to the station. Something about Wilton Road and Memorial Hospital came to him.

All the terrible things flooded. The brutal kidnap-and-murder cases after the Recession – the shocking twists and turns he heard over lunches with his colleagues, even the bunker crisis in 2013 – all were rushing back.

Taking an eye off the road, he read the message again. It said the station, not hospital. That was when the right side shoved him head first into the window. An ear-splitting metal explosion, along with the cracks and screams of glass, banged a momentary shock before the world went for a tumble.

Night must have fallen, dampening those cries and yells. For some reasons, the haunting smell of benzene and burning rubber disappeared for walnut papers. He was in a dark room. In front was her – his hon. "Daddy," said Miri.

Jake took a breath for words that would not come.

"You're always stressed out! Don't think too hard!"

He blinked. Sweet air calmed his throat and fed into his tender lungs. The dark room dissolved into a park, where he saw Miri skipping on a rope.

"Take care of yourself, Daddy." An echo carried her voice on and on, as a prickle bled his forearm. "Do you love me, Daddy?"

Miri was no longer in front.

"Do you love me?" her voice echoed. "I love you, Daddy." The impulse began from the back of his head, hitting with a twinge. "Take care of yourself." The metallic clash sprung him off this blackness. "Don't think too hard, okay?" His body was languishing, crippled and in pain. "Don't think too hard."

His eyes recognized a steel rod, which formed a railing for something like a single bed.

"Don't think too–."

Five faceless figures stood arching over him.

"Don't think–" The first face was Lottie's, looking absolutely in shock. "Don't-" Then it was Rachel's, before Craig's. "Don't–" He was on the bed. And slowly he realized. "Don't! Don't!" He was saying it.

The blackness returned, with Miri standing and grinning. "I love you, Daddy. Take care of yourself. Don't think too hard, okay?" The smile was a mirthless curl against peachy cheeks with her hair falling in locks. Bald, her scalp peeled into dried flakes.

And then those lips moved again. "I love you, Daddy. Take care of yourself. Don't think too hard, okay?"

Miri dissolved. And he found the will to – think… react… scream.

"Jake!"

"Oh, Jesus! Jake, calm down!"

His arms were moving despite the restraints. Things made sense. There was a flatscreen TV upon the ceiling over Rachel. He looked at Craig, who was breathing heavily. Lottie was not there. But there was another woman, whose head of hair was thick and greasy. The plain expression, with eyebags and dimples, caught him. "Ruth?" he sighed.

"I'm here, Jakey."

"Where am I?"

"You got into a car accident. You're okay. Just some cracked ribs."

"Lottie picked you up?"

"Yeah."

"Where is she?"

"I asked her to go. Her boy been acting up. We came soon as we can after her mom told us."

"What the hell happened? I can't remember a thing."

"You're okay now. They're all at home. Your home. I'll call them here."

"Don't. I uhh, there was something I should do." He sucked in, as those vivid hallucinations entered his mind. Not a piece of it escaped, not even the horrendous sight of his daughter liquefying to the ground. He can still hear those sentences before everything fell apart. "Miri. It's Miri," he said. "The police called me!"

Ruth moved from the bottom of the bed to be at his side. "Jakey, darling. Listen to me," she said, holding his swollen hand. "You need to be strong, okay? You have to be strong."

"I can walk, Ruth. I'm okay. I have to go."

"They found her, Jakey."

Jake's heart skipped, his eyes fleeting. "They did?" he said, beaming. "With the Moulins? It's them, right?"

"Not with the Moulins," replied Craig.

There was a throbbing sensation under his chest. "Where then?"

When Rachel approached to sit next to his leg, he understood everything about the blackness and disintegration. Something bad happened. Someone told him about Miriam – but the strong medication was blotting a part of his mind.

Either Craig or Tashtego or that McCrain, he was not sure. But he was sure. "I'm really sorry, Jake," said that stranger. "We found her. She's dead."

10

His chest started heaving. He opened his mouth for nothing; his throat acidified in bile, mucus and gummy saliva. He was shaking from something – almost as if he was in a cloak of flames doused with cold water. Miriam was dead. He heard from Craig again and once more with Ruth confiding the awful truth.

Miriam was dead.

"How? Why? Where? You sure it's her?"

The monitor indicated a rise of blood pressure. "Jake, you have to calm down!"

He did not know how he found strength through the attacking faint. "Stop telling me to calm down!" he yelled, kicking the tray off the overbed table.

Ruth gave Craig a dirty look. "C'mon, Jakey. I'll help you up."

"I gotta be at the station."

"Yeah, I know," she said. "I'll try calling the chief."

Jake struggled into his pockmarked jacket. Nobody protested his urgency, despite the plain fact he looked so white almost like a ghost. There was a sigh of relief after a nurse helped him out of his IV. The hospital staff were nowhere near when Jake stumbled to the side from a searing abdominal pain.

Not that he needed no hand – to be honest, he needed more than just a hand. His nerves whirled toward an epicenter beneath his scalp. Mucus clogged his nasal cavities, painless but disorienting. Ruth's grip never failed, even near the elevator where he supported her brother's whole weight on their way down. "You got a forklift?" quipped Jake, hissing.

The writhing pain grew as Ruth handled his discharge papers. Ruth then had to be on her knees, holding him the way their mother used to do. Her embrace scented a surrealistic maternal warmth from Rhoda Brownfield.

"This isn't happening," he said. "Tell me it isn't."

"It's not, Jakey. It's not happening." Craig arrived with a wheelchair and was reaching for his forearm when Ruth snarled. "Back off, porch climber!" And she hauled Jake into the wheelchair.

"Why is everyone looking at me like I'm in a funeral? The police told everyone?"

"Jakey," said Ruth, doubting.

"What?"

"You've been out for two days."

Color, if there was any, fled Jake. "Two days?"

"Yeah."

"She's buried?"

"Still in the morgue," replied Ruth. "Tashtego needs you for ID."

"What the fuck? Rachel didn't ID her?"

Ruth put a hand over his shoulder. "The cops want you to be there. We're holding her back for you, Jakey."

Jake shot up for a groan as sharp twinges damned his ribs to hell. He had to sit still, bending his head to help with the pain. He squealed upon entering Craig's rented car, half-spitting and half-cursing. Of all the cars in the world, the cheapskate had a hatchback parked so far away.

"I don't understand," said Jake. "How did she die? It doesn't make any sense!"

"We'll explain everything back home."

"Home? No! We going to the station. Call Tashtego! Tell him we're coming."

The chief was pulling a McCrain on them. Ruth tried three times before giving up. "Sorry. He's not picking up."

"Of course nobody's answering!"

The bouncing motion of an uneven road twitched Jake's throat with a nauseous tingle. Colors and shapes stormed around him. "She can't be dead, Ruth," he croaked with a parched throat. "She can't be."

"I'm really sorry, Jakey."

He winced at every step along the driveway, to be welcomed with sullen hugs first from Lottie. Charles and Donna came from the dining, looking mournful. A shaved head stuck out for a peek. "Terry," said Jake, with a bleached smile. "The kids are here?"

"Boys!"

Lottie helped him to the couch when two boys made a quiet entrance. Malcolm and Declan had a hoarse voice stabbing him with dread for sounding similar to Miriam. The last was Rachel who looked like a corpse. Behind that somber, sorrowful pout was not bereavement. Jake refused to meet her eyes. He felt that semblance, a stench Donna gave the most perfect description. It really was a disease, emanating with such a putrid effect.

"Turn on the news."

"I won't do that, Jake," said Terry.

"I wanna see."

Ruth grabbed the remote. "You have to know something."

"What could possibly be worse?"

Jake backed uneasily as Terry held his hand, an awkward gesture from a big man like him. "It's gonna be hard," he said. "I won't sugarcoat this. But the police think it's homicide."

"Muh-murder?" Jake managed to hold back the migraine fit. "Someone murdered my Miriam?"

"It's a torture murder, Jakey."

Jake's jaw shook, his mouth convulsing into a groan, squeal and then scream in a surging emotion that his mandibular joints froze into a brief paralysis. After that, his roars were guttural. Pillows flew everywhere as he thrashed and wrestled against what seemed to be the soft covers of his blanket.

The muscles lining his back were razor-sharp. He got up amid the spasm, not feeling the delicate touch until he saw he was in his bedroom. "Charlotte?" he mumbled. "You here?"

"I won't leave you," she said, holding tightly as he sat hunched.

"I wanna see her."

"The chief said he'll be at the station anytime you're ready, honey. He wanna be there for you."

Jake stared emptily. "He really said that?"

"He called a few times checking on you."

"What time is it now?"

"It's one in the morning."

Jake's eyes closed, stinging. "I'm not dragging anyone outta their bed," he said. "Get my laptop please."

"Sure."

A nictitating insertion point waited for his entry into the oval search bar. A sharp arrow cleaved through his heart because the search history remembered Miriam. Three months ago, she had searched her own name just for the sake of fun. It took a decisecond for 750,000 irrelevant results. Now the hits were different. Google suggested at least two million clicks, mostly related.

And these hits overcame Jake's anguish. After declared missing, Miriam Brownfield was as popular as Jamal Khashoggi. Lottie looked perplexed, noticing the change in his eyes now no longer droopy and wilting. They were not blinking, hot and impassioned over columns and columns of news. The news participated in this form of unconsented hysteria.

Miriam was discovered to his disgust in a ditch far from Farmington Center, hours before he crashed the Honda. The press developed chronological stories. Their special report saved him hours, now replaying at current time. Jake struggled for the living room, where Terry was watching a boring documentary about global warming effects against lobsters.

His sleepy slits widened when he saw Jake. "Don't have to get up," said Jake, bumbling into a couch with Lottie's help.

"I'm making cocoa. You want some, Terry?"

"Sure."

"The news, Terry."

A woman in black was covering a story with a composited chroma key of Miriam. "–but a cryptic voice message to her mother, a recently divorced woman in Huntsville, Alabama," she said. "On August 22, Farmington PD have fresh leads about possible bullying, which saw them suspecting Naomi Moulin particularly after a prank from her father Willis who has his encounter with the law over assault and drug charges while mother Imelda serves time at a correctional facility in Vermont.

"On August 23, comes the heartbreaking end. A local physician also philanthropist, Dr. David Morgan was jogging when he found–."

"David Morgan?" said Jake.

That crooked nose appeared prominently on screen. "I've done cadavers during my residential days. The smell doesn't leave you," he said.

"Immediately after finding out, Dr. Morgan alerted the authorities. And the kidnapping of Miriam Brownfield, despite prayers from California to the Vatican, is now officially a murder case – perhaps the worst in New England history."

The screen split into two, now showing a solemn-faced anchorperson also in black. "Thank you, Kaylie. I am in Farmington where people are denouncing this act all over social media. Reports are still bleak but with one thing for sure – Miriam was tortured to death. We're unable to reach her father who has been in an untimely accident on his way to the police station that day Miriam was found."

"Good God Almighty," said the anchorperson.

"What we know is Mr. Brownfield has been notified." The screen showed a montage of Farmington, while Kaylie talked about the town. It stopped at Jake's front lawn. "The Brownfields are definitely no strangers in town."

Jake switched off the television. "They're gonna walk down the fucking memory lane every chance they get." He said, as Lottie placed a tray of three smoking mugs. "Cocoa, Terry. Please, help yourself. I'm not my dad."

"Thanks."

"What my dad did lost me my sister – and a brother-in-law. Thank you for coming. How long are you staying?"

"Dunno. Took unpaid leave," said Terry. "We just couldn't stay. Ruth – she's dead on the inside asking about Miriam every single minute. We really can't stay."

"It's funny," said Jake, shaking his head.

Lottie turned. "What?"

"Something goes wrong – and it's always the Morgan," said Jake. "I can't understand that – he happens to be there? C'mon." The window rattled as leaves rustled through the lawn. "What's for dinner?"

"Pizza."

"Oh, damn. Again."

Three slices of beef pepperoni sizzled in the microwave. The toppings had all been scrounged and scraped. "Craig got into this one, I s'pose?"

"Sorry about that. Declan–"

"Don't worry about it," replied Jake. "Where's the bastard anyway?"

"Declan?" said Terry, stunned.

Disbelief filled Jake. "I meant Craig. Jesus, man!"

"Oh, God. You had me there!"

"Craig got himself a motel," said Lottie. "After Terry punched him in the face."

"What the hell? What happened?"

"Your ex-wife had the nerve going batshit blaming you about the whole thing. I told her to fuck off. Craig tried playing hero. I ain't having it."

Jake laughed but then groaned.

They turned on the TV, after the memory lane was surely over. The first to hit his screen was a trailer of an anticipated movie. "Oh, fuck."

"What?"

"Miri been wanting to see this movie."

Documentaries, movies and sports veered them back to the news, where Jake was exasperated for something new. They were not focusing on Miri anymore. Wall Street was having a bad day, following the trade war escalation with China. The news repeated twice about a possible recession because of persisting market volatility.

"You're in housing, right?"

"PR," said Terry. "Not investor relations."

"Any rising foreclosure? That can be a sign of market crashes, so you know."

"I dunno anything about market crashes. I mean, I know about them. But I can't predict if it'll happen."

"Trust me, the media can't either. They just speculate, speculate, speculate and be like, whoo-whee we told you so!"

"Hah. I prefer crashes if they're on roads."

"Yeah. Like mine."

Terry blanched. "Shit. Not like that."

"I'm just kidding. You did vehicle crash?"

"A lot. Like two weeks ago, a woman rammed a moving truck and died on the spot. The insurance refused to pay arguing her premium expired. Turns out, it didn't."

"How did it end?"

"Still ongoing. With inquiries and all," replied Terry. "They kept looking for loopholes."

"How many kids she had?"

"Three – now with the CPS, maybe. The husband's dead long time ago."

"They can live with me, if they want," said Jake, mumbling.

"Hey, I wanna ask – about Miri," said Terry. "You don't have to give me the gory details but seriously, she being bullied at school?"

"You saw the news. Almost at daily basis, as I've been made to understand. Why?"

"I've been to this ditch where she was dumped. Been there the first day I got here," said Terry. "I'm asking 'cause I really can't see how those bullies put her there. It's eight miles away!"

"Eight miles?"

"What, they got an Uber to get there? C'mon! We weren't born fucking yesterday to believe in crap like that."

"I dunno. I really have no clue," said Jake. "If only I excused her that day – none of this woulda happen."

"Come on, Jake. It's not your fault."

"Pretty sure Rachel will sue me for negligence."

"Malcolm heard them talking. Don't worry. We got your back."

Jake finished the slice. "Something in me, Terry. Something in me now wished I let Rachel keep her."

11

Sleep was stubborn during these laboring hours. He was wincing under a blanket, a glance over the NSAIDs which could probably be a contributing cause of his pain. He held a particular position that was not aggravating his injury, letting the fabric and foam swallow his whole weight.

Terry had turned in after a spirited attempt to stay up. By the time he was alone, the ceiling started spinning. Branches raked against every window. Light swam into his living space whenever a car passed by Court Street.

It took forever to blow an hour into the clock. Miriam lingered in his mind every single minute, until it was time to face the music. The family surfaced from their rooms after murmuring among themselves. Jake knew they were up. Those toilet flushes and spraying showers had given them away. "Dad's coming with us," said Lottie. "We're taking the minivan."

Ruth went first to sort Malcolm and Declan in the backseat. Jake managed to get out of the house, courtesy of another ibuprofen with Lottie and Terry at both sides. The same acid thickened down his throat. Sweat smeared all over the leather seat. He looked over for every intersection, his hands tightening by the edges.

The town lied. All business joints were vibrant, unaffected and unchanged. He caught a newspaper stand during a stop at the traffic light overlooking High Street. That was the only memory for his dead daughter, a monochrome picture on the front page. That was it. Nobody, he saw throughout the mile drive, cared for Miriam.

Absolutely nobody.

His heart skipped a beat when he saw that small Citgo right before the final turn. His buried scream jolted Charles, who turned with great alarm to find him burying both hands into his face.

"What happened? Jake, you all right?"

"Just drive, Dad!"

Malcolm and Declan went stiff. And Ruth was on to Jake, who whimpered. "Pepsi. Pepsi."

"You can't have Pepsi, Jake."

"N-no! The Citgo. I got her a Pepsi that morning, her last Pepsi, Ruth. Her last at that Citgo."

They missed Terry turning away with a smashed face. Charles made a full turn to stop by a parking space. "This is it, Jake," he breathed. "C'mon, son. I'll help you down."

A small group gathered before the station, all in black and unanimous for no cameras or microphones. The press came with nothing but words. It was something Jake had never seen. He tried shaking some hands and nodding with bitter thanks. Charles steered him out of there within this circle of family members straight to where Tashtego and McCrain stood.

"We'd like to see her," said Ruth.

"Only parents or legal guardians, ma'am." Tashtego reached for a consoling tap on Ruth's shoulder. "Trust us on this. Please."

Now they were exchanging glances among themselves. Tashtego came to hold Jake, whose knees were weakening. "Go ahead, Chief," said McCrain. "I'll take the rest."

The main office had a cordoned section where Rachel stood upon seeing them. Jake this time could not escape her crinkled face. "Jake," she said, a voice without much of a sound.

"Rach."

A waiting officer opened for a room, where there was a man in a full plastic gear. They found steel tables filled with surgical instruments before a wall of mortuary fridges. "I had to keep her here, Jake," said Tashtego. "Can't trust those guys in the hospital. The cat ain't out of the bag yet. The press only got the tail."

"What the fuck does that mean?"

Tashtego gestured to the man, who knew where to go. Frost cracked and shattered when the door swung with creaky hinges. Fogs radiated from the cuboid space, bringing effluvious air along with the body. Within that instant Rachel found Jake's hand, their fingers intertwining for an unholy pause. It only took a look – just once upon the milky-white, brittle thing on the stretcher.

Jake hunched as his stomach roiled with a churning sensation. Rachel gave away an echoing hiss. Tashtego backed away from the fridge, giving a deserving space. The room got a bit hotter, with silence so deafening they could hear the ticks and tocks of the clock on the wall.

For at least ten seconds, the parents did not move a damn muscle. Both stared at their daughter – or what was left of their beloved daughter. Jake no longer felt his body, now standing straight with his expression stony. He was not blinking. He was not breathing.

Miriam Brownfield looked up with a lifeless gaze. Her hair was tucked underneath her broken shoulders, wet with a smell of refrigerant carbons. The face was corpselike, blank but with evidence of the brutality covering her naked body – if it was even a body to begin with. Jake stood there looking at the carnage while Rachel clung on a fridge holder.

Tashtego was right.

The cat was not out of the goddamned bag yet. This murderer was not human or even animal. Miriam's condition was beyond anything. A dermal desiccation started an inch below her collarbones and continued downward on and on to every part of her frail body.

Rachel turned to Tashtego. "This can't be my daughter!" she said, her hands tinged in dried blood across the girl's body. "What, do you have an escaping prisoner or something? Someone cracked enough to do something like this?"

"We're looking at every profile across the country," replied Tashtego. "We're working on this. I wish I can give you more."

Jake's trembling hands reached for a pair of latex gloves. And he looked closely upon those gory lines at Miriam's stomach. "It was knife, sir," said the man with them. "Maybe a pen knife. And if you look at her chest, you will see they uhh – well, they–." No one was able to finish a sentence of that nature. Jake saw a circular redness by her left torso, the place where there should be a nipple. "Right next to that is a cigarette wound."

"She's sliced, burned and poked," said Tashtego. "Our preliminary findings determine she wasn't doused in gasoline. But there is something flammable, possibly bug spray. Something aerosol."

Jake found his voice, uneasily looking at her singed privates. "Was she ruh-raped?"

Tashtego lost his. "We'll have to double check."

"The first check is a yes?"

"Yes, Jake."

"Oh, my God!" screamed Rachel.

"What the fuck got you, baby?" Rachel reached for his hand again, as both clutched their beautiful girl's mangled body. "What the fuck got you?" The amorous embrace continued, so strange and endearing.

"Our baby, Jake," she said. "Our baby!"

With one last look, Jake slid the body back and slammed the freezing chamber shut. Then he left with stumbling steps, returning to the chief's office to meet with those question marks.

"It's her," he said.

"This is not accept-and-move-on," replied Tashtego. "When we catch the bastard, there's gonna be hell to pay. That I promise you."

"What's the point, Bob? It ain't like she's coming back." Jake turned to the family. "Whatever's in there is no murder. She was slaughtered to a slow death."

Craig had an eye over Rachel, who was still sobbing. "Deputy, take the kids to the vending machine. I'll have a word with their parents as well." McCrain led the confused children out as Tashtego picked a brown folder for six A4 papers, each with a photograph from different angles. And every face in the room went pale, except for Craig who remained placid with a strange composure.

"Is this common here in Farmington?"

"Never seen anything like it in my twenty years of service."

Terry groaned. "What's the game plan then, chief?"

"We are starting with that audio piece to see if we can relate to any known serial killer. Meanwhile we're looking if there's any DNA on the body. It's been a few days. The killer must be hiding, tryinna blend in and let everything blow over. In time he'll make a mistake."

"What do you suggest we do, chief?"

The question was self-answering. They were told to do nothing for the moment. That night Tashtego went national in a live broadcast from that waiting room. Sweat beaded on his balding forehead, indicating the lighting setup behind cameras.

"Chief, what have your department done so far?"

"I called for a thorough autopsy to expand our available lead. Just now I've divided my force into six teams to look around the school compound. We're figuring out how Miriam got out of the school."

"You're saying you have no idea who did it?"

"I'm saying I'm looking for this person," said Tashtego. "If I know who did this, I won't be sitting here talking to y'all. This is something–"

"He has no idea what he's doing," said Terry.

"–while we look deeply, we gotta make absolute sure that no one else suffers the same."

"Right now, what's new?"

"For now there is no update," said Tashtego. "I can confirm that Miriam's parents have viewed the body. Mr. Brownfield is still recovering from accident. It's not a condition for a grieving father. And I'm sure more will come after the autopsy. Once the result is out, you'll know." He then excused himself, with the police force enveloping his exit.

"You okayed another autopsy?" asked Rachel.

"Yeah. They'll do it even if I tell them not to."

"You can at least tell them not to!"

"She's a murder victim, Rachel!"

"She's suffered enough! You wanna cut her up for what? She's my daughter!" said Rachel. "If you hadn't fought for custody—"

"Ah shit. Here we go again."

Rachel glared at Terry. "She'll still be alive if she stayed with me!"

"She'd be dead the soonest you get her," said Jake. "She hated you, Rachel. She never stopped saying bad things about you. She said you cheated on us both. And if she saw what happened the night before my accident, she'd probably hang herself." Rachel was shifting from red to purple. "Tell me something, don't you think she tried hanging up the phone every fucking time you called?"

"Why would she do that?"

"You talked to Miriam. One of those time, she heard your boyfriend in the showers! Let's be honest, Rachel. You'll never do the right thing. You're not made for that. You're never a good mother, and we both know that."

"I can be a good mother," she hissed.

"Can you? You can't even be a loyal wife. And as far as your relationship goes, everybody knows you only wanted Craig because you ain't got a fucking choice. Wanna blame me for Miriam? Fine. It is my fault. You said that a million times. You blame me for everything. You even blamed me when I caught you getting anal!"

Craig shot to his feet. "The fuck you on about? We never did anal!"

"Funny I never said it was with you."

The dramatic turn had Rachel cowering into a wall. The house seemed to shake when Terry got up. And they were out of there within seconds, last seen driving away in that stupid Yaris. Things dipped into a cool atmosphere that they heard wind billowing through the front door.

Jake's fingers twitched as all eyes were fixed on him. He was heard repeating on a recliner in the backyard. "*Peter Piper picked a peck of pickled peppers.*" He headed to bed after emptying a Marlboro pack.

Lottie was about to follow when Ruth got her arm. "Helps him sleep better," she said, of the plastic bottle.

"I already got him on aspirin."

"It's for those panic fits he's having," said Ruth.

The living room cleared one by one. Malcolm and Declan kept looking at each other for at least a while, before helping their parents in the kitchen. Lottie went into the master bedroom to find Jake on the floor with both fists shut. "Can I come in?" she said.

"My daughter, Charlotte. Who coulda done this?

"Jake—"

"Why? Why would anyone do it to her?"

"The police's on it."

"Even if they catch him, so what?" There was not much to say. Lottie sat cross-legged as Jake went on about their fishing trip. "I really thought it's a fresh start for us."

"Believe me, honey. I look at her like she's my own daughter."

"She's gone." Jake breathed. "Rachel blaming me. Police will cut her apart. I did this. It's on me."

"Jake, it ain't your fault. You wanted the best for her."

A shiver blocked his words. "What am I gonna do? What am I gonna do now?"

"Look. Where you go, I go, okay? I can't lose you too!

"I'm not gonna kill myself."

"I didn't mean it like that."

"Heh, I ain't gonna do that," said Jake. "Why would I kill myself? Look at me! Do I look like I'm gonna kill myself?" There was nothing in his smile, almost like a husk devoid of humor. "I lost everything. My mom's gone. My dad. Now my girl! Fuck, what I'm gonna do?"

"I'm sorry, Jake." Lottie got his hand. "I'm really, really sorry. You don't deserve this."

"What you got there?"

"It's something for your panic attack. Ruth gave me."

"Diazepam. She's a sniper like mom." Two tablets sibilated through acerbic taste in his gullet. Lottie drew him a warm bath and respected his wish for privacy, knocking every now and then throughout the hour he spent. Terry then brought them a lobster roll seasoned to perfection. "She still got it," said Jake.

"Why you think I married her?"

"Shotgun?" said Jake, which caught Terry. "I wonder where my dad kept that gun."

"I'd snap it to pieces."

"Why bother? It's not even real."

Terry looked as if he swallowed lemon. "Your dad held a toy gun at my balls?"

"Some prop for a school drama."

"Son of a bitch! I thought it's real!"

The story went around like wildfire saying God put Abraham Brownfield in his place. "He was always that holierthan-thou kinda person," said Jake. "Priestlier than priests. You don't do this, don't do that. You raise your child wrong." And the family coerced Terry and Ruth into marriage, after finding them cuddling in bed.

"Sorry, Jake. Fuck your dad."

"Amen."

"I wake up hungry and sleep with a full belly thanks to your sister."

"Amen to that too."

"And I'll still marry her if your dad didn't go crazy with that gun. Might take some more time, yeah."

"And Malcolm won't be born."

Another lemon sluiced down his throat. "Shit, you're right," he said, now realizing.

"Being honest with you. After the divorce, I wanted to go to Utah so bad."

"Why didn't you?"

"I thought Ruth hated me for not standing up to her," said Jake. "I know I should. I hate myself every time I think about it."

"It's okay, Jake. Let bygones be bygones."

"That's what Uncle Obie said."

"Aha. Uncle Obie. Where is he anyway?"

"Probably dead somewhere in the Grand Canyon. The guy's like asking for it." Jake shrugged. "Grand Canyon. Arizona ain't that far from Utah. We should probably go there. There ain't much here. Surely the insurance company wants your ass back."

Terry took a breath. "Jake, I think I better be straight with you," he said. "I didn't take unpaid leave. I resigned to be here for you."

12

Three people knew about the emergency meeting over Miriam's body. They were Robert Tashtego, Paxton McCrain and Roger Gauthier. And they stopped short when it was about the autopsy result. Nobody dared telling Jake or Rachel – especially Rachel – about the long waiting list. The problem loomed over Tashtego, who later sat in his office scratching the white print in between a gray notepad and his black smartphone.

He was the Chief of Police. So, it was his duty to inform the family. The complete autopsy opened the girl's body for a closer examination. Two coroners had undertaken the process, both agreeing to the same cause of death. But there was a problem. "Number Seventeen," he muttered, circling Miriam's name in the list.

McCrain had told him earlier. "It'll take more than a month to get the samples to the lab." In a week, District Attorney Peter Renbarger would be eating them alive. Tashtego snapped a quick decision and the same afternoon won a consensus among those in the State Department.

"Every murder is denounceable," he said in writing. "But there is a fine distinction separating a shooting or stabbing and the kind of criminality Miriam endured. Maine could not and should not suffer from this or the endangering risk of a repeat in the coming weeks."

That letter unnerved the systemic barriers to the Augusta state laboratory. Within 48 hours, they returned the toxicology and histology results with an extra cavalry of investigators. And Tashtego made a personal visit to the Brownfield residence, where their breaths hissed anxiously.

Neighbors retreated from plain sight to scope from behind the curtains. No files or papers accompanied his arrival. But in the living room, he produced a tablet to begin reading the electronic report.

Miriam died on Friday, two days after she was declared missing. The forensics team was unable to determine the precise time. But the conclusive cause was thermal injury. "A quarter to an inch deep over eighty percent of the body," said Tashtego, to the heartbroken family. "A spot by her left shoulder blade is deeper. We found the scapula completely black and charred. It's a burn of all degrees."

"Hot water?"

"They were uneven. From the look of 'em and those triangular stamps, we're sure it's steam iron."

Jake's eyes widened. "That thing can go over four hundred!"

"Four fifty Fahrenheit," breathed Tashtego. "I'm sorry. I have to disclose this to you. You're gonna find out sooner or later when this case goes to trial."

"You have any idea why she was tortured?"

"We have theories. There are only two certainties. Bullying or interrogations. Or both."

"Jesus Christ. She ain't some fucking terrorist!"

"Any of it being political?" asked Jake.

"No. It's not about your drunken thing. Nobody cares about that mayor."

"But is it possible?"

"I don't think so."

"What makes you think this is an interrogation?" asked Ruth.

"On the count of lung damage, brain damage, broken bones. Thin injury line by the neck." Tashtego stopped short for an effect. "We uhh have a case like this. Months back. It's a silly one – some kids tried waterboarding a friend of theirs. Stupid but luckily he survives, with similar injuries."

"This is some fucking nutcase we're dealing with!"

"Wait. What does it mean?"

"The fucker put a cloth in her mouth and pour water on her face. To drown her but not kill her."

"Oh, my God."

"It's why the state government fast-tracked Miriam's autopsy. She was burned and waterboarded. And as for the uhh rape–" Gulps filled their throats. "I had my team start on that first. I'm really sorry but we confirm there's no penile penetration."

"She wasn't raped?" asked Ruth.

"Why sorry if there's no penetration?"

"I can confirm, with a heavy heart, that an object had entered her vagina and anus," said Tashtego. "There is a severe damage to her rectum." He stopped again, this time because of Jake's emotional outburst. "I think I'll spare the remaining details. I must tell you that kidnapping has this thing we call footprints – broken twigs, bent grasses, you name it.

"One always leads to another. We're on every relevant surveillance camera, hoping to catch any glimpse of Miriam.

What I need you to do is hang in there. It's not easy, I know. I want this son of a fucking cocksucker to feel so safe."

Jake nodded. "Let him make that fatal mistake."

"Which he will. One other thing – there'll be a press conference. I've been ordered to disclose everything."

"You're going to show the pictures?" asked Jake.

"No. Not the pictures. We did a graphic outline. That'll be enough for the news."

The conference was scheduled in such a short notice that Tashtego had little time to prepare his notes. Redder than normal, he appeared behind a solid desk to repeat the grisly details before the millions watching him. He looked into the camera lens as he looked into Jake's eyes. He knew Jake was watching.

There was a flinching plastic crack. Jake's closed hand was shaking with the remote in his grasp. "Malcolm, turn it off," said Lottie.

"No," said Jake, as the boy reached for the television. "I wanna hear it all."

"Jake, that's enough."

"Shut the fuck up!" he shouted, flinging the shattered pieces of the remote control.

It did not put a dent on Lottie, who flew forward to yank the plug out. The 40' Samsung went black, much like that flowing fervency in her eyes. "No more of this, okay? No more! For the kids' sake, Jake! Look at them!" she yelled. "Just look at them for once!" His chest relaxed, expelling heat through his nose, mouth and maybe eyes as well. "We can't watch TV every day. Miriam deserves more than what we're giving her!"

"I can't bury her, Charlotte."

"I'm heartbroken too! But for her sake, we have to!"

Terry held Jake's hand. "She's right."

They followed him to the kitchen, where he took his prescription with three glasses of water. "The government flew Sam home in a flagged coffin. Miriam was only two at the time. I stood with her in my arms during the funeral." He looked at Ruth. "She knew something was up. I told her, that's how we'll end up after we die. And now–" His face crumpled. "Now you're asking me to bury her."

"I never met her. I never heard her voice," said Ruth. "I know I'll regret it until I die. Trust me, I don't want to do this. I really don't. But we can't give them more ideas to think of the many ways of cutting her up. She's not a piece of chicken."

Jake closed his eyes, his fingers weaving together into a clutch. "I dunno where to start," he said. "Who do I call?"

"Let me handle it," replied Lottie.

"I really appreciate that."

"Never yell at her again, okay? She ain't your wife. She ain't got no business to be here. But she's still here for you."

"I know. I got carried away with how I used to with Rachel. I just lost it."

"She's not Rachel. You better stop–"

"Ruth!" said Lottie. "He gets it. It's okay."

"We all been crying behind your back," said Ruth. "Last night she went out. When she got back, her face is all puffy."

"I got stung by a bee, Ruth."

Jake breathed what sputtered into a subdued laugh. "Jesus Christ," he said. "Stung by a bee. You're a terrible liar, honey." Lottie's smile was sincere with tears.

It only took a call to prepare all the necessary arrangements. Jake stashed his phone away in a drawer before landing abed next to Lottie, facing to explore each other with their eyes. She was the first to make the move, leaning closer with her lips parting. He pressed his head into the pillow, breathing out as that light tenderness lasted into salivary glue.

Nothing seemed to matter anymore – but this thirst. The floor beneath the bed turned upside down. Walls uprooted with alien wind dispersing the rooftops. Gardens flowed and swayed, as the precious moments stroked a beguiling eternity. His hands found places for a folding pleasure so savory it was sinful even for him.

Those moans soon soaked them within this sweaty duet. They for one priceless moment floated into a peak, soon subsiding with him on her beating chest. And Lottie found him snoring, with a picture in a hand which did not move until he stirred at the sound of a commotion.

At high noon, neighbors began pouring over. Tara Robin gave her condolences three times and apologized for not coming sooner. Jake fielded an apology after another, some with unbelievable excuses. But nobody came empty-handed. The dining table was a feast of butter garlic rice, beef stroganoff and Pico de Gallo.

Some neighbors embraced them with tears, sharing their moments with Rhoda Brownfield. The center of attention (and hatred) was Ruth, who looked stern the entire time. Nobody dared talking about her past. In the midst of comforting words, there was a political talk about criminal justice and gun policy.

Lottie had a heated argument with a neighbor over an insensitive remark about school safety. Jake listened from 20 feet away. Her ripostes ripped the other guy, who teetered with strawman heaps. She had a fine memory, weaponizing his fallacies unfailingly. And Jake turned to look at her Hyundai Santa Fe, now ashamed of his earlier perception toward her.

An incoming call distracted him into a stutter. "Hello?"

"Jake, you okay, man?"

"Doing all right. What's up?"

"Need you at school."

"Now?"

"Afraid so, Jake. I can send a cruiser if you need one."

Jake figured not to trouble Ruth and Terry. He hopped next to Lottie and as soon as they began, his fingernails began digging into the seat. A heavy blue garrison overwhelmed the school compound. At the parking space, they met the crabby-looking principal. "Mr. Brownfield, thank you for coming," said Tashtego. "I know this is the last place you wanna be. But we gotta take care of something."

"Mr. Brownfield, on behalf–" breathed DeWinter.

"What do you need, Chief?"

Tashtego noticed the furious twist behind those flaring curls. "A time machine," he said. "Madam Principal, I need all access to your files."

"You already have them."

"I mean, everything. Discipline records. Teachers' remarks. Meeting minutes. Everything. We need to be a cohesive team. Investigator. Parent. And school. That's what I need. That clear?"

"Okay. I will ask my staff."

"I'm gonna need your safe too."

"It's just my medicine pill, Chief."

"Not gonna ask again."

"Just a minute now! My experience on school administration is over twenty six years. I have–"

"Don't go dick measuring when you have none. Save it for yourself. Now, to your office." Back in this bat cave, Jake dived for the water dispenser. The blinding fluorescent forced him to squint. "It won't take long, Mr. Brownfield," said Tashtego. "Hope you can hang a while?"

"Can we do it somewhere else, chief?" asked Lottie.

"No. We're here. Let's get it done," said Jake. "I wanna go home quick as I can. So, just do it."

Tashtego admired the green safety deposit box. "It's nothing to do with Miriam's case," said DeWinter. The glaring breath locked her in a pumping staredown with Tashtego. "Just my prescriptions, chief."

"You keep prescriptions in a safe?"

"Only the ones over a grand."

Jake's eyes narrowed. "You have cancer?" he said, which DeWinter reacted with a nod.

"I'm fine. Can we please continue?"

"Well, I'm so sorry, Madam Principal. Please, you don't have to stand." Tashtego waited until DeWinter was seated. "We'll start with you."

DeWinter chose her answers with a rehearsed tone. "I arrived usually around seven. Fifteen minutes, give or take." When asked about Miriam, she started with a long sigh. "I never talked to the girl before. But my staff especially Ms. Calvert had good things to say about her."

"What did you do the moment Mr. Brownfield came to you about this?"

"I checked with security and did my best like any principal."

The muttering growl did not miss Tashtego's earshot. "Got something to say, Mr. Brownfield?" he asked.

"She checked the security, all right. After it's clear that Miri's missing, she begged me not to call you guys. She did not act the way a principal should."

"Is this true, Madam Principal?"

That scowl alone sufficed. "I didn't want to alert the authorities, true. Because I think–" She needed a sip from the cooler. "Because I think she's not missing. Just loitering somewhere, and that voicemail is just a ruse."

Tashtego's facial lines pulsated with displeasure. "And you're bragging about your twenty-six years," he said. "You were prepared to handle situations like this." Then he spoke over the radio upon his shoulder. "All teams, switch to Careless Principal. Repeat, go Careless Principal."

After a crackle, there was a response. "Roger."

"Careless Principal, chief?"

"Moving on. Mr. Brownfield, you sent Miriam that morning. What time?"

"I'm not exactly sure. We were a bit late."

"What was she wearing on the day she's missing?"

"Green-red plaid and khaki pants. Black shoes. She like it that way."

"What about other accessories?"

"Red ribbon for her ponytail."

"Is it like a hairband?"

"No. It's a ribbon."

"Define red."

"Huh?"

"Amaranth red, barn red, blood red?"

"I dunno. Dark red?"

"Okay. Did she mention anything about the bullying thing we're investigating?"

DeWinter shook her head. "Our school is a fine institution which we promote the basis for higher learning. We don't tolerate bullies."

"We have a footage confirming it happened."

"I – I wasn't told at all."

"That's one of the twenty things that went wrong, all in your responsibility. Mr. Brownfield, you were saying?"

"Miriam promised she'll handle Naomi."

Tashtego continued about DeWinter's mishandling, treading along the thin line between professionalism and disappointment. They procured three separate bullying incidents, none which she knew. Twice Tashtego turned to Jake, who noticed the overconfidence in this one-dimensional system. DeWinter never experienced police grilling throughout her career. She kept talking about the school success, a clear capitulation that little guys and victims never mattered to her.

And those subjugated students prepared a surprise on Jake's exit. They lined up from the head office, expressing their support for Jake. The kind gesture titled into fulminating anarchy when Naomi showed up with thin eyes. A girl tried halting her hungered advance. But she blew through, cursing. "I'm glad they found her! Deserves what she got."

Jake kept walking.

"What else you gonna tell the cops? You gonna say I did it? Go ahead. Tell them I did it. At least it'll take the real killer off the fucking hook!"

"Miss Moulin!" There was a scream. "Detention!"

"Do whatever you want, you hook-nosed Jew!" said Naomi. "Y'all are big fucking liars, like your stupid daughter! She deserved it, fucker!"

"MISS MOULIN!"

"I'M GLAD THEY KILLED MIRIAM, YOU HEAR ME, BROWNFIELD?"

"NAOMI!" shouted DeWinter.

"YOU HEAR ME, FUCKER! I'M GLAD THEY KILLED THAT ROACH!"

Jake's calmness melted in the car. He punched the dashboard many times that he no longer felt his hand.

"That's the bitch she faced every day?" said Lottie.

"I shoulda rip her throat out!"

"She ain't worth it."

"Call Ruth! I want the neighbors gone! All of them!"

The neighbors were spared from hearing Jake's tirade. Ruth held an unconcealed expression, boiling in rage that she was also shouting. "You didn't do anything, right?" asked Terry.

"I should!"

"Okay, good. She's a minor, Jake. Remember that. We gotta keep it together. Do it for Miriam no matter how crazy this town is."

Declan brought a piece of chocolate cake over a ceramic saucer. "Uncle Jake, want some? I'll cut some more."

Jake gulped. "Sure. Dip the knife in hot water."

"Okay."

The family streamed a Netflix movie over lunch. Right after that, Jake went for a shower. Water jets needled on his scalp, trickling downward to fill the tub. Temperature soon vapored the sliding door, ensconcing his nudity. His head ran through the day again, from the first visitor who greeted him. He recalled those faces. And then a lightning bolt hit his head, blazing and zapping that he was next barreling out in a towel.

"Real killer off the hook! Real killer!"

"Jake?"

"Naomi knows who killed her!"

"What?"

"Naomi! She knows!"

"Jake, slow down," said Lottie. "She's a psycho!"

"No. She said I'm a liar like Miriam!"

"So?"

"Liar," said Jake, shoving a foot into his shorts. "What does that tell you?"

"I dunno – she tryin to get you upset or something?"

"Yes. And no. It's just the way girls talk with girls," said Jake. "How many times you get called a whore back then? For no fucking reason, someone called you a whore. How many times?"

"All the time."

"How about a bitch?"

Lottie raised her shoulders. "Same, I guess," she said.

"But how many times someone specifically called you liar? Like, very specifically over whore and over bitch?"

"Huh," she huffed. "Miriam musta done something, you mean?"

"Water in her lungs. Steam ironed. Beaten. Broken. Sliced. She must have screamed and screamed – because she's a liar. They woulda stop if she told them the truth – or at least, the truth they wanna hear."

"What, though?"

"Of course they can't match this with psychos! Of course there's no hit with escaping prisoners or sexual offenders! It's not a psycho, or a prisoner, or a sexual offender!"

"But they got nothing on Naomi."

"Because Naomi ain't the one!" said Jake. "She never was! She only got into this because she bullied Miri!"

The air in the room was getting hotter. "If it's not her, then who?" asked Lottie.

"Walk with me, honey! If you're missing ten dollars, will you feel bad about it?" Lottie raised both shoulders again, shaking her head. "Okay, but what about you're missing ten dollars when you're Miri's age?"

"That time it's a lot."

"Yeah, picture losing a grand at school."

"I'd be dead soonest I get home." Jake clapped his hands. "But I never took a grand to school," she added. "Why would anyone take a grand to school?"

"Not cash."

"Huh?"

"CHARLOTTE!" said Jake. "Someone lost something worth more than a fucking grand before Miri went missing! I'm sure she told you too!"

Lottie's jaw dropped. "The iPhone! Amelia Morgan!"

"Miriam was a liar because she did not admit she took the iPhone and they tortured her thinking she'll fess up!"

"Oh, Jesus Christ!" breathed Lottie.

"Curious her bigshot doctor daddy found Miri in that ditch so fucking far away from the school, and he didn't even pay us a goddamn visit today!"

"Yeah. Curious."

13

The moment Katherine DeWinter feared had finally come. Those press conferences united the public into a singular force that nobody – not even the alumni – dared backing her "careless, selfish and sluggish" administration. The clandestine operation of investigative journalists was only in their head. The news companies did not need to extend that much, because parents vented online for the lack of care over bullying incidents.

"My son is fifteen! And he's on PTSD therapy!"

"Nothing good comes from that school. Don't enroll."

"Everything in Mt View is fake! The education, the extracurriculars, the noses!"

Pressure was mounting among her underlings. Irene Dedder's resignation paper was still on her desk. Sophia Ratzinsky threatened to do the same, unless DeWinter fixed this mess. She had no idea where to start. So, she paid Jake a visit to talk about a crowdfunding effort from Fundly and GoFundMe. "Thirty fucking grand?" he said, gasping as the principal nodded. "You're buying me out with a damage control!"

"N-no. I don't mean it like that, Mr. Brownfield." His elevating temper stumbled upon that soft touch from Lottie. "I created this account the other day. We got so many volunteers. Figured it wouldn't be nice to have them pay for their own lunch or dinner. But seeing as Miriam is, you know, gone, I believe you should have it."

"You can shove it down–!"

Lottie cut in. "I want information about these donors. You have them? It'll be like a list."

"Yeah, I do."

"We'd like a copy if you don't mind."

"Okay. I'll have my clerk print it as soon as possible."

"Now, I mean. Right now. Just email us."

DeWinter's glance hung over Lottie. "Might I ask why?" she said, after making a call.

"For the eulogy," said Lottie. "We gotta thank the donators. Throw in some names. It's why they donate in the first place."

"Oh. I didn't know things were like that."

"Figures," said Lottie, with a harmless look upon Jake.

The donator list checked into Lottie's business email that afternoon, along with financial statements summing the total amount. "All the donators as of five minutes ago," said DeWinter in a text. "I'd like to again apologize from the bottom of my heart."

"Like you have one."

Jake imagined the scowl upon her face. A doorbell brought him to meet a boy, who stood with a wreathed bouquet. And he was not alone. The entire school must have lined up at Court Street, all looking wanly. "Hello, Mr. Brownfield. My name is John Cadogan. This is for you," he said, giving the bouquet. "We'd like you to know we are Miriam Brownfield."

"Me too," said the boy next to him.

"Me too, sir."

"Count me in, Mr. Brownfield."

"We miss her so much. We are Miriam Brownfield!"

The echo somewhat stirred Jake into a roller coaster. He went from smiling to crying and to laughing before sobbing back and forth. The children, mostly girls, had thoughtful quotes with full hugs.

"I'm your daughter."

"I'm your daughter."

A boy jumped to hug him. "Say not in grief she is no more but in thankfulness that she was."

The teachers' condolences were more flowery, with personal statements conveying their wishes and thanks. After it was all done, they retreated to the dining room where Lottie held his hand. "Someone's missing," she said.

Jake rubbed his face. "Maybe she's absent?"

Lottie put her phone in front of him. "Nope." Amelia's latest Instagram post was a picture at school. "The little bitch's dogging us."

Their whispery conversation ended when Terry brought up about the donator list. "What's it for, if you don't mind me asking? People never specifically mentioned donors during eulogies."

"Maybe I will."

Jake tried a search option for the Morgans, which was fruitless in the five PDF files. The first was anonymous, starting with an impressive $100 kick. Some people chipped in money with meaningful notes and trivial emoticons. Soon things got pretty serious with substantial pledges. Money was coming from Germany, New Zealand and United Kingdom. Even non-English speaking countries such as Argentina, Kazakhstan and

Malaysia were there, though small graces after currency conversion.

"Goddamn. We shoulda asked them to sort from the highest," said Lottie.

Jake smacked upon the desk. "Got a winner! Page nine! With a typo, no wonder."

Swiping the Galaxy, Lottie found the name. "*Mrogan*," she said. "Four thousand! Jesus!"

"David left a note too," said Jake, reading. "*Nothing can describe this loss. To have someone so young and ambitious suddenly taken away at the budding stage of life, to know she was pure and gentle, to believe this is avoidable, it hurts us as a family. We too have a daughter of her age. This is personal to us as well so if there is anything we can do, anything at all, ring us.*" He turned to Lottie, his face swarming with energy. "He knows his way with words, I give you that."

"Oh yeah. It's nice," said Terry.

Jake and Lottie swung to him. They had Ruth at the same table before disclosing their suspicion. All four of them came to the same conclusion. "She stands out," said Lottie. "She lost the iPhone. So they did some interrogations. Then the dad went jogging outta town and found Miri. And this morning she didn't join the school, but her Instagram confirmed she's there."

"We can't let the cops know this."

"How are we gonna pin her down?"

"Not at least we are sure of something – something concrete. This is nothing. It's like a hunch," said Jake. "I've seen how cops look down at parents who start accusing without proof. It won't do us good, not one bit."

Lottie flinched, those beady eyes flaring. "Oh, my God! Amelia deleted!" she said.

Jake's breath reeked in the dryness of his mouth. "For real? Let me see!"

"I shoulda taken a screenshot! She was there, having a wefie with her broads! She was there, Jake!"

"Forget about it. Jake's right. Too weak it's nothing," said Terry. "They'll say she deleted to respect Miri's death. Besides the school take attendances. So, we're good on that."

In the family room the news broadcasted a montage view of Farmington before starting out with public opinions. Some strangers popped up sharing their thought. But then that voice scratched into their ears.

"I'm still shellshocked. Dunno what to say really," said David Morgan, in a zipped-up polyester sweater. "Stuff like this happens somewhere else! But here in Farmington and this killer is still at large? That's just scary. The principal's been very helpful in this troubling time, and I've also encouraged everyone I know to chip in some money for our brother Jacob Brownfield. It will at least help him through this tough time."

"Yes, this donation thing has really racked up in just a matter of days."

"It's a miracle, right?" said David. "Now for those of you still in the dark about this, just visit my Facebook. David Morgan. I have a link for you to donate."

"Jesus Christ. He's publicizing himself!" said Terry. "How does he know the news will be there?"

Jake gritted his teeth, seething. "He knows this rich woman in Manhattan. She's supposed to give me a job." The yellow panel cut under the news to show the sunny 82°F in Farmington. "Didn't know he's a bit of a prima donna like his daughter."

"We gotta be careful, Jakey," said Ruth. "He's a big thing here, like Jesus in Alabama."

The reporter narrated a brief history about the Morgans in Farmington. David grew up in a Dennistown plantation, where everybody knew everybody. "The population remains the same since the Seventies, with only thirty people. And David was one of them living near Crocker Pond." His honor roll earned him a spot in Stanford. And he returned very much a superstar celebrity, ending up marrying Eden and settling in Farmington "to support his beloved wife's mortuary business and advocate a universal healthcare not only by politics rather through an affordable practice on a voluntary basis."

"He treats people. His wife buries them." Declan looked at his mother. "What kind of town is this, momma?"

"You got that one right, Dec."

The Morgan family returned to the news that night, grandstanding about pro-bono services. "Dave and I agreed with the school to extend our thoughts and prayers by organizing Miriam's funeral for free. We won't even take a dime from the fund they've crowded–"

Lottie turned off the TV. "I was listening to that," said Jake.

"You're five seconds from breaking the new remote."

"Three."

"Come on. You haven't had anything since breakfast!"

"I don't have any appetite."

Lottie snapped a photo and showed to Jake. The skin around his orbital bones had withdrawn, leaving some sort of holes where his eyes remained. Blackness blighted his jawlines for a sagging neck he never saw.

"Eat something!"

The stern voice compelled him to the plate of beef sandwiches on the work desk. Lottie prepared a ginger infusion for those sharp burps. Jake was shaking as strength rushed within him. He could finally think.

"They killed her, Charlotte. They killed her and bragged to the world. I lost my daughter and nobody asked me a damn thing out of so-called respect to my fucking privacy!"

Lottie took a sip from his cup. "The chief called," she said. "You'll have to say something live tomorrow during the funeral."

"It's happening, huh?" he said, snorting.

The pouring rain brought back that night when he arrived Farmington with Miri. He managed to stay up for some minutes before Ruth's diazepam spurred time into an acceleration. One moment there was a hailstorm; the next the sun rose against the balcony door.

In between this mad transition, Jake was back at that odd-smelling room where Rachel broke her tailbone. The doctors recommended and performed a caesarean section for that innocent cry of a newborn, which echoed through the agony of his nightmare.

He had been there that morning Miriam was born. And now he had to bury her – also in the morning. His body felt heavy from the drug. But he was strong enough to process the text from Rachel.

"What the fuck?" He heard Lottie's steps from the balcony. "Never mind." Nobody disturbed Jake. Terry was the one to fetch him into a limousine where Tashtego waited with a somber demeanor.

"Jake. I'm here to escort you. First lemme–"

"No more condolences, chief. Been too much already."

"I mean lemme brief you through," he continued. "The state's handling this funeral. So I think you know who's coming."

"You want me to shake Voldemort's hand and blow his nose?"

"Not the last part."

"What else?"

"The Governor closed all schools today. I'm sure there'll be a crowd."

"Put on a game face?" asked Ruth.

"Yeah. It's disgusting, I know. I'm just doing my job, ma'am."

"Anything else, Bob? 'cause I'm uh – I wanna see my daughter again," said Jake. "Even if it's for the last time."

"I'll take you there."

They huddled close together as Farmington streamed in a shaded blur. The journey was no more than two miles. Just as Tashtego said, a crowd waited on both sides of Farmington Falls Road. This procession of black and white continued from Maple Avenue across those closed business stores and straight to the green Riverside Cemetery.

A police officer welcomed them through a rose-filled path. Everyone nearby traded their warm wishes. Rising out of this pack of people was a neatly combed man, whose fiery temper during speeches defined his public image. Today he was cheerless, folding both hands as he took Jake. "I know you been getting a lotta this," he said. "But I'm really sorry for your loss."

"Thank you, Governor."

"The President has spoken about this. We're gonna do all we can to arrest this murderer. I know that won't—"

Roars from police motorcycles diverted them to the convoy encircling a polished hearse. From the belly of this beast, an ornate wooden coffin surfaced to land upon the shoulders of eight servicemen for a procession led by the family. Robert Tashtego took his place next to the Governor, just behind Jake.

Clouds gathered as those rifles directed for three ear-splitting shots. They passed through gravestones and pillars. Five seconds later, Jake was falling apart. The Governor had him by the arm at every clambering step. And they lowered Miriam Brownfield into a hole fit for a child. Lottie was holding Jake. But it was Ruth who fell on her knees, much to her husband's equal despair.

That commotion did not bestir Jake, whose eyes were feeding off a foreign power from somewhere. Right at that moment, Lottie realized. That wretched family stood in attendance, somewhat shining. While all the children attending were shivering in this gloomy weather, Amelia looked as though she was in a boiler room.

Lottie's hands got firmer. "Jake. Don't do it," she breathed. "Not today. Please."

But Jake nodded to that direction, with half a smile so realistic that David took his sweet time calculating a feigned response. Jake turned back to the grave, well away from their sight. And that was when Lottie started shaking. Because he was biting – his tongue, the insides of his cheeks and his teeth. She turned to a sound, which was none other than his gloved fists.

The last respect was gallant and noble to the state. But for Jake, it was an insult. Those salutes, shots and strings did not hide the simple fact, which was thousands of pounds worth of topsoil and a meaningless bed of flowers. And no justice.

14

The Governor's ten-minute speech was a yawning monologue, much like a bedraggling sermon from the pulpit of a church. His talking points reminisced online fervor, vying for justice but promising nothing. The family excused themselves after this rambling rhetoric, in disgust when the Governor used Jake's migraine to justify a hasty retreat to the Blaine House.

Everything stayed the same after the funeral. Court Street remained a street without a court. And Miriam's room felt haunted. They found Jake on her queen bed looking at the stickered study desk. "Uncle Jake," said Malcolm, at the door. "There's someone downstairs. He wanna see you."

"Another neighbor?"

"Maybe. He looks like a priest."

Agitation launched Uncle Obie into a barreling squeal. "I didn't know! I didn't know!" he said. "How – how did it h-happen? Why didn't you call? Why didn't you call me, Jake?" His tongue hung upon seeing the woman with a slight twist of mouth. "Ruth?"

"Hello, Uncle Obie."

They had a cup of coffee under the alfresco. "It happened so fast, Uncle Obie," said Jake. "I was in pain the whole time. I know I should call. I just—"

"I am more of a father to you than Avraham ever been! How can you forget me, Jake? I drove all the way," he said, bawling. "When I know. And I heard about that Moulin girl. You should complain, Jake. Don't let that one slide."

"We're not giving anybody a quarter, Unc."

The boys were spotted in the kitchen, stealing a good glimpse of Obie who called them out. It was a quick change of subject, something Jake so needed. "What was Brooklyn like before you came to Farmington?" asked Declan.

"Ooh. Brooklyn is just a short story," said Obie. "You see, I was born in a moshav somewhere around Mishmar Hayarden. It's like a village, now in Israel. I was too young to remember what happened during the war. But my father died fighting, and my mother married someone who died later from cancer.

"Momma had to work, leaving us with her brother. God, I love Uncle Haim. Those were hard times, boys. I have no idea how my pops look like. There's no picture." Then Uncle Obie darkened, shaking his head. "Uncle Haim. He got in the draft and the Egyptians got him in Sinai."

"What happened after that?"

"The bad sixties," said Uncle Obie. "In one week, I lost two of my half-brothers. And guess what? That still ain't all. Seventy-Three, my last year in Israel – my mom had a heart attack. She was like unconscious at a hospital and we found out about the Arab's surprise attack."

"Yom Kippur," said Malcolm.

Obie gave a light bump to his cheek. "You know our history well! I lost everyone that October."

"Your mom too?" asked Declan.

"They nearly drove us to the sea. There's no power. When I heard, I didn't go back. What's the point? I packed my bags and left for Brooklyn." Obie shook his head. "I was legally a Torah preacher and illegally a bricklayer. Some rabbi helped getting me an asylum here in Farmington, saying I wanna perform some missionary work.

"It ain't really what I wanna do. But one thing led to another. Here I am, your Uncle Obie." He took another sip from the cup. "Now, I'm only sharing to you what I've experienced. My life sure ain't easy. One corner you gotta survive; another corner, many people hate you for no reason. But things woulda been more difficult if I didn't come to God."

"We go to God too, Uncle Obie."

"Really?"

"Terry takes them to Chabad Square from time to time," said Ruth. "Not every Saturday."

"Is it worth it?"

Obie turned to Jake. "You musta heard of Shimon Peres," he said. "Before there was Israel, he purchased arms and found recruits for the Haganah. He died in his nineties. Yitzhak Shamir was someone in the Mossad. Dead in his nineties. And Golda Meir – she woulda lived to her nineties, if ain't for her cancer."

"Okay?" said Jake.

"Jake, look at the enemy camp! Nasser's light went out when he was fifty-two. Look at Anwar Sadat! Now they fight each other for no prize - only power and money." Obie grabbed his hand. "Going to God is worth the whole world. Surrender to Him, Jake. Surrender and He will guide you. I'm sure of it."

Jake sighed. "I'll try my best, Unc."

"That's what I wanna hear," said Obie. "Give yourself to Him, and He'll shine your way."

Escorting him to the door, Jake asked. "One thing I'm wondering – why you think He shined you to Waltham?"

"Believe me, Jake. I've been asking myself that question for forty years. Guess, He wants me here, huh?"

"Sure," said Jake.

Terry was simpering behind him. "That's sure some piece of work, huh?"

"He's a family for a long time," said Jake, massaging the bridge of his nose. "His whole life is a war we're like a buncha sissies really. But he's always there for me, man."

"You told him about the Morgans?"

"You crazy? He been acting like Rabin got a Pegasus from Yahweh. I don't need a scripture quote about prejudice."

Prejudice or no, Amelia Morgan was baking in that cold weather. Those damned Morgans stood no further than 30 feet on an elevation. Heat emanated from Jake's pores, causing that swing of an arm upon the drywall. His anger precipitated from weeks of misplaced patience, clinging on nothing but stupidity while Farmington got closer to catch cold than the murderer.

The outpouring disparagement retracted into countable support from crime enthusiasts. People kept themselves busy with the Boothbay Harbor Fest, a waterfront celebration for local small businesses. Those missing posters deteriorated on corners and walls as Miriam faded away from Farmington.

Media shifted attention to tee time, harvest day and that Permaquid Oyster Festival. They chipped five minutes from the coverage block, looping a diabolical insult with a polished façade. Miri had to share airing time of 300 seconds with other crime events.

Jake descended into a cyclical activity seeing himself repeating a daily pattern. He woke up, showered, ate and slept – and sometimes he had to refuse those harassing calls from Alabama. "She's one complete fuck up," said Lottie.

"That's a start," he replied. "To think she'd take the hint from all those years I been doing this."

Lottie arranged the pillows after straightening the sheet. "Last night she sent you something."

"How come? I blocked her."

"From her sister's number," said Lottie. "A long bullshit with a shitty apology for leaving before funeral. I'm telling you, that bitch thinks she can text you whenever the fuck she wants and I'm sick of it."

Jake got up. "I'll change my number then," he said. "There's not a damn thing I wanna do with Rachel."

"It's okay, Jake. You don't have to do if it it's just to make me feel better."

"What the hell, Charlotte?" he breathed. "It's not that I'm texting her. C'mon. Don't do this to me!"

Lottie moved to a corner, hooking an arm to her forehead with a sigh. "I just had a bad day at work," she said. "Okay, you should change your number. I'm sorry. I didn't mean to guilt you up for that bitch."

"You're just jealous."

"I'm not."

"Yes, you are."

"Not."

"Are."

"Not."

Grief did not diminish his feelings for Lottie, who was a bushwhacker between parenting, privacy and profession. She was his rock, a strong mainstay bobbing an ambience of peace into his soul. It was for her he cried his last tears, fuming only when his mind stayed idle. His head had to be over his heels, clocking things up around the house.

He had been cleaning the house.

He had been mowing the lawn.

He polished the silver, even there was never going to be a formal dinner. He plugged his ears and confronted his babbling sister, who found a golden window in this midst of misery. Ruth had just bounced from Billingsley Supermarket and Pat's for grocery. And every afternoon, the Kenwood mixer groaned to every earshot within a square mile. She squeezed time for family meals and cookies on demand from specific clients.

This whole thing was Malcolm's idea. The boy never believed his business page would be featured in the news as a solidarity promotion to socially support the family. Jake overheard their conversation about someone wiring money for cookie delivery to local parishes. Obie's exclusive contacts broke the ice, that Ruth finally spoke positively of him.

Days ago, a Baptist church approached Ruth all the way from Cleveland. They paid a grand to get cookies for the nearest Baptist congregations every Sunday. Ruth got a subscription from Lewiston Muslims for Fridays. For the first time, Ruth outearned her chapfallen husband who pulled over the driveway every weekday after spending morning, noon and sometimes night to get a job in this remote world.

Jake marooned himself in the periphery of his property. He preferred to recline under that maple tree and surf family albums. Once or twice, he stumbled upon those Farmington-targeted cookie ads. Good thing Ruth had little exposure to social media. And Malcolm was busy at school (not at Mount

View). Jake kept assuming into their business profile to delete those derogatory comments against Ruth.

Jews are always Jews, or so they said about Ruth's financial pursuit.

The Internet was quick to jump on these animals. Facebook sometimes was quicker to zucc them all to hell over community violations. He struck a schedule to clear those pestering mofos out of his sister's page. There was an installed reminder app to keep at this task before Malcolm returned from school. And he was still doing it, when Tashtego was there. "How are you coping?" he asked, puffing the Pall Mall into open air.

"Taking it slowly. How about you?"

"Hell of a week at the office," he said. "The press been hounding my wife even, asking if she knows anything."

"They like it when cops got nothing. Keeps the story going."

"I have something actually."

His fingers twitched again. "Well, go on!"

"We took our time for cross checking." Miri's first day at Mt View was on August 12. "She went missing on the Twenty-First. We've looked into this to find any correlation. We know there's no bad blood or anything personal about your bar fight."

Jake nodded. "You told me that before! I was drunk when I insulted the mayor."

"Right. Since it's not politics, we move to sex offenders," said Tashtego, ignoring Jake's scoff. "August Twenty, we have five sex offenders roaming around."

"And?"

"Judge Rodeback sentenced these offenders years and years ago. They served their time, but he made sure they report every day or every week. By doing that, we can track them." Tashtego raised a finger. "One of them we think has something to do with Miriam. But the man has an alibi. He was out of town two days before."

"So you have nothing."

"Not done yet. Let's say he did it. It doesn't explain a few things. If he did it, he did a very good job washing Miriam's body before dumping her there." Jake nodded. "The method of murder wasn't stabbing or blunt force. She succumbed to her injuries." Tashtego saw another nod. "It was too clean. No fingerprints or DNA. Super clean even for a sex offender who was arrested for using Google Pay!"

"Okay, that's something."

"Before the funeral, we've run a lot of DNA analysis. There's just nothing. Not an inch of her body had anything that could link us to this offender. Whoever did this, they're professional."

"Bob, I'm gonna need you to be honest with me," said Jake. "You think this case can end up cold?"

"I'm deploying my teams to make sure it doesn't. It'll take some time, Jake. They did a lotta homework to cover their mistakes but we'll get their tracks soon."

"Any possibility they make that mistake to divert us?"

"It's not just me they're diverting," said Tashtego. "The feds are involved. They hate cold cases. By next year, we'd have a quarter a mil of unsolved murders. The going rate is six thousand a year. And there's no way in hell I'm letting Miri in that number."

"So – there is a possibility."

"Everyone wants answers. I want answers. Why, big cases like this the government want answers. Even DeWinter is having a hard time. Her credibility is coming into question. She may have to resign."

"You're not answering the question, Bob."

"Yes, there is a possibility. A murder like this will happen again, if I may speak bluntly. That's why we have hundreds of people in this county brainstorming anything and everything. I'm keeping it local. It's my battle, not some bigshot from the J. Edgar Hoover!"

Jake glared at him. "This is no battle," he said. "She's my daughter. Get your fucking grip and work together, man!"

"I know, I know. If I may speak personally, I may have to resign if this gets cold. And I have a family. Two girls near Miri's age. I tuck 'em in and I wonder if they're next. So yeah, I want you to know – I'm on your side. Because this shitshow has to end. Not for my daughters even. For you. For Miriam."

After sending the chief back to his cruiser, Jake joined the family in the living room. "Things aren't going well?" said Ruth.

"Not for him. I played the sad dad. He told me everything," said Jake. "Miri's body was washed before being dumped. There was no fingerprint. Now we all know there's only one woman who cleans that well. And I don't mean Vanesa Valdez!"

"A doctor with a mortician wife."

"Got me wondering," said Jake. "If the Morgans can dump my girl just like that, what else they been doing?"

15

Fall began with a sneeze attack ruining much of the day for the family. Blobs of phlegm dribbled down their noses during a hot shower. Jake had another reason to grunt. His Bangor Daily News subscription expired for now a limited access of five articles. And Lottie had blown three into the stricture, sparing him to contend with an official statement from the State Department about a certain vaccination petition.

Not intending to blow his last door, he meandered to an article about Autumn equinox. The Sun had no problem putting an uncensored picture of the North East Skinny Dip in Northumberland.

The British enthusiasm spiked beyond the border for Farmington. The horror film Miri wanted to see smashed the box office with solid reviews. Baby Boomers opted for the exciting *Rambo: Last Blood*, divided between thematic elements overindulging violence and the need of a proper character development.

The rest of his Facebook depicted boring lives. Jake then felt inclined to head out for the mailbox, where the first hiccup came gnashing at his resolve. He stopped breathing for at least ten seconds, fumbling into the driveway with the brown envelope in a hand. Ruth scoped him from the living room.

"Jake? What's wrong?"

"Nothing," he said. "Nothing's wrong."

"You're brooding out front for nothing?"

"I just lost a kid, Ruth."

"What's that you got?"

Seeing no cause to hide, he dropped the envelope on the countertop. "Just go through and tell me how much." Inside Ruth found a three-page document with the first honoring Jake's loss. Miri was then mentioned to be a direct dependent under Jake's custody in the eyes of the law. It all built for the impaling claim in the last page. "So, how much I owe him?"

Ruth looked horrified. "Thirty-five thousand dollars!"

"Shit. I totally forgot about it."

"Jake, that much?"

"It wasn't a short battle. The bitch had guns."

"You – you have money?"

"I'm not gonna think too hard."

True to his words, Jake took the document to his desk and sat while humming *Ave Satani*. It was a song from ironically Obie's favorite film. The divorce took a turn for the worst, when a killer switch flicked a U-Turn in Rachel's head. And she went on a sudden gambit, gun-blazing for full custody. Jake got the better of her, with the best lawyer in town.

"Hey, it's me, Jacob Brownfield."

"How's it going, Mr. Brownfield?"

"I apologize - I missed your emails."

Rufus laughed. "I take it you got our claim?"

"Yeah. I gotta be honest. I really can't pay it all now."

"Ah. Don't worry about it. We understand what you're going through." Rufus' voice did not change, even a bit. "It's just for formality. We do cut corners and give clients more time. I can't see why we shouldn't do it for you," he said. "Here's the thing. Pay whenever you feel right. Take as much time you need."

"Oh, my God. Thank you! I feel so guilty now."

"Please, don't be. I do this a lot. Last thing I want is a buncha depressed dads squandering my win."

"Thank you, Mr. Pyke. Thank you again!"

He punched the air with a quiet whoop. The death of a daughter sufficed him a grace period enough to figure out what the hell he was going to do. And he knew he had to act before Rufus' killer switch accused him of malpractice. Ruth agreed to his notion, still at shock of the humongous overdue. "Don't worry. Terry will get a job," she said. "We'll do our part."

"This part is mine," said Jake. "Miriam was there for me. Turns out I can solve things if I don't think too hard."

After breakfast Jake found himself biting his fingernails and rubbing his face. These habits were often repeated, even in the privacy of the bathroom. He rearranged the living room to eliminate Miri's double seater from his glimpse. About an hour later, he caved into the heavy block in his chest. And he moved the sofa back in its place, before questioning his decision again.

The television gave a short distraction. Glaring scenes cut into action with an anchorperson updating about the Abqaiq-Khurais incident in Saudi Arabia. Still in the Middle East the news pounded the same old story about the US's strained relations with Iran. Jake slammed the red button hard when the story started on Sahar Khodayari.

"I was watching that," said Ruth.

He shook his head back and forth, trembling. He had enough about self-immolation and third-degree burns. "*Don't think too hard. Don't think too hard.*" The front door swung for

Terry, whose forced grin was a hideous expression. "No luck today?" asked Jake.

"Not even a handshake out."

Terry turned the TV back on. "The questions about Miriam Brownfield's horrific death are mounting as we approach a month without a lead. A petition was set up in the White House website two days after the funeral, calling for Principal Katherine DeWinter's dismissal. As of today, over a million people have signed and the White House released a statement last week about an inquiry into her community school."

"Holy Christ, one million?" gasped Terry.

"She's still holding on," said Jake, bristling. "Just fucking resign!"

"We've talked to the community in Farmington and they are all expressing what they describe as abject fear.

"One of the prominent residents in Farmington–"

The scene sequence riled Jake. "You gotta be kidding me!"

"–David Morgan as we all know is a practicing doctor."

"I have a daughter, almost the same age. It's just sick," said David. "Very sick. It's hard to imagine how some maniac can do something like that to someone as young and sweet as Miriam."

Jake kicked the couch backward for the stairs, where the house spun in a mad blur. "How some maniac can do something?" The black bag from the top of his bookshelf swung upon a yank, pivoting with the force of an arm straight to his desk. "How some maniac can do something!" he muttered. "I'll show you what maniacs do!"

He stuck a hand in, feeling through nylon and polyester for a metallic device. It was his loyal stinger, a close friend with two deadly buttons to compromise his target. After that he reached for the 2006 Nokia mobile phone in a pocket. "Whoa, you still have that?"

Jake blanched. "Dec, when did you get back?"

"Just now." He showed a worn-out baseball. "Play catch, Uncle Jake?"

A brick fell down his throat. "I have to run some errands. Maybe around five, if it's okay with you?"

Declan smiled. "Five's good."

"And Declan, don't say anything about this, okay?"

"Sure."

He leaped across the room to lock the door. "That baseball!" He was not putting this off for another day – not even for Declan. It had to go down the moment that pretentious asshole appeared on television showboating for personal popularity. "Fucking murdered my daughter – now you're tryinna be famous, huh? I'll make you famous, bitch boy."

His spate of fury toed a thin line to provide a reason for Terry's Toyota. He was out of there in three minutes, bound for a slow drive to the willowy Fairview along Perham. This intersection took him to an elevated seclusion that was the almighty Granite Heights.

"You bastards live closer to trees than you do with people!" said Jake, passing by the motley-designed houses.

He pulled Terry's cap upon nearing a cape cod, where the Gabbays resided for generations. That Lord-loving family turned up at his house with the rest of the neighbors that day when Naomi Moulin went batshit at school. Jake kept nodding into a microsleep when Chaston Gabbay was lecturing about godly plans. But there was another piece of memory hibernating in the meaningless side of his mind cave. It was after Lottie turned the debating Strawman upside down. She was about to resume chatting with Erina Gabbay, before leaving for Mt. View.

They were close, really close. For that reason, Jake was not waiting for Lottie's Santa Fe. Up ahead was the turn for Heritage Circle, and he stopped beneath the shades of a yellowing basswood. There was a colonial house with makeshift potting arrangements – without that black Mercedes AMG. With Amelia posting on Instagram, Jake knew he was good to go.

His chest stirred into a thumping motion, threatening to break through his rib cage during the silent observation for movement, any movement whatsoever. Seeing none, he made his way for the bell to be greeted by a slender woman.

"Mr. Brownfield?" she said, with the strangest smile.

"Hello. You must be Mrs. Morgan?"

"Yes." Eden extended a hand. "What brings you here?"

"I was in the neighborhood visiting a friend. He told me you're living here." Eden stood there, frozen with the same simper. "Err, bad timing?"

"Oh, no, no. Not at all. Please, come on in."

The frontmost section of this house was a scented vestibule where they kept awards, medals and trophies in great glass displays. Jake did not miss the big portrait holding the family together with a plastic expression. He was brought to a decorated guest hall. "Quite a house you got," said Jake, as Eden went straight to the adjacent bar. "I hope I'm not troubling you, Mrs. Morgan."

"Please, please, have a seat. Just Eden, by the way."

"Eden–" Jake stopped before an acrylic work of hue and tone blending a familiar luminescence. "Is that from Charles Reade?"

"Not sure. Dave's a sucker for art. You drink?"

"Of course. Everyone drinks."

"I mean, alcohol, Mr. Brownfield."

"Oh, silly me. No, I don't." Eden returned with a tall glass of grenadine mocktail with a slice of lime teething by the rim. "That's really something," he said.

"Thank you. You looking quite thin, Jake."

A blast of heat hit him. "Still shell-shocked. I can't be at home honestly," he said. "Just wanna head out for some air, thank people who helped me along the way. You know, just to take stuff off my mind."

Eden sorted her empty words. "You know we are very sorry for your loss."

"C'mon. Don't be. It's not that you did it."

Right then and there, her face locked, loaded and launched those tense curls beneath that glowing skin. "I didn't mean it like that," she breathed.

"Jesus. It's just too many condolences. I'm sorry. Of course you meant well."

"We have a girl too. She means the whole world to us and more. I really can't think if anything like this happens to her."

"Yeah. The whole town been buzzing about it. With many moms working, they're just scared of their kids being home. I haven't talked to a friend of mine yet. You know Cassie Blount, the gal working at Dunkin'?"

Jake had to pause for an unnoticeable squint studying Eden's reaction. He never thought a person could ever flutter both eyelids in that kind of way, perspiring like a pig in a slaughterhouse – if there was such a thing. She managed a reply. "I'm on keto. So I don't go to Dunkin."

"I see. Well, I meant to say her girl is about ours." There was a momentary silence, brief but terribly corrosive. "I guess, I'll be off. Just wanna thank y'all. Give my regards to David."

"Wait, Mr. Brownfield. Since you're here – would you like to have dinner? You know, you and all three of us?"

"Right here?"

"I was thinkin' somewhere else – but sure, why not? Say, tonight?"

"Super!"

He felt Eden staring on his back. He did not turn but for one solitary second, he landed a good view from a reflecting angle. She was grimacing with a misshapen contortion, almost akin to someone having a tattoo in doubt. Back in the car, Jake hid the Nokia by the door and pretended he was reaching for something in the back.

It took a while. But Eden went inside to answer.

"Hi. Is this the Morgan Morgue?" he said, with a huskier voice.

"Yes. Eden speaking. How can I help you?"

"My uncle just passed away."

"Oh, I'm really sorry to hear that.

"Thank you. Do you have an office or something? I'd like to talk."

"You can come to my house. Know Granite Heights?"

Jake gripped upon the steering wheel. "I'm still at the hospital. Got some things to sort out. Can you come here?'

"The hospital?"

"Yeah. I really can't go anywhere."

"It's okay, sir. I'll be there in a few. What's your name, by the way?"

He saw a warning sign not too far away. "Warner. Head out for the cafeteria."

About five minutes later, the silver Chrysler backed out of the house for Maple Avenue. And he was out of there, smiling as the burner phone deflected Eden's calls throughout the day. He returned to the Morgan home after sundown. The whole family was there in formal to greet him.

"Welcome, Mr. Brownfield. Been wantin' to have dinner with you."

"As long as we have that mocktail again," said Jake.

Eden laughed, dryly. "Really sorry to tell you this. We had to order."

"Oh? You don't have to! We can do this tomorrow."

"No way, man. Tonight's tonight. Just that some dude asked for a funeral service but we got stood up." David raised both hands. "Just happens sometimes. People don't take things seriously."

"Shit. That's not okay," replied Jake. "Can't go around wasting someone's time."

They went into greater detail about that in the dining room, which was a spacious expanse of teakwood and more displays. Amelia was still pale, avoiding Jake's eyes the whole time. No more than half an hour later, she excused herself. "We're really sorry about that," said David. "She's just not herself since the funeral."

"Why?"

Another warning sign flew across the table bouncing between the power couple. "Miriam uhh was in her class," said David. "They know each other."

"Oh. Yeah. Yeah. Miri told me a lot about you. Just that she never got the chance to tell me anything about school. Always Amelia, Amelia, Amelia – like she wanna ask you out for a barbecue."

His inflection was perfectly placed, neither accusatory nor confiding. "Yeah. Wish we could turn back time," said Eden, first to fall in the tangle.

"I lost my mom months ago. It was painful for weeks. But then I figured out she was in a better place with God and all. And it just goes away. With Miri – it ain't easy. Trust me, it ain't. I try not think about it – or something else will come in my mind."

"Like what?" asked Eden.

"A noose around my neck."

"God Almighty!" exclaimed David. "Sweet Jesus. Be more sensitive, honey!"

"It's okay, doc. You must have some experience on this. I feel trapped like I want some justice but the cops are downright wondering what the hell happened." He had David's undivided attention. "I'm just heartbroken, doc," he said, wheezing. "I'm heartbroken. Someone did me something very wrong. I just wanna know – why my girl?"

After dessert, David invited for a smoke in his home office. And Jake jumped right at the chance. The office was next to the master bedroom, with a balcony where David lit his cigarette.

"I don't smoke, by the way."

"Really? Why didn't you say so?"

"Just want someone to talk to," said Jake. "I know some hippy docs. Just never seen one who smokes."

David laughed. "That's a really good one."

"But, if I may ask – how's Amelia really holding up?"

"She's been quiet. First someone stole her iPhone earlier on. Now this – it just didn't go too easy on her."

"Yeah, I heard about that iPhone thing. Miriam talked about it. You found it yet?"

"That's the thing. It's just gone like someone chucked it in space or something. I'm telling you, 2019 sucks!"

"Yeah? Wait till next year. It'll get a whole lot worse."

"Huh. I didn't like the idea her having an iPhone. You're basically like a king with an XS."

"Can I see her, by the way? I really wanna talk to her."

"Why, sure. Right this way."

The golden opportunity got them to the lower floor for a right turn toward a white door. Amelia shot to her feet. "Hey, I just wanna talk to you," said Jake. "It's all right. Sit."

Amelia did as bid. "What is it, Mr. Brownfield?"

"Do you know Miri?" he asked, moving his wrist for the stinger ensconced in a sleeve pocket. "Ever talked to her? Eat with her?"

"I wish I did, sir. She was in my class."

Jake nodded, taking a knee next to her. It was then he dropped the device and put a foot over it. "I just want you to know this. You're like a princess to her. She even googled how to get back your phone. She just adored you."

"Really?" breathed Amelia, her brows up.

"It's just too bad what happened," said Jake, smiling. He kicked the stinger under the bed. "Just don't stay down too often, yeah?"

"Okay, Mr. Brownfield."

16

Mozzarella melted into stretchy filaments pasting over his hoary beard. Terry shrugged with the back of his hand, munching those scones as he peered over his credentials with a vacant expression. He already lowered his pay scale, cutting corners with a decade worth of accounting which should be a mouthwatering pitch. But there was no call back, not even one. And he soon realized he was dumber than a fucking jerboa. Because he spent too much time polishing his work description that he overlooked the critical error in his contact information.

He had given an old email and criminally inverted his phone number. There were rejections, citing with respect that he was of course overqualified. But there had been so many calls for second interviews which he missed. Now he had to circle around town again for the remaining hunt.

And the very next day, he was on his way to a Sandy River bend along Farmington Falls Road. The woodworking company had a small profile, without a website. At this point, it would make no sense to tell Ruth about his doltish mistake.

He had to assess the operations for a better understanding. But within the hour, he was certain to work in this moribund company. And Jake only found out on the third day, after not seeing Terry for hours and hours at a time. Jake had been busy being an operative with a headphone tapping that large reach from the Morgan home.

The device was like a sound black hole sucking things from Amelia's room. After that dinner, she had an earful for being rude toward Jake. David yelled at her without that apologetic tone for a girl who lost her friend.

Jake paid attention to those frequencies and soundwaves on the monitor. Most of the time, Amelia's room was a static bat cave. She never talked, not even to her friends if she had any. His suspicion never dwindled throughout this period. Doubts never clouded his judgment.

He knew he was listening to the killer.

What he did not know however was another story.

Those wavelengths saw him scrambling back for the headphone to hear something he never expected. Coldness wrapped his face, upon listening to those moaning gasps. He froze without movement, one moan, two moans, and the third that soon became a thousand even at 1 in the morning. Those heavy breathings and muffled screams kept penetrating his ears against a creaking background.

One night, it was an hour – literally an hour – of pleasure that Jake threw the headphone. "Still nothing, huh?" asked Lottie, reading at the balcony.

"She's not a human."

"You ain't that different when you were her age."

"I murdered no one."

"Honey, as much as I want justice, but I gotta say. You can go to prison for this, y'know? She's a minor. What if they find the device?"

"They don't have a maid. Her room was a mess I'd say the fingering fuck ain't a cleaner," he said. "Besides, they can't prove that's mine."

"How long you have?"

"The battery goes to standby. It sleeps if there's no sound."

"Jesus. Where did you get this stuff anyway?"

"Some people in Los Angeles I won't even hang out with or risk being in the DoD's radar. You gotta go around legality to push your cause. It's always like that."

"You sure they can't trace you back?"

"Nope."

"Still doesn't make it right, Jake."

Jake turned to her, glaring. "Puh-lease! Don't go moral on me now, Charlotte!" he said. "They killed Miriam! You didn't see the mom's face. I saw it in her eyes when I first walked in. She was very afraid, like a whore at church standing there her eyes wide like I'm God! They did it, Charlotte. And I gotta prove it. And if I have to burn this fucking country to the ground, you bet I will do it!"

"I will too," she replied, her voice unchanging. "But I don't wanna lose you."

"You won't be. I wouldn't even be alive if that thing is traceable. The rich fuckers ain't too smart covering their own tracks. They won't be following mine – they're too afraid."

After school the next day, Amelia came home grumpy like always. Jake heard everything, from the loud thud of her book bag and those creaky stiff spring in her mattress. Yet again she got lost in the deep end, paddling her pink canoe with oar-like fingers. After about an hour Jake heard a heave. First mistaking for the obvious, Jake then realized she was voicing something.

She was voicing. "Fucking roach deserved it."

"Mean young lady, this one," said Lottie.

"So, if a convicted sex offender was responsible for the murder, how come *this* sex maniac thinks of Miriam after jacking off? I mean, you don't think about bad things that happened around you after having sex with me – right?"

"Having sex with you is bad enough as it is. So, no," said Lottie, keeping her straight face. "But, you're right. And why David scream at her like that just because she ain't talkative. You're a stranger. What's the big deal about being quiet?"

"Unless if they hidin' something and got scared about it."

"This is something," said Lottie. "Her being rude to you ain't really about rude. It's about raising questions or asking for troubles. We just need to find more, something enough to take this young lady to church."

"David never asked about the Manhattan job. He was too friendly with me. Eden was jumpy. Amelia was quiet."

"Anyone else in the house?"

"I'm sure they have a gardener. They keep one helluva lawn. Why?"

"Gimme a minute," said Lottie, ringing her dad. "Yeah, dad. I'm at Jake's. We're thinking of doing something in the backyard. Mason tripped over a rock. I was wondering if you know any good gardener around? Say, I saw some houses up at Granite Height. Those guys musta have someone." A pause ensued. "Oh, the Morgans? What's the name?" The second pause was agitating. "Okay, text me the number."

"Where did you learn to lie like that?"

"You're welcome," she replied. "His name is Marcell."

"Who?"

"Their gardener."

"Okay?"

"Miriam must have screamed and screamed when Amelia tortured her," she said. "We know one thing – Amelia never skipped school. She was there when Miriam called Rachel. They musta jumped her and somehow got her out of the school before you started looking for her."

"And if they tortured her in that home, this gardener Marcell woulda known."

"That is if they tortured her in the morning. But they can't torture her in the morning and be at school the same time."

"Then they tortured her in the evening."

"The neighbors woulda heard. I've seen people there, when I was with the Gabbays. They'll go for evening walks. Some nights, they'll walk their dogs. Can't be at night. They'll hear."

"Maybe they didn't torture her there?"

"Where else? The clinic? The mo–"

The realization hit both of them. "It's the morgue! The fucking morgue! Eden has a basement there!"

"How are we going in there?" asked Lottie.

There was nothing they could legally do to prove about the funeral home. Perham Street from TD Bank took them to Edgehill Lane, a dirt road in the fore of an autumnal thicket. The Morgan Morgue was on the right of that turn, surrounded with red roses over black loam.

Those walls had a two-foot brick barrier with a colorful fill. A cross was shining on top of a conical roof. Jake drove around the parking space to find no opening. "How are we doing this?"

"Too risky. We gotta do it with Eden around."

"How's that not risky?" exclaimed Lottie.

"Because you're a good liar."

Her jaw dropped. "You want me to go in there with Eden Morgan?"

"I have a way."

The wipers fought a mild precipitation as they doubled back to Moore Avenue. The slippery Middle Street was a long stretch through two schools, meeting a credit union halfway to a convenience store where Jake bought a spray paint at $18.69. "What's that for?" she asked, managing through the subsequent disquiet and not expecting to be at Riverside Cemetery.

She followed him to the grave now with a flat marble: *HERE LIES MIRIAM BROWNFIELD, the Farmington angel whose future was unjustly stolen.*

"Touchy," said Jake, shaking the paint can.

"Whoa! Jake, what the fuck?"

It happened too quickly. Jake's arm and wrist swung and twisted, forming a green swastika upon the plaque.

"What the fuck, Jake?"

"Snap a picture," he said, walking back to the car. And when it was all done, he turned to Lottie who was red-faced. "Show Eden that picture. Tell her you wanna change it before I see it."

Her voice was scolding. "That's your daughter!"

"*Was* my daughter, Charlotte," said Jake, turning away. "I know what I'm doing."

"What if I go there – and she gave me a view of the place – and we found nothing?" she replied, straining for words. "You know who they are in this part of town. Anything happens, you can scoot and skedaddle – but you ever think what might happen to *my* mom and dad? They have a business here!"

Jake blinked a few times, realizing. "I'm so angry," he breathed. "The thought didn't really come to me." That made things worse, as Lottie punched for Eden and then shoved her phone over the dashboard. Lottie took the car for the appointment at the morgue. "Wait. Take this." He handed her a rectangular device. "It's the stinger bug."

"Jesus. How many you have?"

"Four more."

He was then listening on two fronts. Eden was caught telling Amelia about the appointment. *"Vulture's flying."* Lottie's phone beeped through the earpiece, which produced a distant engine roar. *"She's on her way."*

"Okay," said Lottie, through the stinger bug. "She just texted me." They continued this voice-and-chat communication, until the Chrysler arrived. "She's here."

Some footsteps afterward, Jake heard that wretched voice. "Hello. Been waiting long?"

"Oh, no, Mrs. Morgan. I live around here. I think you know my parents? The Reades?"

"Oh, of course! Charlotte, right?"

"Wow. You know me?"

"I heard a lot about you. What are you doing here anyway? Your dad isn't dead yet."

Lottie kept her cool. "I'm not booking a funeral. It's just—" She combed through her handbag. "I was at the pizza, the one across the graveyard. I saw some kids doing some spraying."

"Oh, God. On a gravestone?"

"Not some gravestone. The girl's gravestone."

Eden blurted after seeing the photo. "Oh, my God!"

"They ran soon as I called at them."

"Does Mr. Brownfield know?"

"Oh, no, no, no!" said Lottie. "He cannot know! My dad had to talk him out of a suicide attempt some days back! He cannot know this, Mrs. Morgan!"

"What the fuck?" whispered Jake.

"Jesus."

"I heard about you doing some pro-bono. But I'm willing to cover this on my own dime."

"The governor paid more than what I usually charge. I can fix this. But we gotta tell the cops, Charlotte."

"At least after replacing?"

"Sure."

Those echoes indicated the interior space of the funeral home. It was a mere glimpse for Lottie, who was ushered to the office section. "D'you have the gravestone here? Not in catalogues, I mean," she asked. That played Eden, who led her to another door. Jake heard the slight whisper, not too soft for his headphone. "Basement," breathed Lottie.

"It's a mess down here."

"Oh? Should I wear gloves?"

"That won't be necessary. I can give you if you want," said Eden. "Look, I never had anyone else in here before. Please if you see anything, just ignore it, okay?"

"What kind of things?" asked Lottie, stammering.

"This is where I do the—"

"The cutting?"

"Yes!"

"Jesus. I thought you meant a ghost or something," said Lottie. A while through the walk, she asked, "you never get afraid here?"

"I was scared of ghosts when I was a kid. But now the living scares the crap outta me. Sorry for cursing."

"Like my ex-husbands," said Lottie. "But hey, I never knew you in forensics doing cutting and all?"

"I don't investigate how they die, Charlotte," said Eden. "What I do is, I embalm bodies. I don't wanna go into details. Don't wanna ruin your appetite."

They agreed on a tombstone, and she refused an advance. Upon returning home, Jake hugged her. "They have an indoor dumpster," said Lottie. "In the basement. I saw it. The trash collector has the key."

"You're sure?"

"Yep. He goes in. Comes out with the bin. That way Eden doesn't have to be there."

"That's our way in!"

"I saw something inside," said Lottie. "There was a cutting table. You know that steel-made thing? Eden was so not comfortable when I looked there many times. The basement ain't hot at all. But she's–"

"Sweating."

"Yup. A whore at church."

Jake clapped. "It's where they tortured her! We gotta find who's on duty. Think we can call the garbage company and find out?"

"I know who he is – at least he's on duty tomorrow. But it ain't gonna be easy. He's widowed with three kids. We get caught; he gets fired."

"How well you know him?"

"Not too well, why?"

The pen clicked against his thumb. "Widowed with three kids, huh?"

"Yup."

"You think he'll cooperate if we threaten to do something on his kid?"

"Are you outta your goddamned mind?"

"I didn't say *we* hurt his kid," said Jake. "How long before Amelia suspects one of his kids and go crazy again?"

"But will she? She's scared as shit now."

"One way to find out."

They waited at the morgue for the truck. And by noon, it came roaring down Perham Street. "This is crazy, Jake."

"It's gonna be okay."

The jumpy-looking man in a jumpsuit was jumpier up close. "Jesus Christ! What the hell you think you doing?"

"What's your name?"

"Gerry. You ain't cops, are you? I swear to God she told me she's nineteen!"

"Calm down." Jake took Miriam's photo from his wallet. "You ever seen this girl?"

"Yeah. She's in the news. Wait, you're her dad, aren't you? Brownfield?"

"I'm gonna need your help. I'll even go down my knees. But please, let me in the morgue."

"I can't do that," said Gerry. "I'll lose my job."

"Only for a minute or two."

"Wait, why you using your daughter to go in? What's she gotta do with it?"

"They raped my girl, Gerry," said Jake, which got his attention. "They raped her. They fried her. They killed her. In. That. Morgue."

Gerry stood unmoved. "You telling me the Morgans did it? No. They're good family. Can't be! How you know this?"

"I'm running my own investigation. I wish I can tell you more. But please, let me in. You can watch. You can even tie my hands behind my back. But please, let me in! I know you have the key."

Gerry turned to Lottie, who gave an assuring nod. He scratched his scruffy head and croaked. "Okay. But our lil secret, yeah! I say leave, we leave 'cause believe me, the dumpsters can kill anyone. Last time they keep those smelly bottles – you know chemical stuff." He then put a hand on Jake. "The Morgans ain't got nothing to do with this, you know. You saw the news, how Dr. Morgan keep supporting you."

"Look at it this way, Gerry. How many times the Governor or the Mayor come up the news to talk about Miriam?"

"I dunno. Once. Twice."

"But how many times Dr. Morgan cover this story?"

"Shit," said Gerry. "Shit. I see your point."

The dumpster section smelled like hell. Jake followed Gerry through the trapped air and into the hallway where Eden had taken Lottie. It was imperfectly built, with cracks and chips all over the place.

"Can't be long here, okay?"

The phone flashlight illuminated the area in a circular projection. Jake found stone slabs and pre-registered tombstones on a heavy working table. There was nothing in that area. He moved to the storage section where Eden kept files and folders. Ahead, they took a left for the cutting table. Upon hitting the switch, the whole place came to life with signs of death against steel and tiles. Jake began looking, ignoring as Gerry started being pushy.

It soon dawned that Eden got everything. The racks, shelves and ceiling were spotless. The floor reflected the glaring overhead bulbs, mopped perhaps ten times over much like the ventilation fan. Not even a speck of dust was there – or anywhere. Just as Jake was about to give in to Gerry's insistence, he saw the stairs toward the upper home. "No, man! Come on!" said Gerry. "I ain't got the key for that!"

"You sure?"

"Oh, for fuck sake, I'm just a trashman! C'mon! We gotta go!"

Lottie had to come in for Jake. And they went back after Gerry locked the place. "It's okay. Just a setback," she said.

"They're fucking good, Charlotte. The hallway is a mess. The file room is a mess. But that damn autopsy room was squeaky clean. They mopped it up and blow-dried everything."

"We'll keep on looking!"

"That's our only place," said Jake. "They all had her there. And they cleaned it up."

Lottie banged on the wheel.

"They burned my daughter."

"Jake."

"Fuckers burned my daughter, and they're smiling over dinner and all!"

"Jake!"

"She's diddling herself while my daughter rots!"

"Jake!" said Lottie, a bit louder.

"What?"

"They steam-ironed her with something electric."

"Yeah. So?"

"It'll show on the bill!"

Jake straightened himself. "No, it won't," he said, resigned. "It won't do us good. They can say they spent a night or two in that morgue. And that'll be that."

The last turn to Court Street had them on edge. Ruth was seen looking very upset, standing next to a police officer who saw them coming. "That fucker dime us out?"

"It's all right, ma'am. I got it. You Jake Brownfield?"

"Can I help you, sir?"

"We got a situation at the impound. Your dog attacked someone."

"Attacked?"

"Declan walked Spud out!" said Ruth, out of breath. "He just jumped at a bunch of girls!"

"I suggest you go to the impound now, Mr. Brownfield. Afraid what might happen to him."

"Thank you, officer." Lottie breathed. "We'll head there right away."

Jake charged at the officer. "My dog never attacked anyone the past eight years I adopted him!" he said. "Who did he attack? You know those girls?"

"Everyone knows them," said the officer. "It's Amelia Morgan."

17

Jake was so glad to see the woman in the impound that he kicked the floorboard, thrashing with a deep growl of excitement. Kendra Whipple was alone behind the glassed counter, someone he shared more than mere friendship in his greener days. He considered her as a sister. She however fought for an impossible relationship, wanting to live in an affluent region as a supermodel someday. She never stopped harping about Downtown Hollywood and Upper West Side.

She earned her red carpet, which was a dusty doormat behind that automatic door. She told them to be quick with Spud, before her supervisor returned from a break. And they were out of there in no time. Jake brought Spud upstairs where Lottie saw him removing what appeared to be a micro-SD card from the collar.

"Gosh. You put a stinger on Spud?" she said.

"We had a break-in back in Huntsville. Spud chased the burglar away," said Jake, putting the memory piece into a reader. "Since that day, I put a camera in the collar. Never took it off. What date is today?"

September 24 started with spiders in the ceiling – spiders they never knew existed. Spud took a liking of them, watching for minutes that Jake had to cursor through this 360p video.

He guesstimated the time around by afternoon. And they leaned back when Declan was heard talking. "Come on, Spuddy," he said. "You're a cool dog. I always want a dog. My mom won't get me one. But it's okay. I have you."

Spud was looking at the Riverside Cemetery. "Oh, God," said Lottie, hissing. "He knows Miri's there!"

"What is it, Spud?" said Declan. "You miss her? C'mon, let's go see her."

"Jake! He's gonna see the spray!"

Declan was skipping toward the cemetery when a bark fizzed through the speaker. "Spud?" Another bark followed, much louder. "Whoa! Spud! Stay, boy! Stay!" And then the ground moved. "Spud! Stay!" The dog had seen something so provoking that his feral instinct triggered that unwavering King Shepherd ferocity.

His strong legs brandished the vigor burning deep in his chest. He was old. But he covered the gap in a short, blinding flash. And up ahead, they saw what Spud went after in the midst of barks, howls and screams.

Amelia froze on her ground, staring wide-eyed at the speeding dog. Her friends dispersed, abandoning a ship to its fate. After that was a screaming sequence of frantic movements. "He just went off to her," said Lottie.

There was no reason for Spud to go wild. "What got in him?" he said, an eye over the sleeping dog. He replayed the part again. They came to the same ending. And Jake found some solace seeing Amelia on the ground, writhing in pain. It was until Lottie asked him. "Jake – what's that?"

"What?"

"That." Her voice was raspier. "See that? The hair ribbon!" Her trembling hand scrolled into his phone's gallery. She needed a photo, the one during which time they had a blast with herself in that hydrophobic shirt. "It's Miri's! Miri had that on during our fishing trip!"

In that second alone, Jake blinked a million times. It was not just a resemblance. The hair ribbon was the exact same, a carbon copy passed between two classmates who never befriended one another. The crimson fabric looped over her head in a similar style to Miri's choice. The mediocre visual quality did not miss that sandpaper-like, homespun design.

They had Ruth in the room for this appalling video. Jake held that timeframe and noted the ribbon in comparison with Miri's photo.

"Heavens Almighty!" she exclaimed.

Terry came home tired of work. "You nailed it! This is it," he said. "This is proof."

"No, Terry. It's not."

"Why?"

"We can't go to the cops yet. They'll start asking to put Spud down for attacking the not-so-innocent girl. And the ribbon thing, they'll argue it's a coincidence."

"I can keep him," said Lottie. "Nobody ever seen him here. All Shepherds look alike anyway."

Jake scratched his head. "Miri loved him. We can't let them put him to sleep."

"I'll take him to my dad's, 'till it blows over."

"Uncle Jake, someone's here!"

A young police officer was standing among a group in black. The day Abraham died was the last they ever heard of Beth El Congregation. Father had a certain fondness of that synagogue in Portland. And their representatives looked tired from the drive. And it had been long since anyone greeted him with a high note of accent.

"Shalom, Mr. Brownfield."

Anton Yermolov had a round stomach tucked under a tight vest that seemed to constrict when he took a seat. The next on the couch was Yigael Peretz, smiling through a trimmed beard. And they rammed straight for an accusatorial conversation, with a cold grip on history. It was something Jake did not expect, what more appreciate for the kids were well within earshot.

The family tried brushing away with a gentle joke, without looking much of a gentile. But the guests were not smiling. Those natural frowns were collective steel masking each of them. And they did not touch Ruth's cookies, so fixed in this broiling effort to win Jake over the fence.

"I understand where you're coming from," he said.

Yermolov hit back. "No. You don't. If you do, you sure don't look like it," he said. "Don't you see what's happening here? Your daughter is a murder victim of hate. That same hate is all over this country now."

Their interpretation stayed within Jake for a while. They saw Miri's murder as a confluence of tributing aftershocks. The Jewish community to them was standing on a collision course, with assurances from people who would later put a knife on their back. Democracy had given them a meaningless voice as those in power sliced and diced them into a clawing partisanship, to be regarded a champion of an inexistent global cabal robbing the working class.

"It was always a subtle label," said Peretz. "Your daughter was called a lying roach. Surely now you can see how this is anti-Semitism."

Shimon Elazar cut in. "I can understand this is all too far-fetched for you. We respect that you've built quite a life in the secular world. We can't blame you for that. But we are what we are, Mr. Brownfield. No matter how much you try, you are always a roach in the eyes of those who hate us."

"The motive of my daughter's murder is undecided. They cannot find anything against Naomi Moulin."

"Then perhaps Naomi Moulin is not the one responsible for this hate crime."

Jake nodded in agreement.

"It's not about the Moulin girl," said Elazar. "She's just one name. If a Jew girl steal for example, she'll get a slap, a kick and a punch until she's half-dead. And they won't stop, even if she's dead on the ground. You can shake your head, Mr. Brownfield. But it happens."

Jake had a delayed response after Peretz showed the screenshot of a news article. He had to pretend, first with the squint of a convincing myopia. The picture had to overwhelm him in front of them. And it did. "Oh, my God! Who can be so cruel!" Ruth shared the same sentiment, nearly dropping the tea tray because of the condition of Miriam's gravestone. "Why would they do this to her?"

"The chief has a team combing through social media hoping to catch the asshole responsible," said Officer Mizrahi.

"It's unlikely we'd catch him," said Peretz. "But we think you should say something, Mr. Brownfield."

Vandalism was an urban ulcer in a society. But the swastika graffiti was denounced, renounced and pronounced a social cancer. It was an abomination worthy for international organizations to weigh in within hours. If asked last year, Maine was the least likely state to be scorned by nations from distant shores. Now Nazism bred tyranny within its border. "To do it upon the grave of a recently murdered girl while regaling Adolf Hitler—" Yermolov quivered, his temples swelling that Jake thought he was having a heart attack.

"You lost a family, Mr. Yermolov?"

"My father fought in the Sixty-Fourth Army. He was never found."

"Moscow force?"

"No, sir. Stalingrad. We have his bloodied diary."

Gavriel Yermolov's sacrifice delivered this world from malignant hate. It only took a simple order from the *Bundeskanzleramt*, and six million people were consigned to oblivion. And no one remembered their names. Jake made certain to throw in about Yermolov in the short video they filmed in the dining section. He mentioned the impact of the graffiti against his Jewish lineages.

And then he said what he needed to say. "I condemn those behind this! I can't believe how low you'd go. I lost my baby! She's innocent, damn you! Damn all of you to hell! It's not funny!" he said. "Miriam was killed! And to use that Nazi symbol is pathetic. People lost lives in that war. Millions in Russia where Mr. Yermolov fought. Millions more in Germany." Jake paused for a second, out of breath. "We have failed as a nation and I hope to God we find this animal before he – or *she* – claims another as his or *her* victim!"

Before leaving, Yermolov handed him an envelope. "A little something from us," he said. "Use it well, kid." When he opened the envelope, he was the one to schedule for a heart attack. The check cashed a solidarity of over $15,000, in no way a little something.

Lottie came with a big question mark. "You ever think of applying for Hollywood?" she said, groaning with both brows up toward Jake.

"Okay, I'm so not proud of what I did. I never thought it'll be this big."

"Don't pull off something like this again, hon," said Lottie. "I don't mean to be philosophical. But whatever our goal is, we can't justify our means like this."

"I know, I know. I just want Amelia."

The killer had a cache of secret. But Jake was not running a covert defamation mission. He listened to every second, not sleeping from dusk to dawn. The stinger stopped picking anything new; maybe the battery depleted. He learned nothing of value from Amelia. So, he assembled his stash into a sound editor to mute everything but background noises. The editor had a preset for this purpose, cleaning the things Jake did not need for a three-hour exporting process.

His shoulders grew heavy against that ache now splitting his back. He was tired, so tired with grief and mental death. Of late he cannot stop thinking about Ike and Sam, no longer needing to wonder how his mother really felt. He never knew Ike. Things were different with Ruth, who kept to herself like a princess in their younger times.

Sam was a duplicate of the same mold. He missed Sam, who was a significant part of his childhood. Their unshakeable bond however fueled him with a sobering lesson about growing up. And he cried that night. He cried a cry so hard that even Lottie cried. He cried for Sam. He cried for Miri. He cried for Mother. And yes, he cried for Father too.

He cried for not spending enough time. He reflected with little joy of the last time he and Sam were in the basement playing Madden NFL. And the final tournament they hit together was in the 2003 game. None of them knew that last match was indeed the last, when one after another started separating for their destiny.

Time gnawed his childhood piece by piece until he had cherishing moments stuffed in permanence. It was his fate with Sam, later his mom – and now Miriam who was wronged. He was exhausted; dear everyone in this fucking world, he was too exhausted to continue the exhaustive cat-and-mouse pursuit for justice. He had changed. His sweat had a pungent smell the more he thought of the murder. He could not go five hours without craving a shower.

His body had never been the same, always acerbic with an unusual heartbeat. These things, he accepted, might never go away. Nor that sugary spring at his side. His fingers ran across her back, nudging by the neckline where he kissed. He undid the clasps holding her clothes. And the full-frontal nudity invited him downward, lower and lower until both were ready.

"I miss you," said Lottie.

This was forever his wife, a wonderful woman he owed a great debt and that no other woman would ever come close to a possible perfection that was Charlotte Reade. Stupidity led him to Rocket City, when what – or who – he sought was always here hiding in a dynamite body.

And when that bomb blew, Jake realized what he had done. For once he did not care. Neither did Lottie, who approved with a kiss on his head. There must be a blessing in that kiss.

Sleep consumed them both that they did not hear the ensuing storm. Nobody knocked on their door. Mason must have been up for hours; they found him on the floor watching a cartoon video. Jake finally pulled himself out of Lottie, whose smile brought him back to her ample chest.

Her morning breath smelled so good under the blanket. "You hungry?" she said.

"Don't go."

Lottie giggled, caressing his head. "I won't."

The tummy croak tickling his ear told another story. "Yeah, right."

"I'm really hungry, honey."

Jake got up, frowning at his private. "Holy shit."

"It's okay." Lottie held his hands. "We'll be okay!"

"Your time of the month is anywhere close?"

"Just got over it."

"Shit."

The balcony door rattled with the maple tree wavering in the wind. The whole district hung in a momentary suspension as neighborhoods simultaneously went dark.

"Lock everything!"

Jake had air mattresses and fleece blankets in the basement. The cool white LED bulb swung with the cable on a hook, dangling at a safe stretch to the gator-clipped car battery. Mason was stiff, cupping his hears at those thunders. Malcolm and Declan had to distract him with a bumping ball.

Lottie had a dining chair with a stud finder and cordless drill to string their wet clothes with hangers. "She's a keeper, I'll tell you that," said Terry.

Ruth smiled. "Do it right this time, Jakey. And stop this spying thing. You're not getting anything from it."

Jake stared as lightning flashed through the frosted hopper window. "The system sucks," he said. "That's why we have murder, kidnapping, domestic abuse – and lawmen can't do shit because the law is stopping them. That's why I had to do it my way. I never got caught because I don't slack. I get the job done, Rooster."

"You're a pitcher, Jake. You know it breaks if it goes down the well too often."

An ear-splitting thunderbolt cracked like a whip, breaking the rain within 15 minutes. As Terry and Ruth explored the damages, Jake went to the MacBook and banged the desk in joy. The conversion was complete.

Putting on a headphone, he listened as the surroundings now replaced the main sound. Those soundwaves were plateau, with some irrelevant notes – except for one distinct tone he kept picking.

That tone repeated here and there for hours. He shot up the volume at the expense of bass and treble, trying to identify the particular sound. "Dear God, help me. What is it?" he said.

The sky opened up. Light shimmered. And a concerned message from Uncle Obie gave him the answer. Those repeating audio returns were WhatsApp replies, set so low only for Amelia's ears.

Jake did his best to magnify the quietness between those ringtones. What he heard was obviously the sound from an electronic keyboard. "Vibration," said Lottie.

"She's messaging someone. And she ain't stopping."

"Why didn't we think of it before?" she breathed. "We get her phone – we get to the bottom!"

"Actually, we don't need her phone. Not hers." Jake went for the video from Spud's collars and paused right at the time when the four girls were in the frame. He pointed at the one in yellow and red. "That's Addy Blount. I know her mom. She's working at Dunkin's. Single mother. We gotta find out where they live. You think Amelia will post that on her Insta?"

"If she doesn't, we'll have to follow her."

"Fine with me," said Jake. "Quick replies. Quick keypad. It has to be a WhatsApp group. As long as they don't clear their messages. We get that group. We get Amelia!"

18

The neighbors had taken the brunt of the storm, leaving them behind a seeming shield to suffer from nothing more than a roadside deluge. Tara Robin was seen surveying the scene muttering something about damages. She looked displeased, this time fully-clothed from neck to toe. Jake wanted to ask her, if not for the hour-long conversation with Charles who complained about plastic pieces and leaves in his garden.

Radio stations informed about fallen trees on Belcher Road and Eastmont Square. Windows cracked and broke. In a week, homeowners would find themselves dealing with black mold. Jake saw no cause to worry about it. His house needed no repair, only some cleanups when Alabama rang.

"We saw the news."

"Okay?"

"The Nazi thing," said Craig. "You know who did it?"

"Is there something I can help you with?"

"Jake, I'm only calling—"

"Why does it matter to you anyway? You fucking left before the funeral. Now you're perked up concerned and all. What? Someone tipped you about the money I got?"

"Money? What are you talking about?"

"Go fuck yourself, Craig."

185

Craig was not worth his time. Ruth might have given more words. But he was busy grasping about those majordomos around the Instafamous piano caper. "We know the Blount. Dirt poor, after the mom was doing a Rachel," said Lottie. "The dad didn't want Addy. Demanded a paternity test. No alimonies. No child support."

"The brunette?"

"Christie Hayes. No idea. Mom's a Boomer in a Gen X body," said Lottie. "And that last one, Debra Smith. Her dad asked me for a fuck."

"That fucker."

"Fucker with a dead cock."

Jake gulped. "How d'you know he has a dead cock?"

"Oh, please, spare me," said Lottie. "Addy looks like an easy prey. If she gets her mom's brain, that is."

"Can't go to war today. Too many people in the streets 'cause this storm. We do this when the thing blows over."

Power returned in some parts of the town, though not in the central area. Speculations were rife for the rest of the day. That evening, the administration confirmed a suspension of schools and issued an emergency directive asking everyone to boil water. The treatment plant had an operational shutdown, resolving 18 hours after the last of the trees were cleared.

The downtime gave Jake and Lottie an opportunity to drive around for their target. Their theory about Addison Blount proved to be true. She was the easiest over Christie Hayes and Debra Smith. On Monday, the girl walked out of Dunkin's for half a mile on foot. Lottie reported her sighting to Jake, who waited in the Santa Fe by Grove Street.

Addy saw Lottie blowing a cup of coffee with a book in front of TD Bank. "*Duncecap turned. Be ready.*" She had her earphones plugged into Spotify, never once imagining what was about to unfold within the minute she appeared in his rearview mirror. Jake stepped out of the car and stood well within her sight.

That dramatic moment was just as he imagined. Her strides dithered into caution, swerving for the bootstrapped house. She gave one last faltering act, turning only after Jake called out. "Mr. Brownfield," she said. "I didn't see you there."

Jake had many things to say. But he managed his voice to wangle just the thing he needed. "Didn't you?" Apprehension overtook her forced warmth. She stood unblinking in those solitary seconds. When Jake made a cursory move, she started backpedaling. "I already know, Addison," he said.

That was it.

Those lips under her mooning eyes bubbled and drooled. "What d'you mean?"

"Miriam sends her love," said Jake, approaching.

"Leave, now! Or I'll call the cops!"

Jake waved his phone. "The chief is on his way here. I've told him everything about you, Christie, Debra – and Amelia!" Something started rocking her jaw. "You're smart. But not too smart, for your own good."

"Please don't hurt me."

"I've thought long and hard about what I'm gonna do to y'all," he said. "I have a steam iron too, y'know?"

A whimper escaped her foaming mouth. "Please–"

"I would love to use it on all four of you little bitches but – you're lucky I'm close to your momma. So, I'm gonna cut you a small deal. I'll figure how to make it easy on you, so long as you give me your phone now."

"My phone? N-no!"

"Addison! It's over! You can either go down the road on my side – or be tried an adult and spend life sentences with Big Momma, Killer Kelly and Lucky Lucy."

Lottie swooped from across the street, holding as Addy's legs bended for a fall. "C'mon, now. Stop being a pussy," she said. "Let's go inside and have a drink."

In the unkempt living room, Addison had a breakdown. And Jake stood over her. "Why, Addison? Why my girl?" he asked. "What did she do to you?"

"I'm so sorry! I'm so sorry. I didn't mean to, Mr. Brownfield! It just happened so fast. Amelia – it was Amelia! She's the one who did it!"

Jake perspired as his blood boiled. "I want proof," he said. "You must have proof in your phone!"

She stared in disbelief. "How you know?" Her answer came blurting after Jake swung a fist onto the coffee table. "Yeah! Yeah! It's still there!" Fear thickened over her hesitation. She produced her Oppo for Jake. "Please, I'm sick of this! I'm really sorry for not doing anything!"

"You think I'm gonna believe you're this innocent accomplice on a fucking one-way ticket? Password!"

"Just 1-2-3-4."

It was simple, too simple for a moment Jake had a slight doubt. He keyed in those numbers. And it worked. He was in her phone. It worked. His stiff thumb went for WhatsApp. It worked. There was that group. And now, he took a deep breath for the moment of truth:

It worked. The chats were there extending all the way to the top. Jake stopped at August 18, because Debra texted at 0715. *"It's the new girl! She took your phone! Naomi told me!"*

Jake's chest tightened, bulling through Amelia's xenophobic obscenities mirroring her anti-Semitic nature. They had a plan. They were going to *"corner that bitchy roach like a fucking rat"* and did something far worse than what they did to Dora Styler.

They were told to be alert the whole time. *"Darling Amy, can I be honest with you?"* asked Christie.

"What?"

"You donno that slut! She'd munch your carpet and wont wash her mouth. She likes you that lot I think she loves you, that freak lesbo! If you get close to her, she'd probably ditch that four-eyed frogger nigger. We do it like welcoming her to our gang. Take it from there. I got my dad's turnip to surprise her front and back."

Addy echoed in agreement to everything Amelia said. That silver spoon was like a mother hen dominating her chicks with a temperament that was rebellious and so juvenile.

On August 21, that fateful day, there was no conversation. The group was silent for two days straight – two days Jake could imagine what they were doing because Addy broke with three crying emojis. *"Darlings, what do we do now?"*

"Darling Addy, its all been taken care of. Dont u worry."

The group talk edged for trivial things. Addy threw a panic fit most of the time, confessing her fear of jail. Christie echoed Amelia's confidence for a time. But she cracked later on about death rows, electric chairs and lethal injections. After the funeral, everyone was panicking. Amelia was the only one placating the sorority slaughterers.

"Were safe. They too busy with that homeless bitch." Amelia took pride for dodging the police. *"We did well, Darlings. I love y'all."* They shared pictures and videos of what they described as an amazing interrogation that *"even the CIA will be fucking proud of us."*

"*I love you, Darling Amelia,*" said Christie.

"*I love you, Darling Amelia.*"

"*Yeah. Love you a lot, Darling Amelia.*"

"*I love y'all too. Darlings for life!*"

But in September, Amelia turned into a new leaf quivering about the "*dumbass dad*". The darlings gave her comforting support.

Addy stood by her, replying a lot.

"Addison," said Jake, out of ideas. "Here's what we gonna do." Right after he outlined, there was a brief pause. "Is that understood?"

"Yes. I'm sorry, Mr. Brownfield."

"Do as I say, or you'll regret it forever."

"Okay. Believe me, I just like to be with Amelia. I should–"

"Maybe good of you to shut the hell up just as you did the whole time." Jake used her phone to call someone. A while later, Cass answered. "It's Jake. Jake Brownfield."

"Jake?" She sounded smaller. "You got Addy's phone."

"Come to your house quick, Cass. Quick and quiet. Don't say anything to anyone."

"Is Addy okay?"

"No, she's not okay. Come quick."

The mother came blundering through the front door like a rogue elephant. "Addy! Addy? Jesus, what is all this?" In her face was nothing but that sincere motherly worry. She had not a damn clue about her damned daughter's crime. Makeup was still in her face, blotched and smudged from anxiety.

And after Addy fessed up, her temper rocketed. Not a sob. Not a gasp. It was pure outburst with a knifelike scream. "HOW COULD YOU?" Lottie had to jump in between them.

"HOW COULD YOU? YOU FUCKING IDIOT! HOW COULD YOU DO THIS TO ME?"

"Cass, come on now," said Lottie.

"Jake. Jesus, Jake, I'm really sorry! I didn't know! I shoulda been a better mom! I'm so sorry!" And she fell to his knees. "Please! Please! Don't go to the cops! Don't! Don't go to the cops! I–please, don't do–" The rest were hard to sense. Jake picked her up for an embrace. "I'm sorry! I'm so sorry! Miriam–I didn't–" she broke free to lunge at Addy. "You fuckface! You little bitch! You saw the news! YOU BURNED HER TO DEATH!"

"Shh! Shh!" Lottie held her back again. "The neighbors, Cassie!"

"Jesus! Oh, Jesus, Mary, Joseph!" Cass fanned air around her head, crashing to the single couch then finding her feet again. "Oh, my God!" What she had just now was on the floor after an abdominal strain. And Addy looked at the scene, altogether whole but in separate pieces. "What have you done, Addy? What the fuck have you done?"

Fate was unkind. Cass had slaved for a baby girl who grew to be a demon now defeated on the floor of her own home. The house was like a crypt for several minutes.

"I won't lie. You have no fucking clue how difficult it's been for me!" said Jake. "It's all up to the law. But if I have my way, no jailtime. No death sentence. Nothing. All you need to do is testify to the cops and court. And that's it."

Cass snapped. "She'll go to jail, Jake."

"My daughter's dead, Cass," said Jake. "I swear to God, I ain't giving back her phone. You charge me for theft; I'll charge your daughter for murder. We see who wins." Cass blanched, clawing those tears out of her dehydrated body. "It's all there. Everything. With videos."

"Is this true?"

Nodding, Addy breathed. "I'm sorry."

"Take my offer. Because in five seconds, I'm out of here."

Cass reacted suddenly, rummaging her hair with a groan. "You fucker, Addy! You little fucker!"

The mother and daughter came to an understanding. Nothing would help. Addy never stopped sniffling through the ride back to the station. The railing helped them up the stairs. And Jake had a hand on Addy's wrist, dodging the front desk straight to where Tashtego jumped from his chair.

Addy stumbled for balance after a push. She put both hands on the desk. "My name is Addison Blount," she said. "I helped murdering Miriam Brownfield."

The change in Tashtego's eyes stunned her. "I promised we can do something in exchange of her testifying?" said Jake.

"You *helped* murdering Miriam?"

She turned to Jake. "You said you've told him."

"Answer the fucking question!"

"Get a tape recorder, chief," said Jake.

Tashtego raised a hand to his direction. "You have something to do with this, Addison?"

She hesitated for a moment. "Yes, sir. We killed her."

"Addison Blount, you're under arrest for the murder of Miriam Brownfield, and all the other charges that may be placed upon you," said Tashtego. "You have the right to remain silent. Anything you say can and will be used against you in a court of law. You have the right to an attorney. If you cannot afford an attorney, one will be provided for you."

Jake closed his eyes, drinking it in. The spectacle cleared his throat. He was free from the shackling acidity. Addison surrendered with an unwilling heart. And Cassie was taken for questioning in this resounding victory. He reached for Lottie, squeezing the air out of her with all his strength. He dragged his weary feet to a couch and waited. He just waited; for what, he cannot tell.

"That was something," said Tashtego, almost an hour later. "What the fuck just happened?" He gripped on the back of his seat, starting a slow laugh which Jake reciprocated. "Did you really just waltz into her house and threaten them with a death sentence?"

"Pretty much."

"Doggone, Jake. Dog-fucking-gone. You fucking did it! I've signed for Renbarger. He'll start on arraignment."

"He's the D.A., right?"

"Yep. And I got a call from the Bureau. Imagine this – those fuckers weren't entirely sure about you. They were considering an unhappy home as a possibility."

"Unhappy home?" gasped Lottie. "What the fuck they on about? Like Jake murdered Miriam?"

"A neighbor told 'em hearing a scream – your scream, Jake. And looking into Miri's Instagram captions, they're convinced Miri was troubled because of the divorce."

"Who heard the scream?"

"Hey, I can't tell you that."

"I just gave you one of the four murderers, damn you."

Tashtego looked through him. "One of the *four*?" he gasped. "Who else?"

"We'll trade, motherfucker!"

"Now, you look!" Tashtego bit his lips. "Oh, what the hell – it was the Ten Tummy. She told the Feds."

Jake nodded. "I was fixing a car. I got zapped. I took a nap. That time Miri called me – the voice thing. We believe somebody chased her, didn't we? And guess what, we're right."

"Go on."

"My daughter was lured into a trap. The Mount View school has this, I dunno, some sorta groupie like Mean Girls," said Jake. "The Darlings. Addison is in that group, with three other girls."

"Who are they?"

Jake spoke their names. And Tashtego went pale when he said, "Amelia Fucking Morgan. Now excuse me, I have a call to make." Inside the Santa Fe, he had a phone over an ear. "Tara? How you doing?"

"Hey, Jake. I'm okay. How are you?"

"Chief had a word with me. You told him I screamed at Miriam?"

"Uhh, no. I didn't."

"Don't lie to me!" said Jake. "Did you?"

"Seriously, I didn't tell anybody you screamed *at Miriam*, Jake," said Tara. "Just a coffee talk with Eden. I told Eden I heard screaming. But I never said you screamed at Miriam."

Jake narrowed his eyes. "Thanks, Tara."

"What?" asked Lottie. "More plot twist?"

"We gotta get that bitch."

19

The cops in the State of Maine were different than those in California, Texas and Florida. Public criticism was not so rampant here. The state never needed to reconsider a death penalty against cop killers. Enmity was never a case, especially in Farmington where people loved the bluecoats – until August 21.

That was the day, when their honeymoon of happy meals (nothing to do with fast-food) and petty crimes unraveled into a full blown sweatbath. Family dinners and late-night buddy gatherings disappeared, uprooted from the town culture.

The abduction rear-ended them to a spiky curb. And the murder plunged the whole department into a drowning depth. There was a petition asking for casualwear to avoid another heckling discontent. The officers faced animosity everywhere, even in this very station where superiors and underlings disapproved one another.

It was a pressure cooker, bubbling, steaming and scalding into a pressurized lock that Tashtego had the Blounts in a separate detention room. Peter Renbarger had given him a direct order, believably from the Governor. "Keep them safe from your dogs," said the District Attorney. "We don't want police brutality on us."

Renbarger must have a crystal ball. Because Tashtego caught McCrain oiling a baton. There was no reason for that, because Addison already sang like a canary. She explained why Miri was the suspect. "Because she's a Jew! She's a Jew! Amelia thinks Jews are thieves!"

"What do you think, Miss Blount?"

"I dunno. It went missing after Miri came here."

"Apple made a mechanism for this. Did you have proof that Miriam Brownfield took it?"

"Nossir."

"D'you believe Amelia?"

"I dunno. She's dead sure about it."

"So, you believe Miriam took the iPhone?"

"She admitted it, chief."

"When is that? Before or after you burned her?"

"When they were burning her."

"*They*? You mean you didn't participate?"

"Nossir."

"You didn't torture Miriam?"

"Nossir."

"You didn't even taunt her?"

"Nossir."

"You didn't even lay a finger on her?"

"Nossir."

"You're telling me – that you're one of the damn darlings. They held her, tortured her, brutalized her, murdered her, dumped her and you did absolutely nothing?" Tashtego scowled after her nod. "I promised you court leniency, provided if you're honest. Looking at the evidence against you, it's clear you're lying. If you wanna play this game, you lil bitch, fine. I'll recommend you be tried an adult! You're going to prison for the rest of your life!"

"Okay! Okay! Wait! I'm sorry!" A whizzing sound stopped Tashtego. Addy contracted with a shameful success at holding her regurgitation – but not her bladder. "Amelia told me to burn her! And I did, chief! I did!"

"How many times?" Tashtego's foot started twitching when she counted with her fingers. "Ballpark a number. One to twenty. Twenty to forty."

"Ten to fifteen, chief."

Tashtego pounded the steel table. "Clean your own piss! MURDERER!"

Within the hour, Tashtego sent the recorded testimony for transcribing. Amelia was hell-bent at getting her iPhone back that she used a steam iron as a tool of torture. "Miriam was tortured over twenty-four hours, give or take." Her death should be at night of August 22. "She was not raped. Addison told us it was – I'm really sorry to say this – a turnip."

"Crazy bitch!" yelled Jake, spitting.

"Addison said you have her phone?"

"The mother has something to do with it?"

"Cassie? Not sure yet. She was just crying and saying she doesn't know."

Jake brought out and placed the phone on the desk. "I had to bend over backward for this," he said. "Can I trust you won't fuck this up?"

"I want this to end too, Jake."

"Why haven't you gone after Amelia Morgan?"

"I've unleashed the hounds," said Tashtego.

Jake got up. "Okay. If that's all, I'd like to be home with my family."

Tashtego stood. "From one friend to another."

They hugged.

The tide had turned. It had fucking turned. Jake was there when the police surrounded the Morgan home. Eden wailed like a banshee, her legs curling on the lawn. Seeing the overzealous brat squealing when the officers grabbed her injured arm was satisfying, even for Terry who took an urgent leave just to be there.

Christie Hayes had a stomach bug for weeks, leaking watery stool over the bathroom floor in her mobile house at Sawtelle Lane. She cursed and swore with a smoking butthole which zipped shut after the police arrived. It was the first time she got dressed in front of strangers, who handcuffed her father and slapped her mother.

The last was Deborah Smith. They tracked an online ticket purchase for a comedy film. Gasps filled the theater room when Deborah tried breaking for the exit. And she was body slammed in front of the speechless moviegoers. She was slammed again, this time in the detention room where Christie soiled through her clothes.

By afternoon, Tashtego was breathing fire. "Do you have any idea what you've put this whole town through?"

"I want my lawyer!" said Amelia. "You ain't got proof."

"Why don't you ask your Darling Addy?"

Amelia gathered her confidence for rage. "You lesbian bitch! You fucker! You fucking sell out!" Tashtego slapped her back into her chair and got Addison out of there.

The girl was like a helpless baby. She needed Cassie's help to her drinks. "I'm really sorry, mommy."

"Do you know Miriam?"

"She gave me a dollar for breakfast once."

It was her turn to get a slap. "She was there for you!" said Cass. "And you still help killing her!"

"I'm sorry! I just wanna be a Darling, mom."

"Darling!" said Cass, scoffing. "Fucking Darling! You wanna be a darling so much you'd kill someone? I have to pull double shifts to put food in your mouth and you gonna throw away for that Amelia? Is she gonna save you now?"

"I'm scared, mom. I don't wanna die."

"You killed Jake's daughter. Fuck, can't believe you're making me choose – my best friend or my stupid daughter!" Cass was whimpering. "That's it, then. I'll be fired. I'm gonna lose the house. We're already two months late! All because of you! You fucking idiot!"

The next day, they had a visit from the D.A.'s office. Peter Renbarger initiated the arraignment process, leaving Cass out as she was not a complicit in this crime of four perpetrators. Jake was not informed, until Cass showed up at his doorstep looking like a mugged victim. "Your daughter, Jake," she said, slurring. "Your daughter – my daughter – our daughter. They need help. Please, take Addy away."

A patrol arrived just in time as Cass was unbuttoning her shirt. Jake gave the spare room to Lottie's parents and spent an hour with Spud. "You good boy! *You* solved it. Who's the big champ?"

Spud did what he always did. "Woof." He slept through the night with a belly full of homemade peanut butter treats. Jake's treat was upstairs, curled up naked with a glistening grin in this candlelit room. He stopped thinking. No more strategy against the Morgans. Amelia was in chains. It was time to unchain his burning carnality.

And he slept the longest, canceling the whole morning and the most part of afternoon. That night he had a video call with

Obie, who was not in good health. "Yeah, some virus. For a week now," he said, with a small voice.

"You got to a doctor yet?"

"I just got discharged."

"What did the doctor say?"

"I wasn't young as I was anymore."

"See? I told you that. You been going everywhere!"

"Life is short, Jake."

"Get a good rest there, Unc. I can't lose you too."

Uncle Obie laughed. "A little cold won't kill me, boy."

There was a shadow outside. "Unc, I gotta call you back, okay?" It was Cassie again at his doorstep. "Oh, you gotta be kidding me."

"I need to talk to you," she said, a lot fresher.

"You're not gonna do a lap dance, are you?"

"What?"

"Never mind. What is it?"

"I just wanna ask you something. My daughter did something very wrong. Very, very wrong."

"Cass—"

"No, please! You promised her, Jake! You promised you'd talk the chief for a lighter sentence!"

"I did."

"But the chief told me she's gonna be tried an adult," she said, her voice breaking.

"I'm not the D.A., Cass."

"Please, try talking to them! You promised her!"

"And you believed me." Cass put a step back, her mouth forming a hole that Jake could fit a fist. "I was your friend, Cass. Your daughter knows that. But she still burned *my* daughter," said Jake. "I don't give a fly fuck about Addy. You're a moron for taking my word. That's why you're still here working a minimum wage."

"You can say whatever you want. But Addy is all I have!"

"Miriam was all I have, Cass. The way I see it, Miriam's dead. Addy is still alive. You get a better bargain without fucking asking."

"Alive in prison, Jake?"

"Look. I'll talk to this Renbarger. She'll testify and we'll recommend leniency. To forgive her is up to God, Cass. But if the judge ruled against leniency, you better believe I won't lose any sleep over it."

Near evening, Jake and Declan hit the backyard for a throw with Miriam's baseball. Terry came home and joined them, revealing a secret about his arm. "It's never the same after that fall," he said. Then Jake went for grocery shopping, mingling around the community who asked about his wellbeing. The store owner swung by, giving the grocery for free. "It's a sad day for all of us, I tell ya'," she said.

Jake had to accept upon those approving nods. After that he made a stop by the closing florist to deliver his love on Miri's grave. The grassy soil was already motley-colored with fresh flowers. "We did it, hon," he said, a hand on the new plaque. "You can rest now. We nailed 'em."

All was going well. Jake read the comments over dinner, hosting a special guest from the station. After clearing the plates, Terry poured the bubbling Piper-Hiedsieck champagne and posed a question. "How long you been chief here?"

"Some good years," said Tashtego. "I didn't start here. The town needed a chief, and someone put my name in."

"Who did?"

"No idea. Some guys didn't like it. McCrain was an asshole for the good year before he got along."

"He wanna be the chief?"

"Who doesn't? It's a small town. Everyone's a wannabe," said Tashtego. "It's an easy job I think I can even part time somewhere else. You go to work not worried about anything, before Miriam's that is."

"You have any update for us?" asked Terry.

He did not miss the fleeting glance from across the table. Ruth felt inclined to change the conversation before Jake threw in the nod. "It's okay," he said. "What you got for us?"

"I been taking some heat from up top about this being hate crime and all," said Tashtego. "Amelia said she was only getting her stuff back, like it's self-defense. She been cheeping about Miriam confessed. But Miriam kept changing the story, saying she sold the iPhone to Naomi. Then she said Naomi didn't pay her. After this Naomi and that Naomi, Miriam said she didn't take the phone."

"Get a fucking clue she didn't take it!" said Terry.

"That's the thing. Amelia is so stupid some big dogs come to my yard deciding it's anti-Semitic by nature."

"Will it help at court?" asked Lottie.

"All I heard, Renbarger will try them as adults. That's 25 years at least."

"Just that?" said Terry.

"*At least.* The way Miriam been going she's the real victim, she'll get life with no parole. Her bitch darlings said Miri's innocent. I dunno if it's honest or just plain bullshit. Those videos didn't have much of a face – except for one, just one."

"Who?"

"Debra had an insect repellent over a gas lighter and sprayed fire over Miri's *under-the-belly.*"

"Not Amelia?"

"The brat was smart. She was never in the video," said Tashtego. "But we have her voice. And she sure ain't a nun in this thing."

Jake finished his drink. "They'll cook something up to get her out."

"Oh, yeah. David went batshit at the station we nearly arrested him."

"You should."

"I haven't found dirt on him yet. The fucker had a good standing in this city. Everyone loves—"

"HE IS NOT ABOVE THE LAW!" His fingers bled from the smashed glass. "Yeah he's a prodigal son! Yeah his wife is a sweetheart! Well his mother was a whore! His father was a whore! Every motherfucker in his fucking family is a fucking whore, you fucking hear me?" Jake took a breath as Tashtego raised his hands, startled. "Listen to me, Bob. There's no way the girls did this alone. Who drove the body from the morgue?"

Tashtego looked interested. "The morgue?"

"That's where it happened," said Lottie. "That's where they tortured Miriam."

"You know this how?"

"Know what how?"

Tashtego shook his head, grinding his teeth. "If you told me a month ago these girls did it, I'd probably arrest you," he said. "But you went god knows how and got them, saved us from everything. So, I gotta ask you this – you just say yes and no, and I'll file a warrant for David."

"If I tell you, will you do something for me?"

"What is it?"

"Amelia has something that belongs to my daughter. I understand you're gonna need it for evidence. You have to take it from her."

"Sure. Now, did they torture your girl in Morgan Morgue?"

"Yes."

At the perch of his smoking area, David made seven calls for a recommendation he had through testimonials from his wealthy patients. The tip saw a burly man swinging out of a Lincoln sedan for the police station. McCrain had a long conversation with this stranger and later cursed under a breath.

"Their attorney," he told Tashtego.

The lawyer had a wicked smile after failing to get Amelia out of custody.

"What's his name?"

"Bastard won't even introduce himself."

Tashtego acquired a warrant and assembled his knights before sunset. For a long time, he dreamed of this moment – to feel this energy, supposedly akin to the braggadocio of a conqueror. He was at the head of a cavalry, modern and metal with wheels. Information spread like wildfire, beating the four-minute gap to the green Granite Heights where those aristocrats stood disapprovingly.

David sat waiting for them. In his hand was a glass of sherry, clinking as he twirled his wrist. It was the only sound they heard from him. He said nothing even after they towed the Mercedes-Benz and Chrysler. Eden imitated the same guileless gesture next to her husband. Holding hands, they watched as honor crumbled in their very home. "Dr and Mrs. Morgan, please hand me your phones," said Tashtego.

They relinquished their iPhones without a word of protest. But those steel faces finally twisted when an officer came downstairs holding a strange-looking thing. "Chief, we found this in the girl's bedroom."

"What is that?"

"Oh, she talks." Tashtego stashed the object into his pocket. "It's my beeper," he said. "Must have fallen off."

"That doesn't look like a beeper!"

Tashtego turned to the officer. "And the other thing?"

"Got the hair ribbon, chief."

"What do you want with my daughter's hair ribbon?" hissed Eden.

"That's the thing. It's not your daughter's," said Tashtego. "Kevin, read these morons the Miranda and take 'em away."

Tashtego did not have an easy ride back to the station. "You can't confiscate their phones," said McCrain. "We never had a warrant for 'em."

"I know what I'm doing."

"Really? 'cause from where I stand, you clearly don't," said McCrain. "Riley Versus California! We didn't include their phones in our warrant."

"Correct. But Chimel versus California stated clearly that an arresting officer may search the body of the person without a warrant and the area into which he might reach to protect material evidence. So technically, I'm in the opposite side of the same legal world."

McCrain's voice grew sharper. "The side of law when Obama was an American kid living in Indonesia!"

"You don't really have to say *an American kid*. He was the president."

"You're missing the point."

"No, Paxton. You're missing the point. Once we get to the bottom of this, none of it matters! I'm done talking about it anyway!"

Tashtego went through an encyclopedia about the Fourth Amendment and reacted with a scoff. When the forefathers penned these legislations, none of them preconceived the future of this republic. They were too busy prohibiting slave trade only as a foreign policy tool against the British influence. The Slave Trade Act 1807 was not a benevolent gesture, because it did not abolish the practice of slavery. Yet these authors had no shame going with an absolutist belief about freedom, freedom and freedom.

It had to be done. Tashtego produced a Stylus pen from a drawer to start on David's phone. While doing so, McCrain recorded their statement in the other room. About an hour later, Tashtego joined the questioning. "What were you doing before you found Miriam?"

"Can't really remember. Jogging?"

"Eight miles from here?"

"Pretty sure it's a lot less than that," said David. "Even if it is, what's wrong with that? It ain't Dubai. People do that, y'know? Too many people know me here. So I put some miles out of town. Last I checked, that ain't a crime!"

"And you went to Weld the night before. What were you doing there?"

"Emergency patient."

"Nobody called you on that night or the night before."

"He called my wife."

"I didn't find any information on your wife's iPhone!"

"They called the Morgue's phone."

"Someone was sick. And they didn't call your number. Or your wife's number. They called the number of a funeral home and you conveniently went straight to Weld without even calling them back for location?"

"I know the place."

"And where is that?"

"Check my phone. There's GPS in it."

Tashtego punched the steel table hard. "Don't fuck with me, Morgan! Give me a straight answer!"

The setup may have broken Amelia. But not David. "That's exactly how it is."

"I wanna see the patient file."

"Confidential. You're gonna need a warrant for that."

"The evidence law does not recognize physician-patient privilege! Don't tell me how to do my job when you suck at yours!" He left to attend his phone. "What d'you want, Jake?"

"He didn't confess?"

"You're gonna tell me how to do my job too? Is it how things are going now? Everyone wanna tell the chief of police how to do his fucking job?"

"Bob, that's not why I called."

"Then why did you call?"

"Those bastards cleaned the morgue before we have the chance. That's tampering with evidence," said Jake. "But Charlotte been wondering. They had Miri for two days, stamping her with steam iron. You know how steam irons work. They guzzle power like a hooker guzzling–" he cleared his throat. "Charlotte been thinking if it'll show in the bill. Do the math. A thousand four watts per hour."

"I'll call you back." Tashtego burst into his own office, repeating, "one four zero zero. One four zero zero." He wrote those four digits on a piece of grocery receipt. "Times thirty-six hours." The unconvincing 50.4 kilowatt should cost Morgan Morgue absolutely nothing. "Six bucks is like a toothpick!"

"Tally up with the morgue at that particular time when there's nothing registered. No dead body. A quiet funeral home. Nothing running. Somehow, some way, it's like you baking pineapple-topped pizza for seven busloads of Italian tourists. I mean, c'mon, man."

"David probably will run with that at court if you ask me."

"Pretty obvious you got nothing from them."

"I can't tell you that."

"I know. That's why I'm asking," said Jake. "Where do you want me to?"

"What the hell is that supposed to mean?"

"Your hands are tied to your balls. We both know that. Set me loose, and I'll help you out."

Tashtego pondered for a second. "This is crazy," he muttered to himself. "He went to Weld probably the same night he dumped Miriam. I dunno, maybe before he dumped Miriam. He told me he got some emergency patient there – in Weld. But he can't back it up. It's like he's having an affair or something."

"With that kind of wife, even you would. How do we know he really went to Weld?"

"His Google Map. He arrived near ten at night."

"I'll call you once I'm there." At that time Jake was pressing his latest photo into his old journalist badge. "You wanna go for a date?"

"Anywhere special?" asked Lottie.

"I hear there's this joint near Webb Lake. We're taking Mason too. He's driving Terry crazy. Been laughing at him even when he's not making funny faces."

Lottie giggled. "He's excited – that's all. Been years since somebody treat him this good."

"Can't blame him, really. With his dad been out of picture and all. Now everyone around him."

"His dad is not out of the picture."

"What? Your ex-husband's back?"

"You're his dad now."

Jake's cheeks glistened as he smiled. "Nah. I'm his grandfather."

"What are you on about?"

"That night you went down on me, and I pulled your hair. You called me daddy. So that makes me a grandpa."

"Oh, fuck you!" said Lottie, blushing.

20

In West Farmington, there was a six-mile byway cutting to Colby Miller Road through an untouched forest with countable houses that Google Map however was discouraging. Jake was wondering why, at first. But soon he regretted taking that road. It was not even a road, more like a passage with five different names. And after bumping their way for at least 15 minutes, they finally passed the country club next to Wilson Lake.

The next eight miles finished Mason who was sputtering through the stop at a gas station. "I just filled up," said Lottie, looking across the dashboard for the oil gauges.

"I need to buy something." Jake went to the counter. "Good evening," he said, showing his journalist badge. "I'm Jacob Brownfield."

"Brownfield? Like the girl's dad? I'm really sorry about your daughter, man."

"Thanks. I'm running point with my own investigation," said Jake. "I'm assuming you heard of the Morgan girl. Someone tipped me she and her father dumped my girl the night they drove for Weld. I was wondering you see them coming here?"

"Nossir. But if they did, our cameras coulda picked 'em."

"Oh, of course, you have surveillance! Can you wind back to August Twenty-Sec? At night somewhere around nine to ten." The man had a bad leg, hobbling across to key something into a computer. "You okay, man?"

"Parting gift from Afghanistan."

"Jesus. My brother served. Fucking IED got him."

"Damn IED got couple of my pals too."

"Always in gratitude of your service. What's your name?"

"Gonzalo."

"Gonzalo?"

"Gonzalo Salas, Corporal. Any specific I can look for?"

"Black Mercedes Benz or silver Chrysler."

Salas hit a fast-forward function, speeding the footages up to 18x. Three minutes later, he told Jake. "No Benz or Chrysler."

"Can you run it again?"

The overhead camera captured a car at 2137. It was a Ford, gunning to outrun a devil. And Jake called Tashtego. "I found something."

"Me too. But you first. What is it?"

"David shoulda pass Hills Pond on his way to Weld. I'm at a gas station not far off Hills Pond. They didn't get a hold of a Mercedes or a Chrysler. But there's a Ford."

"Hmm. He coulda rent a Ford out."

"Exactly," said Jake. "Back to you. What did you find?"

There was a brief pause. "We found the steam iron, Jake."

"Where?" asked Jake.

"This is the wrinkle there. I know you gone feisty with that Reade girl," said Tashtego, who imagined Jake turning to the car. "Jake, we found the steam iron *in her fucking basement*!"

"What the fuck?"

"I'm at her home, and she ain't here! So I'm asking you—"

"You think she's got something to do with this?" said Jake. "This is horseshit, Bob! And you know it!"

"Maybe. But I gotta take her in."

"What?" he said, almost yelling.

"Jake, you know where she's gone to?"

"You're not taking her in."

"We already rounded up her mom. Gothy's going to the bookstore for Mr. Reade."

The swaying pines whirled into a tailspin. "Jesus, Bob! What the fuck is all this? It coulda been planted there!"

"I know!" Tashtego was shouting. "But we can't get to the fucking bottom of this if she's on the run now, can we? Look, make it easy on the whole thing. I don't wanna go around Maine chasing a single mom."

Jake's heart twisted. The woods whispered, hissed and roared as he marched to the car. "What took you so long?" she said. "You didn't – you didn't buy anything!"

"They found the steam iron."

"Seriously? Where?"

"In your basement, Charlotte!" said Jake.

Her fingers tightened on the Lenovo smartphone. She tilted her head, baffled with a shade of fear. "What? How?" she murmured. "How did that thing get into my dad's basement?"

"Bob saying it like you got something to do with it!"

"And you believe that sonofabitch?"

"Fuck, no! But what can I say? You weren't with me that time. I already told him I got zapped doing your car! They coulda say you gave me your car to distract me or something!"

"Oh, my God! This ain't happening! I have a son!"

"We gotta go to the station, Charlotte."

"And let them arrest me? I have a son!"

"They planted it there! They couldn't get your fingerprint on it!"

"You sure about that?" Her raspy breath squeezed Jake's insides. "This is nuts. I'm not going there, Jake. They're gonna arrest me! If they put it there, they musta have a damn good reason to blame me!" Her voice was breaking. "I can't go there, Jake! Christ, I have a son!"

"If you run, they'll suspect you're involved!"

The barrage of phone calls sent chill into them. "I'm shaking, Jake!" she said, sobbing. "I don't have nothing to do with Miriam's murder!"

"We gonna hire a lawyer. It'll set everything straight. They probably distracting the cops or something, I don't know. But you won't go to prison for this."

Everyone was there when they reached the station. Near the entrance, Lottie kicked the ground and slumped over the throbbing sensation in her midsection. The queasy reflux remained in her throughout the process with those law enforcers. "I don't know how it got there," she told McCrain.

"But it was there and there was no sign of a break-in. Until you're cleared, you're considered a suspect."

"Chief, I have a son. I can't stay here!"

"Shoulda thought about it before you aided and abetted in a murder," said McCrain.

"I didn't do it!"

"If you're worried about the child, we can have the Child Protection until we get to the bottom of this."

"Child Protection? She had nothing to do with this!" Jake said in the chief's office. "This is fucking nuts!"

"Mr. Brownfield, I suggest you take your tone where it belonged."

"Fuck you!"

The room echoed in Tashtego's roar. "I can handle this, McCrain! Gettefuckoutta here!" The Deputy did not expect that. He glared at both men, before going through Terry who had to move away from the door. "Now, Jake–"

"Bob, she couldna done it," said Jake. "She loved her, Bob. That damn thing musta been planted there!"

Tashtego's gesture was a false hope. "We're running it through forensics. Until we get the result, she has to stay."

"And how long is that?"

"Three business days at least," said Tashtego.

"You fucking insane! You know her! Her dad has a bookstore for crying out loud!"

"David Morgan is a philanthropic doctor! He created fifteen jobs here! The way thing's going, he'll be going down. That's fifteen families going hungry!"

"It's come down to fucking money in the end? Let the wrong one take the fall?"

"I'm not saying that, you son of a bitch! This whole damn town has gone crazy, and I'm still catching up because I can't do anything now because we found that damn thing in her basement!" The one-breath tirade defeated Jake's retort. "I asked the Governor for house arrest. I asked him for supervision. I asked, damn you! Believe me, I fucking tried and he threatened to fire me! You coulda say thank you. So yeah, YOU'RE FUCKING WELCOME!"

Jake fought for air. "Chief, go to Hills Pond. Talk to Corporal Gonzalo Salas. He has the evidence to get the bastards. You already have 'em here!"

"The lawyer bailed 'em out. Nothing I can do."

"Fuck. All of them?"

"No. Just the Morgans, Hayes and Smith," said Tashtego. "The Blount girl tried killing herself. She's at the hospital."

"And you don't see how fucked up this is?"

"Matter of fact, I do," said Tashtego. "This whole iron thing could be something or nothing at all. Until we get to the bottom of this, I can't be seen talking to you."

Jake gave up with a long sigh. The officer did not allow another visit in the custody section. Terry took over the wheel and drove him home. "What's at Hills Pond?" he asked.

"Just a mystery Ford ripping through the same night Miri died," said Jake. "God, I dunno what to do anymore. He's fucking smart, too smart he didn't use his own car. He dumped my baby with that Ford. If we can nail which car, might be a DNA or something."

"How many rentals are here?"

"C'mon. He ain't that stupid to rent something here. He coulda gone outta town. Bangor even," said Jake. "Someone coulda rented it for him."

"This doesn't change the things about his daughter, right?"

"Nothing's changed but Charlotte," said Jake. "The D.A. been going for adult trials. But dunno why I think they'll get juvies. No life imprisonment. In some years, this fucking town will book funerals from Morgan Morgue. And fucking Amelia be the one faking condolences for blood money!"

His living room was scalding. Jake had a thumb over his lips, his mind ricocheting every second. He fumbled for something – for anything, drawing blank with the hiss of a pine snake. Come next morning, Mason woke up without his mother. The boy sat cross-legged, a forefinger tracing the rain on a window. His burgeoning mind permitted a murky understanding that things had gone wrong. He refused to play with Malcolm and Declan.

"We gotta get her out, Jake!"

And then there was that voice. David Morgan was on the television. "We're being charged by someone with mental issues," he said. "We know Jacob Brownfield got himself fired in Alabama. That's the reason why he came back. He didn't wanna be there.

His attacks tested the waters. "And because of this revenge seeking bigot from the Lord's La La Land, they suspended my license. I can't practice. Hundreds of people see me every day. And because of this unholy man, I can't give my friends in Farmington an affordable healthcare they deserve."

That interview reeked through the WhatsApp community group, now with a blistering conversation too offensive for Ruth who could not steady her hands. Those chat bubbles were her cookie customers. And they turned on Jake, festering rumors into a gang of dozens. The family locked and dropped the blinders, doubling back to the basement with bats, knives and a portable Sawzall.

"Get outta here, you fucking Yid!"

"Go back to Alabama!"

"Jake the Cuck!"

The neighbors called 9-1-1. And when the crowd dispersed, some arrested, the damages triggered his panic attack. "*Don't think too hard. Don't think too hard,*" he said, almost like praying. "*Don't think too hard.*" He had to think hard. Those people had bunched around his house, their deadly weapons leaving permanent marks over the planks. The front door came down upon a light nudge from Declan. The postbox was missing, as well as the trashcan.

A sulfurous odor permeated into the basement. They found a way to burn the American flag on his roof. The pole pointed skyward, with cauterized fabrics still flowing. They later found their postbox inside a window, where the trashcan was flat next to Terry's car smashed and smeared with human feces.

A switch flicked in the back of his head. Jake remembered an overreaching paralysis from his toe, which felt cold and apathetic. Then he was looking around what seemed to be an ankle-deep watery expanse. Behind him was a concrete embankment. Or at least that was what he thought; when he got there, his barefooted heels sank however in mud.

He did not stop to think about it. Because dead in front was the small figure of a longhaired girl. "Miriam?"

"You think?" she replied, though a while later he realized her tone was nothing inquiring. "Too hard."

Jake sank to her feet, crying. "Honey, I missed you so much! Come home!"

"Don't think too hard, okay?"

"Honey! Say something else! Please! I want you back!"

A giggle broke out. "I think of you, Daddy."

"I think about you too. I missed you!"

Miri moved in the shifting mist. And there was that gas station at Hills Pond. She remained static as the wind shifted around them. He clawed the ground toward her; his legs were immobile – then his arms, and head.

"Honey, look at me."

"I love you, Daddy."

"No! No! Please, don't go!"

"Take care of yourself."

"Miriam! Look at me!"

"Don't think too hard, okay?"

"HON! I'M ASKING YOU TO LOOK AT ME!"

And Miriam did. Her radiance was shredding into pieces and specks, until she was a charred, balding corpse. "I love you,

Daddy." Those blackened lips moved. "Take care of yourself. Don't think too hard, okay?"

Miriam dissolved with a long, guttural roar which Jake resumed in a bright, cramped room. Jake became aware of the presence of a woman behind those curtains. "Morning, sunshine," she said, dryly.

"Miriam! Where's Miriam?"

"The bitch is dead." Jake's face burned with anger. "Probably got fucked by worms in her grave, I'd guess."

"You! The fuck you doing here?"

"My daughter's here because of you!" said Cass.

"That bitch ain't dead?"

That hurt her. Her hand found his face. "*You* did this, motherfucker! You didn't talk to the cops! She coulda been home with me! You left her there! You wanted her to go to prison for life!"

"You're right," he said. "I didn't care about her."

"She helped you, Jake! She had trouble getting friends. And she sold her Darlings for you!"

Jake coughed a laugh. "Because she's trapped like a fucking rat. I heard those animals bailed themselves out. They left your Addy to fend for herself."

"I'll talk to Eden," said Cass, her teeth scraping. "I know she'll help!"

"G'head. You're good at kissing asses. I always know that. I just never thought you're a narcissist. Go to your daughter. Hope she makes it. I mean that."

"Who's being narcissistic now? Just so you know – I'm pressing charges against you. For breaking and entering."

"Whatever."

Cass rocked his bed, holding back a scream. And she got out of there when the door opened for Tashtego. "I'm sorry," he said. "She ain't supposed to be here."

"Neither are you."

"I came here for you, honestly. You okay?"

"Is that a trick question?"

"There's a patrol in your street," said Tashtego. "Everything's fine now."

"*Fine.* Nothing's fine! My daughter's dead!"

"Look, I had to throw you under the bus," said Tashtego. "I didn't know what to think when I found the steam iron. I was too tired. I got emotional."

"Why are you here, chief?"

"Got word from Renbarger. It's a go. All four will be tried as adults. What David did is sick but it won't change a damn thing. He'll get an arraignment of his own."

"That's good to know."

"Speaking of David, I followed up on Hills Pond. It was a Ford Fiesta. We got the license plate but a hiccup, the car's missing."

"Surprise. Surprise. What about Charlotte?"

"Nothing yet, Jake. We allow some mother-son time."

"Is that all?"

Jake had nothing else to say. It was supposed to be good news. But he could not come close to muster a smile, even to Ruth who came the next day for the discharge papers. Against his better judgment, he checked his timeline in which the town had nothing good to say. Philip Braybury opened a baker shop about two miles from Court Street. His words cut deeply. *"Abraham is ashamed of you, Jacob."*

That was nothing compared to Bill Nickelworth, a father of three based on his display picture. "*You, your mom, your dad, your bitch girl – three done, one left. Fuck y'all*"

It clung.

"*Christ killers!*"

It stung.

"*The dad murdered Miriam!*"

It flung.

"*The dad did it!*"

It wrung.

"*The dad!*"

It hung.

"*The dad!*"

Farmington became a pit between a saint doctor and his hallowed mortician wife, with the divorced duo of a bereaving father and a single mother. It was not a fair fight. David publicized a video talking about Jake's supposed Manhattan job, inflaming the Internet about "*biting the hand that tried feeding him.*" The worst of all kind was the self-styled experts, who must have acquired their degree from CSI. "*DNA can solve this murder!*"

That dark mood however had overtaken the town. Terry was spotted at a traffic light by Intervale Road, where three men began charging with liquor bottles at ready. He made a tire-screeching turn, barreling toward a semi-truck with a close shave in that honking pandemonium.

He dodged another head-on collision with a mid-size SUV. That was when the siren started out, initially he believed to his advantage. He had to fight a patrolling officer who accused him for reckless driving and evading arrest. He was breathing hotly about it. "I didn't sign up for th–" he said, stopping short as Jake passed.

"Didn't sign up for what?"

"I nearly got mugged."

"You didn't sign up for what, Terry?" said Jake. "Coming here?"

"For working! I didn't sign up to be mugged!"

Jake wasn't listening. "I woulda been there in your Zion curtain if you're in the same shit I'm in. Go back to Utah if it's too damn hard."

"Oh, don't take it on me, Jake!" said Terry. "Some guys wanted to kill me! I been on my toes, taking in those shit from work! I did not mean what you think I meant!" Terry never stopped huffing for air. "I always thought of Miriam, damn you! We always wanted a daughter!" Those fiery eyes welled up. "We always looked at your Facebook! I wanted Ruth to call you when you're going through a divorce! Then this happened. We wondered what'll happen to our Miriam! Our Miriam, Jake!"

"The first photo you put online–" said Ruth.

"She was five and she was riding a pony, am I right?" Terry yelled. "Don't you fucking tell me to go back. I ain't Craig. I am here because I wanna be here!" He took a slow breath after Ruth tapped on his forearm. "I need some air."

"Terry, wait. I'm sorry." Jake went for an embrace, locking him tight for so long. "I'm heading out."

"Didn't you hear what I said?"

"I'll risk it. Can't leave her there, guys. She's in there. Her parents are in there. Just – can't do it."

"If you're going, I'm coming with you. You won't last five seconds out there."

21

The world converged, collided and crumbled on Jake, who had to pick up the pieces in that groggy carcass that was his body. Fever was baking him in that turtlenecked sweater. And he was fighting to hold on – to make sense – and to accept the unfurling reality from the moment those police officers announced an imminent arraignment hearing.

Peter Renbarger's team was there, spending two good hours after which Tashtego came to answer them. "We got the result," he said. "The steam iron is the murder weapon, they used on Miriam."

His tone suggested a problem. "And?" asked Terry.

Fingerprint analysis struck a lightning bolt, proving Lottie did indeed touch the murder weapon at some point. During questioning, she stuck back with an unchanged story. "She told us she never saw it," said Tashtego. "But that's that. We got hers on the handle. The DDA will arraign her."

Jake's mouth was wet with an acrid salivary foam. He was looking at something – the dashboard, the coffee table in his living room, the plate on his dining. He was holding his bladder, too tired to move. And he had to relieve himself, after finding out Charles and Donna were on their way. Blood was in his urine with the shrinking bathroom on a floaty spin. Donna fixed him with a cutting glare, placing a step forward one after another full of energy. When she spoke, it was clear. "Jake, we have a plan!"

Her soft voice flowed with an imposing maternal fury. They did not blame Jake; that was for sure. They did not think their daughter was innocent. They did not *believe* either. "I fucking *know* she's innocent!" said Charles. "This is a fucking setup! We're gonna stop this in the hearing."

"We need a lawyer," said Ruth. "A good lawyer!"

"I already got her one," replied Charles. "My niece, well, not *my* niece – she's my cousin's daughter – I used my phone call to get her. She can straighten this one out. Now, Jake, I know Miriam is important but–"

"You don't have to convince me, Mr. Reade. I know Charlotte didn't do it. We're gonna get her out."

"So we're relying on the D.A. for Miriam, and we're fighting the same D.A. for Charlotte."

"It's rigged, Terry. It's fucking rigged."

"But it's on our side, right?" said Ruth. "They don't have a motive to put Charlotte out."

Charles took a slow breath. "They have a motive."

"What?"

"Not a strong one but there's a chance she might get murder even."

Jake was fidgeting. "What did Charlotte do? She said something about this?"

The forensic system required some vital tests before the arraignment hearing. A health official had been there with her, while the deputy district attorney discussed with the chief of police. Lottie surrendered her biological samples to create a criminal profile. Her blood test determined she had no medical disorders. But the thorn in their temple was in her urine.

"She's not a junkie, Mr. Reade!" exclaimed Jake.

"C'mon! They found meth in her blood or something?"

Donna took Jake's hand, a gesture holding the whole living room in suspension. She took a second that lasted forever. "Honey," she said. "Charlotte's pregnant."

It was good news. Jake cannot contemplate how this could be used as a possible motive – until Charles played a voice message. "Okay. That's not good. It'll be like Froggie wants him and the girl Miriam didn't want them together. And Froggie kinda uprooted her out of the way to get a fresh start with Jake."

"That's the lawyer."

"It sounded like an assumption to me!" said Terry.

"She found this on her Instagram," he said.

It was a screenshot of Miriam's Instagram post. Among the comments to a photo of their fishing afternoon, someone asked "*ooh, a new mom?*" And Miriam replied, "*not in a thousand years! My dad is a lone king!*"

"She was joking!" Jake cried out. "That's nothing!"

"I wish I can say the same, kid. It won't do any of us good. They'll go with she's pregnant just to put you in a trap. They'll go with you got her pregnant like uhh out with the old, in comes the new. With that sonofabitch doing that coverage, we all gonna need a lot of protection if we wanna even make it in the backyard!"

"That family is rotten to the soul! A buncha fame-mongers and attention-seeking hookers!" said Donna, her chin quivering. "We can't give them the satisfaction they got even!"

"We won't, love. Queenie will get her out!"

"How much your lawyer niece is charging us?"

"I got that covered," said Charles. "It's enough to cover her retainer. She's only asking to fly here."

"It's my fault," breathed Jake.

"No, kid. It's not."

"They put the iron in your basement because she's my girlfriend. They know it'll hurt me a lot. If she ain't my girl, Mason will still have his mom around."

"Jacob," snapped Charles. "Those bastards murdered Abraham's and Rhoda's granddaughter! Makes this our fight as much as yours."

The fingerprint revelation was a spiraling discussion around town. Jake did not care to know how everyone found out. Since the madness at his home, the press was forced to censor all contents involving David Morgan. They adopted the same old tactic for damage control, inviting experts to criticize each other.

Jake was dusting those framed pictures of Miriam at Clearwater Pond and Allens Mills. "Look at these, Terry. Lottie printed 'em and put 'em here. No reason she'll do this if she really wanted Miri dead."

"We'll get her back, Jake," said Terry. "I checked on that lawyer. Couple years back, she went to war for a homicide. Homeless man. The Black dude was beaten to death in a park."

"Robbery went wrong?"

"Some White kid jumped on him. He lost both eyes. A piece of his nose went to his brain. Dead on arrival."

"Shit."

"It gets shitter," said Terry. "When they got that bastard, there was I dunno something in the law. First murder, then manslaughter – after that inconclusive, unconvincing, indecisive. The bastard woulda walked if Quinn Ganderton didn't come in."

"Wait a minute. She's a D.A.?"

"It's Kentucky. They allow private citizens initiate criminal cases. The D.A. got too much dick in his hand. They told her to win this. And guess what – she did. Worked night and day – and the sonofabitch got life with no parole. He appealed, all right, got overturned twice."

"Wish she can be on the Maine prosecution team."

"She'd legalize the death chair!"

"Amen!"

The sun peeked over the horizon illuminating the wide-body American Airlines on its way to Augusta Regional Airport. The particular lawyer – all-powerful and mighty – became a little girl after the carousel section, where Charles and Donna stood waiting for half an hour. That doorbell jolted them into the living room.

Her long legs swayed toward the coat hanger, an arm over Charles' shoulder laughing at a joke. Quinn Ganderton stood taller than everyone, even Terry by an inch or two. "Lovely place you got here," she said.

"I'd sell it to you, if you want."

"No, thanks. I got three of my own and still renting a squalor." After exchanging pleasantries, Quinn went right to the point. "I'm late into Miriam's, honestly. Till a week ago, I had no idea what the hell was happening. Handled three crazy domestic violence," said Quinn. "One of them was a Filipino illegal alien, married to our citizen for seventeen years. But she wasn't registered so she's technically here illegally. The husband kept using that piece of technicality as a weapon. When I found her at the State Hospital, she was broken everywhere – the jaw, backbone, cracked ribs and all."

"Jesus Christ. Is he cheating on her?"

"On the scale of one to five, I'd say twelve." Quinn took out some photographs of this Filipino, wrapped in bandages. "She got the house, the kids, some big fat check. I won – but she didn't. Syphilis, gonorrhea and last time I checked, HIV from his orgies."

"That's sick."

"Not a happy ending. Reason why I'm telling you this 'cause there's a reason you can spell rot and rut from court. You can really rot in a rut. It's bloody. It's a fucking warzone. But I guess you already know that."

"It's getting a hell lot complicated."

"The guilty will turn this world upside down if that's what it takes to weasel their way out. But in the end, they will squeal. They will always squeal like Ted Bundy the night before his execution."

Quinn went on with the details. The arraignment hearing to her opinion should remain between the immediate family. It was a nicer way of saying she did not want Jake anywhere near the courtroom that day. And the first battle scored a good win, because the magistrate judge approved bail after considering Lottie's clean record and good behavior while in jail.

"How much was it?"

"Ask me again. And I'll cut your tongue," said Charles.

Jake found Lottie massaging those red marks by her wrists. In front of her on the night stand was an uncapped pain relief ointment. "I'm starving. Got something to eat?" she said.

"Go on ahead, Jake," said Quinn. "I gotta talk to her. Alone." She closed the bedroom door, pulling a chair closer to help with the ointment. "Hospital last Thanksgiving. Arraignment this year."

"You don't have to be so mean, Queenie. I didn't ask for any of this."

"Of course, you didn't," she said, kissing her forehead. "Those handcuffs can be a lil mean. Gotta do the usual fuckattahea, I guess."

Lottie sputtered a laugh. "Yeah. I guess. Thank you for coming."

"No biggie, Froggie."

"I hate it when you do that."

"Heh, I been saving that one out. But seriously saying, I'm used to saving your lily-white ass 'cause it needs a lil smacking." She closed an eye, pushing her tongue to a cheek. "But looks like you already got a few smackings."

"You never fucking change!"

She pinched her nose. "You got a good one, by the way. Don't blow this!"

"Yes, mom."

That smile was still there. "Don't blow this," he said, poking her tongue now. "Blow him."

"Already done that," whispered Lottie.

Queenie giggled. "Tell me what happened!"

"Fuck off, you pervert!"

"I mean, when you're in jail, stupid!"

Lottie's grin disappeared. "No, I don't wanna talk about it, Queenie."

"You're talking to your lawyer Quinn Ganderton now, Miss Reade. What happened in there?"

"What d'you mean what happened?"

"Were you beaten?"

"No."

"Were you given your rights to phone call?"

"Yes."

"Were you given meals?"

"Yeah. Some sandwiches. There was a bug in mine."

"Were you groped?" Her eyes narrowed when Lottie fumbled. "Froggie, did they sexually assault you?"

"Please, don't tell Jake."

"Fuck!" mouthed Quinn, taking a breath. "Was it the chief?"

"No."

"Who, Froggie? Tell me!"

"It was Roger Gauthier," said Lottie.

"Where did he touch you?"

Lottie shook her head. "Where he shouldn't."

"Specifics, Charlotte! Up or down?"

"B-both. Pulled my hair when I told him to fuck off."

"That son of a bitch. Was there an indecent exposure?"

The night was cold and dark for a cold and dark reason. Gothy came into the custody section over a phony examination pretext. He would have violated her, if not for the jangles from the main station where someone was fiddling with keys. "There was a rape attempt, Queenie. Now please, leave it at that."

"One last question – did he disrobe you by force?"

"He did," said Lottie, holding a breath. "I beg you. Don't make a scene outta this. I don't want Jake to know."

"You're making a mistake."

"It's my life, Queenie. I fucking know he won't even look at me if he finds out."

"There's no way I can help you without him knowing." It was too late, because the door swung for Jake who was shivering in rage. He shoved a paper bag at Quinn and leaped for Lottie, holding her into his chest. "Imma be downstairs."

There was an unspoken understanding between them, a meeting of minds so tacit and sympathetic. They circled on Lottie's case, working to disestablish her pregnancy as a motive. Jake never let go of Lottie's hand, their fingers intertwining.

Quinn had gone beyond her responsibility as a lawyer and a second cousin. The whole time she was wheeling between a maternal responsibility and sisterly concern, sometimes both. She explored the possibility of PTSD, giving her personal insight based on the many victims she prevailed in the battlefields.

But in the privacy of the bathroom, her emotion leaked from that lean body of an athlete. She sat in the tub with her lips pressing together to contain a heartache. Those beady eyes tempered an endearing memory of their past. In those days, Lottie never had to fear a damn thing.

She straightened herself out before surfacing for the news marking the three-way war in Farmington. It was long overdue, but the Federal Bureau of Investigation was finally showing up in defiance against David's philanthropic efforts.

The entire frame was given to Richard Halgriffin, a superagent who made his career taking cold-blooded murders out of the national unsolved list. "The Bureau is assisting mostly behind the scene thus far," he said. "But we're getting little progress with farcical twists."

The scene cut to Tashtego who was sweating and stammering. "Our investigation is narrowing into two teams now—"

"He and his teams," said Terry. "Something bad happens, just create more task forces and fuck things up."

And finally the devils emerged, well-dressed behind a bulky African-American who was too young to have snow over his roof. He articulately arranged his words almost as if he was reading from a book. "–doing this, but we're complying. This investigation has taken a toll. We hope to clear our names so that my clients can move on which hopefully after the preliminary hearing, we can walk away and start on finding the real killer."

"Get a load of this guy!"

"That's Marcus Frankopan," said Quinn. "He doesn't care what his client does. He rights the wrong. He wrongs the right. And he's gonna fight for Amelia."

"You sound worried."

"This man is a monster. If things aren't going his way, he'll try firing for a mistrial. Three years ago, he successfully turned a rape charge. He convinced everyone it was a false accusation. The rapist walked free. The victim was fined down to the last penny in her bank account and the judge had to resentence her. She's still in correctional." Quinn grabbed the remote to switch off the television. "They have Mark. He can help them walk away innocent. Renbarger has to expect that – or else he'll lose. I wonder what he's planning to do right now."

22

The lamp craned from the furthermost extension of a metal swing arm. Its light flickered in failing power, much like the future of the man under the bulb. His throbbing arms shot the clutter into an orderly arrangement in the available space on his big desk. And under the pile, he fished out what appeared to be a clean, uncrumpled envelope that spelled death in every conceivable way.

His puffy eyebags must have dropped another inch after peering into what was inside. His scream echoed in this cavernous office. Exasperation thrusted the whole envelope into a thick ball. And he hurled it into the air, missing that steel bin next to the clothes-littered couch.

"Fuck! Fuck!" Peter Renbarger was still screaming. "FUCK!" He would have kicked the Nordic desk. He would have broken everything in this office. But he decided to do what everyone would do if twisted in a tangle. An hour later, the last of his tears had dried up. He had enough for the night, setting his phone alarm, shaker alarm and that screamer alarm for early morning.

Somehow, he woke up every hour to stand before the toilet bowl, looking at the one thing that landed him in hot waters.

And the first person to come into this office was a relatively unknown secretary from the district court. "Really? I came here half an hour early and you're already here!" she said.

"Is there something I can help you with, Sheila?"

"What time you come here anyway?"

Sweat beaded on his forehead, after her cursory glance toward the bin. He stood to hand her a file. "It's for Reade's case," he said. "It's moved to next week. Make sure her lawyer gets that information."

That cool sensation nibbled at him again. He looked at those account statements, now gashed with wrinkles. He did so again that night on the couch, shaking his head in the same rush of anguish.

The preliminary hearing seemed too distant when he was languishing in his stupor. But he never stopped wondering how the hours seemed to jump when he was busy. Mornings turned to afternoons in a split second. And time slowed after sunset, when the last of those prosecutors, secretaries and clerks went to their beds – sometimes in the same house.

At least they had beds. He had a couch; the same couch gave him cramps after a week. The nipping wind rattled against the window, confronting him with a realization. He never had a sniff of fresh air, not at least since that brunch among those shifting souls in the cramped pizzeria. And that was six days ago. Six days in this stale air, an eternity of headache with thumping emotional throes.

The rotting burden left him hamstrung throughout their current phase on Charlotte Reade's case. Criminal courts mandated a "discovery period", during which prosecutors were to share evidence with defendants to avoid an ambush at trial. Yeah, nothing like the crap seen on TV. The deputy district attorney and investigators were not too shy to spill their thoughts. And Renbarger had to concur.

It was a shameful discovery period, all hyped with nothing to point but that worthless fingerprint analysis. His deputies listed a number of people for questioning through Chief Tashtego's network. They took statements and more statements before coming to another circle.

Nothing was prosecutable (again, aside from the contestable analysis). No witnesses could be called to testify against the defendant. And Quinn Ganderton struck the first blow. "They don't intend to have a plea bargain!" said Thomas Wilkins. "She's going for our throat and we got nothing!"

"Nothing on them?" asked Renbarger.

"There ain't no damn thing. The gun is in our hands. But it's pointing back to our fucking dicks!" Wilkins kept pestering him on behalf of the rest in the office. Three deputies had both feet deep in the mud, tap-dancing on however a slippery surface for Renbarger.

And they were banging the desk, throwing stuff and yowling like cats on heat.

Christopher Archambeau was heard from across the hallway. "I already had that file on his desk last week!" he told Wilkins.

"You sure?"

It was the same with Arthur Rowe. "What d'you mean he doesn't know? I told him four days ago. That witness is no good."

And Patricia deAlaris. "No, no, no, no!" she was shrilling. "The chief never said Charlotte Reade admitted to the murder! God, where's this coming from?"

In the final days, Renbarger picked up the pace to organize his arguments. The defense team opted for clean tactics that did them no good in front of the media who continued speculating. And it all came down to the court, rousing into action when Judge Gregory Rodeback squeezed through a gap for his position.

Renbarger gulped from a glass of water to drown that spicy flavor of his morning sandwich.

Hearts were pounding.

Weeks of preparations had come to this frightening reality. Renbarger did not miss the defendant's smile after a nod from Jacob Brownfield. That smile disappeared when everyone sat. The judge's prominent jaw hid whatever neck he had under that wisp of a beard. He looked over the case file, finishing with a rather ogling glance, "Charlotte Reade – against the State over aiding and abetting and tampering with evidence in the murder of Miriam Brownfield. How does the defense plea?"

"Not guilty."

The opening statement flowed in a fluid motion, describing Lottie as a co-owner of the Bookstore on the Left in Chevalley Street. "She escaped an abusive marriage, coming back here since March this year. She put it to rediscover herself, during which time she met Jacob Brownfield and his daughter Miriam in mid-August."

Renbarger sat unfazed through this 15-minute statement. Upon his turn, he delivered the version of his narrative. "Your Honor, Miriam Brownfield was an innocent child in the face of a new environment," he said. "There was no denying that Farmington was not a mingling town like Huntsville, where she was born. Her father had never thought of bringing her here. That was until the death of a relative. An American hero that was Miriam's uncle, who was also a victim in this twist and turn of a dysfunctional family due to Abraham Brownfield. And no surprise either – for the memory of this same man gave her only daughter a shotgun wedding causing this poor Ruth Brownfield to fly straight to Utah – again never to look back.

"Here we have a setting of a dysfunctional family. Not just a divorce or failed marriages. It's not just about Jacob Brownfield or Rachel Tempner. Miriam was born in Alabama and exposed to the concepts of sister wives, domestic violence and Bible bangers of the Pentecostal persuasion. Such was the influence she grew up in. The flight to Farmington to her should be as liberating as anything you can imagine!

"This sounds like a baseless assumption," said Renbarger, reaching for some papers. "I'm passing to the bailiff some evidence to confirm my statement. Screenshots from her Instagram posts – need I remind, deactivated account."

The bailiff passed the second copy to the defense desk, a mere formality to put them up to speed. The evidence was a two-year-old post, about a fight between Jake and Rachel. Renbarger constructed an argument on the basis of Instagram posts. "As the months went on, Miriam kept talking about it almost like a scene update sequencing together what that is indeed a dysfunctional family.

"Obviously, your Honor, the environment was toxic. You may also notice that once she got to Farmington, her posts were more and more positive," he said. "She was happy. She was like I said liberated. Until a few comments from none other than her biological mother herself. A follower of hers insinuated of a possible marriage between Jacob Brownfield and the defendant Charlotte Reade. Which Miriam replied remorselessly with offense. She did not like the idea of them marrying. The case is simple, your Honor. Very simple." He paused for an effect.

"Third marriage is only possible – with Miriam Brownfield out of the picture, completely."

Quinn shot up for a riposte. "Your Honor, I'm not sure you understand his irrelevant logic." She continued, after an explicit confusion from the judge's table. "The going divorce rate is nearly sixteen cases for every thousand married American women. The most common final straw is infidelity. It was the established cause in the Brownfield-Tempner divorce. The lack of loyalty killed their functioning home.

"Second place behind infidelity is domestic violence. I assume you of all people know that, Mr. Renbarger. From what I heard; you're having a marital problem as well."

"We're not divorced, I'll have you know," said Renbarger, disapprovingly.

"Order in the court!"

Quinn gave a buttonholing comparison with divorce rates from the national median and state average. "Arguments in marriages are very common. I'm sure you argue with your wife, your Honor." Rodeback's lips curled into a smile. "Ooh, that's a yes there! Who won that round?"

A small chuckle broke out. "Bring it in, Ms. Ganderton," said Rodeback.

"What I'm saying is, your Honor, that one comment from Miriam to a follower means absolutely nothing. We all know what this is all about. She got jealous, and that was it. If we consider that comment alone, we gotta consider on all the other reasons – one of 'em being the reason why she's happy here in Maine. I mean let's be honest, she met my client the defendant after which her Instagram sounded more positive. This shows my client's positive influence in Miriam's life."

The war of words fired up, with more speculations. Rodeback listened to Renbarger's ingenious approach to embroider hostility between Charlotte and Miriam. And Quinn retaliated with crystal-clear conjectures. She gave her client's smartphone, already scrolled to the plenty Instagram posts which Miri commented.

"*Take me dinner. What's Mason doing? You're hot – what's your secret?*" said Quinn, reading every comment she memorized. She faced Jake. "*Think you can braid my hair, tagged Charlotte underscore Reade. X O X O. My dad sucks at it!*" The laughing reaction was priceless. "This is proof, your Honor. Miriam is not in my client's way. Not by one bit.

"Miriam and Charlotte got along fine. She asked for braiding advices. How many stepparents – or biological parents for that matter – have that kind of experience with their daughter? Camilla Palmer wrote for the Guardian two years ago, about a dad sharing his braiding experience: how braiding made him a better dad." Quinn angled against the defendant desk. "It's obvious they're having a good time. Good time that if my client wants a step further with Miriam's father, there's no need to clear the table. The bedroom door is already open."

The battle seemed to have converged upon a solid wall. Quinn erected a strong defense but yet again, the prosecution went around her argument. "There's a thing when it comes to grief," said Renbarger as the bailiff vaulted another piece of evidence. "You can see in the attached report is a urine test from Dr. Alfred Huntley, a state-approved OB/GYN for the defendant, Charlotte Reade. At this point, it is scientifically too early to determine the father's identity. But we are assuming it is Mr. Jacob Brownfield–"

"You don't have to assume. It is him!" said Lottie.

"Order in the court!"

Quinn acknowledged. "We apologize, your Honor."

"Thank you, Ms. Reade, for that piece of information," said Renbarger. "Your Honor, losing a daughter through murder is nothing short of a shell shocker. What happened to Mr. Brownfield is terrible." He approached the defendant's desk, looking straight into Lottie's round eyes. "Would you mind telling us how you got pregnant, Ms. Reade?"

"Objection. The prosecution is badgering my client. This ain't the place for a human sexuality class."

Renbarger turned to Rodeback. "Your Honor, her pregnancy is clear proof that Mr. Brownfield was able to move on so quickly after the murder!" he said. "And for her to be pregnant during those sensitive times is another proof. He lost a daughter, and you're that innocently quick to make him a new one. One bread out, another goes in."

"Objection."

"Sustained!" said Rodeback. "Will the prosecution and defense please approach the bench?"

Renbarger and Quinn strode to engage in whispers with the judge. And then they went back to sit at their respective desks. Rodeback sorted out his desk. "I always live by the means that correlation does not equate to causation," said Rodeback. "Being pregnant at this time – it's not easy. This is the last place I'd want for an expectant mother. But the law is the law. It wields power over all of us." Rodeback sighed. "As such, I am exercising my power to adjourn this session to a later date, thereby giving more time for both parties to obtain and organize."

Voices circled around the room.

"This hearing has been – strange," said Rodeback. "My advice for both teams, organize a better exchange and stop speculating! Or else I'm dismissing this case with prejudice!"

23

Antiseptics and iodine nibbled under those bloodied wools. Lottie was not complaining, and she had no reason to do so. Her lawyer and second cousin staved the criminal case from suppurating into the prosecution's favor. It was far from victory, very far. But she held her head high outside the courtroom, the building and in the car. Those heavy police motorcycles escorted them home. And Lottie was reminded to stay indoors the whole time.

Charles converted the study to accommodate their purposes, storing away his painting equipment for a war-like décor. There was a 7' x 4' pinboard, laying out the details regarding Miriam's murder. "Renbarger went for the superweapon the first day," said Lottie. "But that didn't do him any good."

"It did us no good either," replied Quinn. "That's the thing – nobody gets to sleep soundly at night."

Donna's coffee goosed them for another debate. She returned later with Red Bull in an ice bucket. "Lord knows how much I don't like you drinking this sugar stuff."

"Lord knows how much I like you serving them, Aunt Donna," said Quinn, smiling as she frowned. "Okay, I promise I'll quit sugar."

"You promised last year, and the year before!"

"Next year and the year after that too," said Quinn, sipping with a purposive sound.

"Queenie," said Lottie. "Something doesn't sound right. That D.A. kept railroading about Jake being my baby's father and all. The fuck he on about? Like I'm some sorta hooker?"

"That son of a gun doesn't have anything, that's why."

"Didn't expect it'll turn that way," said Donna. "I mean, do prosecutors really pretend to be snoopy assholes?"

"Some don't have to pretend, Aunt. Don't be too caught up about that Renbarger guy. The man only has two hands."

"You have two hands, Queenie."

"Yeah. But I don't have a dick or a shell company."

Lottie took some time to process that. "Wait, he's taking bribes?"

"From what I'm told."

"Shit happens, I guess."

"Yeah. Like your baby," said Quinn.

"That's mean. We didn't plan this to happen."

"I did some math. You guys went birds and bees after the Morgan's arrest. How is it possible you're pregnant already?"

"Now you're questioning Jake being a dad."

"No. I'm questioning the power of his sperm! What are they? Flying like the Christmas scene in Iron Man Three?"

Lottie laughed. "We were celebrating!"

"I guess I have to run with that during the hearing."

"Is that even legal?"

"Sex out of wedlock?"

"Celebrating a person's arrest, you idiot!"

241

Quinn looked at her. "Hundreds of people went on cheering while Ted Bundy was being executed."

"Okay. It's legal. That's all you gotta say, dork."

The adjournment allowed them more preparatory time to mount a stronger defense. Someone later worked magic behind the scenes, twisting and spinning yarns to catch the prosecution team with a surprise date. Quinn pretended not to worry. But Renbarger was upset. "Glad I have a moron for a prosecutor," said Lottie, the morning when they were readying.

Renbarger went for another round of hare-footed bantering. Lottie again had to certify Jake's parentage, a pre-planned response to assume Quinn's victimization strategy. "Your Honor, I'd like to have the particular person called as a witness," said Quinn. "Jacob Brownfield."

Upon Rodeback's approval, Jake got up and proceeded toward the bench where the bailiff waited with the Bible. He was about to place a hand when he caught the sight of a disapproving man with a kippah. "I don't have to swear by the Bible," said Jake.

"He doesn't," said Rodeback. "Just the hand, bailiff."

"Do you solemnly swear to tell the truth, the whole truth, and nothing but the truth under the pains and penalties of perjury?"

"I do."

Quinn wasted no time. "Mr. Brownfield. You're the father of the fetus in conception?"

"Yes, I am."

"Can you give us your account on it?"

"It's been hell," said Jake.

"Define hell, Mr. Brownfield."

"My daughter wasn't just murdered. She was slaughtered. It affects our lives, even right now. It wasn't just about Miriam being dead. Not just that. It's about her killers walking free and posting on their Instagram and all. But yet somehow, we are here talking about that one comment that would not matter if this district has a reputable attorney on their behalf." Renbarger turned away. "But what I can tell is this. When I cornered the persons I believe to be involved – I felt like justice is served. The satisfaction. The peace."

"It was a planned conception?"

Jake took a breath. "N-no. It wasn't," he said. "Being divorced at my age really switch something off." He snapped his fingers. "Just like that. You feel like you don't wanna get married again. You feel like you had enough. And when you meet the right one, it happens and that's what happened."

"But in the weeks after your daughter was in your own words slaughtered?"

"Not exactly," said Jake. "It was after Amelia Morgan's arrest. I mean, after she was charged."

"It felt like a victory for you?"

"Absolutely."

"Not planned?"

"Not planned."

"At all?" said Quinn, waving both hands.

Jake imitated the same gesture. "At all."

"You see, your Honor. It was accidental from a prolonged period of sexual latency. Could be of a psychological cause. Or performance anxiety. Whatever it is, this pregnancy does not have anything to do with Miriam's murder. It will still happen regardless, just the matter of time," said Quinn. "But since we're on this subject. I'd like you to have a copy of an article from *Health Immediate*." She handed the bailiff two copies.

"One for the witness, bailiff. Mr. Brownfield, would you read the title and the first paragraph?"

Jake perused the rehearsed content. "*Does Sex Combat Depression?*" Jake started reading. "*Depression can deprive you from sex, diminishing your motivation and at the same time your libido. Yet safe sex can help with the effects of depression, on your way toward a start in recovery.*"

"Thank you, Mr. Brownfield. That excerpt was from a medical research report written by Niranjan Singh, MB Bch BAO PsyD. But we're Americans. We're not familiar with these abbreviations. Let's just say, he passed USMLE for Medicine, Surgery, Obstetrician and Psychology. What does that tell you? It tells you that two consenting adults are tangling the blanket. And it has nothing to do with Miriam's murder."

"Your Honor," said Renbarger, after Quinn finished her argument. I'd like to cross-examine the witness."

"Proceed."

His stride was akin to a marching wild boar, especially with that broad chest. "You're telling all of us this is an explosion of warm and wonders, huh?"

"Yes."

"The aforementioned doctor was talking about safe sex. What you did with the defendant doesn't sound safe, does it?"

"It was between me and my girlfriend – it's none of your fucking business."

"Watch your language, Mr. Brownfield," said Renbarger.

"Objection. Under the First Amendment, the witness has the rights to free expression."

"Best we don't do that here, Mr. Brownfield."

"I'm sorry, your Honor. I have deep respect for you," he replied. "You can't just sit there letting him question my privacy but somehow got a problem with my language. I didn't rape. I love her. Ask if she consented to our relationship."

"I consented, your Honor," said Lottie.

"This conception was not planned. Stick with that. But we do intend to take full responsibilities, in the upbringing of the child." Jake dug deep into Renbarger's eyes. "Sir, this is my child we're talking about. *My* child. Let's just not continue this. It has no basis or bearing against why we're here in the first place."

"And why are we here then, Mr. Brownfield?"

"You're asking me?" snapped Jake. "Ain't you the one filing against my Charlotte about the fingerprints upon the murder weapon?"

Rodeback shrugged with a mutter. "You have the floor to ask whatever you wanna ask the witness, Mr. Renbarger," he said. "Do it and let's move on."

"Mr. Brownfield – how do you describe your feeling after being told of the pregnancy?"

"Shocked. Scared. Worried. She was in jail at the time. That's why we're here, Mr. Renbarger."

"Basically, after your daughter died–"

"*Murdered.*"

"After your daughter was killed–"

Jake shouted. "Say it for what it is. She was murdered!"

"Mr. Renbarger! I stood by with what I said the last time we're here!"

"Okay, okay. After she was murdered, your child in the belly was–"

"I'm not answering anything more about my baby. It's a proof of our undying love. Sure, not what I expected. Agreed, timing wasn't right. But I made her that baby. And we're damn well gonna keep it. We stuck with each other until the very end

– managing to get those who murdered my daughter. Why don't we talk about that Amelia Morgan?"

"Amelia Morgan is not the purpose of this hearing," said Renbarger.

"Neither is our child, you pompous fuck!" shouted Jake, so loud that the courtroom shook.

Renbarger's retort was lost. And after he declared a retreat back to his legal den, Quinn managed a small grin to Jake. "No further question as well, your Honor."

"You may please exit the stand," said Rodeback.

Jake should have punched Renbarger in the face. The next hour saw a tedious elaboration of wrongdoings during his divorce battle. Those marriage problems were as Quinn described: "a perfect ammunition for defamation." But the instrumental part stood out. Renbarger was not able to substantiate his own claims to determine Lottie's guilt.

Everyone played along and listened to Renbarger with apathetic postures. In the middle of a contention, that low, rumbling resonance started out. "–pure display of arrogance, instability and immorality for a divorcing father with a growing daugh–" Renbarger had to stop because of that gripping plangency.

Right at that time, Ruth elbowed her snoring husband. And Terry shook out of an exhaustive doze, eyes widening. "Please respect this courtroom!" said Rodeback. "Go home if you're tired."

Both arms up in apology to the judge and Quinn, Terry cleared his throat and rubbed his eyes. "As I was saying before I was rudely interrupted," said Renbarger. "Mr. Brownfield's behavior on record insulting the mayor was perfect to show the kind of upbringing Miriam had, prompting some sort of a social shock when introduced to the calm cultures we practice in Maine."

"Objection, your Honor. For the third time, the father is not the murder suspect."

"Sustained."

During a recess, Quinn started with Terry. "What the hell was that all about? I didn't ask for that!"

"Sorry. I really flat out."

"Don't do that again. Looked like you were making fun of him!"

"No!" insisted Terry. "You're whooping his ass without our help."

That was the first time they saw Quinn blushing, short-lived as an officer interrupted. "Excuse me, sir," he said, offering a hand. "You're Jacob Brownfield, right?" Jake felt something in that handshake. "I'd like to shake the hand that killed your daughter, sir."

Quinn stared, agape. "What the fuck is wrong with you? Get outta here!"

The young officer made a gesture, and Jake looked at the folded paper in his hand. His eyes whitened after reading. "What the hell?"

"*Pete's withdrawing*? Pete? Like Peter Renbarger?"

Jake recognized the handwriting. "It's the chief's."

"I don't like this. Kill this game quick, Queenie."

The court battle resumed with Renbarger doing the same thing. Quinn decided to stonewall everyone with a contesting objection. "Your Honor, the prosecution refused to back away from this conception nonsense," she said. "I would like to request your consideration to dissolve this hearing on grounds of lack of evidence."

"Overruled."

Quinn grimaced. That was fast. "So, I would move to request," she said, almost growling, "the murder weapon be brought here to the stand." Everyone shifted on their seats. "Because I believe that'll be enough to prove my client's innocence." Renbarger's jaw fell, revealing the lightly shaded pink of his tongue dry.

The waiting minutes became a game of knitting brows between the prosecution and defendant. Two police officers were permitted into the courtroom, hauling a blue Panasonic steam iron on a flat trolley.

Ants skittered across Jake's spine. His nervous revulsion was a loud huff. "Jesus Christ," he breathed.

"It's barely thirty dollars. A good brand for a daily use," said Quinn. "Would the prosecution please acknowledge if this is the murder weapon?"

"Why would you ask?"

Quinn stood unmoved, facing the judge. "Yes or no?"

"It is, your Honor," said Renbarger, hesitating.

"Your Honor, I would like to request," she said, "the prosecution describe why *this* is the murder weapon."

Rodeback's brows dropped to furrow over his narrowed eyes. He waved toward Renbarger. "Your Honor, *this* is the murder weapon," he said.

"Describe, Mr. Renbarger!" said Quinn, still not moving.

"I was just starting, Miss Ganderton."

"Oh, my apologies."

Jake shivered, his shoulders twitching.

"If you would look deeper at its plate, your Honor." Renbarger held the iron with a gloved hand. "You may notice a clear hint of something right there." He pointed at the wavy smudges in black and brown. "That's what happens when a hot titanium burns through flesh. It's a, with respect, tissue leftover from Miriam Brownfield. Therefore, it is unmistakably the murder weapon used upon the poor girl and from the fingerprint analysis, used by the defendant, Charlotte Reade."

"I'm confused," said Quinn. "If used by the defendant, is this hearing for murder or tampering with evidence?"

Renbarger stammered.

"You know what, don't even answer that, Mr. Renbarger. You gotta look at yourself in the mirror next time you do that." She snapped two fingers, and the bailiff passed the judge a file. "Your Honor, enclosed within you'll find two different pictures from a forensic analysis. The one on the left is from *that* steam iron, presented as the murder weapon. The other one is a steam iron in my experiment with Mrs. Ruth Stapleton, Miriam's aunt. She's here at court by the way."

They swung toward Ruth.

"Your Honor, this is a legal ambush," said Renbarger.

"No, Mr. Renbarger. It isn't," replied Quinn. "I filed it during the discovery." She turned away from his bleached demeanor to give Rodeback a little more space. "I would like to explain, your Honor."

"Please do."

"The purported murder weapon had the wears and tears of flesh wound. Same for the second picture, the not-the-murder-weapon steam iron. Two irons – same effect."

"And?"

"Allow me simplify it to you. Two pictures in that file – left, the steam iron presented by the prosecution; right, the steam iron Ruth and I experimented! Yes, this object of evidence has the mark of burned flesh. But that does not make this the murder weapon."

"Objection. This is plain denial."

"Sust–." Rodeback paused. "Overruled! Elaborate, Ms. Ganderton."

"Has the flesh residue been analyzed?"

"Yes, it has."

"DNA matching Miriam?" asked Quinn, to which Renbarger stumbled after a brief intention. "DNA matching with the murder victim?"

"I–"

"Did the DNA of *that* flesh on *that* steam iron match with Miriam Brownfield, Mr. Renbarger?"

"Your Honor, I request for– request for some–"

"It does not match!" said Quinn. "Two pictures! Two irons with the same burn marks! It means, my iron burned the same thing as the prosecution's iron. And your Honor, I burned the flesh of a pig, meaning that *that* is *not* the murder weapon!"

Those murmurs reverberated as Renbarger sat straight.

"Order! Order!"

"She didn't tell me what it was for!" said Ruth.

"ORDER!"

"You know this?" asked Terry.

"ORDER! I CALL FOR ORDER!"

Jake breathed. "It's over. She won."

"And therein," she said through the maundering acclamation. "And therein, I call in question the legitimacy of a criminal trial, because this is not a piece of evidence. Whatever the reason my client's fingerprint is on it, there is no relevance for a trial."

Another flare went out. "Order!" shouted Rodeback

"Shut up!" retorted a spectator.

"That's it! Bailiff, get 'em outta here!"

Quinn stayed in her seat, a hand wide to curb Lottie's excitement. When the chaos died down, she continued. "There was not a sign whatsoever to relate this steam iron as the murder weapon, your Honor. It was brand new!"

"Objection. Speculations. Besides, the torturers could have purchased a new steam iron."

"Sustained."

"Torturers, Mr. Renbarger? You have yet to get a conviction on the next case. How exactly d'you know there's more than just a killer?"

"Uhh."

"Do you believe in those video footages?"

"I—"

"Of course, you do. It's your case after all," said Quinn. "So, let's run this again. No wear and tear. Very brand new. Animal flesh. I dunno why it's been called the murder weapon. Read my lips: *it is not.*"

The disarray was the first sign of the incoming sweetness. Renbarger was sitting with both hands on his head. And Rodeback appeared to be teetering. "This hearing will call for a more experienced forensic team to assess the legitimacy of this claim," he said.

"You don't need experience, sir. All you need is a team full of integrity in the name of justice."

"My – Ms. Ganderton. Do you doubt the purity of our justice system?"

"I don't, your Honor. But I'd humbly ask you burn a pig and an unclaimed corpse with two steam irons of the same brand – and see which matches this so-called murder weapon." Quinn continued. "This Reade case has drowned Farmington too little too long. The effects will stay. The Reade family bookstore has suffered from dropped sales, due to this hearing. So, you should understand the reason of my disillusionment."

"Alright. I'm convinced." Lottie held her breath as Rodeback spared a few seconds. "I've come to the decision that the case against the defendant, Charlotte Reade, be dropped and dismissed with prejudice."

He pounded the gavel.

And Renbarger was gone within seconds.

Lottie screamed upon the bang, throwing herself into Quinn's arms. She then spun to latch on Jake, kissing with passionate fire.

"You're amazing! You're really amazing! You killed it!"

"Never thought it was that easy."

Lottie had a big bear hug from Terry. Her mascara was all over her face, those tears dotting her sleeves. But she did not care. The whole thing was behind her now.

She was a free woman.

24

The study was gushing with positive ambience, and it was not because of the perfumed humidifier. The family was sitting on a four-person velvet chesterfield sofa. Jake was given a single tufted chair. And they were there for Lottie who was going through the words on a tablet. After finishing, she gave a shudder.

"You sure I should post this?" she asked.

Quinn took her hand. "Absolutely. Read it again."

"Okay," said Lottie. "*My name is Charlotte Reade. I'm sure you know who I am. I am famous for something I wish I can take away. It will forever remain on me, despite my acquittal.*" She took her eyes from the screen. "Hmm. Acquittal means I'm free, right?"

Jake nodded. "Keep reading."

"*I'm not writing this to get my five minutes of fame. I don't need it. I'm writing this because I believe a woman's voice when united can break down every barrier upon the face of this earth. I'm writing this because I believe a lot of women will suffer the same if I keep my silence. I'm writing this because I believe what I went through has been going on for a very long time.*

"*I'm writing this because I believe. I have been a victim in the court of law, in the system purportedly built to protect me, and in a world justifying its innocence. When I was in jail, I was subjected to an undeserving treatment. My captors proudly wear their badge as if it means something. But for one of them, it is power to take advantage of and I was in a perfect position to be vindicated with an unforgivable degree of sexual assault.*

"My lawyer advised that I keep this down. Until I am proven innocent, to prevent any supposition that I am making things up to weasel my way out of trial. It is disgusting if you think about it. Because it is so true. Even to this day, a lot of people (especially women) will proudly rally up to defend a sex offender just for the hell of it.

"But I shall keep my silence no more. I write this knowing the risk that waits, because I am not a celebrity. My life does not interest the media. If this happens to a famous singer, there is no doubt it will be hot in the news. But I am Charlotte Reade. Nobody cares what I've been through. Not even women safety supporters, I'd assume, because this is our reality so superficial that the world is only safe for the fame and the rich.

"And please, don't debate me on this – women were assaulted for decades; y'all turn a blind eye asking 'how long her skirt was' and 'why go to a dark alley' and 'why she's being out at night', then some celebrities posted Me Too, and everyone suddenly got stunned and surprised.

"So yeah, being a woman is being at war every single day. Matters not you're beautiful or fugly, loaded or sagging, wet or dry, in this war we're being seen for one thing. And in no way I can change that. But I can at least speak the name of the monster who laid his hands upon my breasts, tearing my privates with his fingers and flashed his short penis to my face. Not only that – I will tag him, his wife, his mother and his daughter. Know this, Officer

Roger Gauthier, this is a small town and everyone now knows you for what you really are."

"That's good," said Quinn. "Post it."

"You sure about this, Queenie? I mean, it's a lot! He can get imprisoned for years!"

"Don't worry. It's only up to thirty years."

"Thirty years! I'll be a grandma, by then."

"You already look like one," said Quinn. "To hell with it. He has to pay!"

And it was done.

The world slept lauding Roger Gauthier for his service. They would wake up in eight hours to find Farmington at a hurtling crossroad. Lottie clicked the standby button, gripped the tablet so hard her hands were shaking. Jake watched as Quinn moved closer to hold Lottie into her chest. "It's okay," she said, her eyes welling. "You did the right thing. He got what's coming. You're not what he made you. We all love you, Froggie."

The men exchanged a look and excused themselves, leaving for a walk. They said nothing; their boots against dried leaves and pinecones were the only sound to fill this hour of the wolf. Up ahead was a small gazebo, built in brick and mortar with a singular glass panel for roofing. And right there, they talked – not about criminal cases, oh no. Not about paintings. Not about women, of course. They talked about the Moon and stars.

About distant galaxies. And the beauties that formed clouds of gas in designated superclusters. The farcical hearing tripped Charles into a hole that he emerged back to his former self, with facial hair styled into an inquisitorial Vandyke. And he kept repeating about a Thanksgiving dinner, even at breakfast. "It's still over a month away, dad," said Lottie.

"Yeah, Uncle. Not sure I'll still be here now that my work's done."

"You're leaving?" asked Jake.

"Some of my guys are already calling."

"Something wrong, Jake?"

"That Renbarger scares the hell outta me. He's like that guy who lied in his résumé and got the job," he said. "He was really, really incompetent with his arguments."

"Took him down, didn't we?" said Lottie. "I'm free."

"Am I the only one seeing this? Renbarger is going up against that Mark Frankopan! He's gonna fuck things up, and they'll get away. Tashtego's tip didn't work out. Renbarger did not withdraw. You had to defeat him, Quinn. Scaring the crap outta me."

"I understand where you're coming from. But, I don't think I can do anything. I'm not with the district attorney's office."

"Can you apply?"

"It doesn't work that way, Jake."

"Shit. Can we like choose who to prosecute Amelia?"

"That I'm not sure," said Quinn. "We really have to put our faith in that guy. I just don't see how we can do this without him."

"I'm not about to let some moron run this case to the ground, Quinn."

"Me neither. But we gotta take baby steps for a while. It's not over until it's really over."

Jake kept biting his nail from that point. He could not bring himself to join the family. Spud was having the time of his life, flipping and turning in a rough play with Malcolm, Declan and Mason. That night, Spud was asleep after a long period of running while the family played Monopoly without Jake. After bankrupting both children and cleaning Donna out, Terry was on a roll. "We gotta talk to him," he said. "The man look like he's gonna have a heart attack."

"I'll do it," said Lottie.

Her forfeit gave Terry the ultimate chance to win the game. She went to a bathroom and found Jake in a bubble bath. She threw herself onto a recliner and later realized he was no longer there. She roamed around the big house, a head craning through doorframes only to find him standing in front of that pinboard. "Weren't you in the tub?" she said, heaving. "How you got here so fast?"

"You dozed off. Didn't wanna wake you up."

"Oh. What you doing here?"

"Nothing."

Lottie's lips curled into a sincere smile. "It's gonna be okay, Jake," she said. "Dad already talked Quinn into staying. She'll stay at least until it goes to trial."

The next morning, Quinn had another reason to remain in Farmington. She wiggled out of a decent sleep for a drag race to Court Street, where she bulled toward two police officers in the living room. "I'm the attorney for Charlotte Reade," she said, sharply. "She's been cleared from any wrongdoing. So, if you have anything to—"

"I'm Brad Crayton, Internal Affairs." The man produced his badge. "We'd like to have a word with Ms. Reade here about what she posted on Facebook last night."

"Officer Roger Gauthier has been suspended pending a criminal investigation," said Ashleigh Murdaugh. "We're looking into surveillance footage and his log files. Some of our people are meeting other women detained these few months while he's in the station."

"What do you need from my client?"

The officers treaded lightly with harmless questions in the beginning. Physical assaults had gained grounds in the correctional system, normalized after a prolonged course of unprosecuted actions. Crayton and Murdaugh were able to canvass through this clear act of constitutional violations. But they were not here to ask about physical assaults.

That was when Lottie's breathing went erratic with a wild convulsion. She was back in that wretched jail, her head slumping against the tiled wall. She caught a brief spell of intermittent sleeps, too distracted from that shifting light. And when the cell gate creaked, she saw a friendly face – or at least, a face she considered friendly all this time.

"He came to you at nights only?"

Gauthier had smiled. It was the smile she expected from serial killers, never cops. "Just nights. I dunno if anyone else knows," said Lottie. "He never came during the day."

"You hear anyone else in the station?"

"No. Or I can't remember. He'd have me cuffed." She showed those marks upon her wrists, now easing into mild pink. "He gagged me. I tried spitting it out but I can't."

"Did he say anything?"

"Oh, Jesus."

"He said, *oh, Jesus*?" asked Crayton.

"No, you idiot!"

Lottie closed her eyes. A searing pain cut through her abdomen from the crotch. "C'mere, you fucking bitch," she repeated Gauthier's words.

"C'mere? Not come here?"

"Yes. C'mere."

"What is it? An accent?"

Lottie nodded. "Yes. And I didn't like it one bit. Then he smacked me – the backsides. Kept doing it over and over again."

"Ms. Reade, this is not just sexual assault."

"If you're asking what I think you're asking, yeah, he raped me but there was no penetration. He–" A wave of flush went through her. "God, I can't forget that," she said, her eyes sparkling. "He masturbated over me. There, I said it! Enough! No more about that!"

"Okay, okay, we understand," said Murdaugh.

"I think that'll be all for today," replied Quinn. "I suggest you go check something else. His body cam footage maybe."

"That's the cat," said Crayton. "The cameras were covered."

"Oh, that's perfect."

"Yes. Yes, it is perfect," replied Murdaugh. "He can't cover his body cam. Prosecutable by law."

"We can work things around, seeing who did it. Maybe a footage from a different angle confirming Gauthier going around the station with a piece of cloth or something. And we'll charge him with what we can find."

"Is there anything else you can tell us, Ms. Reade?"

"Enough for the day, Officer."

"Please, Ms. Ganderton," said Murdaugh. "I'm asking this as a woman. We believe her."

Jake's arrival saw an end to their questioning. There was no time for pleasantries. They refused to meet his eyes and decided straight for their cruiser. "I came as soon as I can," he said.

"It's okay. I got things covered."

"Fuckers shoulda sent an all-women team!"

Those officers were there because her public post wrung a tailwind position generating a tempest of 200,000 reactions in three days. In the comments, there was an online rally that nobody dared downplaying Gauthier's wrongdoing. Her voice blazed a political trail ahead the upcoming presidential primaries. Even a year away, the election was slated to be the incumbent's defense against Joseph R. Biden who threw down the gauntlet that dark day when Huntsville lost a child with bright future. Nigel Shelby had taken his own life, after going through an unforgivable torment of bullying for being gay.

Jake remembered the boy's sincere smile glistening in sunlight, recollecting how the world moved on. Nigel was subjugated for his sexuality. Miriam suffered a similar malignance for being Jewish. And Lottie was leaving that crossroad for being a woman. "She's been through a marriage abuse once," said Charles, dusting his shotgun. "Beaten like she's some animal. But she walked into the family court like a champ. Like nothing happened. Like she never had a stitch." He pulled the pump, a grunt escaping his mouth. "But what that Gauthier did to her. Why my daughter, Jake? God Almighty, why her?"

"Funny."

"What?"

"It's funny, Mr. Reade," said Jake, clearing his throat. "I kept asking the same question myself. Why my Miri. Jesus Christ, the Morgans have everything. They can fucking get a new iPhone! Now look at them."

The gushing support for that family had dwindled to nothing more but a lick. Quinn continued checking for updates. The justice system seemed to have met a stumbling block. "I got no information from the DOJ," said Quinn. "Maybe Renbarger or Frankopan petitioned for more time to get things done."

"Who, you think?"

"The prosecution side, maybe. Some guy named Wilkins told me to stop being cunty and go get laid. So I asked if his wife would like my eight-inch strap-on."

"Jesus Christ, Queenie!"

"You got an eight-inch dildo?"

That was, as dads would say, how the fight started. "That's none of your business, Jake!" It was nothing a dinner can't fix. They swerved through the winding roads for Weld. Both gave that apprehensive glance upon the gas station, where their world dangled upside down. But nothing happened. Tashtego did not call again. And those horizons beamed with gleams much like their hearts, which poured out after finishing that $60 porterhouse steaks.

Lottie pulled a blanket. "Been thinking, honey. Can we like leave Farmington? For good?"

"You sure?" asked Jake, tight-lipped with a smile.

"I'm just done I really wanna leave. Drive somewhere. Keep driving. Maybe go to Canada."

Jake kissed in her glossy lips. "After the trial."

The idea floated in Jake's mind, keeping him awake for hours to peer into his woman's fluttering eyes. Those same eyes dug into a book by the backyard, under a comfortable shade of an overcast sky. Jake loomed by the kitchen, an unchanged resolve beating in his chest.

"Don't get up," he said, as she stirred.

"I gotta pee! The lil meanie' been at it on my bladder."

"That soon?" exclaimed Jake, which she did not respond. "The hell is that all about?" She was next rapping her knuckles, with half a scream even to Spud. Jake swung her by a restaurant for bagels in a variety of whole grain, cinnamon raisin and double dip. Then they had an unexpected visitor. "Bob? What are you doing here?"

"My wife works here, Jake."

"Really? I didn't know that." Jake had to cut in, after Tashtego turned his attention to Lottie. "Now's not the time for whatever you're thinking, Bob."

"It's okay. You wanna arrest me again, chief?"

"I just wanna say how sorry I am for being careless."

"Just that? I had to sit through a fucking hearing because you got careless and you're sorry for it?"

"Uhh, I mean I'm sorry for what Rog did."

"Oh. You're not sorry for putting me in jail. You're just sorry for what happened in jail. Got it. Anything else?"

"I got you some things. I'll be right back." He went out, returning with a basket full of baby products. "Got you some hair oil. Lotion. Some socks. Some clothes."

"You seize it off some Customs?"

"C'mon, man. I bought it!"

"Seriously, Bob? For real?"

Lottie's swing of an arm sent everything flying. "You can shove 'em up Gauthier's ass and go fuck yourself!" Jake had to walk over the gift, chasing after her. "Coming up to me thinking it's all forgiven and then use our baby for his dirty work? Oh, I hate this town! I fucking hate this town!"

Jake stayed quiet.

"If it was legal, I'd throw that ketchup bottle to the bastard's head! God, I shoulda done that! I shoulda done that! The fucker!"

"Honey."

"You weren't there, Jake!" said Lottie. "I had to go through it by myself! Because I was the weak link! They can't touch you.

So, they went for me! Wonder how much they're being paid! The fucker!"

"I never wanted any of that especially to you, Charlotte."

"It happened anyhow. All the places in this fucking world, you had to take me to his wife's! Felt like I wanna throw up!"

Jake had both hands over his head, reclining at the balcony as the maple tree whispered. His phone then rang. And he lurched two steps at a time to lock the door and sit on the toilet bowl. "I can't talk long," he whispered. "What d'you want?"

"Filling you in about the Ford."

"Keep talking. Keep talking."

"We tracked the Fiesta to Olsen Rentals, the one near my station. A junior repair dude got it in his garage for some servicing. That's point one. It didn't go missing. Point two, there's not a hair or hide of Miriam. Just someone's anal matter."

"Jesus Christ," said Jake.

"Ain't his either, I tell ya'. That's what the forensic guy told me." Tashtego said. "We thought it was a lead to the killer. But just a blind alley. A cold one."

"But who rented the car?"

"Point three. Not David. It was Sarah Hayes. Christie's mom," said Tashtego. "Connected and prosecutable. Just that we didn't know how it went. We didn't even know if Miri was in there. If she was, must be in one helluva body bag."

"Probably frozen first," breathed Jake.

"That's possible. Or they didn't rent it to dispose the body." He continued, as Jake sighed. "Look, I also got this funny thing from the Morgan home. It's a small device."

"I dunno what you're talking about."

"Yeah, sure. If the feds find it, you're dead!"

"I said, I dunno what you're talking about."

"I still can charge you for being a perv."

"Fuck you."

"Heh. Just doing you a favor. I moved the patrol guy an hour late. He usually goes there around eight. He'll come around nine tonight."

"Why?"

"Because after eight, a cop car will swing by. I'm in it. I'm gonna leave your listening device in your mailbox."

"We got no mailbox. Thank David."

"Okay. Leave a shoe next to your garage. I'll put it there."

"How you know it's mine?"

Tashtego laughed. "You're not the only eagle in the sky, Jake."

"I had to do it."

"Yep. I'd do the same if this happened to mine," said Tashtego. "It's fucked up anyway. Never had an inquiry like this all my life. Felt like I wanna retire early."

"And do what? Work at Costco?"

"Better than being called incompetent! And that Internal Affair thing."

"Yeah. Brad Crayton from the Affairs was here."

"They always like a sniff. Can't blame them."

"Look, I really wanna talk to you," said Jake. "But you gotta do something with Gothy. Why is he suspended?"

"What d'you mean? He abused her."

"Yeah? Why isn't he fired, you fucking idiot? You can't seriously be going with innocent until proven guilty."

"Jake, the man has a wife and kids."

"And a short dick!" said Jake, full-voiced. "My girlfriend got kids too, and one of 'em is in her belly! You go humanizing

Gothy again, and the next thing that goes flying won't your baby oil, chief! I mean that."

"Look, I'm sorry, okay?"

"I heard that every single day, chief. Fire Gothy or else you can consider our friendship goodbye and go talk to Quinn Ganderton if there's something you wanna talk about. But all the same, you piece of shit, thanks for giving back my device and thanks for the note. Now we know how useless it is!"

"What? What are you talking about? What note?"

"You sent that police boy to us? Giving us that note during the hearing?"

"Jake, I didn't send any note. What did I say?"

"You didn't? What the hell? You wrote me saying Renbarger's withdrawing!"

"Hell no! I don't know what you're talking about!"

"Jake? Door's locked! Open up! Open up, now!"

He had no time to end the call. He threw the phone onto the anti-slip foot mat. And he saw Lottie's face, curled in surprise. "What happened?"

"They're dropping! They're dropping Amelia's case!"

"Quinn still here here?" exclaimed Jake.

They found Quinn watching the news. "Renbarger withdrew!"

"For Amelia?" shouted Jake. "Not Lottie?"

"He fucking withdrew!"

"Can he do that?"

"He said there's lack of evidence."

"WHAT THE FUCK?"

"Jesus, this ain't happening! The girls got cleared?"

"We lose," said Quinn, resigned.

Jake's head got heavier in a split second, his vision darkening. Then he retched, upchucking his lunch onto the vinyls. "*Don't think too hard. Don't think too hard.*" He was mumbling. "*Peter Piper picked a peck of pickled pepper. Peter Piper picked a peck of pickled pepper.*"

And by evening, Tashtego was on the phone. Quinn said nothing in that paralyzing suspense. When it ended, she took a deep breath and turned to all of them. "We're gonna do something you won't like," she said. "We're exhuming Miriam."

25

Cooped at a corner between Rumford and Carry was the unincorporated village Oquossoc 40 minutes away from Farmington. They had to come here. "What's gonna happen will raise some hell," said Quinn. "And when it does, I want you gone. Just until we take a look at the body again. Could take a few." And Oquossoc was just the place, unpredictable and too difficult to pronounce. The press would have to take time just for the spelling.

Nothing beat a good break from the town, to see those red tractors hauling whatever they always hauled. And those high greenhouses were teeming with life, pruned with gentle hands. And the best part was the lake, opening up after a long-awaited turn to Marina Road.

"I can't get Internet here!" Malcolm complained. After an umpteenth time, Ruth made a snatch and held his phone out of the window. "Mom! What are you doing?"

"I hear any more of Internet—"

"You won't! You won't! You won't!"

Declan pointed at him, closing an eye with a stifled laughter. The kids helped unloading the minivan before setting up camp without Jake's help. He was glued to a foldable chair, taking in the biting cold of breezy air.

"Remember, guys. No smiling, okay?"

It was a demand. "Look unhappy. Do whatever you want," said Quinn. "Cry if you have to. But don't laugh – ever. We don't need bad publicity right now. Keep playing the victim."

Nobody recognized them. That was the thing Lottie loved about Oquossoc. She did not have to cowl her head with a hoodie. She could enter an overcrowded souvenir shop unnoticed. So, she took Jake's cap away, leaving him to look like Theodore Herzl at a lake with that half-inch hair on his gaunt face.

The souvenir shop sold a white box, with a requestable engraving. Lottie waited until the kids were away before handing it to Jake. "*Thanks for the orgasms,*" he said, allowing a thin, smileless laugh. "Where the hell you got this anyway?"

"Trust me. The carving man was stumped. Lucky I still got a hang of French."

"Ruth will kill us if she finds out."

"She had a shotgun wedding. She ain't allowed to an orgasm."

"You're crazy, Charlotte." In that brief silence, he added. "Last someone gave me something was a mocha. Miri always looked out for me." His long face came back. "She said I was driving to her d-death. Huh. She saw it coming, I guess."

"There, there now."

"I really miss her, Charlotte. Been thinking of going back. Just to see her. One last time."

"Jake."

"It's only been some time. She should look–"

"You don't wanna do that, honey."

"What else you got there?" he asked of the other box.

"Avocados. If it doesn't work, get me ginger tea."

"What's going on?"

She took his hand to her belly. "We're having a family, Jake. That's what's happening."

"You're having morning sickness?"

"Morning sickness. A heartburn. Some mood swings," said Lottie. "Same thing I went for Mason. Rachel don't go through this?"

"Meh. That psycho don't have to be pregnant to have mood swings and a heartburn."

Jake diverted his attention by doing everything for Lottie, even bending over to file those slippers into her feet. He walked her around, to a garden of green grass, lilac lilies and gray cobblestones for selfies and yes ginger tea with a provoking aroma. But at times he reverted to his doldrums, staring, staring and staring. Hunger brought him to the barbecue. Duty had him spiriting around for Lottie. And despondency mowed his ground back to melancholia. Even three pieces of sausage took nearly an hour to go through his twisted throat. He was half-asleep on the chair, when Terry's Huawei rang.

"Yeah. What's up?" With a glimpse upon Jake, he said. "Yeah. He's doing great. We just – yeah, what is it? Uh-huh. Okay." After that, his voice broke into a squawk. "What?" Another squawk came. "N-nothing? Noth-thing at all? Like the hell? You serious?"

"What is it?"

"Oh, fuck! Jesus Mary Joseph!"

Lottie took the phone. "Queenie? What's up?"

"Froggie, we exhumed the body!"

"And?"

"There is no body!"

Quinn did not need to elaborate. They knew their retreat was over. She promised she would not call, unless if there was a matter of urgency. She did call. And there was a matter of urgency, to a point Terry threw everything (including glowing charcoal) into the Santa Fe. Jake was kept on a need-to-know basis – until they were at Fairbanks. And he was out for the police station, before the car even stopped. "Where is she?" he asked at the officer outside. "You saw a lawyer in there?"

"The cold room, Mr. Brownfield."

Tashtego took a blow to the face when he tried stopping. "Jake! Jake! Wait!" said Quinn, crying out.

The doors parted for the same brightly-lit chamber he swore he never wanted to come. That malodor clung upon the freezing air. There was a steel table in the middle. But something was different this time. On its surface was his worst nightmare that both halves of his face twisted toward different directions. He approached that plastic shroud covering the frailty.

And he was knocked backward into the freezers, eyes widened with his jaw crippled for some painful seconds. It was as Lottie put it. *He does not want to do this.* "No! No!" His screams were incomprehensible. "No! No! Oh, my God! No!"

Skin and sinew were the only fiber holding the girl's head to her lower extremities. Her arms were detached, veiny and striped in black lodes of inflamed nerves. The same dark threads coiled around her appending posterior. The buried girl was a corpse of 200 bones and trillions of decomposing cells. The exhumed girl was a liquefied carcass over something beyond the reams of regular microbial rigor mortis.

Miriam Brownfield was nothing but noodles, noodles and noodles.

"Jake, I didn't want you to see—"

A grip pressed her maxillary muscles into sinus cavities. "You called us telling there ain't no body left!" he was screaming at Quinn. "What the fuck do you expect I'd do?"

Lottie reached to break him from Quinn. Then she turned. "Oh!" Her throat tickled. "Can't! Can't! Imma go!"

He did not see her scurrying outside. "My girl! What happened to my girl!"

"It's chemicals, Jake," said Tashtego, holding his purpling cheek.

"Chem– chemicals?"

"Something like a dissolving agent. I've seen corpses. Even four months old, they'll be brown black. This is a tissue collapse. Gotta be chemical."

"Eden!" said Jake. "Had to be her."

"We don't know for sure," said Tashtego.

"She handled her body!"

"Jake, we need proof otherwise–"

"Proof? What proof do you need? She handled the goddamned body!" A gasp stashed his apprehension. "The trash man! Gerry! He got her dumpster some time back, I dunno when! Says it got some sort of a chems."

Quinn turned to Tashtego. "That'll be enough for proof, chief! She was the last and there was a witness."

"Okay! I'll arrest her tonight."

"Look at this idiot! Tonight? Just go already! She'd probably on her way to Mexico the moment we start digging Miri out!"

"He's right. We gotta do this now, chief." Jake swung for a look upon his daughter. "That's not Miri anymore," said Quinn, moving her jaw to relieve the pressure pain. "Miri is in heaven, Jake. She's happy. I need you to come with me."

"I wanna stay here!"

"Someone been asking for you."

His knees were shaking from a pounding sensation. He could not steady his steps, on the way back to the car for the snaking road leading to Chevalley Street. The Bookstore on the Left was closed since Lottie's arrest. Today must have been an exception, because the door was ajar. Inside, they saw a square-faced man in a HUGO suit sitting with Charles Reade.

"You're the guy from my arraignment!"

"Christopher Archambeau," he said, holding out a hand which Jake did not take. "I'm a deputy district attorney. And yes, I filed against Ms. Reade that day."

"What d'you want?"

"Take a seat, kid. You want to hear this."

"Peter Renbarger had not been himself the past few weeks," said Archambeau. "And I found out why." He slid out a timestamped photo of a figure in black placing an envelope on a big desk. "My guy's working on to identify this guy. He broke in on the night we had that storm cutting our power. But he didn't know our surveillance runs on a circuit with a backup generator."

"What's in the envelope?"

"Compromising material. The thing is, Renbarger been living in his office, we found out, for over a week. When we asked him, he said he's too busy he can't drive home. That's bullshit, I told him. So when he dropped the case, I looked into surveillance. He living in the office is nothing too serious. Maybe he had a fight with his wife. But this—" he tapped the photo with two fingers. "I confronted him alone. And he broke fessing up he's been taking bribes. The envelope had account figures from his shell company. And this—" again, he gestured at the photo. "—is not the only envelope they sent."

"Son of a bitch!"

"I'm not sure why Renbarger dropped the ball. Maybe he took bribes from the Morgans. Or he was threatened with exposure if he didn't comply."

"It's intimidation, meaning that we can work it out for a new trial," said Quinn. "And we don't have to prove anything. It's clear as day."

"Who was the judge for Amelia's hearing?"

"Same guy."

"Rodeback didn't even check why it's been dropped?" asked Lottie.

Archambeau scratched his thick-haired head. "Who d'you think threatened him? David Morgan? That bitch boy can't even hold a warm spoon!" He told them. "It's Rodeback. I got a lotta dirt on him. He did a lotta things, demanding favors from a lotta people. He's a freaking Nazi with a black robe. I choose the word Nazi for a reason."

"What reason?"

"What else, Mr. Brownfield? You're Jewish. Why should he uphold justice for a dead Jewish girl? To him, probably one less Jew to worry about."

"Oh, my God," breathed Jake.

"But Rodeback dismissed my case."

"Because Ms. Ganderton gave him a good reason not to do so. The argument is solid and see-through it can build Trump's wall."

"And Mexico didn't have to pay her," quipped Charles, cracking a smile. "But how come they have a choice to pick a judge?"

"Hardly a choice," said Archambeau. "Rodeback is a local. He doesn't have any love for David Morgan but he doesn't hate him, that's for sure. He's that bowl they'd bake a cake in. And before the charges were dropped, Rodeback was in Renbarger's office. It all fits."

"How come he drop the charges? We got a video!"

"Amelia's lawyer told our investigators saying Debra has been digitally inserted into the video."

"It's not fucking Deep Fake!" said Jake.

"I know it's not," replied Archambeau. "I ran it with a filmmaker in Chicago. He confirms that can't be Deep Fake. The shadows and lighting were all consistent, too consistent to pass a professional fakery."

"Can we do something?"

"We can and we are. There's only one shot at this."

"Please, don't treat my girl like Renbarger did."

"Nobody in the D.A. office cares for your girl, Mr. Brownfield. I mean no offense but that's the truth. Renbarger left a mess we gotta clean. Wilkins is going for Renbarger's job. I expect Rowe will do the same, and deAlaris gave her resignation letter. They got each other by the balls."

"What about you? What's in it for you?"

"Nothing. I do this or not, I still keep my job," said Archambeau. "I do care about justice. I believe in it. That's why I'm fighting for Miriam. And I'm gonna have Ms. Ganderton here as my legal consultant."

Jake clawed a smile through his hot cheeks. "I thought you can't do that."

"You can't drop a case like that. But it's happened. I don't see why Ms. Ganderton can't sit by my side. But before we go anywhere with Miriam, we gotta know what happened to her body," said Archambeau. "Chief Tashtego is on to it. Eden Morgan was the last to be with Miriam. She musta liquefied her right before the funeral."

"That's gotta be why they looked so scared that day!" said Jake. "Like they shit their pants."

Lottie's incessant knock on the desk was distracting. When they turned, she began. "Were you there the whole time they dug her out?"

"Yeah," said Quinn.

"Was it easy?"

"Uh-huh. Don't need an excavator, if that's what you're asking."

"How easy was it?"

"Where are you going with this?"

"I went to see Eden because of that swastika spraying," said Lottie. "I talked about a new tombstone. And she did replace it. I'm thinking that's when she chemmed the body."

"Could be."

"That's a problem," said Archambeau. "We're assuming on a hunch."

"You have investigators in the D.A. office!"

"I'm not gonna deploy them for this, Mr. Brownfield. Miriam is important. But she's the main course. We need to get through the appetizer first."

"We're going for Rodeback first, Jake," said Quinn.

"Right now we're working with the feds because he'll be collecting favors soon."

"Like what? Sex?"

"Possibly."

"That mofo can find his dick under that belly he got?"

"The Morgans have the money to pay him. I think they're gonna pay for Christie and Sarah too."

"But not for Addison Blount."

"Because she's been poisoned. And she's gonna die from it," replied Archambeau, without emotion. "But if she recovers, she goes straight to court. So, my question is, what will her mother do to stop that?"

"What can she do?"

"That's exactly what I'm thinking. *What* can she do?"

"She mentioned about asking Eden's help."

"Eden would've paid if she really wanted to help. Here we have Cassie Blount. We know she can't pay Rodeback. Not with cash at least. And this is Rodeback, the devil we overlooked for a long time. He's not gonna be sloppy like Renbarger when it comes to hooking up."

Quinn squinted, pondering and weighing. "Can we trust Tashtego?"

"No!" said Lottie.

"This is bigger than us now! Can we trust Tashtego?"

"Depends on what we're trusting him with."

"Is he a crook like Renbarger?"

"Not sure."

"We're not going with Tashtego, Ms. Ganderton."

"Then?"

"I have guys on this already."

Later that night, they came upon another startling turn of events. Tashtego did as he said. His officers spoiled the festooned revelry in the Morgan residence after sundown. And they confronted David, who lied to everyone. "Where is she?" he asked.

"I told you, she's having a stomach bug! She's in the bathroom, probably."

"Take us there now."

"You have a warrant?" asked Frankopan.

"I can arrest a suspect for violating a state law!" said Tashtego, shouting. "Now take us to the fucking broad, or I'm gonna arrest you as well!"

David maintained that pretentious grin, at least until Frankopan backed down with a nod. That was the last straw. And the crumbling pieces stitched together for a wild chase which ended in Errol, next to that brook pouring into Umbagog Lake. McCrain argued about interstate paperwork, because they had no authority in New Hampshire.

His reasoning fell on deaf ears, because they had Eden into the Maine border within the hour. In the questioning room, Eden lashed out. "I don't see what's wrong about visiting my mother! I'm bringing her here for Thanksgiving!"

"You can bring her after you're done here."

"How did you find me anyway?"

Eden avoided attention by paying cash for everything. Or so she thought. Surveillance footage confirmed her stop at Rangeley, where she purchased a cup of hot macchiato with cash. But her membership account in that coffee chain floated a marker for the police to follow. Her tough act did not help during the polygraph test, earning herself another arraignment story in this town.

"We've exhumed Miriam Brownfield for another autopsy." Tashtego told the press. "But we are surprised ourselves to find her in a condition that might have been chemically tampered. I'm splitting a team, to conduct a new investigation for this part. And I hope it'll bring us to justice for Miriam Brownfield."

He took questions from the press and gave confident answers before moving on to talk about other crimes. By then, the news reported about something else perhaps to avoid a drop in viewership.

"What in the fly fuck just happened?" said Terry, laughing. "They're falling just like that!"

"They got what's coming, that is!"

"Damn straight."

"Hope this is over soon," said Jake. "I really can't stand it anymore. Felt like I wanna grab a gun and shoot them all."

"We're winning this, Jake. Don't go down like that."

Jake nodded. "Hey, you still got your home in Utah?"

"Yeah. Been thinking of selling it. Why?"

"Don't. Keep it. We're leaving Farmington soon as this shitshow is over," said Jake. "We're gonna get the fuck outta here. We gonna go far. And we ain't fucking looking back."

26

Tashtego had a lot of things in his mind. He had to thank the media for overplaying this story. For that reason alone, public expectations soared beyond reasonable levels. Now everyone learned that his department had been condemned with budget constraints for many years. Of course, the Governor promised to break bills as long as he delivered a winnable closure before predictably the next election.

But he had to be honest. It was not easy to be the chief right now. There was a steep price to pay. He started this campaign as a clean official, free from being a minion in this puppetry. Now he had mouths to feed and cocks to milk. All for the daughter of his old friend. He made some outcalls, and as usual, the Governor denied his request. To clean his chin, he nudged Archambeau who was a classier hooker.

"We have been careful but we might have missed something," he said, in his phone call. "Miriam has been doused with some sort of acid to speed up her decomposition rate. There was barely a body to work with. We believe this is done when the suspect replaced the gravestone."

"Are you absolutely certain this is chemical, not natural?" asked the Governor.

"Positive, sir."

"Look, I'm about done with your town. It's been a pain in my neck for months! Your chief has no clue. Then your district attorney fucked things up. And what I'm about to say might sound tasteless and unprofessional, and I don't care if it does. But if you fuck this up, you'll be next to drink that acid, you hear me? Use whatever resource you need to get this done and don't fuck this up. You hear me? No more fuck up!"

This plan had no guarantee. Nor the one he had in motion. He held a pen with both hands, spinning as he pondered with a look at the telephone. Then he reached for the receiver, dialing. "This is Christopher Archambeau," he said. "I'm a deputy district attorney for Farmington, and I've been presented the prosecution powers for the murder of Miriam Brownfield. Is this understood?"

"Y-yes, sir."

"Good. Right now, I'm impaling your daughter for murder and accessory to murder," said Archambeau. "If found guilty, and she will be found guilty given the evidence, I will make sure you lose your appeal and she remains behind bars for the rest of her life. Is that understood?"

"Please, Mr. Archambeau. Have mercy on her!"

"I'm not the God. I don't do forgiving. I prosecute, that's what I do. And your daughter is no good to me, according to her medical report."

"She's doing good one day, and she got bad the next. It's been up and down for both of us. So if there's something I can do—"

"There is, Ms. Blount. The man next to you is Richard Halgriffin, an agent for the Bureau. You do what exactly as he says, and I'll charge your daughter for Class B instead of murder and accessory of murder. It's the least I can do, not what she deserves but it's something."

"What's Class B?" asked Cass.

"A criminal law for all assaults committed with deadly weapons."

"And how long will she go in if she's found guilty?"

"*When* she's found guilty, Ms. Blount, she'll serve no more than 10 years."

"N-no! She'll miss college!"

"I can see where your daughter gets her brain," said Archambeau. "This is never a negotiation, Ms. Blount. You do as Agent Halgriffin asks for your daughter's lightened charge. That's the deal."

The phone vibrated against Cassie Blount's ear. She looked to find Archambeau's name in the call log. Right after that, the agent took it away. "Looks like you have a choice to make," said Halgriffin. "What's it gonna be?"

Cass sucked in to help with those pangs in her chest. "We gotta do it," she said. "You'll keep your word?"

"That depends on you," replied Halgriffin. "Give us everything and we'll do the same."

"What do I do?"

"I can't have you in there with listening devices. He's gonna see because with respect, you'll be without clothes," he said. "We gotta go down with the basics. You'll find everything you need in this backpack here." He pointed to a Matein bag on the backseat. "When you're there, the guy will check your phone first just to make sure it's not recording and all. Before doing your thing, you call us, go loudspeaker and we'll mute from our side."

"Do I have to have sex with him?" asked Cass.

"No. Again, depends on how you run things. The sooner we have what we need–"

"What do you need? Just tell me that. I'll keep in mind and bear trap him right there but please, my daughter gets Class B. Not murder."

"She will. You go in there clean like a bashful virgin. You come out the same, meaning you ain't got a clue we're doing this."

"Huh?"

Halgriffin turned with a growl. "You must make him talk about Addison's sentence. He needs to talk about it. Or else he's gonna say he paid you for sex. Or you're his mistress," he said. "This afternoon must be about you buying Addison's sentence by having sex with Rodeback on your own, meaning if you fuck this up, Addison won't get what we promise her – and you *will* have sex with him. Is that understood?"

"Yeah," she breathed. "You prosecute; I prostitute."

"Exactly. Except the fact you're *our* hooker. Don't forget the backpack."

Richard Halgriffin must have balls made of steel. He betrayed no sentiments of empathy or hatred. He walled his face in passivity, fully accepting this was a job to nail this son of a bitch. Nothing more. Nothing less. And Cass was an asset. She got out of that Ford Expedition and returned to that jalopy she bought with her first pay at Dunkin's. She eased on the racketing clutch for a crawling pace along Vienna Road.

At a dirt road to her right, there was a spotter in a heavy-tinted sedan. Another spotter waited on her left before Crowell Pond. She ignored and drove ahead, turning once or twice at those shimmers upon the surface of the sunlit pond.

"Damn you, Addy!" she cursed under a breath.

She had to curse again after her car broke down at the shoulder, just before the last turn. It was a quarter mile push with free brakes. And she arrived Besse Road looking rough with dirt and grease. The heavy haul forced a smelly discharge staining that expensive thong she bought from Wish. And the underside of her breasts was flooding. She knew damn well she cannot meet Rodeback in this condition.

"You fucking idiot. I thought you're at it with him!"

"I know. I know I shouldn't call but I'm a mess right now," said Cass, puffing in heat. "My car ran some trouble. And I have to walk to see him!"

"So, walk!" snapped Halgriffin.

Again, her ear vibrated. "Fuck!" she huffed. "Damn you, Addy!" She took the backpack out of her trunk and set out on the rising trail. Her teeth pressed on one another, fighting the scraping pain in her swollen knees. At one time, she had to sit on the dirt with both legs stretched. Her eyes welled out of agony and anguish. A mild fever was growing as she turned for a house. And she threw herself onto a vacant chair in the open-air porch.

Wiping those tears, she looked around for a car. He was not here yet. She went back to the front door and looked under a pink pot just as told. There, she found a key and went upstairs. The splashes from a showerhead ran across her skin, lumping her dandruff and sweat into a dirty flow toward the whirlpooling drain.

She got out for a towel, slippers and a scream. "JESUS!"

"Afternoon, Baby," said Rodeback, with a rumbling voice. "I'm feelin' durty – why don't we showah togethah."

"Jesus Christ," breathed Cass, disgusted but so low it did not reach across the room. "I'll wait you there."

"Uh. Uh. Uh. What did we talk about?"

Cass shot him a glare, her knuckles popping. "I'll wait you there – Daddy!" she said, sweetly. Fortune did not favor her, because Rodeback fit into that bathtub. His horrible kiss stabbed a distaste down her throat. That unclean tongue swept and grazed over her chapped lips. It took a prayer not to puke into his stinking breath. Those big hands bristled against her bony shoulders, squeezing with thistly sensations.

With a push, she was down to his crotch where a stench singed the hair in her nostrils. She kept her thought to herself and took the meat under those meaty flaps.

Those grasps were tightening. She told him not to pull her hair. But he answered with a light slap on her head. The third slap triggered a gnawing fury that she decided to play along with her wet mouth. It was so innocent at first before she introduced a barbed delicacy with her teeth. And her eyes – those submissive eyes – were killing Rodeback.

When his knees looked rubbery, she winked. That was it. The whale stretched its ugly flaps for the curtain, losing his ability to stand.

"I'm sorry, Daddy!" she said. "I thought you like it!"

"I do, Baby. Just – go easy, yeah?"

Cass swallowed her nausea and said, "sure, Daddy."

"I'm not as young as I once was."

"You don't have to stand. Let's take it to the bed. You can rest there and–" Her voice was husky after she reached his junk. "–I can give you a massage." He took the bait and rumbled out of the bathroom with quaking steps. Just as he sat, Cass went barreling into him for a kiss. She explored the Big Daddy, who seemed to enjoy with closed eyes. That was her chance to probe around the room – for her phone.

Her handbag was at a corner, unzipped and rummaged. Her clothes were piled at a corner in the bathroom. And her honor – whatever was left – was in full display of a man indeed old enough to be her daddy. Just as Halgriffin said, her phone would be the first line. And she found it at a side table next to the bed. She twisted and turned for an aggressive foreplay, lugging herself closer for a swing of a leg.

The phone fell silently onto the carpeted floor. "Daddy," she whispered into his ear. "I gotta pee."

"Now?"

"I really can't hold it."

"Okay. Go! Quickly!"

Her spare tires were proof of her weight history. She always hated that part of her body. No matter the diet – Atkins, military, plant-based, intermittent fasting or the DASH – her waistline remained bulging with a middle-age spread. But this afternoon, the flabs came to her rescue. Her hand was firm over her urethra, an arm holding the phone against her belly. And she ducked as a silly front of holding her bladder.

"Don't close the door."

"No way!"

Those tremors from the bedroom sent chill down her spine. He was coming. Her fingers – so used to the digital ordering monitor – tapped the screen, and right after that she hit the loudspeaker. Rodeback got there when the phone was already safe on her pile of clothes. "You gonna show daddy how a babe tinkle?" That lusty voice traveled to the Expedition, which now waited in between the black sedan and Cass' car.

"Okay, Daddy."

She tried not blushing. "I'm a bit uncomfortable," she moaned.

"It's okay. You doin' good. Just let it go," said Rodeback, smiling as she did her business. "There we go. See, it's not that bad. Nice and easy. Keep at it. Yes. Now, lemme clean it up." Her feigned eyes widened after he bowed for a lick in the area.

And he carried her back to the bed.

"Daddy, you have a big dick, you know that?"

"You want it in you?"

"If you promise we can do this again maybe tomorrow?"

Rodeback smiled. "You like me, don't you?"

"What's there not to like, Daddy?"

"Okay, baby. We dance again. Now, where were we?"

Cass grabbed his sad-looking, creasing pouch, letting her tongue do all the *hard* work. "Mmm." That hum delighted the fat bastard, still with the same fucking smile. "Daddy," she said.

"Yeah, Baby."

"My mouth is hungry."

"You're already having it."

"Not this mouth," said Cass, wagging his tongue. "The *other* mouth."

"Ooh. Well, what d'ya waiting for?"

"Your okay for my daughter?"

Rodeback's horny smirk curled into a twisted expression that he was normally known for. He sat up straight and wrapped Cass into his hairy chest. They lied abed for a light kiss. And then he said, "don't worry, Ms. Blount," he said. "I'll let Addy go. I know how difficult it's been for you, with that fucking Jew at your throat. But I'll do a convincing release. Your daughter will get out of that court with a clean record. It'll be like it never happened."

"You promise, Daddy?"

"I promise, Baby. If you promise one thing?"

"What is it, Daddy?"

"Today I'll open your door," said Rodeback. "Tomorrow I'll open Addy's door? Then one day, I'll open *Cassady*'s door together? What d'you say, *Bay-Bee*?"

A door opened, all right. Those heavy footsteps across the wooden stairs announced the arrival of federal agents in blue. They converged upon the bed, guns-blazing for which Cass screamed at the top of her lungs. "Shut the fuck up! Shut it now!" Halgriffin punched her in the face and then brandished his badge to the great white elephant in the room. "Gregory Rodeback, you're under arrest for criminal conspiracy," he said, completing the Miranda rights. "You have ten seconds to get dressed. We are authorized to use extreme force should you wish not to comply."

Rodeback had a dirty, defeated look upon everyone. He held a long glance on Cass, who sat covering her body and sobbing. Then he complied with the federal agents and was taken into the Expedition. "I'll have your job for this!" said Rodeback.

"Or I'll have yours," replied Halgriffin.

"You don't have anything on me!"

"Trust me, Greg. The last place I wanna be is anywhere on you."

Cass had done a good job to tap into Rodeback's conspiracy. And the reward was a blanket to cover her nudity. And the prosecutor came to her home later, with a suitcase carrying a document. "This is an agreement to our understanding," he said. "Your daughter will be given leniency of Class B, pending her testimony at court."

"She still gotta testify for this?"

"Addison has to testify against Amelia when she's healthy again," said Archambeau. "It's one part of the process."

"One part?"

"The other part is that you will testify against Gregory Rodeback during his trial."

"Wait, what? I didn't agree to this!"

Archambeau pretended he did not hear. "After you sign it, I will delay her arraignment process and charge as I promised. And we'll try going for a six-year sentence, three in prison three in suspension." After Cass signed the document, he added. "This is a non-disclosure agreement. You'll say and write nothing. The media will be told what they will be told. You will not approach any reporter for anything regarding this operation we did."

"But I will have to testify against Rodeback! They'll find out I'm the one he slept with."

"You will testify through a written testimony, anonymous and private given to you before the day of trial."

"What if he said he's in a relationship with me?"

"You sue him for defamation."

Cass was in no way a master of law. But she saw through his bluff. The odds for her identity to remain a court secret was a hill to climb. Alone in the living room, where it fell apart, she came to a realization. She was not a victim of rape or sexual assault. She was made an accessory of a conspiracy to blot another conspiracy, though protected behind a systemic filament at the Feds' mercy and leisure.

She delivered Rodeback at the cost of her moral image, now forever branded as the judge's hooker. But at the very least, Addison would be off the hook.

The motherfuckers promised that.

27

Halgriffin kept the corrupt judge away from Tashtego's reach. He did not want the media to catch a whiff of his investigation, at least until after this interrogation. Rodeback was wincing in this dark, isolated room. The digital recorder ran a count-up, guzzling their conversation as future evidence. "Rodeback and Renbarger. Two coins from the same fuckbowl."

Rodeback smirked. "It was consensual!"

"Sure it was," said Halgriffin. "I take it she's your girlfriend?"

"She is!"

"Just out with it. Where did you meet her first?"

"Rome."

"Like in Italy?"

"No," said Rodeback. "It's a town twenty minutes from here."

"Hmm. Funny because she said she saw you first here in Farmington."

"She's lying!"

"Or you're lying."

"I'm a judge!"

"Gonna have to take that as a yes," said Halgriffin. "Isn't it a conflict of interest to bang a woman whose daughter will be standing trial for murder?"

"She's not the one charged with murder."

"Greg, just come clean. What were you doing there?"

Rodeback presented a bastardized version of his relationship with Cassie Blount. It was outlined to perfection, almost scripted for good measure. He had known Cassie for many years and banged each other until their brains started oozing out of their ears. She was his secret cherry topping a cupcake that had gone vanilla over decades of marriage. And he admitted to have secret frosting, secret marshmallows and secret whipped cream.

But his version was shot to pieces, after Halgriffin told him, "right now I want to set things straight. That woman is a mole working for us," he said. "And you don't want to go to prison for someone who bought her daughter court leniency by calling you Daddy."

"Fuck!"

"Here's the rundown, Greg. We're investigating as a case of murder and conspiracy now," said Halgriffin. "A suspect used a lot of acid on Miriam. Her body is now tangling up like a goddamned zombie. Unless you wanna get pinned for that, do start telling me the truth about your involvement! I already know what you're gaining by testing Baby Blount's depth. So let's start with the twenty grand in your account!"

"Twenty grand? What you talkin' about?"

"I have your bank statement."

"You have a warrant for it?" exclaimed Rodeback.

"We have your wife."

Rodeback went whiter. "Th-that was for my heart. David is my doctor."

"My guys are checking David's medical files. You're telling me, if I make a call, they'll confirm you're his heart patient?" Halgriffin nodded when Rodeback stiffened into silence. "Last chance, Tubby. You tell me who's in it with you. Every name. Everyone. And I'll recommend a lighter sentence."

"I know how it works. I'm a fucking judge."

"No. You were the judge who fucks. There's a difference." Rodeback swung onto the table and opened his hands as a gesture. "Good. Now that we have an understanding, let's begin. What is that twenty grand for?"

"Amelia Morgan,"

"Good. That's easy, right? Just the Morgan?"

"Just the Morgan. I'm gonna be meeting the other girls' moms after Cassie Blount."

"They are the other secret toppings you got on your cupcake of a wife."

"Y-yes."

"You didn't try Eden Morgan?"

"They're too rich," said Rodeback. "The rest don't carry a damn tune. So, they sell themselves."

"How long have you been doing this?"

"What d'you mean?"

"You decide in their favor. They decide in yours. How many cases am I looking at? Cases that shoulda been declared mistrials for perverted justice?"

"A lot. I dunno."

"You presided over thirty murder cases. You tellin' me your judgment depends on what your dick said?" Halgriffin exploded. "D'you realize how many killers got free because of you?"

"I know," said Rodeback. "I just – I know that."

"Okay. So, who's on this with you? Other than the Morgans, Hayes, Smiths?"

"Renbarger. I told him to stand down."

"You fucked him too?"

"No!"

"What about Charlotte Reade?"

"I liked her," said Rodeback. "But she has a good lawyer. That moron Renbarger lost to a woman!"

"Who else?"

"No one else," said Rodeback, shaking his head. Halgriffin made a bolting move that in the next second, there was a Glock cocked at Rodeback's head. "McCrain! McCrain! He's on it too!"

"Deputy Paxton McCrain?"

"Yes! Yes! Paxton McCrain!"

The room was steaming. "Start talking!"

"He wanna be the Chief of Police. He thinks the Democrats did something, giving the job to Tashtego. He's the one planting the fake steam iron in the Reade's house. I told that fucker to burn a body. But he did it on a fucking pig! That's all. He just wanted Tashtego's place. That's all."

Halgriffin scowled, in horrors. "You're telling me, the Reade trial is because of McCrain wanna be chief?"

"Yes, sir."

Halgriffin got up for the next room, sitting with a cigarette poking in between his teeth. The embers hissed as he breathed to ruminate about the whole thing. And by evening, Franklin County was wobbling into the chasm of a humongous inquiry, perhaps the largest ever seen in the State of Maine with cans after cans of worms. And Jake had to read the whole lot of it from newspapers.

"This is a big problem," said Quinn. "Oh, fuck, this is a big problem. We may have to fight for Froggie again!"

"What? You told me it's with prejudice!"

"His trials will be declared mistrials!" Lottie's fate depended on this inquiry, which would take months, probably years. Because officials had to assess the impairment of each trial. And there were just many, because so many people began spilling the tea about their run-in with the law under Rodeback's dictatorial capacity.

A man named John Billett left New Sharon after being jailed for a crime he did not commit. His wife was still traumatized over the repeated searches, all without warrant. The Billets (and almost everyone) accused Gregory Rodeback as the main cancer behind this corruption. Halgriffin lauded Jake's bulldogged effort for the world to hear. "This is an amazing recovery on the road of justice," he said. "It's all because of Miriam Brownfield. If not for this poor, innocent soul, none of this will be exposed. I was sent here to investigate a poor execution of the law. But what I uncovered was the rotting cause of it.

"I cannot express how Jacob Brownfield feel. To have a daughter slaughtered and her murderers almost got away. This misconduct is in simple words crazy. We will keep investigating but for now, how low has the mighty fallen."

Jake watched the news with satisfaction. Not just that, he enjoyed seeing a shot of the police swinging David Morgan to the ground. Amelia was there, shaking in front of cameras. The police arrested Christie and Deborah at school, meeting their handcuffed parents in jail. Tashtego was told to stand down from departmental powers. But Halgriffin persuaded him to continue working in the station under his authority.

"Just for the time being," he said. "You know how politics work."

The national news ran about Farmington over and over again. Their features quelled the Morgan maniacs into shame. Some of those crazy enough to attack Jake came back apologizing and were told to fuck off. That afternoon, he used a public photo of Miriam's grave for a written content. He reproved everyone he could think of, telling nothing but the truth in which David was mentioned 48 times.

That content rode Lottie's momentum, reaching 132,000 timelines within a day. Prominent pages and news outlets shared that post to further their reporting. His appetite returned with vengeance. He devoured three chicken legs over mountainous dollops of mashed potatoes and ratatouilles. And right in between, his phone rang out from an unknown caller.

"Am I speaking to Mr. Brownfield?"

"Yes. This is Jacob Brownfield."

"Oh, hello, sir. My name is Pam Kearns," the caller said. "I'm a junior assistant to Mr. Andy Rewells, the editor-in-chief of Paxington Publishing."

"Okay?"

"I'm calling to inquire if you're available for an interview."

"What you wanna write a book about me?" asked Jake, stirring everyone.

"We've already commissioned a ghostwriter on your behalf, Mr. Brownfield."

Jake put down his fork. "Wait, this is serious?"

"Of course, sir. Can you give me your contact information? I'll send our offers." She called him back after emailing the details. "Okay, so right now, we're publishing this after the murder trial. I'm authorized to offer you one hundred grand in advance."

Jake shot up, his knees hitting the table. "Son of a—" he wheezed, limping out of there. "When are you guys coming?"

"I'll stay in touch, Mr. Brownfield."

His face flushed with excitement and vigor. The grass suddenly looked greener. Those clouds hanging under an azure-white sky were waving. More phone calls flooded. Literary agents were racing to represent him for the best publishing deal; he invited them for negotiations. Book deals turned into documentary offers and live show invitations.

"Damn, Jake. If you ever get a movie, get me a cameo!"

Jake googled about Paxington Publishing. "It's in Salt Lake City," he said. Spoons and forks hung in between plates and mouths. Ruth was about to speak, when a yellow cab pulled by the street for a woman with a luggage.

"Rachel?" said Jake.

The ex-wife embraced him with a kiss upon the cheek. "How are you, Jake?" said Rachel.

"Where's Craig?"

Rachel gave a sad smile. "We broke up."

Jake threw his brows up. "Why?"

"I think I owe the family an apology."

"You *think*?"

"I never wanted to go back. I wanna stay for the funeral. But he insisted. When we got home, it just didn't work out."

"Where's this coming from? It's not that I don't know you! Why come here even? I left you a house!"

Rachel had no answer.

"I think it's best you go, Rachel," said Ruth.

"Jake, I know you're with that woman. And I respect that."

"That *woman*'s name is Charlotte."

"Yeah, her. I respect your relationship," said Rachel. "I'm only here for Miriam, Jake." Tears were spilling from her eyes. "For God's sake, let me be here! I heard everything! The exhuming! The chemicals! Everything! Just please, I'm begging you! Let me be here!"

Lottie's voice came from upstairs. "It's all right. You can stay," she said. "C'mon, Jake. Just for a while."

Jake shook his head. "You're leaving after the trial."

"Thank you. Thank you. Oh, God! Thank you!"

He joined Lottie in the bedroom for a massage. "I can't believe she's here. She left us high and dry. And now I'm getting these deals – she shows up."

"She's a moron, Jake. But she's the mother."

"The bitch cheated on me. She left me for Craig. Now she left that Craig."

"Ow! Easy on the leg!"

"Sorry."

"Like I said, she's a moron."

Rodeback's fall from grace was too important not to be on primetime. The presenters started with opinion pieces about corruption. "If Gregory Rodeback is a hurricane, I'll name him a Category Five," said an analyst. "What he did proves what the women movements have been saying."

"I'd like to point out a correlation in this whole thing. Here we're seeing sex solicitation," said another analyst. "But there are some other red lines. Administrative misconduct from Paxton McCrain and sexual assault from Roger Gauthier. It's a freak avalanche. Rodeback and McCrain both were anti-Semitic and xenophobic. And this McCrain have three fake accounts – Bill Nickelworth, Tom Edrington and Eddy Kline."

McCrain went far with these masks, that he trolled a family member of a shooting victim. "Eloise Hill started taking antidepressants because of him."

They highlighted his chronic inclination to White supremacism. Nickelworth was seen congratulating a mosque stabber. Those against his opinion were branded as *Muslimbeciles* and traitors to the Union. And yes, he hated that same Union because to him the truest form of freedom died when the Confederacy lost in 1865. Upon a closer look, Jake remembered when he was being clung, stung, flung, wrung and hung. There was a comment from a certain father of three, named Bill Nickelworth who said, "*you, your mom, your dad, your bitch girl – three done, one left. Fuck y'all.*"

It was Paxton McCrain, surfacing as Eddy Kline after a monthlong suspension. "He wanted an open shooting on the Indy Pride Festival," said the presenting analyst.

And this was only the beginning of a very long story from 2011. "This guy is a maniac!" said Lottie.

Done with McCrain, the presenter returned to Rodeback. "I'm of the opinion he's checking social media to determine his verdict." Because Rodeback exacted a maximum sentence toward White people who were of the LGBTQ+ community. "To name a few, Brett Mattins, Cheryl Chandler and Marcus Ophright are transgenders. Their sentencings were maximum. Ophright got a heavy-handed sentence, despite a stainless traffic record. Traffic record! I mean, how did we overlook this? How is this remotely possible?

"We're reaching Miss Chandler for more comments. But another SGM woman in Gilbert Avenue – doesn't wish to be named – shared to us about being harassed and vandalized just because she made a gender change. And Rodeback dismissed the harassment case. Her appeals went on deaf ears, before she found herself in a dumpster stripped and beaten half to death."

"It's a question of public safety in Farmington. Whether it is safe to walk in the streets again."

"With a corrupt in the law enforcement, it is not. I don't doubt we will know more about this in the coming weeks. But in my view, Farmington should not be a focal point. I've been there. I've known some people. It's an amazing community, truth be told.

"This is not about the people. This is about two or more public servants misusing their power. This is about hatred. Once we uproot these weeds, we'll see a brighter, better not only Farmington – but the whole Franklin County itself. The only questions right now, is McCrain alone? Is there any more McCrain out there in Avon, Carthage, Chesterville, Industry all the way to Wilton and the five plantations?"

The detailed assessment was a prologue to start about the Darlings. The analysts were of the opinion their mothers were mere chips of a putrescent iceberg. Because more women came out of the closet about reduced bails and shortened sentences, in exchange of sexual favors.

Lottie stared from the couch, unblinking. "I coulda been one of them," she said. "Can you believe this is happening?"

"I know," said Quinn, eating peanuts on the floor. "Not the first time I saved your pussy."

Lottie turned for a kick to her shoulder. "Fuckattahea!"

"Guys, you guys sure we're safe here? I mean, even the Governor gets an inquiry for pushing the funeral," said Terry. "They might hire some mafia to rub us out for this mess."

"They killed Miri. Why should we be afraid?" Lottie put a hand on her belly. "We didn't do anything wrong."

"He's right, though. We can't be too sure. How are we on the Morgan case?"

"Can't share that, Jake," said Quinn. "We're keeping it tight. But all I can say, we're doing good. I'm getting calls from LA, Miami, Seattle, Portland – you name it. Since I handed Renbarger's ass, I been popular."

"Portland is just two hours from here."

"Err. Portland in Oregon, Jake."

"Oh. You're not thinking of going. Are you, Queenie?"

"I can't," said Quinn. "Christopher been cooking something up to have me in the prosecution again."

"That's awesome!"

"Telling you, this state's gone crazy. But we're starting all over again, and we just got the arraignment part done. No plea bargaining. And they're gonna be tried as adult."

"Meaning they get the chair?" asked Ruth.

"No chair here, Ruth. Life imprisonment for Amelia."

"What about the rest of them?"

Quinn sighed. "I dunno. They'll get a reduced sentence, I'd say."

"Wait, what?"

"To prove a murder, you need an intent or you gotta prove that homicide was committed so brashly," said Quinn. "We can do both. But murder has its degrees. Right now Amelia is done for. First degree. There's intent. They premeditated, yes. But when it comes to executing that premeditation, I'm very sure the Darlings will abandon ship and blame it all on Amelia."

"And we're allowing them?"

"No," said Quinn. "We're prosecuting Morgan, Hayes and Smith for first degree."

"And Addison?"

"Her mom helped the prosecution by fucking Rodeback. Don't say that in public! The State promised her Class B for Addison. Less than ten years," said Quinn. "The justice system isn't perfect. You know it. I know it. But we have one bullet straight to Amelia. If you ask me, it's worth it to clip a dying girl out of the picture. Besides, Christopher been saying you got 'em through her phone. That's something, right?"

"We got 'em 'cause of Spud, Quinn. He's the one. Damn he got Rodeback too, I'd say."

Lottie raised a finger. "You been on and off about your old cases," she told Quinn. "But this is the first time you say someone's done for. What's going on?"

"Everyone been getting angry they're leaving bad Google reviews on Frankopan's law firm. Mark just unpublished his Facebook page to stop the hate comments."

"Hope he backs out!"

"You just ruined the surprise."

"What, he is?"

"Yep. He's walking out," said Quinn. "The Morgans are going to court with no lawyer and no favorite judge. Miriam is getting justice."

"We're winning this!" said Ruth.

"They're sitting ducks. But they can still duck outta this."

"How?"

"I'm willing to bet my wedding ring they're gonna plea for insanity," said Quinn. "That if all else fails."

"Queenie, you don't have a wedding ring."

"Idiot, that's the point," replied Quinn. "What I'm saying is, they can still walk. If Amelia gets her insanity plea, they'll institutionalize her and wait for another corrupt to suddenly declare she's fine and she walks, and all is fucking forgiven!"

28

The hospital staff were running around the clock to save Addison Blount. The girl had been through an eleven-hour liver transplantation, after acquiring a matching organ from a donor. The rocky waters calmed right after a successful surgery, before three seizure bouts ambushed the battlefield of high fever and low blood sugar. Cass was called late at night. When she arrived, the head doctor rushed to remove the liver and declared the time. Addison's death was a frustrating conclusion, especially for her wailing mother who did not realize Archambeau's instrument walking across with an icebox.

It was another strike upon McCrain, who would be held culpable for this tragedy.

The State was tilting toward a hopeful bid to restore the system. Jake cannot be happier, after the hearing. "December Four," said Quinn. "Judge Paul Avery will preside in the trial. He's been awesome in the hearing. Clean record. Then again, so was Rodeback."

Paul Avery was nothing like that pigheaded swine. Rodeback was morbidly obese with a breath of processed cheese. If the rumor was true, his groin smelled like musty fungus. But Avery had a straight posture with a scholarly look. And he did not have to squeeze to get behind the bench.

The tables had turned. Quinn secured an access to assist Archambeau in this fight. They were positioned in the prosecuting side, where next to them was shockingly Mark Frankopan. The barrel-chested lawyer kept his nose over papers and his glass of water.

Jacob Brownfield brought the whole clan to the courtroom. They occupied a long bench, with Uncle Obie at an end giving no space for Rachel. He dropped by at dawn to be there for them and ditched the clichéd garment for a classic-cut suit. Patience was thinning in this airy hall. Those mumbles and mutters shadowed an overpowering temptation that was nothing but animosity. And when the Darlings were brought in handcuffs, everyone in this eight-juror battleground was hissing.

Christie Hayes had an obvious bump in an eye. Tear-tracks painted a watery path on Deborah Smith. And the devil in flesh did not have that moping expression. There was a smile at the precipice of her lips, almost taunting the spectators. These defendants were to be tried as adults. With their parents taken out of context pending hearings of their own, they had to stand their ground themselves. And Amelia was enjoying it.

"This murder has a trial of its own, upon Farmington, upon Franklin County, upon the State of Maine," said Judge Avery. "I am sure we will overcome this stain. Personally speaking, I wish all of you luck today. And may God judge us fairly."

"Amen," said Jake, among the echoes.

Avery read the case, ending with, "how do the defendants plea?"

Frankopan was scowling. "Not guilty, sir."

The attendance turned into a jungle. "Order," said Avery, without pounding. "I've been authorized to allow leniency to all defendants – provided there is honesty." Quinn's face changed. "So I ask you again–"

"Objection, your Honor. We've not been counsel–"

Avery raised a hand. "I ask you again," he said. "How do the defendants plea?"

"Not guilty, sir."

"Very well," said Avery, reproachfully. "Will the prosecuting team make an opening statement?"

Those perfunctory glances mapped across the courtroom for Archambeau. "Your Honor, for months Miriam Brownfield gets mentioned in every corner of this god-green Earth. Some countries take greater interest, compared to the rest. This is normal. What is abnormal however is the impact on our country, particularly this state – the scorn, the criticism, the insult – simply because one girl led a group in the murder of another."

"Objection, your Honor. Speculation."

"It is an opening statement, Mr. Frankopan."

The space allowed Archambeau to repeat his statement, more seditiously. "Miriam Brownfield left a loving father and a coming half-sibling. About this half-sibling, let me remind everyone in this room today – this unborn baby has been the forefront of mockery by my own office, as if he or she is a taint proving Charlotte Reade's involvement behind Miriam's murder."

Upon completing the summary of the previous hearing, Frankopan objected again to no avail. "You may continue, prosecutor," said Avery.

"The charges against Amelia Morgan, Christie Hayes and Deborah Smith are incomplete without walking back the painful details," said Archambeau. "Miriam was falsely accused to have stolen Amelia's iPhone. And she was tortured in a form of a military-style interrogation. It's uhh – excuse my language – *damn if I do, damn if I don't* situation. Admit, they burn her out of anger. Deny, they burn to have her admitting it. And she admitted all right but since she wasn't the thief, she was unable to tell them where the phone is."

After Archambeau sat, the judge turned to Frankopan. "Would the defendant make an opening statement?"

Frankopan conjured another round of murmurs. "No, your Honor. We won't." And the three girls turned to him in unison.

"What the hell?" said Jake, pretty much the thought of everyone in there.

Everyone except the prosecution. It was Quinn's turn. "Your Honor, I'd like to call the third defendant to the stand – Ms. Smith," she said right away. As soon as Debra swore, Quinn made her first move. "Ms. Smith. How are you feeling?"

Debra raised her shoulders. "I dunno."

"Are you afraid, Ms. Smith?"

"N-no. I'm not."

"Why are you sweating when you say that?"

Debra paused. "I d-dunno. I guess I am afraid."

"What are you afraid of?"

"It's my first time taking this stand."

"Isn't it your first time murdering someone?"

"I didn't murder anyone."

"Then could you please explain to us who the person in this video is?" A footage appeared on the flat screen. "Who is that person, Ms. Smith?"

Debra turned to Frankopan, who stared right back into her.

"The prosecutor asked you a question," said Avery.

Frankopan mouthed. "Look."

She obeyed. "It's Deep Fake," said Debra.

"I already have a team of experts analyzing the authenticity of this video. You sure you wanna go down that road, Ms. Smith?"

Debra did not move. "What do you want me to do?"

"Do you recognize that girl in the screen?"

"N-no."

"You don't recognize her? Hmm. How many times you look at the mirror?" Debra raised her shoulders. "How many times today?"

"Once. Twice."

"Twice. Surely you can see yourself, unless if you're a vampire," said Quinn, well received among the crowd. "Now can you see yourself in that screen?" Debra nodded. "You've sworn to the court you'll tell the truth. Are you saying that's you in the screen? Do tell us, before I charge you for perjury!"

"What's a perjury?" she breathed, her eyes glistening.

"Lying at court. You said you don't know – but clearly you do know. You will look at the screen again – and you will tell us who that person is!"

Debra sniffled. "That person is me."

"We didn't hear you."

"I'm that person," she said, wide-eyed upon the hostile reaction at court.

"Order! Order!"

Quinn nodded, walking around. "You admit you're the person holding poor Miriam down," she said. "Who else is there?"

A moment of doubt hung, surrounded with stifled susurrus as everyone leaned to listen. Frankopan sat unmoved; from the corner of his eye, he saw his clients on edge. "Amelia Morgan, Addison Blount and Christie Hayes," she said.

"All those persons are here?"

"N-no. Addison died."

"You three were released on the same day. What happened to Ms. Blount?"

"I dunno. I was asleep."

"We have footage of her poisoning," replied Quinn, striking her with an intense look. "Do you want to correct your statement?"

"Okay. This is what happened – Amelia said something to her. I don't remember. It was just too fast. And then a police officer came, giving her something. Like water. When she drank it, she complained of a stomach ache for about an hour."

"Anyone helped her?"

"Nobody did."

"Do you recognize that policeman?" Debra nodded. And Quinn produced the official portrait of Robert Tashtego. "Is this the one?"

"N-no. That's the chief. I think it's his deputy."

"Thank you, Miss Smith."

Frankopan then got up. "Ms. Smith. You're saying Deputy McCrain poisoned your friend?"

"Addy's not my friend anymore."

"But McCrain did poison her?"

"Y-yes."

"That was your plan all along? Kill Ms. Blount?"

"Nossir."

"What about Miriam? Did you kill her?"

"Nossir! Christie and I kept telling Amelia to stop!" And so, it happened as predicted. "We thought we're playing the hard ball, like we used to do with the sling."

"The sling, Ms. Smith?"

Debra bit her lips. "It's just a silly game."

"Care to tell the court?"

"It's when one of us gets outta line. We always give it to Addy," she said. "One of us will hold up her skirt. She'll have to spread her legs. Amelia will whip her lady bits."

"What the fuck!" exclaimed a man.

"Order!"

"What happens afterward?"

"If she screams, we'll repeat. That's what we thought when we're doing at Miriam."

"Did you sling her too?"

Debra looked stunned. "Uhh. Yeah."

"You little bitch!" hissed Jake.

"Mr. Brownfield – keep order," said Avery. "I understand how difficult this must be for you. Please, don't push me. I don't wanna ask you out."

"After you sling – after those painful burning, what did you learn about Miriam?"

"Miriam didn't take her phone. That's the truth. We kept saying. But Amelia won't listen. I was slung just because I told her to stop."

Jake could not speak for the others. His eyes kept bouncing between the defendants. Even from behind, he noted the furious lines upon Amelia's jittering jaw. The next was Christie Hayes, who confirmed Debra's testimony. Amelia's role in this murder was larger than the rest. "I can't stand Amelia beating Dora," said Christie. "But I swear I wasn't the first to accuse Miriam."

"Who else did?"

"Naomi Moulin. Amelia showed us the text."

"No further question, your Honor."

Archambeau lunged into action. "Ms. Hayes, what is the consequences for lying at court?"

"I uh-no."

"Imprisonment. And should you be found guilty of murder, it'll add to your sentence. You'll get more years."

"Okay."

"So again, Naomi Moulin accused Miriam?"

"She's the first to accuse Miriam. I didn't want Miriam dead. I swear to God," said Christie. "I'm so sorry. Mr. Brownfield. I don't think what I did is just a mistake. I know the difference between a mistake and a crime." Christie stopped for a drink. "I wish I can go back and stop myself."

Jake eyed at her icily, diminishing when Archambeau continued. "Your Honor, this Ms. Moulin is with us today at court. I'd like to call her as my next witness."

"Proceed."

Behind the clumps of people sitting tightly together, a girl stood upon the insistence from her father. Naomi hesitated for a moment. Then flanked by two officers, she made her way to the stand. "Ms. Moulin. This is not an arrest," said Archambeau. "You have nothing to fear. I believe you know the murdered victim?"

"Yessir. She's a–" Jake noted her father's nod. "She wasn't close to me. I heard her talking about the iPhone."

"What did she say?"

"Something about the iPhone."

"So, you're not sure yourself?"

"Not too sure. But I did hear iPhone."

"How did you come to that conclusion that she took the phone?"

With both brows and shoulders raised, she said in a deadpan manner. "She's a Jew?" And the seething crowd threw a rancor that took 15 minutes to calm. "I didn't mean it like that."

"No further question, your Honor."

Frankopan shook his head.

"Very well. Get off the stand, kid," said Avery. "Get off the stand before I have your tongue scrubbed with your own foot."

"Even Jesus can't fix that family!"

A dark cloud covered the sun, dimming the courtroom when Amelia Morgan walked to the stand. The eyes followed her from the moment she got up to raise her hand for an oath. It was a dramatic theme for their imaginations, too superstitious in reality especially with a foreboded tiding involving Quinn. She got up, putting the papers together on her side of the desk. The chair scraped backward. Her premium soles clopped on the floor, making her approach to the rosary window where she was swimming with light as sunshine made a sudden permeation.

"Ms. Morgan, you are accused of murder by not only the State, also two defendants among your own," she said. "Yet your lawyer began the plea with not guilty. Tell me, what am I to make of this?"

"I'm not guilty. I am the victim here!"

"Correct me – how is it you're the victim?" said Quinn.

"I didn't appear in that video!"

"But you talked about it on your Darling group."

"Just kids talk. That doesn't mean I did it."

Her sole expression from then on was to look at her thighs, as questions flailed from both camps. Saying nothing helped during the arrests. In this courtroom, she was shaking. "Your Honor, in that video, we could see that Miriam was undressed," said Quinn. "It's a footage of a naked minor, a tremendous felony which the defendant's parents should be questioned so we may ascertain their knowledge about the matter."

Amelia took a while to process that statement. "No! Please, my father doesn't know!"

"Then help him, Amelia. Help your mommy and daddy. Start by explaining why you're accused by Darling Debra and Darling Christie!"

Amelia's eyes darkened. "Alright. Alright," she breathed. "I wasn't in the video. Because I wasn't there!"

"Your Honor, I move in motion of perjury!"

"Young lady – if you're found guilty of lying, you can get five years. I suggest you not do this."

That was the moment. Amelia no longer flaunted her elation. She was wincing. "Say something!" she mouthed. But Frankopan turned away.

Quinn crouched to be at eye level. "Did you torture Miriam Brownfield to death?" A brief silence later, she slammed the flat surface of the stand with a full-voiced roar. "DID YOU TORTURE MIRIAM BROWNFIELD TO DEATH?"

"I did! I did! I tortured her! There!"

The rest was history. The murderer's walk was a reduced sashay, almost as if she was sure to get out of jail with a card. Now Amelia Morgan quailed into accepting her fate. "Start from the beginning," said Quinn. "What happened that morning at school? What happened on August Twenty-One?"

That career-ending Wednesday began when school security Pat Wilson had to deal with another student brawl. Dora was jumped again, this time by Addison for an unintended shoulder bump. With Pat out of the picture, Amelia had ample time to stop the surveillance in the security room. "I know how to do it," she said. "I saw on YouTube. It's not too hard."

"How did you get Miri out of her class?"

"I got Addy for that. The class hasn't started. So, it's easy." Amelia, Christie and Debra were waiting at the garden behind William King Block. "The school cleaners grow some things there. But it's just us that time. They were blowing leaves someplace else."

"Keep going."

"Miriam asked a lot on her way. I asked if she took my phone." Miriam denied any involvement. "I kinda believe what Naomi said. Miriam came here, and I lost my phone. She's using that ugly Xiaomi. So what'm I s'pose to think?"

"And then you jumped on her?"

Amelia nodded. "Christie should have hit her in the head." But the baseball bat swung overhead with a blinking whoosh. Addy blocked Miri's escape, causing her to tumble aground where they began trampling her. "She did not go back. We were scared when she leaped over the wall – out of the school."

"Where is this exactly?"

"There's an open field outside," said Amelia, of the meadow between Mount View and Whittier. "She tried calling people. We chased after her. She kicked a rock and went down face-first."

A small commotion stopped her. A woman had to excuse herself, getting too emotional at that point. That was when

Quinn saw Jake in a trance with his mouth dropped. Those long tears were already drenching his collar. "Proceed, your Honor?" said Quinn.

Avery nodded.

"Move on from the fight. I wanna know how this becomes a felony."

That fall disoriented Miriam, something so pivotal for them. What happened between the open field and funeral home however was a shocking story. "We dragged her back and tied her, taped her mouth." Amelia locked the empty storeroom, until that evening. "I took my mom's Chrysler."

"You can drive?" said Quinn, calmly but with a hint of surprise.

"Grandpa taught me. That's how we took her out of the school."

"Did she fight back?"

"Yeah. We softened her up with pepper spray."

There was a whisper in the air. "Jesus."

"Where did you get a pepper spray?"

"I can't remember. I had it all along."

Quinn shook her head. "You took her to the funeral home, where you tortured her. And it was all because of a damn iPhone?"

"She admitted she took it!"

"And did she tell you where she had it?"

"No. She kept saying here and there. Everything she said wasn't right. That's what got me mad."

"Wasn't it so clear that she just wanted you to stop burning her?"

"She shoulda tell me the truth!"

"The truth which she did not take your phone, you rich idiot!" said Quinn. Amelia was taken aback. "What else did she say?"

"Nothing."

"That's not true!" yelled Christie.

"It is!"

"Order!"

"Not true!"

"Enough there!" said Avery. "Mr. Frankopan, you might wanna rein your own client there!"

"Not going to jail for perjury!" screamed Christie. "Miriam begged us to take her to her daddy! She promised she'll lie if the cops asked – as long as we take her to the Mr. Brownfield!"

That was the straw. Amelia's hands smacked her own face, before the stuttering sobs stung their ears. "That's not true!" said Amelia.

"You animal!"

"Liar!"

"Lying bitch!"

Paul Avery's voice boomed across the courtroom. "Keep order in my trial!" He was on his feet. "Keep order now!" After the last of the outcry dissipated, he turned to Quinn. "Continue."

"Let's just say you're telling us the truth," said Quinn. "The problem right now is, Miriam died. When did your parents get involved? Is it before or after she died?"

"Before she died."

"Keep going."

"Miriam was dying," said Amelia, softly. "We know that. She wasn't breathing too good. There was a scary sound coming from her mouth and nose and all. She had no voice anymore. And there's this something like a pus coming out of her butthole."

Quinn found a bit of difficulty to keep her voice calm. "Aren't you forgetting something in this story?"

"N-no."

"Something like turnip?"

Amelia's eyes ran widely as Christie retracted. "Yes! Turnips! It was *her* idea. She brought 'em to the morgue."

"How many Christie brought?"

"I dunno. A lot."

"How many you put in her?"

"I didn't put in her!"

"How many Debra put in her?"

"Neither did Debra."

Quinn nodded. "How many Christie put in her?"

"EVERY SINGLE ONE SHE GOT!" That was true, on the count that Christie not contesting. "IN HER BUTTHOLE! IN HER LADY BITS!"

The commotion in the benches hit the pause button, as people went to console Miriam's family. Uncle Obie took Jake into his arms, glowering toward the stand. "Who first saw Miriam?" asked Quinn. "Dr. Morgan or Mrs. Morgan?"

"My mom."

"How did Mrs. Morgan react?"

"She slapped me in the face. She slapped all of us."

"That's when your dad got in?"

"Yes."

"Was he angry too?"

"Never seen him like that. He tried saving her."

"Do you want to know what was happening to Miriam that time when you're torturing her?" Amelia raised her shoulders. "The thermal burns were terrible enough. But those turnips were worse. You stuffed it into her internals. And I can think those turnips weren't washed?"

"They weren't."

"The cuts and tears in her reproductive and digestive systems – you're smart enough to understand my scientific terms – acted as highways. Highways to what, your idiotic mind might wonder?" said Quinn. "You see, when you were turniping her, those soil microorganisms went into her system through these cuts and tears. She was fighting a bacterial infection at levels her teen body wasn't built to take!"

Amelia had a flush of guilt at long last.

"Your Honor, this is a despicable act of murder tantamount of a new level above first degree!" said Quinn. "They did this, before or after cutting her nipple and rubbing the wound with salt! Miriam died – they washed her body. And I take it your family insisted to be there for the funeral?"

Amelia nodded.

Quinn approached her, each step with words. "Amelia Morgan – your dad drives a Mercedes Benz AMG C63. Your mom drives a Chrysler Three Hundred. You have a big house. And a very expensive lawyer here!"

Frankopan's eyes narrowed.

"You have this fancy lifestyle. You are what people describe living on a lap of luxury. God, your school even paid you a lotta money for selling your painting! But stop for one second and look around.

"Addison Blount lived with her mom working at a dead-end job. The Smiths aren't any better. Don't let me start on the Hayes. But you? Oh, wow. Not you, no no. You don't need your father. You can get a new iPhone on your own. So, why go through all this? It's exhausting, isn't it? You fought. You beat people. You talked to your principal and all. And then you throw not only your lifestyle! Your parents' hard work!

"Everyone's future was up in the air, thanks to you! And all for an overrated gadget that overheats easily. Enlighten us, Amelia Morgan – why do this? Why offer rewards more than what the iPhone's worth. Why?"

Amelia searched everywhere. She looked over Quinn's shoulder for the door out of the courtroom. From there she explored the disdain in every face, locking upon Charlotte Reade's daggering scowl. She turned to seek a reprieve from the curious judge, before settling upon her only lifeline. But Frankopan decided to stay hushed yet again. He was not objecting. He was not getting up.

With a deep breath, she opened her mouth. No words crawled out of her throat, just air stinking of dryness, sulfur and curiously nicotine. "That iPhone is–" A struggle ensued, as more air puffed. "It's important for me."

"Why is it important that you'd tear down this town?"

"No. You don't get it."

"What am I not getting here?"

She took another breath, this time deeper. "My photos are there. And I wasn't dressed," she said, blushing when the crowd projected their scorn. "I'm sorry!"

"How undressed were you?"

"C-completely!"

"Ms. Morgan, it's very common for a teenager to take photographs of naked body! You're being curious! I'm a lawyer for many, many years, and I do feminine issues! I know damn well that's not the only reason why you did that!" Her roar returned. "Now would you tell the court the real reason why you beat Dora and torture Miriam?"

"It has videos of me."

"Doing what? TikTok dances with no clothes like girls with daddy issues?"

"N-no. My private videos."

"Define private, Ms. Morgan."

"I was having sex!"

Quinn stood there with her nostrils flared. The people around her, including Avery, were having a heavy reaction in the glutting profanities.

"Slut!"

"Morgan whore!"

"Fucking tramp!"

"Order! Or you're leaving the court!"

Quinn did not wait for the judge's clearance. "Did it occur to you that maybe your boyfriend took your phone?" she asked.

"I dunno. I asked them–"

"*Them?*" exclaimed Quinn for an effect to blow the crowd again.

"Order! Order in the court!"

"How many, Ms. Morgan?"

Again, Frankopan was not objecting. "I don't know," said Amelia, sobbing. "It's the football team. All of them."

Her raised hand stifled the reaction. "You have an orgy with the school athletes in the football team?" asked Quinn. For one dramatic moment, Quinn stopped being a lawyer. Her emboldening charisma was that of a politician. She was this supernova, enrapturing in a peak of publicity. She was going for the throat, her killer instincts bursting in flames. She waited – for that nod from Amelia. When it came, her hand went down. And just as she did, the crowd was screaming again.

Amelia was reduced to shame, humiliation and derision. "No further question, your Honor. No further question."

29

The first day at court ended with a beautiful sunset and Dom Pérignon in tall glasses. Amelia's confession was a celebratory call, strong to land her a good retirement in a federal penitentiary. Jake remained cautious whenever the Darlings dragged her name back into action. In the weeks ahead, the trial further reduced Amelia to shame. Frankopan mounted a bold defense to get Christie Hayes and Deborah Smith out of the first-degree murder charge. But it would seem, even for morons like Rachel, he was handing Amelia to the guillotine.

Jake was not cutting some slacks for Christie and Deborah. The prosecution agreed, bolstering their arguments while the Darlings were locked in a handicapped match with Amelia. Their deathblows solidified grounds for Amelia's conviction. Frankopan used every trick in the book for manslaughter charges, deflecting with bullying issues in which he brought Miri's bus driver as a witness.

The closing statements wrapped this murder case. And at long last, the decision was up to the jury. Avery announced a four-day deliberation to come up with a verdict. And it had been four days since. Today was the day. Jake was fixing

Declan's tie that morning. His heart was pounding over a mismatched feeling.

Euphoria filled him with a salt of worry. Anxiety was peppering across his face. Terry for the first time declined breakfast. "Should I call 911?" said Lottie.

"Very funny. The cops are coming anyway."

This morning's ride was special. Halgriffin arrived in his Expedition. They squeezed in for a quiet drive to the courtroom where all three defendants were standing beneath the judge's desk. "I don't have to emphasize how long it has been," said Avery. "Is there anything the prosecutor or defendant wish the add?"

Quinn, Archambeau and Frankopan remained where they were, all three of them unsmiling and unnerved.

"Very well. Has the jury reached the verdict?" A twitch zapped Jake's spine. The jurors nodded in unison. "And what is the verdict?"

Jake had to hold himself together. "*Don't think too hard. Don't think too hard. Don't think too hard.*"

"On the murder of Miriam Brownfield, by one count of first-degree murder and one count of abduction, we found the defendant Christie Hayes guilty."

Christie's mouth dropped.

"On the murder of Miriam Brownfield, by one count of first-degree murder and one count of abduction, we found the defendant Deborah Smith guilty."

Debra's knees gave out.

Two convictions scored first-degrees, setting up for a hattrick. "On the murder of Miriam Brownfield, by one count of first-degree murder, one count of abduction, one count of accessory to criminal conspiracy and evidence tampering, we found the defendant Amelia Morgan–" This was it. The moment of truth Jake had been dying to hear. It had been long time coming upon an excruciating path for justice. The spacious hall deadened into a spasmic hush that even a sneeze can be heard from a mile away. "–not guilty!"

Jake's heart skipped a beat. He turned to meet the culminating gust of exhalations from the others. They were grimacing at the standing juror, who was looking at the judge. Then he realized he had imagined that particular verdict, which the juror was about to deliver.

"GUILTY."

Jake closed his eyes, laughing with tears. So did Rachel. Lottie leaned in to hold Jake. None of them caught the emotions from those Darlings. None of them gave much thought about how they felt.

"I take no joy from this. I myself cannot comprehend how girls with such promising future can become mindless criminals," said Avery. "The sentencing date will be later determined in which we will conduct a sentencing hearing and the prosecution can seek a greater prison sentence." That gavel saw an end to this crazy drama, the sweetest music for everyone.

Frankopan did something none of them expected. He congratulated Quinn and Archambeau before disappearing amid the crowd. "To Quinn!" said Terry, holding a shot at a restaurant.

"Quinn!"

"Quinn!"

"Quinn!"

Jake put the pint glass with a clinking thud. "I gotta ask," he said. "That Frankopan wasn't really fighting for Amelia. What was that all about?"

"Yeah. He's like a lion going kitten."

Quinn pursed her lips for the straw. "When Renbarger quits and Rodeback fucks around, his law firm took a hit," she whispered. "Those Google reviews kinda smoked the DOJ in for a *look*. So I persuaded him to do the right thing for once in his life."

"That's why he came back?"

"Yep."

"Wait. Is that even legal?"

"Nope. But I'm sure eavesdropping minors ain't legal too," said Quinn. "Or breaking into the funeral home. Or whatever else you guys did before I came."

"You spied minors, man?" asked Terry.

"Nothing like that," said Jake, his eyes dancing at the thought of a particular shoe he had forgotten.

"Yep. Nothing at all."

The victory swung Archambeau to the frontlines. It took some official steps. But everyone was sure he would replace Renbarger, a cursed position which meant he had to sacrifice two Christmases because he would be up against David, Eden, McCrain, Rodeback, Gauthier and Renbarger himself.

"Start on DeWinter too!" said Jake.

"Anyone see her at the trial?"

"She ain't gonna come. To her, this case ain't got nothing to do with the school. As far as she could care, the attack happened out of the compound – so were the torture and murder."

"Sheesh. Pretty sure he'll keep her job," said Jake.

"Speaking of jobs, I gotta bounce to Houlton."

"Houlton?"

"Murder case," said Quinn. "This old man killed his friends. Claims they abducted his grandson. If his story's true, I'm gonna have to clear his name."

"What about the sentence hearing?"

"That's on Archambeau. I was just an assistant."

"And my case?" asked Lottie. "We don't have to fight again?"

"Haven't heard anything yet."

Jake looked into Quinn's eyes. "Before you go, I have one last thing to ask," he said. "You guys don't really need the evidence anymore. Can I ask for just one of them? Just one."

"I'll see what I can do," said Quinn, smiling.

Lottie and Quinn shared a long hug in front of the Reade residence. The affection they had for each other was marveling. Quinn leaned to kiss Lottie's forehead, sniffing the sweetness in her hair. "Stay outta trouble, Froggie," she said. "Better year next year, yeah?"

"You betcha – baby sister," replied Lottie.

Back at his home, Jake threw himself upon the couch and then turned to find Rachel alone. "You're still here, good," he said. "I just wanna say, thanks for coming back. Miri deserves it."

"Speaking of her. We gotta do something with the body."

"I'll handle it, Terry," said Jake. "There's something else I been thinking about. I'm gonna take the publisher's deal. Paxington offered me enough to start over in Utah, I suppose."

"Utah?" asked Declan.

"You're coming to Utah?" said Malcolm.

"Think about it, Jake. You really wanna move out west?"

"Heh. You see how fast Quinn skipped town. Even she's done with Farmington. Imagine how I feel." Jake took out a piece of paper from his coat. "Ruth, momma wrote this. I'm listing this house. She wants you to have some from the sale. There's just too much memory here. Mostly the bad ones. Dad. Mom's death. Miri. Our lil brother Sam."

"Urgh. Keep the money and dump the sucker, Jakey."

"I'll call the agent tonight," said Jake.

"If you're moving, what about Lottie?"

Surprisingly, Rachel was the one to ask that.

"She'll follow me till the end of the world," he said, smiling. "I mean that." The weight in his pocket was his reason. Lottie was in the backyard, treating herself a pitcher of lemonade for the nauseating throat. He sat on a wooden chair, holding her hand. "There's something I mean to tell you."

"No need to be dramatic about it."

"I'd never make it without you. You were there for me. You know I love you. But I don't want this to end. So–" He took the weight out of his pocket, which was a small, velvet box. Her mouth dropped for a croak, the book in her hand launching into the air. "Charlotte Reade, will you be my wife?" He presented the diamond ring which had been in his mother's safe.

"I will! I will! God, I will!" And she threw herself into him for a kiss, stunned as claps and cheers echoed from the house where the whole family stood in hiding. Charles came out of there with a cake, flanked by Donna and Ruth. Following far behind was Rachel, smiling a blank smile.

She had the house all to herself for two nights. Jake wanted the ceremony private but meaningful. Donna pulled her sleeves and declared. "You been married twice. You keep this one or I'll kill you myself, Froggie!"

"Three time's a charm, Mom."

Uncle Obie learned about the wedding through Facebook. He liked the pictures without commenting. "He's like a father to me," said Jake. "But I can't have him there. He ain't gonna be happy about me marrying you."

"Why?"

"You're not Jewish. He kept telling me about looking for God and stuff. So, I figured it's probably the best not to have him around."

Quinn spoke for about an hour, congratulating three times. "Yeah, yeah, you said that already," said Lottie.

"I know. I didn't congratulate you for your first two marriages."

Lottie smiled, which then disappeared into a groan. "Screw you! You always make me feel like I'm wearing a kick me sign."

"Nah, I'm just joking. Sorry I can't be there. I'm taking this case!"

"Really?"

"Yeah. Sure he's innocent. I gotta get back to him. Talk to you later, yeah? Remember, stay outta trouble!"

It was the last thing they wanted. Jake was no longer at the balcony. He preferred his days outside, keeping a good distance from the papers. He unfollowed the news pages for the sake of personal liberation. Now nobody reminded him about the Morgans. David's case was complicating with a tango of sexual harassments, a development that Jake of course did not know.

The town lost interest, if the stupid WhatsApp group could be believed. They were banging about politics because Joe Biden was leading in national polls. Lottie and Ruth read the final bits of their rabid debate before leaving the group.

Moments later, a group admin messaged them both. But they did not reply. They did not even open the message. Terry negotiated a fair price with a long hauler to Utah, where he rented three storage outlets. Jake went through his documents, stopping when he saw those discharge papers from that day he was told of Miriam's death. "Nine grand," said Jake. "So America. Thank God I still have my insurance!"

After the last of the furnishing was loaded, the house felt like a ghost. Air breezed through the crevices and half-opened windows. And Jake took another stroll, his heart locking up when he neared her room.

That room on the right – the one with the ornamented door – was emotional for Rachel, who helped with the clearing. Jake held out Miri's Ybenlow crewneck sweatshirt. "I want you to have this," he said.

"Really?" she said, without a voice.

"You should have something of hers. Still has her smell. Just don't wash it."

Together Jake and Rachel shed more tears in the chilling memory of the girl they lost.

"Good luck, Jake," she whimpered.

"You too." At the door, he stopped her. "I'm happy you came back by the way. Would've been better if you stayed for the funeral. But it's okay. It's done anyway."

"I have something to tell you."

"Nah. I know you're gonna press charges saying I was negligent," said Jake. Then he reached in for an envelope in his pocket. "Before you do that, just think of something. My wife and I think you should have this. It's not a lot – but that's how much we had when we started in Huntsville."

She flipped with a look of astonishment. "Jake! I can't accept this."

"You're Miri's mom. Nothing can change that."

"We had five grand when we started house-hunting."

"Six actually."

Tears rolled down her eyes. "I won't press charges, Jake. You have my word," she said. "I never get to apologize for cheating."

"Move on, Rach. That's what I'm doing," said Jake. "This money doesn't mean I forgive you. Being honest, you don't need my forgiveness. It's over. We're done. Miri's gone. We got nothing together. It's just over. I just want you to know that. Don't contact me again. I don't wanna see you anymore."

"I understand, Jake."

"There's a cab waiting for you outside. It'll take you to the airport. The extra thousand is for your ticket back and some other stuff you might need to buy. Good luck." Rachel put a step for a hug, which he raised a hand. "No. No. Just go."

And she was out of the house. In the cab, Jake saw her head drooping. The woman had nothing else to do. Now single, her lowly modeling career crashed thanks to the five-inch scar upon her belly. And she had to start over. Lottie reeled in from behind, putting her arms by his stomach.

"What did Miri last say to you?" asked Jake. "Was it about her?"

"Nope. It was on the phone," she said. "*Don't worry about me. I'll be okay.* Jeez, I'm getting goosebumps thinking about it."

"You know what she last said to me? *I love you, Daddy. Take care of yourself. Don't think too hard, okay?*"

"Christ."

"I still wish she stayed with Rachel."

Lottie swung to his side. "Rachel won't be a good mom, Jake. Miri told me herself. She was glad you got her. Miri will be dead on the inside if Rachel got her."

"Miri's dead inside out with me."

"Not because of you."

"I dunno if I can even move on."

"Don't have to, Jake," said Lottie. "We'll keep her in our heart. It's where she'll be for the rest of our lives."

With one last look to the house, Jake braved for a smile. "Miriam, if you're here – be good to Uncle Reggie."

And that was the final time they saw the house... ever. Their first stop was the police station, where Tashtego greeted them with flowers.

"I'm heading to Utah," said Jake.

"For a vacation?"

"Something like that, yeah."

"Well, when are you coming back?"

"When I have a serious buyer."

Tashtego nodded. "Congratulations on the wedding, Jake. Look, I gotta say this. I know I fucked up. But you understand what I hadda do, right? I mean, I'm a cop."

"Just drop it, Bob. Charlotte doesn't need to think about it. I don't wanna think about it. I'm just here for some arrangements I gotta do."

"Let's have a drive."

Jake pondered for a moment. "Sure. Gimme a moment." After telling the family, he hopped into the cruiser. "When I first moved out, I hated this town a lot. Never thought of coming back here. But now, sheesh."

"Heh, imagine what I feel," said Tashtego. "Just the two of us, okay? I'm leaving Farmington. Next year will be my last."

"Didn't see that one coming."

"I already packed my bags. The fuckers here blamed me for being too slow. They also blamed me for everything McCrain did."

"McCrain. Who woulda thought, huh? First time I met him, he was really good," said Jake. "I bet he knows about the real murder weapon."

"He does. He told us already."

Jake turned to Tashtego. "Lemme guess. He kept it all along?"

"The Ford, Jake. That time Miriam was sure to go. There was nothing they can do. David disposed the murder weapon in Webb Lake. Our divers are at it."

"That's why he went to Weld."

"Yep. You shoulda apply for detective work."

"No thanks. I never thought I have to crack my own daughter's case."

Tashtego chuckled. "About our arrangements. You really sure?"

"I've already made my mind, Bob."

"Think about it, Jake. You know there's no going back once we hit that button."

"No. You think about it," said Jake. "There's no going back now. There never will. Please don't ask about it. I don't wanna second-guess myself when I'm doing the right thing. I mean, I'm not talking about now – if I live for another fifty years, it's a fifty-year pain. Stuff like this never go away, Bob. It never will."

"Yeah. You're right about that. Sorry I asked."

"Do me a favor, Bob. For as long as you're here – for a month or so, maybe the whole year, who knows? Don't let this happen to anyone else. There'll always be leeches in the system. I've learned that the hard way."

"Farmington will never be the same. I ain't surprised if the President wants a visit."

After a cup of coffee, Tashtego drove him to the hotel they booked in Augusta. He departed, wishing his best for the whole family. "Had fun?" asked Lottie.

"I gotta see him, Charlotte."

"Oh, no. I mean, you had fun?"

Jake looked through her. "Not much. He kept talking about David and Rodeback."

"What did you tell him?"

"I told him to fuck them all," said Jake.

Room services had their final bill at a substantial $500 before tax. Terry swiped his credit card, before heading out with his kids. From Lumpkin Road, they were bound for the landscaped Doug Barnard Parkway. It was just straight from there, until Aviation Way where they cleared the ticket in a terminal that looked like an R&R.

The American Airlines flight punched on time and took off within the hour, crossing the neighboring states in a liberating hum of compressed air and full thrust. Jake had a sound sleep, drifting and dreaming. The lump he had in the back of his head for so long was no longer there, when he woke up. In those days he slept with a sense of guilt and got up with a headache. But he stirred painlessly out of sleep when the captain announced their landing.

They were fetching Spud from an airway kennel when that announcement rang out. "Your attention, please. Will Mr. Jacob Brownfield from Augusta please approach the helpdesk? Thank you."

"What the hell?"

"It's okay. Come on."

Terry led the way, looking worried. And at the particular helpdesk, a young woman managed them. "Can I see your ID please, sir?"

"Is there something wrong?" asked Terry.

"Oh, no, sir. Standard ops for special packages. Just a moment there."

Jake moved to the nearest bench to wait. "You wanna tell me what's happening here?" asked Terry. He shook his head, as Lottie and Ruth came with their children. "Dunno what's going on. Something about special packages."

"Special packages? You brought a weap-- contraband or something?"

An officer brought a box to the desk. "Mr. Brownfield?" he announced, handing Jake the paperwork for signing.

"What is it, sir?" asked Terry.

"It's an urn," replied the officer.

The family paused. "An urn, Jake?" asked Lottie.

"My arrangements with the chief," replied Jake. "You think I'd leave her with Uncle Reggie?" After signing, he brought the brass urn out of the box and reached into his pocket for the homespun, crimson-colored ribbon. "A little magic our Queenie worked out with that Archambeau."

He tied the ribbon around the urn. "Miri will love it, Jake," said Lottie.

"She'll always be with us – now then, and forever."

Author's Note

I omitted the sentencing chapters, as you might have noticed. I have my reasons. We know Amelia Morgan would be spending her days with Big Momma, Killer Kelly and Lucky Lucy. But what about the other Darlings? We can't forget the Morgans for aiding and abetting. We won't forget Roger Gauthier for what he did to our Charlotte. And don't let me start on Gregory Rodeback, Paxton McCrain and Peter Renbarger.

Here's the thing – throwing three chapters to cover the timespan of their trials is a narrative suicide. These antagonists would be mentioned on the news, read by the main characters of my next crime novel, *The Burlington Bull*. So, there is a window of opportunity here. I think their fate should be in your hands. You deserve to be the judge, jury and executioner. How long do you think they should be sentenced?

You can recommend on my Facebook page.

Made in the USA
Middletown, DE
02 April 2022

63529281R00198